I0670112

King of Star-Cast Skies

Kaitlyn Carter Brown

Whimsical Publishing

Copyright © 2025 by Kaitlyn Carter Brown

All rights reserved.

No part of this book may be reproduced in any form or by any electronic or mechanical means, including information storage and retrieval systems, without written permission from the author, except for the use of brief quotations in a book review.

NO AI TRAINING: Without in any way limiting the author's [and publisher's] exclusive rights under copyright, any use of this publication to "train" generative artificial intelligence (AI) technologies to generate text is expressly prohibited.

ISBN: 978-1-998195-24-4

For information address Whimsical Publishing, whimsicalpublishing.ca

Edited by Micheline Ryckman and Deborah O'Carroll
Cover art by Salome Totladze
Cover design by Micheline Ryckman
Map by Hunter Ryckman

To Michael, who has given me starlight and has walked through the days of small things with me, never growing weary of life. I love you.

KAITLYN CARTER BROWN

KING
OF
STAR-CAST
SKIES

SANCEN DESERT

INSTANOLDE

TEMPLE

PALACE

DOCKS

THE GUNGOLE

DELTA LANDS

Chapter 1

Razhar

P assing from shadow to shadow, Razhar crossed the
stone courtyards and gilded chambers of the palace in
a delicate dance of stealth. Steps he knew, well accustomed to sneaking about, but not in a palace brimming with
Jarkin invaders. Drawing a sharp breath, he pressed himself
against the wall as the shapes of two hulking warriors crossed
the courtyard. Armed to the teeth with short battle-axes and
quivers of black-fletched arrows, they prowled like lions laying
claim to their territory. Men of the far east mountains who
survived by the edge of the sword.

Conquer or be conquered. The way of survival in the harsh
desert. And Razhar was no stranger to survival.

The warriors passed. Razhar sagged, releasing the air in his
lungs. Tilting his head back, his gaze swept the pillars of
polished marble stretching up to the ornamental mosaics that
shimmered like gemstones.

The world that adopted him. The home that he'd
borrowed. And he didn't intend to lose it. Not for anything.

Slipping behind a row of potted palms, he rounded the

edges of the courtyard, never venturing into the afternoon light. A purple tassel from his tunic caught on a draping branch, and he unsnagged it.

Hardly an outfit for a harrowing operation, but he had no clothes for the shadows, only bright turbans, silk scarves, and tunics embroidered in every shade of the spectrum. A clever disguise for an orphan from the Kushite canyonlands.

"A poor defense if ever there was one," he muttered. But defenses were in short supply these days. Memories of last night assailed his mind like Jarkin arrows. Of the city square, bathed in harsh firelight and burning buildings to illuminate the battle.

No, not a battle. They hadn't the battlements or the armies. Instanolde had one man—a cursed man.

Elerek had looked nothing like the prince Razhar had grown up alongside, the skilled strategist, and, not to mention, the most impossible, insensitive man Razhar had ever known.

And this man—this *king*—had become something else, transformed by the curse that lurked in his skin and doomed its victims to die, drowning with a single touch. He'd faced Gaudab Batu-Khasar, the Jarkin warlord, without a weapon; the water dripping from his outstretched hands was treacherous enough.

A bold move—one that Razhar couldn't risk Elerek making. Not with so many lives at stake, cursed lives already fading like starlight.

Reaching the end of the courtyard, Razhar wiped a sheen of sweat from his brow and swept into the palace corridors. Patterned light fell across his vision from row after row of lattice windows. Familiar routes, places where laughter and tears were shared.

Places they lived.

The hearths lay cold in the kitchens and the jars of oil and flour were sealed now. Everywhere Razhar looked, he saw only ghosts. Azraa over a month back. Fin two days ago. Myra just yesterday. Those whom he could not save.

Azraa had died at the temple, but Fin and Myra had both perished before him. Only Myra had known how he'd kept them alive despite being doomed to drown with their king. It had helped, sharing his burden with the maid who'd freely chosen to take the curse...

Now she was gone—not from the curse, the Jarkins took care of that, but dead all the same.

Swallowing his grief, Razhar grabbed a round of flatbread, a small wheel of cheese, and two oranges—the *last* oranges. The rest had been used for a birthday cake to celebrate another year won for a cursed soul.

Razhar stilled, moving his thumb across the oranges' waxy surface, feeling every pore and wrinkle. A year that he'd bought them, and they had no idea.

A cold, cynical thought. One that didn't belong in his world of golden palaces, spiced coffee, laughter, and swirling dancers. Much like a Kushite orphan with a disgraced history and shameful secrets didn't belong in the palace at all. In that, he and the Jarkins had something in common. He stuffed the oranges into his pants pockets and left the kitchens.

This isn't your fault. A tiny voice spoke in some deep, empty part of his heart.

Oh, but it felt like it was. And the fact that he walked freely, without guards, without chains about his arms, couldn't be overlooked.

Razhar paused in another corridor, waiting for a contingent of Jarkins—and the guilt pounding in his heart—to pass.

I didn't know it was going to happen like this.

They'd known the Jarkins were coming. The mountain men struck with deadly accuracy when they took the Darcress Kasbah, the fortress guarding the edge of the Sancen Desert, and killed King Cormek. One summer to live, they'd claimed, and the players took to their places much like the golden figurines of *barjee*, the strategy game he loved so much. Surely there had been hope, pure and as bright as the dancing constellations themselves.

Even so, Instanolde had been conquered.

Not with the strength of armies, but with blood, cursed water, and . . . sand.

The remainder of the night replayed in Razhar's mind—the night that he might regret forever. Myra falling with the knife in her side. Norbah, Instanolde's general, dragged away.

Lystra.

Grace and elegance and ferocity. The queen who survived the Sancen Desert and became Elerek's wife out of devotion to her people. The one meant to save them all. Something like steel had overcome her features as she watched Elerek face his enemies alone. Razhar couldn't stop her, couldn't protect her as Elerek had charged him.

She'd run to him. Touched him. Took the curse.

Elerek's best-laid plans shattered as pain twisted Lystra's lovely and noble face. The roar from the king's throat had pierced Razhar's heart with the accuracy of a Kushite archer. He'd spent his life attempting to uphold all that Elerek—all that *he*—held dear.

Enough.

Dashing out of the shadows, Razhar had planted himself between the Jarkin warlord and Instanolde's cursed king. The water pummeled his body, but no curse tainted him. He'd lifted his hands and sand, fine as the Sancen dunes, poured from his palms, breaking the current of Elerek's waters. The secret he'd spent his life protecting.

"If you kill him now, you'll die with him."

They would all die.

"There's only one way to break this curse."

One way. One horrible way.

"And I can help with that."

Razhar clenched his fists. A clever lie. One that both the Jarkin warriors and the royals of Instanolde believed. One that burned like a bitter betrayal in the eyes of the king. Was that all Razhar would ever amount to? A clever liar? A man hoarding secrets? But he'd kept Elerek and Lystra alive. Not indefinitely. If there was one constant in their world, their struggle for survival on the edge of the desert, Razhar knew that nobody could be completely saved.

No one tried harder than him.

The relentless summer sunlight fell over Razhar's shoulders as he hurried across the stone-cast yard. Before him loomed the keep belonging to the palace guard, along with the entrance to the underground prison.

One way in, guarded by five immense Jarkins. Razhar hesitated, eyeing the jagged blades of their knives and the heavy heads of the axes strapped to their backs. Weapons made for cleaving bodies.

But he had to get inside—to find Elerek.

Once he hears the truth, he'll understand. He must. Doubt nagged at his scalp, like sand caught between the folds of his clothing. Another clever lie to tell himself. Razhar carried no weapon, knew no stance. The only defense he'd ever needed was a dash of wit, a flair of flirt, and a winning smile. He doubted any of those tactics would work on the invaders, still it was all he had.

Razhar walked right up to the warriors with his head high and a bit of swagger in his step. He cleared his throat. "Afternoon."

The Jarkins' shoulders, capped with the skulls of wild jackals, tensed. One brought his hand to the knife at his belt.

Razhar withdrew the round of flatbread, his eyes darting to the prison's dark shaft, visible between the towering Jarkins. "I've brought dinner for the . . ." *King*. Perhaps not the best choice of words. "Prisoner."

The warriors glared at him. "Move along, Kushite." One muttered a string of words that sounded far from friendly.

He squared his shoulders. "Let me pass."

The closest Jarkin drew a short sword, the blade screeching from its sheath. "I said"—he stepped toward Razhar—"*move along.*"

Razhar raised his arm in a feeble attempt to defend himself. And sand. Fine, amber grains cascaded from his skin, drifting down in a soft curtain from his forearm, piling on the stonework at his feet. He didn't control it. It just happened. After all, what was more sand in the desert?

Shock subdued their leathered faces. The same terror that the sight of Elerek's powers provoked—now turned upon Razhar.

His face flushed. His abilities were meant to preserve, to keep people alive. Surely this was no fearsome thing. Razhar didn't know how to react when eyes looked upon him in spectacle.

Elerek knew. If only he could talk to him.

"Don't make me ask again." Razhar forced a snarl into his voice.

This time, the Jarkins backed away, clearing the path. They remembered the horrors they'd seen last night.

Darkness engulfed Razhar as he hurried down the rough-cut steps. A long tunnel stretched before him. Weak torches flickered from their crudely constructed sconces, and despite getting past the guards, Razhar felt as feeble as the flames themselves.

No sound stirred. No shuffle of boots, clank of shackles, or moan of prisoners. The silence unnerved Razhar, making him long for the sounds of music and laughter.

After the first row of empty cells, he found a guard. Another Jarkin.

This one was *cursed*. Instead of skin, the man's arm was encased in a shimmery sheen of water. Beneath, pale bones, taut muscle, and spidery veins were visible. This man had been touched, whether directly by Elerek or the unnatural water that flowed from his fingertips.

"What are you doing here?" The Jarkin took a step closer, his stance threatening.

Razhar lifted the bread again. "Take me to the prisoner."

The Jarkin grunted. "No one gets in."

Why did that have to mean him? Fighting the urge to scoff, Razhar mustered his bravado and let his head roll back on his shoulders, the bones in his neck crunching. "As I informed your superiors, it is imperative to keep the prisoner alive and that includes feeding him a decent supper."

The guard stomped forward, his height and girth by far out-measuring Razhar. A growl rumbled in his throat.

Razhar took a step back. Shifting the bread to one hand, he extended the other, sand coating his palm again. He wished that he could wield it as deftly as Elerek did his waters, create a dune to shift this guard off his feet.

Scoffing, the guard grabbed Razhar by the scarf, throwing him off-balance. "You think you can intimidate me? Even with your mongrel king's curse, you dirty river rats are nothing to us."

Before Razhar could react, the guard knocked him to the

ground, ripping the bread from Razhar's hand. "I'll save him a few crumbs." Tearing the flat loaf, he stuffed one half in his mouth. "Get out." He spoke with his mouth full. "Or I'll do worse."

Razhar dragged himself to his feet, feeling as defeated as that disk of bread as he scampered back the way he'd come. *I just . . . I need you to understand.* The air between him and Elerek hazed, a swirl of sand charging across the desert, blocking the skies and drenching all in confusion.

Turning a corner, he leaned against the wall, rubbing his fingertips together as grains of dust caught in the ridges of his skin. Even if he knew how to control his sands, blasting this guard in the deep of the prison didn't seem the safest option.

It wouldn't be the first unusual death among these cells. Hardly a week had passed since Elerek had come to interrogate the Jarkin assassin—and drowned him.

Razhar shook his head, the shell-shocked terror in Elerek's eyes haunting him even now. What does one say when your best friend commits a murder? When water dripped from the king's hands and gathered beneath his wheelchair? When the curse suddenly changed the rules?

Turning Elerek to water and Razhar to sand.

Could he do it? Snuff out a man's life? *No, El wouldn't want me to.*

He shuffled back up the corridor. Maybe he ought to be in one of these cells, his failure enough to secure the bars.

"Fahwal."

Razhar stopped, his boots anchored to the stone.

A whisper. A name. A ghost that haunted the deepest recesses of his soul.

"Come closer."

No. He ought to turn and run the other way, back up the corridor, and into the sunlight. Still, he couldn't help but peer through the shadows, to the nearest cell, where long, wrinkled fingers encased in jewels gripped the bars. A pair of eyes flashed in the torchlight, watching him.

"You and I know each other. Do you remember?"

Razhar gulped. He wondered if this was what Elerek's victims felt just before they drowned.

"Fahwal sent you here? Curious." Dalmah of House Arghan cocked her head to one side, her long black hair draping like a mourner's veil. "You look so much like him."

Dressed in elegant silks and lips as red as blood, she still looked like the queen she'd been before Lorkin's conquests deposed her and placed the throne into House Karim's control. But Razhar only saw the villain responsible for the curse's binding, for the fate of the king doomed to drown—and the host of secrets he'd been forced to carry.

Secrets that belonged to an archer who lived at the bottom of the Kushite canyons. The first to fly off to battle, mounted upon a great condor, when summoned by scrolls tied with orange silk ribbons. Because the king of Instanolde said so.

Razhar remembered curling up on his bed, a barely stuffed pallet in their carved-out hovel. A child left alone in the dark while his baba fought away in wars for a far-off kingdom.

"Someday," Fahwal had said, "there will be no more wars and kings that send lowly men to their deaths and make them pay for what they weren't meant to pay."

Lofty words. But Fahwal had made a bargain. One that came with a signed contract and a dagger etched with starlight. One that demanded a cost. Razhar pinched his eyes shut. *"I'll pay it."* Even after all these years, he still heard the courage in his baba's voice. The resolute stance of a soldier.

But you didn't pay the cost, Baba. I did.

The cost of casting a curse.

"Surely it's been at least fifteen years . . ." Dalmah spoke the words slowly, letting them fill the darkness. "Since they killed him."

Executed. Razhar tried not to think of it. Whatever joys he could find to amuse himself in the present typically outweighed the sorrow of the past. He'd surrounded himself with life, with thrill, with comrades, with hope.

Until this last summer, this last summer to live.

"Tell me, is it true?" Dalmah watched him like the glassy, predatory eyes of the Kushite condors. "About you?"

Clenching his hands, Razhar hoped the shadows might hide him. An impossibility, considering his colorful choices in clothing. Anything to distract, to deter, to keep anyone from looking too closely and seeing the secrets written deep in his eyes.

"Baba had theories . . ."

"And that's why you're here? In the palace of Instanolde? The only son of a lowly Kushite soldier who committed a terrible crime?"

What's a lowly Kushite to the king of Instanolde?

Razhar ground his teeth. "This is my home." He belonged nowhere else in the wide, wild world. But it wasn't just the palace, the markets, and the lively streets. His family was here.

"Ah." Dalmah lowered her hands, leaning against the bars as if they were a marble pillar and she an ornate piece of decor. "Tell me, do they know? About you?"

His insides churned. It was only a matter of time—after what happened last night. And look what it had accomplished. Everyone he loved thought him a dirty traitor.

"All these years, and you've kept such secrets?" The countess clicked her tongue. "Secrets concerning a curse . . . and a doomed prince."

"King, actually." *And I'm doomed to share his fate? How is that fair?* Razhar lurched toward her cell. "Tell me how to break it—*curse binder.*"

Dalmah chortled, oblivious to the title, to the truth that her knowledge of the fell art had designed the curse and its atrocities. Razhar's baba had only carried out the casting—earning him the cost to be paid while Dalmah suffered no injury.

"Surely you must know. Per your baba's wishes, I sealed the writ of sale in the archives myself."

With a huff, Razhar adjusted the collar of his vest, his hand sliding across the creases of parchment stowed within an interior pocket. He'd taken such a risk showing the writ to Lystra. Even now, with the Jarkins occupying their kingdom and the curse more powerful than ever, a simple piece of parchment held the power to damn both himself and Elerek.

"What happens to the cost of the curse when the curse is broken?"

The countess narrowed her eyes. "So unusual. Look at you, a walking consequence—a punishment."

Razhar bowed his head.

"Consequences are to be paid, aren't they? If the firstborn of bloody Lorkin is to die, shouldn't you as well?"

Heat flared up his neck, burning at the stars tattooed on his chest. "Not all who suffer are guilty."

Dalmah stepped toward the bars again, the torchlight striping her face. Darkness and light glimmering in her deep eyes. "Perhaps, but you may well be guilty by the time this is over."

The woman seemed intent on hearing her own voice echoing in this dank cell. "Tell me what you know."

She heaved a resigned sigh. "Nothing for certain. Your circumstances are beyond unusual. But if you intend to see this

11

curse broken, your best chance is to be the one holding the dagger."

She's lying. Razhar knew his face betrayed him as a sinister smile curled across the countess's blood-red lips, reveling in the horror of her words. *El is going to die anyways, isn't he? Stars above, it might as well be you.*

Ending the curse that had haunted him all his life, freeing himself from wrongs that he'd never committed, and proving once and for all that he wasn't just a lowly Kushite.

All at the expense of Elerek's life.

Dalmah laughed. "Imagine, the last thing your pathetic, cursed *king* will ever see is the face of his opposite, the cost of his curse, driving a curse binder's dagger into his chest."

"Insult him again," Razhar growled, his posture rigid, "and I'll make sure the Jarkins know who you are. They're not too keen on curses at the moment."

"Jarkins. Even they won't keep someone like me locked up forever. They have weaknesses, pressure points, like anyone else." She eyed him warily. "I've found yours."

His blood began to boil.

"And I suspect my granddaughter shares your sentiments." The slightest of clouds, the kind that burned off easily in the desert heat, eclipsed Dalmah's gaze. "Is she all right?"

A strange question, considering that Dalmah had bartered her own granddaughter off in marriage to a cursed man. Lystra herself had imprisoned Dalmah, having gleaned enough suspicion from the woman's clever cobwebs. Razhar admired her audacity. "They won't harm her." He didn't doubt for a moment that Elerek's demands wouldn't be met. A king who had the power to drown his enemies could be quite persuasive.

Dalmah didn't reply, her gaze turned back to the darkness.

"I'll check on her, if I can." If he couldn't talk to Elerek, Lystra was his next best option.

"Hmm." The countess let her bejeweled hands slip from the bars. "Send my regards."

Razhar turned and stomped back down the hall. He had to get out of the darkness, the shadows where his secrets seemed to dwell. If only they'd stop following him altogether.

Chapter 2

Lystra

The door slammed shut, quivering on its iron hinges, and the lock clicked. Lystra took one step into the desolate silence, and then collapsed to her knees.

Tears dripped from her eyes while blood oozed from her shoulder. Her hands bore the mark of the curse that would doom her to drown, the fate of all who had been touched by the cursed king of Instanolde.

Air assaulted her lungs in chaotic pants, as if the depths of the curse's waters would come swift. But everything within her heart, broken into a thousand tiny shards, screamed *not yet*.

Not when all had gone so, so wrong.

Bowing her head to the floor, she wept.

"A queen stands to meet all who defy her, looking her enemies in the eye and bidding them to kneel." Grandmother's words meant nothing. Lystra was a queen no longer. But the voice lingered in her mind, mocking her.

A single drop of crimson blood hit the floor.

She drew a shuddered breath. Her fingers, numb and unfeeling, moved to her shoulder. Beneath tattered shreds of silk, her skin was sliced and ruined, cut by a knife in the hand of Instanolde's conqueror, Gaudab Batu-Khasar, as he tortured her before the king.

She turned back to the door, slamming her fist against it. Blood splattered across the desert scene carved into its panels like red drops of the rains that fell so scarcely in the Sancen.

After what seemed like hours, the handle turned, and the cruel face of the Jarkin guard appeared.

"Bring me water," Lystra demanded.

The Jarkin shut the door, but a few minutes later, he returned bearing a clay jar, heavy with clear, cool liquid.

"But you will spare the queen. No one will harm her. Every drop of her blood that you've shed this day will be demanded of you tenfold. She. Will. Live."

How bold his words sounded, rippling over the pool of cursed water covering the marble of their throne room. Demanding her life when she had handed him over to death.

She took the jar, setting it in the center of an ornate rug. All around her, the chamber lay furnished in lavishness. Draping silk curtains, luxurious couches, chairs with curved armrests overlaid in gold. A place adorned for royalty, for lovers, another layer of lies hanging like sheer silk across their paltry attempts to save what remained of their broken kingdom.

Biting back a whimper, she unclasped her bloodied blouse and let the garment fall to the floor. Dipping a cloth into the jar, careful not to waste a single drop, she washed the blood from her shoulder. This she could clean, heal. But not the curse, the curse she had chosen, that which would make her king's declaration that she would live null and void.

When she'd done what she could, she entered her own suite with its fourposter bed, ottoman, a painted screen for dressing, and a balcony overlooking her golden kingdom situated between the death of the desert and the life offered by the river. Her world lay in tatters as ripped as her clothing, and she could do nothing to mend its threads.

Approaching the mirrored vanity with timid steps, she turned her bare shoulder to its glass. The knife's slashes were sharp and defined against her amber skin, forming two interlocking diamonds.

The Jarkins' mark, the same they carried on their flags and armor, carved into her flesh.

The image in the mirror blurred by another onslaught of tears. Lystra could hardly keep from trembling. The mountain men had stolen everything she had ever loved—would they take her too? Now that she bore their mark on her skin?

Lystra bound her wound and donned a plain kaftan of soft linen. She blinked against horizontal shafts of glorious light that fell across her room as the sun leveled with her balcony.

One summer to live.

And like the sun, sinking slowly toward the shimmering horizon, their time was fading. Night would soon fall, and not even the starlight could guide them home.

Starlight.

Cradling her shoulder, Lystra left her chamber and crossed the parlor, sweeping back the second set of silk curtains. A chamber designed to mirror her own, though sparsely furnished to accommodate a wheeled chair.

She perched on the edge of the bed—*his* bed—and turned her gaze toward the window. Another hour or so, and stars would spin in dancing constellations above the jagged line of the eastern mountains. Each of those stars bore a story, tales that had been spoken in a gentle voice and eyes as severe as the sky itself.

She'd seen the wrathgiver constellation here on the night of her wedding. Back when she'd known nothing of the stars and the dagger or how they were tied to the cursed king doomed to die. When the distance was placed between them, when they could *not* fall in love.

Lystra's gaze dropped to her hands. Where skin ought to have been, a thin, wet film revealed bone and muscle. They'd been given a fractured future, but they'd given vows. King and queen, husband and wife. They'd chosen to fight, to strive, to hope against hope that they would survive the next sunrise. And she had chosen *this*.

Was I a fool? As Grandmother had said, a foolish girl with a fragile heart?

She didn't know. Her fate, like that of Instanolde, would not be parted from his.

"I would never do anything to hurt you."

Lystra thought of him, the night she'd snuck into his chambers. He lay still, his eyes softly closed and framed by thick, glossy curls. His bare shoulders sculpted and pale in the starlight, every ridge of his chest tight with muscle. Still and beautiful. Save for the curse mark curling over his ribs, he looked so very much like his brother, Cormek.

But that wasn't why she loved him.

"Do you see ... I ... I need you?"

The resolve in his jade-colored eyes, shining like a star quickly running out of light with a fierce desire to burn. She'd seen him fight demons that she could only imagine. He strove for a world that he knew he would never see, choosing her to guide Instanolde into the light.

And despite the arrangements of their political relationship, Elerek knew the burdens she bore, the grief that had torn her soul to shreds. Like so few ever could.

It had happened little by little, like droplets felled in the desert. In soft words of stars and stories. In the breath of lonely desert air as they'd mounted cardants and ventured beyond the city. In their shared intensity to fight for their kingdom with each precious breath.

And then everything fell apart.

Careful of her aching shoulder, she settled atop the blankets, her arms wrapped around herself. The scent of sandalwood and vanilla filled her nostrils—of him. The bed hadn't been slept in. Their world had begun to crumble, and she'd thought he'd been strategizing a plan brilliant enough to save them.

But she wasn't so sure anymore. Maybe he'd been with Myra the entire time.

El doesn't love you. He loves her.

The price for loving a king was steep, and Myra had paid with her life. She hadn't deserved such an end, Lystra knew that. But she also knew there was no value in loving someone who couldn't return affection.

Her fingers slid down a crease in the folds of his pillow and she buried her face deeper into the linen.

The disaster had come, as they always knew it would. Instanolde needed her tenacity, her fierceness, some sliver of the hope she'd tried her best to inspire in her kingdom. It had never needed her to love a king doomed to die. No, only their "unconsummated, political arrangement."

Anything else belonged atop a funeral pyre, one that demanded her heart laid out upon the kindling. Her kingdom needed her—and Elerek did not.

"I . . . I only wanted to free you . . ." she whispered into the lingering breath of his scent. Could she explain herself? How, since that night, she'd been seeking a way to break the curse? To save those whom he loved and let not one more soul drown in the desert?

She didn't know the cost would be so high. A queen would

pay it. Swiftly. After all, one death—even a king's death—was a worthy price to set the curse's victims free.

Grandmother had taught her a strength to raise the sun itself. Lystra had tasted power and knew her arms could wield it.

But her heart could not.

Power knew so little of kindness, of compassion. It held weight upon the scales but left the measures horribly unbalanced. Grandmother's ideas had cracked her perception before, but she wouldn't let it skew her desire to preserve innocent life.

Not that Elerek was innocent.

What remained for her to do? Her days were numbered now, same as the king's and perhaps the kingdom's. Battles were never without sacrifice and soldiers took up weapons knowing they might lose it all.

Then, I must fight, and I will not love him.

A shiver crept up her arm. She curled herself into a tighter ball and clenched her eyes shut, wishing that this nightmare would end and be over.

Thrust from her slumber, Lystra's heart hurtled into her throat as the thunderclap of the chamber doors strained against their hinges. She hardly had time to push herself up from Elerek's bed, her shoulder pulsing with agony, before the silk curtains parted in a great gust.

Gaudab Batu-Khasar strode into the chamber.

Lystra jumped to her feet, planted between the bed and the open window. The sun had set, the first stars salting the skies, but the presence of the Jarkin warlord seemed to absorb all light.

He stalked farther in, the width of his massive shoulders making the space feel small. The stout, leather armor he'd worn had been discarded, but he still bore a scimitar at his belt and a pair of battle-axes strapped across his back.

The axes that cleaved Cormek's chest open. Lystra's breath came in shallow, terrified pants. The stories concerning the wild mountain men failed to articulate their savagery, their desire to conquer, the kings' blood that stained their hands. Nothing would mar Lystra's memory like that of riding for her life across the Sancen after watching her betrothed die in the sands.

Gaudab's dark eyes fell upon her with the intensity of a famished predator finally seizing its prey. He took a step toward her, and then another. His fingers—rough, calloused, and as cursed as her own—brushed across her cheek.

"Rest well, river lily?"

Air hissed through Lystra's teeth as she retreated from his touch. Her frame trembled, betraying her fear.

Gaudab scoffed. "Ungrateful wretch. I'd thought to spare you from the prison rats."

She'd take the prisons. After all, she supposed that's where they were keeping Elerek.

"Y-you made a bargain." Lystra tried to speak with authority, with the severity of the crown. "You promised me safety."

The Jarkin laughed. "I promised I wouldn't *kill* you, river lily. Your king left no further specifications."

Casting her eyes to the room's corners, she shuddered. *No. He didn't.* Her lungs felt as if her ribs had become the thick coils of snakes, slowly constricting. Even the wide spaces for Elerek's wheelchair seemed too small, but she knew only the great expanse of the Sancen would be distance enough between her and the Jarkin warlord.

"Understand, little queen." Gaudab leaned forward, his eyes leveling with hers. "Your lives mean nothing to us. Your kingdom is conquered. The only reason your king still breathes is because of this curse—this great complication."

Elerek only lived because he was cursed to die.

"As for you." Gaudab seized the collar of her dress, yanking the fabric back from her shoulder, exposing the clumsy bandages. "You'll wear that mark till the end of your days. You belong to *us*."

Lystra tried to remember what it felt like to have courage, to summon boldness. But such endurance lay afar off as the wrathgiver hovering in the heavens above the eastern mountains. Now, she knew only fear, the shadows encroaching like the Jarkin had when he stepped closer, his hand still on her dress, his breath on her collar.

"You'll be *mine*, little queen."

She braced a hand against his chest and pushed, but he was a mountain and didn't give way. "I'll drown first."

One small proclamation. An ember in the darkness. A sliver of the soul she used to have, but she owed it to her kingdom, and to herself.

Gaudab narrowed his eyes, studying her. Then, he released her and crossed the room, his eyes searching the shadows. "If the curse is broken, nobody will drown. You spoke of a dagger, essential to the curse's breaking."

Lystra rounded Elerek's bed, clearing a path between her and the silk curtains. Though she knew she wouldn't get far, the route of escape eased some air into her lungs. "I did."

Gaudab withdrew a gleaming blade from his belt. "Is this the one?"

As her eyes skimmed over the dagger, small in the warlord's

massive hands, everything inside Lystra recoiled. Its polished, ornate handle gleamed gold, but it was the stars—the constellation—that drew her eyes.

The wrathgiver caused terror whether they were etched in the sky, the dagger's blade, or the flesh of Razhar's chest.

The stars that could break the curse.

She tried to mask her apprehension, but Gaudab saw right through it. A smug smile came over his face. "My soldiers found it among your belongings. We were drawn to its exquisiteness, and the stars on its blade. Our lives hang in the balance, little queen. I suggest you practice honesty before I need to knife your skin again." He sheathed the dagger on his belt. "I've not known Instanolde and their bloodthirsty kings to be so noble. The dagger's presence on your person implies that a plot was in order to break this curse." He laughed a deep, throaty laugh. "Perhaps my campaign interrupted."

Lystra looked away. Her stomach, empty and queasy, knotted itself into tight coils. "I haven't known long."

Was it only yesterday that she'd gone to Kushan, the canyonlands with its stubborn tribe and condor-mounted archers? There, in the deep caverns of the greatest archive known to her world, she'd read words inked in red and sealed by her grandmother's hand. A secret that Razhar had no right to keep.

This plot, this feud of hatred and revenge, began long before her birth. And she'd become a part of it, a pawn in her grandmother's hands as she promised Lystra the crown, schemed her into marriage with Elerek, and sent her with the star-etched dagger into her king's chamber on her wedding night.

She needed to speak to him, explain that she hadn't known that her grandmother was the curse binder or that Razhar's own baba had cast the curse.

That she certainly didn't desire his death.

Gaudab folded his arms. "So, then." He narrowed his eyes. "This dagger must accompany the stars and slay your mongrel king. That will break the curse? Save our skins?"

The weight of his cold, hard words shredded her heart to pieces. But this was her task, to save her people from the Jarkins, which now included breaking the curse, and there was no way out, no path to freedom, without sacrificing Elerek.

She was always destined to lose him and was never meant to love him, but now she'd become complicit in the act of killing him.

Without the will to hold them back, her eyes flooded with tears. She gave a timid nod.

Then, to her great relief, Gaudab stalked from the room and through the veil of silk curtains. The door slammed and locked a moment later, leaving Lystra in the shadows and the deepness of her misery.

Chapter 3

Elerek

Deep in the prisons beneath the guardkeep, the darkness seemed infinite. Like drowning beneath a sky without starlight.

Cast from his crown, dragged from his own throne room, the king of Instanolde stared into the blackness, every breath of his still-beating heart laced with fury. Elerek let it freeze him from the inside out, sealing him within its cold void, much like the curse that had doomed him to die.

Of all ironies, the curse had become his only source of solace. Though the water no longer dripped from his fingers, it lurked just beneath his skin. Violent torrents of cursed waters, pounding like waves, thundering the call to *drown them all.*

A dank chill swept over his still-wet clothing and hair. Elerek reached through the darkness with a shackled hand and dragged it across his face. The chains ground over the stone floor, shattering the silence.

He'd been close, so close. With his curse-given powers seizing his heart, dealing swift justice upon the invaders who threatened his kingdom lay within his grasp. Instead, he'd been betrayed by those who claimed to love him.

Elerek braced his shoulders against the wall at his back. No, he couldn't direct his rage at them—especially at Razhar—not yet. The time would come. For now, he still had breath in his lungs and water in his veins. This last summer to live belonged to *him*, and though Instanolde hadn't chosen or wanted him, he still honored his vow to save it.

And if everyone insisted that he must die, a necessity to break the curse, well, then.

I will live.

The curse had given him years to wallow in the shadows of his own self-pity; surely he could last a few more days, long enough to settle the scores and save his kingdom.

The fall of heavy boots echoed in the darkness. A torch appeared, casting striped shadows across the prison bars.

Elerek steeled himself, preparing to meet the next stage of this nightmare.

Three hulking men approached, clad in stiff leather armor and cruel weapons. Their skin was weathered from the sun and the thin mountain air they called home. Keys rattled and the bars swung back on rusty hinges.

"Get up," the tallest of them barked, marching inside the cell.

Elerek squinted against the torchlight. This Jarkin looked as travel worn as the rest, but he bore no weapons. His long beard was braided and his fingers were stained with ink. It seemed strange to see a Jarkin who wasn't a warrior. He wondered if they'd write their own histories, telling how the golden kingdom of Instanolde fell because its king was weak.

The Jarkin swore. "I *said*, get up!"

Elerek looked away, pretending not to hear him.

"Datem." In their ranks, the equivalent to captain. The second soldier stepped into the cell. "He's a cripple."

Not a cripple. Just crippled. Elerek possessed no memories of walking, or even the knowledge that he'd ever learned. His legs, weak and twisted, never recovered from a bout of the skeetos plague as an infant. No physician could heal him and no priest could lay a hand upon him for prayer, on account of the curse.

He missed his wheeled chair and wondered what had happened to it, regarding the contraption with a fond affection, an extension of himself. He'd found little that his disability prevented him from accomplishing—except obeying the command of this ranking Jarkin.

Another string of curses polluted the air. Elerek felt he could choke on their rancidness. "Instanolde doesn't kill its cripples?" The man looked incredulous.

The soldier huffed. He unchained Elerek from the wall and clasped a pair of shackles over his wrists. Elerek's gaze skimmed the curse mark snaking up the soldier's forearm, the mark of his wrath upon his enemies.

"Datem, he was the king."

Am. Elerek ground his teeth. If he still breathed, then he was still king of Instanolde.

The datem shook his head. "A crippled, cursed king, what a sorry invasion this has turned into. Well, I can't touch him. Hurry up."

Elerek grunted as the soldier unceremoniously dragged him from the cell and down the prison corridors. Unable to brace himself against the uneven ground, his bruised and battered legs ached. When they reached the stairs, the two soldiers came on either side of him, heaving him up the passageway.

At the top of the stairs, the prison's darkness was replaced by the amber glow of the last hour before sunset. A brief touch of sunlight alighted on his shoulders, the end of a day that had seemed eternal. A day of far too many failures and too few triumphs.

Mosaic floors spun beneath him as they entered the palace. Marble pillars marched past, as confining as the prison bars had been. The golden palace had belonged to both Elerek's vengeful father and perfect brother. The home he both loved and hated. A magnificent symbol of Instanolde. Everything he'd lost, the kingdom he had failed.

They took him to the library, dumping him onto the lush rug in the center of the rounded tower room.

His fingers curled into the rough wool, worn from the wheels of his chair. He'd often taken refuge in this place, perused its tomes, and reclined on its couches. The maps, a haphazard pile, still lay where he'd left it. Back when he thought to scheme a way to combat the Jarkins' brutality.

A pair of worn boots filled his vision. Elerek slowly lifted his eyes.

At least I cursed you.

Gaudab Batu-Khasar glared down at him. Even the high ceilings seemed too small for the Jarkin's hulking form. His two battle-axes were strapped to his back in leather straps, their heads still darkened by Instan blood.

King's blood. His brother's blood. Elerek clenched his shackled hands. The plague scars across his knuckles tightened, white against the pale shade of Tribe Karim's skin. All this rage, this consuming fury. He needed something to do with it.

Someone to *kill.*

At first, he thought to silence the notion. He had enough blood on his hands. Too many innocents had fallen prey to the curse, even when he shut himself away and barricaded himself from everyone. He knew humanity's fragility better than most, and knew it was a thing to be protected.

But the Jarkins had no such honor, no regard for the children they slaughtered.

"We ride with the dawn." Gaudab stalked to the desk, his massive shoulders hunching as his placed his fists on the star chart spread across its top as if he intended to crush the very heavens themselves.

Dawn. Elerek sucked at the air as if his lungs were full of water.

The Jarkin with the braided beard scoffed. "You're sure?"

Gaudab snarled. Elerek tensed, certain that the warlord didn't appreciate being questioned. He pushed himself up and scooted to the couch, stretching his legs out in front of him. Every bit of him felt sore from his night on the prison floor.

"We need the warmaker stars," Gaudab snapped. "Have you a better plan, Tangu?"

Warmaker. Wrathgiver. Different names, but the two peoples had given the same stars the same attributes. Elerek cast his gaze over the star chart. Every child in Instanolde knew the stars, the dancing constellations, and the stories they told. The assassin attributed to the wrathgiver had been hunting him all this time, starlight chasing him to his doom. The same stars on Lystra's dagger. The same stars on Razhar's tattoo.

Elerek's insides knotted. He didn't understand. It seemed unfathomable that this link, this constellation of distant stars, could connect his childhood friend, his queen, and his curse. Yet upon this their betrayal had been wrought, and it hurt him far deeper than any dagger.

Tangu, the ink stained Jarkin, approached the desk, his brow furrowing. "This curse has addled your thinking, Khasar. Since when do we listen to the tales of dirty river rats? Surely you can see through the flimsy words of their queen?" He huffed. "Or has her sun-blessed skin turned your head?"

Elerek stilled, his hands curling into fists. Water gathered along his knuckles, snaking down his wrists. The image of an elegant hand filled his mind, clothed in the color of the desert with callouses lining the fingertips from the leather reins of cardants. Hands that weren't meant to touch him.

Why Lystra?

"If the curse is broken by his death"—Tangu gestured toward him—"then kill him. This stupidity with the stars is a ploy to draw us out of the city."

No, he hadn't any interest in permitting anyone to kill him. Not until Instanolde emerged from beneath the shadow of the Jarkins' threat.

Eyeing Elerek from hooded eyes, Gaudab scowled, his voice rumbling deep in his throat. "The stars are necessary, and to kill him too soon will threaten us all." His gaze shifted back to Tangu. "But he will die. Him and his filthy line of pathetic kings and paltry bargains."

Elerek glared back at the warlord. He'd made only one bargain—that Lystra would live.

But he couldn't let her live like this. No matter what she'd done, what curses she'd taken, she was still Instanolde's best chance. A ruler who loved her people. A fierce survivor. He needed her safe—from him as well as Batu-Khasar.

"I need you with us, Tangu." Gaudab rose to his full height, folding his massive arms over his chest. "If we're to hold the Darcress Kasbah and the entirety of the riverfront, we need the desert mapped, routes established."

A cartographer. The thought that the Sancen could be tamed was laughable. To survive, one lived with one's head reverently bowed to the vast wilderness. The desert served as a natural defense against their enemies, hedging Instanolde against the river with heat, light, and a thousand mysteries and monsters.

The Sancen could kill a man in a day. No one dared to ride out during high summer.

But they would. Cross the impossible Sancen to chase the stars, spill blood, and break the curse. Elerek shut his eyes, this reality bearing down upon his shoulders with a weight that he couldn't carry.

"Which means you too must be cursed."

The water on Elerek's hands soaked into the couch, dripping onto the rug below. His curse-induced anger building. Seeking a victim. And here stood this Jarkin with his mocking tongue and his compliance in the invasion that had brought Instanolde to its knees. The perfect vessel to fill with water until he burst into a shower of diamond droplets.

Perhaps they had kept him in chains, threatened his queen, and flaunted banners of victory from every spire, but one fact remained—they would drown.

And if the curse took Gaudab Batu-Khasar, the most fearsome of Instanolde's enemies, the victory at the end of this starless night would belong to *him*, the cursed king of Instanolde who carried death in his hands. He would destroy them.

If he destroyed himself in the process, so be it.

Tangu expressed his disgust in a terrible string of oaths.

Towering over his underling, Gaudab's face transformed into a thing of nightmarish wrath. "I've permitted you to question me, Tangu, but not to disobey me."

The mapmaker's jaw tightened. His eyes shifted toward Elerek. "You've gone mad, Khasar. This is a *curse*. It must be destroyed, not perpetuated."

Gaudab growled. "This will be done. But the stars lie across the desert, which will destroy you long before the curse will."

Elerek kept his gaze on Tangu, unblinking. When he'd declared to Batu-Khasar that he could cross the indomitable

Sancen, he'd made no bluff. The desert was sand and sun and death. Water was life and survival here among the canyons and dunes, and Elerek *was* water.

He lifted a hand, his fingers outstretched. The droplets surged to his fingertips and, one by one, dripped onto the rug below. They amassed themselves into a steady stream, soaking the rug and pooling across the stone.

And Tangu watched, shriveling in fear.

Elerek closed his hand. The waters stilled, held in stasis in a wide circle about Tangu's boots. Then, he looked at Gaudab, his stare cold and calculated. "Khasar." Elerek spoke with all the powers of command the crown had given him. "Curse him yourself."

Gaudab's eyes gleamed, wholly undeterred by Elerek's challenge. *Power.* The Jarkins wanted it, craved it, and risked everything to invade a kingdom to gain it.

Sometimes the curse spread secondhand, and sometimes not. Sometimes it required skin contact and sometimes not. Perhaps it might prove useful to know if the Jarkin warlord could spread the curse's vile intent.

"What do you—?" Tangu's eyes darted back and forth, but Gaudab promptly seized him by the wrist. The skin-turned-water on his hand shimmered in the lamplight.

And nothing happened.

Elerek released his held breath. Not even the man who murdered his brother, threatened his queen, and conquered his kingdom could destroy like he could. "Ah, it seems you do *need* me, Khasar."

Gaudab snarled, his eyes glinting with a fire made of darkness. Muttering an oath beneath his breath, he yanked Tangu into the puddle of water, across the dampened rug, and approached the couch that Elerek had made his throne.

Foul words dripped from Tangu's lips. "This is lunacy, sheer lun—" He gasped, air hissing between his teeth.

Elerek could feel his terror, his fury, his *helplessness*, all from one brush of his wet fingertips across the back of the man's hands.

Cursing him.

He felt it. A cold chill swept over his skin and surged in his veins, the terrible power of death seeping into the skin of the man's forearm. Claiming another soul to drown.

For a moment, an intoxicating thrill shot through Elerek. The rush of a cardant at full speed, carrying him across the vast desert. The sense of authority and power as the weight of the ceremonial crown wrought of fire opals rested on his brow. The way Lystra looked at him, her eyes full of grief, hope, and a longing made of both.

I . . . I cursed Lystra.

Like the flash torrents swelling the Gungole into the fertile deltas, his lust for blood dissipated. The curse-induced rage subsided, his humanity restored to him. His mind became a familiar landscape, a horizon of sorrow and loathing.

Give her starlight. Give her the hope he'd never possessed for himself. Lystra had become his queen out of devotion to her people. Together, they took vows before their kingdom, devoting themselves to its survival.

As for Elerek, he'd committed himself to *her* survival.

But Lystra, the sunlight to his starlight, had done the unthinkable. In the place where Myra had died, Lystra stood to support him. Her eyes—the moment she'd touched him—pierced his heart. Fierce and bold and shimmering like the golden sands themselves—and yet, laced with horror, with pain, with the *knowing*.

She knew what it felt like now. She knew him. Perhaps in a way that no one else did, no one else could.

The thought broke him.

Elerek turned away from the sight of the cursed man clutching his arm, swearing and grinding his teeth. Tears filled his eyes, and he wondered if they too held the curse or if they belonged to him—the man inside the monster the curse had cultivated.

He deserved death—not the two women who held a claim on his heart. Two realities that were never meant to be. Myra had met him in some of the darkest moments of his life and loved him. How many nights had he spent in her comfort? Guilt would burn at his heart with the dawn's break for his self-ishness, his indulgence, but he had loved her. It'd broken both their hearts when he swore to uphold the vows he made to Lystra for the sake of their kingdom. He would be faithful to her, the wife he could never touch.

But Lystra's heart didn't remain unscathed. Somewhere in the stillness, the unspoken, the moments where they'd fused together like steel, something had changed.

And he'd broken her heart too—along with his vows.

Well, I suppose we're even now.

Lystra had stood before their throne, cast in marble like the rest of the grand hall, and spun a tale so ridiculous that it dared postulate that his curse *could* be broken. Broken by his death. Was that what Lystra wanted? Even after all they had shared, how they had grown, and how, despite their best efforts, they'd dared to slip into this forbidden territory? A raw and uncut place amid the desert, an affection grew like some rare and determined flower and bloomed in a defiant contradiction.

Elerek closed his eyes. Whatever Lystra's motive had been in the throne room, whatever impossibilities he felt within his own heart, for her he would set aside his fury. His love for Myra had cost her life. He couldn't permit Lystra to share her fate. It had always ended with his death. No other outcome existed beneath the blinding desert sun. He was meant to die and Lystra was meant to live. No matter the storms, the deceptions, the intrigues, *this* was the story he had to write in the stars themselves.

But not yet. He drove his fists like stakes into the cushions of the couch.

If indeed the curse could be broken, he would pay whatever price he was required to pay—but he would see that the Jarkins also paid their share first. And when it was over, and the blood repaid to the stars above, he could only hope that the Starkindler, the Maker of the heavens, could forgive him.

Chapter 4

Elerek

The sun had set when Gaudab called for the soldiers to return Elerek to the prison. Between each jolt and jostle, Elerek craned his neck, scanning the inky blackness.

Searching for stars.

In Instanolde, the stars each belonged to a constellation, and that constellation danced, spinning and twirling, as they followed a delicate pattern that stretched from the dawn of time.

The Starkindler, the Maker of the stars, set them on their course. The stories of the constellations passed from parent to child to share histories, teach lessons, and evoke a sense of wonder.

In a broken world of curses and death, Elerek had always looked to the stars. Their light was pure, illuminated by the glow of their maker, unsoiled by the sorrow and the toil below. When the curse took him, he hoped to see their light with untainted eyes. To see the Starkindler face-to-face.

But now, he feared starlight would only gleam upon the blood on his hands and expose the wrath burning in his soul.

Tangu walked ahead of him, clutching his cursed hand, the mark encircling his wrist like a coiling snake. Before long, it would spread, stealing skin and working inward, drowning him. Elerek had lost count of how many leering skulls he'd seen just before the curse's victims burst into a shower of droplets, absorbed by the desert sands. And every time, it had torn his soul to shreds.

"Cease your muttering," Gaudab snarled. He marched ahead of Tangu, his cloak streaming behind him like the great black wing of a condor. "We will conquer the desert, break this curse, and Instanolde will be ours."

He would drown them all before that happened. Elerek clenched his jaw in resolve just as his foot struck a rock amongst the gravel and exploded with pain. A reminder that he was only a man, and a cursed one. A subtle fear took root within his chest. That his anger and vengeance wouldn't be enough.

"What's in the prisons that interests you?" Tangu bit out through clenched teeth.

"A prisoner. One we didn't imprison."

Elerek scowled. He hadn't imprisoned anyone, except the Jarkin assassin who had attacked Lystra, and he was very much dead.

The black opening of the underground gaped ahead. The thought of another night upon cold stone, pressed on all sides by the deep darkness, made Elerek's lungs squeeze and his blood riot with panic.

A flash of color appeared on the path in the form of a figure who had no business amongst the strut of soldiers and the gleam of weapons. No, the man standing in the gravel ought to have been carelessly dancing the night away at the markets or cracking terrible jokes over a cup of spiced coffee with his companions. A man clad in the bronze skin of the Kushite tribe and eternally clothed in every garish hue Instanolde had to offer.

Razhar.

Elerek's hands clenched into tight fists. Heat burned in his chest, boiling the cursed waters in his veins. At last, here stood the intended recipient of his ire. The brother who had betrayed him.

"El!" Razhar's eyes grew wide as pomegranates as he hurried toward them, the tail of his bright green turban flying behind him.

Water gathered at Elerek's hands, cascading down the leather armor on the soldiers' shoulders. They panicked, letting him crumple. The ground slammed against his chest, knocking the air from his lungs. When Elerek pushed himself up, his wet hands and arms were coated with sand.

Sand.

He fixed his gaze on Razhar, eyeing the dark skin lining his thick forearms and large hands. Skin caked with unnatural—cursed—sands.

"Ah, the Kushite." Gaudab stalked between them, an immense river vessel sailing between two opposite shores. "I'd wondered where you'd been hiding. I've an assignment for you."

Elerek scoffed. The idea of Razhar "hiding" with his typical ensembles was ridiculous.

"What do you want?" Razhar's sand-covered hands drew into tight fists.

"You too will prepare for our expedition. I need someone to interpret your strange stars."

Elerek wished he could laugh. Pity that the Jarkins didn't

ask for a guided tour of Instanolde's bakeries and sweet shops, a skill actually within Razhar's abilities.

"M-me?" Razhar stuttered. "B-but I . . ."

Gaudab feinted toward him. Razhar was broad-shouldered and well-muscled, but still, in the Jarkin's shadow, he looked like a small child. "You seemed certain that your information regarding this curse is accurate." Gaudab drew a knife from his belt, holding the blade eye level with Razhar. His hands, both bearing the curse mark, shimmered in the starlight. "If I find that you are lying . . ."

Razhar's jaw tightened. "I'm not."

"Then you will aid us in its breaking. That is what you want, isn't it?"

Razhar bowed his head, the shadows claiming his gaze.

You want me dead. Elerek couldn't imagine a world without Razhar. A constant steady as the summer sun. No one knew him like Razhar did, in all his shattered brokenness, and still chose to pull him up from his despair with a word of hope.

"To think," Elerek said slowly, allowing the poison to fill his words, "that I ever considered you my friend."

Razhar jerked his head up. "El, it's not like that at all. If you'd listen, just give me a chance to explain—"

"You were my *brother*, closer and dearer to me than any relation of blood." And now, he hated him. Hated him as much as the Jarkin that killed his real brother. Elerek clenched his fists, sand and water squeezing between his fingers. Trying to hold back his rage was akin to restraining the river.

"I haven't the time for this," Gaudab thundered. He seized the front of Razhar's vest, the knife buried in his scarf. "You will aid us in the breaking of this curse, or I'll demonstrate to this reeking river rat kingdom how I really feel about disgusting Kushites."

Tiny clouds of pale sand drifted from Razhar's fingers,

piling about his boots. His eyes, wide and terrified, shifted between the Jarkin warlord and Elerek. He wondered which of them was the more fearsome in Razhar's eyes.

Then, casting his eyes downward, Razhar gave a timid nod. Gaudab released him and sheathed his knife.

"You're a weak, sniveling coward," Elerek growled beneath his breath.

After all they'd been through, dark nights and lonely hells, *barjee* games, terrible jokes, Razhar's patronizing optimism—and he'd lied to Elerek. Worse, Razhar's sands—his own strange curse—had come between him and the work of saving his kingdom. Elerek *knew* he could've done it, avenged Cormek, avenged Myra, and swiftly put an end to this invasion. The Jarkins would no longer be a threat and Instanolde would be free to prosper beneath the glorious desert sun. Its crown would rest on Lystra's noble brow and some semblance of rightness would have come from his cursed hands.

Not even a comradeship like theirs could survive this betrayal.

"Now." Gaudab folded his massive arms. "You'll gather the best maps and star charts your kingdom keeps, and give them to Datem Tangu here. Together, you'll chart our course to follow the stars. The moment you start lying to us, lowly Kushite"—his eyes narrowed to terrible slits, like those of a cobra—"we'll leave your bones for the Sancen."

Razhar gave another timid nod.

"We ride out at dawn, as soon as I can procure enough fresh cardants from this miserable kingdom."

Elerek clenched his jaw. Gaudab himself had slain most of the cardants in the ambush that killed his brother. What lizards remained were procured from the racing committee and donations from the great houses. This had been particularly hard on

Lystra, for there was none in the kingdom who loved the reptiles more.

Gaudab pulled a ring of keys from his belt, removing one cast in polished gold. He handed it to one of the soldiers. "Take the Kushite into the palace. Once he's done with Tangu, let him inform the river lily of our expedition." A horrible, leering smile twisted the Jarkin's face. "Have him tell her that she'll be joining us too. Something pretty to look at in that desert of damnation."

Elerek snapped his head up.

Razhar raised trembling hands, a posture of pleading. "No, Khasar, I beg you. She must remain here. This curse has nothing to do with her."

The sound of his tone, of another man begging for his wife's safety, dragged something dark and terrible from inside Elerek. He lifted his hands, the shackles rattling between his wrists, the water dripping from his fingers as poisonous as a scorpion's.

"No, it *didn't*." He spoke in a low voice. "She was meant to live. Now she's just as cursed as the rest of us."

Razhar stared at him. "El . . . it isn't my fault that she—"

Elerek did not care. Growling, water streamed from his palms, wrought from a curse dark and vile. It launched toward Razhar, who swiftly danced back, small puffs of sand falling from his hands again.

This time, there would be more water than sand.

Bam! A fist contacted Elerek's face, knocking him backwards. His head smashed against the stone pavement. The waters ceased as pain subdued his senses. The world spun overhead and the scent of blood filled his nostrils.

Gaudab stood over him, eclipsing the skies. "You try anything like that, our bargain is off." He scoffed. "As if your queen's life lies in my power. The desert or your own waters may take her first." He grabbed Elerek's shoulder, yanking him upright. "Did you consider that it's in *my* best interest that the river lily lives?"

Elerek's pulse pounded in his head as if his skull were a drum. Blood dripped down his nose and the fringes of his vision darkened.

"Stop! Please . . ." Razhar's voice sounded as if it belonged to an abandoned pup set adrift on the streets. "The curse . . ."

"I've no use for begging, Kushite. I do hope the little queen will do her part and keep the both of you in line." Gaudab stalked toward the yawning pit of the prisons, dragging Elerek with him. Gravel tore at his weakened legs, cutting into his pants and slicing at his bare feet. "I've no idea why this curse concerns you, but we'll keep the king alive until it's time to kill him, just like you want."

Razhar wanted him dead. Elerek closed his eyes, focusing only on the pain and letting it consume him. It was easier. There was nothing, no apology or future, that would repair what had been severed.

The prison echoed with the footfalls of Gaudab and the rattle of shackles around Elerek's wrists. These two sounds went to war with the pain in his head and he wondered when he'd black out. Such a thing would be a mercy at this point.

But they halted. Elerek collapsed. Had they arrived back at his cell? Blinking and grinding dust between his teeth, the glow of torches seared his vision. He lifted a hand to shield his eyes. A cell lay before him, but this one wasn't empty. A slender shadow, like a desert wraith, stood within, clad in elegant silks.

"Who are you?" Gaudab's voice boomed.

"No one that matters to you, man of the mountains."

Elerek tried to push himself up, head aching. He knew that voice. Dalmah of House Arghan. Lystra's grandmother. He held no fondness for the woman, having witnessed the manipulative hold she held over her granddaughter. Around her, Lystra became someone else, someone frightened and unsure of herself. Nothing at all like the bold queen he'd come to love.

Why was Dalmah here? Elerek wiped the blood from his face with his sleeve. Had Lystra done this?

"We've taken control of this city."

"As expected. That boy never had the resources or the time to hold off such an invasion." Dalmah's voice dripped with venom. "This was always Instanolde's destiny."

Elerek tried again, breathing deeply through his bloodied nose, to bring himself into a sitting position. He braced his hand against the wall, leaning his head on his elbow.

They'd done their best to hope, to see the starlight through the murk. Only together had Elerek dared to believe it—him and Lystra becoming something whole. He needed her to help him, and he wanted to hope that he'd done the same for her.

Then why did she do it? Touch me? Take the curse? Declare my death as the only way?

Did she want him to die for her?

"Now I see that you must next conquer this curse." Dalmah's lip quirked with amusement. The jewels on her fingers reflected a red as deep as blood. "Perhaps some good will come of this yet. This curse has held far too long."

Elerek froze, overcome with the curse's numbness again. The void surrounded him, robbing him of all feeling. Dalmah knew? About the curse?

Did she know back then, when she'd proposed Lystra's marriage to him?

"We know how to break it." Gaudab puffed out his chest, overconfident.

"Do you?" Dalmah's eyes twinkled in the torchlight. Then, she smiled. "That is fortunate. If you release me, I'll do my best to spread that good word. It may earn you some merit within these walls. Instanolde will see some good done in this desert—a debt finally paid."

Elerek stared at her. His pain morphed, transcending his physical self and spilling into his soul, which had already taken more than it could bear.

Her smile echoed a feeling that Elerek understood, one of desired vengeance upon one's enemies. And when Dalmah's gaze moved, falling upon him and burning with heat, he finally realized the truth.

Dalmah of House Arghan had cursed him.

A lifetime of wondering, of telling himself that it didn't matter, and now, with his death before him, he'd found his answer. The Arghan queen who'd lost the throne to destructive House Karim. The war widow who had as much reason as anyone to hate Lorkin, Elerek's father. The countess who had worn black to his wedding.

"You . . ." he whispered, his voice no more than a wheezed breath.

Only then did Dalmah meet his gaze. Her eyes were cruel and wicked. Elerek had no difficulty imagining the ornate dagger with the wrathgiver stars etched into its blade fitting into her wrinkled, slender hands.

The same dagger that Lystra had carried into his chamber on their wedding night, dressed in black. A soldier acting on orders.

Her grandmother sent her to kill me.

If Dalmah wanted to punish House Karim, then she'd received what she wished. But Elerek had lived too long, long enough to become king, and that meant he had to die to give Lystra the throne.

Well, that was still his intention.

But had Lystra known? Their marriage had nothing to do with the lofty goals of saving a kingdom, of surviving summer's end, and seeing Instanolde through the night and into the sunrise. No, a deception. A manipulation. Another layer of plot to see his doomed life destroyed.

Elerek closed his eyes again, feeling his limbs losing their strength. Lystra had become a gift he'd never deserved. She'd burned through the darkness, illuminating his world, bringing life and hope where there ought not to be any. He'd kept her at arm's length to protect her, raising his battlements to keep them both from the battle they were doomed to lose.

He only knew that he loved her when he'd already lost her.

But maybe Lystra had never loved him at all. Just another manipulation by a player more skilled than they.

"Guards, where are the keys?" Gaudab barked. The Jarkins shuffled as one of them produced a ring that jangled like bells in the marketplace. "Release this woman. She looks like she belongs among the top of river rat society. Perhaps she has honor enough to keep her word."

"I'll do it," Elerek whispered, his body sagging. His head throbbed without mercy. "Break the curse and die."

"Yes," Dalmah whispered as the Jarkin guard jammed a key into the door of her cell. "You will."

"Take him back to his cell." Gaudab stood tall, filling the hallway with the width of his shoulders. "Let the cursed king rest before we ride for the stars."

Chapter 5

Lystra

Lystra stirred a second time, waking from a fitful sleep atop Elerek's bed. The wound on her shoulder sent spasms down her back. Blood had already soaked through the layers of linen, causing them to stiffen like funeral wrappings.

The sound of a soft knock echoed through the empty chamber.

With a whimper, Lystra pushed herself off the bed. Her body ached with weary sorrow, the kind that didn't come from lack of sleep. The fatigue of battle, of a soul that had been mourning, for far, far too long.

She entered the parlor, approaching the door. The knocks couldn't belong to the Jarkins, particularly not when the door was bolted. But the handle turned when she tried it.

Beyond, the soft glow of torches illuminated the sheen of verdant silk on Razhar's turban—but did nothing to pierce the deep darkness in his eyes.

He lifted his head in expectation. "Your Highness, I—"

"You *coward.*" She spat the words. Her anger was an arrow set against a bow, its string taut.

Razhar dropped his shoulders, her aim true. His eyes shifted to the Jarkins in the corridor, whose numbers seemed to have multiplied. "Your Highness, I must speak with you."

Lystra sniffed and stepped back, holding the door open.

He shuffled inside, his footsteps noiseless on the rug. Once Lystra shut the door again, the chink of the Jarkins' armor filled the void of silence, followed by the turn of the lock.

She folded her arms. "They're locking you in here *with me?*"

Razhar sighed, no more than a shadow in the murk. "We don't have much time."

They never had. She suppressed a scoff.

Hunching over a lamp on the table in the center of the luscious room, Razhar struck a match. His voice was low, little more than a murmur. "They're taking us at dawn. To the desert."

A shudder scurried over Lystra's skin, like the many limbs of a scorpion across the gentle rise of a sand dune. "That's . . . that's impossible." Even the breath of her words felt cold on her lips. "It's high summer."

Could the curse sustain them in the desert even as it turned their bodies to water? The very thought seemed ridiculous, a strange and twisted semblance to the deadly balance of their survival, their existence lingering precariously between life and death.

Razhar hung his head, his bent figure a picture of defeat. Gone was the dancer in the market who'd pushed back the bitter shroud of grief as he had the veil covering Lystra's face.

"The curse is moving swiftly. I doubt that El will survive until the next rotation of the heavens—and we need the wrath-giver to break the curse." When the oil in the lamp burned,

Razhar rose to his full height, watching her with an empty, vacant look in his amber eyes.

Lystra didn't recognize the man standing before her now. Had he so quickly transformed over the course of a month? The short, cruel reign of the third Karim king and his Arghan queen? A man of far, far too many secrets, who wore as many masks as he possessed colorful scarves.

"You sold us to our deaths, Razhar." Hot tears pooled in Lystra's eyes. "Did you know that this would happen? Is that why you took me to the archives? To show me the writ?"

"You already knew that your grandmother was guilty. I gave you the truth, hoping you'd know what to do with it."

"The truth." Scoffing, Lystra stepped past him, moving to the window. The beautiful kingdom of Instanolde stretched before her like a map, illuminated by pale starlight and the warm glow of torches. On any other night, she might have heard the distant pounding of raw-hide drums and the ring of laughter and tambourines. Life pulsing beneath the stars in a kingdom built of survivors, who lived and danced not in defiance of the desert but thrived despite it.

Instead, she heard the shouting of people and the march of soldiers. Even now, in the darkness, puffs of dust covered the roads as people fled. She wondered if her family, her father and cousins, had also fled.

Lystra shut her eyes. She meant to save them. Instead, the cursed queen of Instanolde had failed, all on account of her foolish heart.

"You gave *me* the truth—and I gave it to *him*." She glanced back at Razhar, her heart pounding. "Exactly what you should have done a long, long time ago."

Razhar bristled.

"And now, they're going to kill him." Another onslaught of hot tears flooded her eyes and, one by one, dripped down her cheeks. "They're going to kill him because *I* told him the truth. He thinks we've betrayed him."

"I know," Razhar's voice was barely audible.

Sniffling, Lystra sank onto the couch, her hand moving to her shoulder. She wondered how anyone expected her to carry a kingdom.

"You're hurt?" Razhar phrased it as a question, but the sorrow in his voice implied that he already knew his answer.

"Khasar carved the emblem of their people into my skin. Branded, like an animal." She flashed her eyes at him. "If it wasn't for you, Khasar would have drowned. El had him."

"You don't know that. The tides could have turned like *that.*" Razhar snapped his fingers. "You, Your Highness, more than almost anyone, know what we're up against. The might of the whole Jarkin army against one man? An impossible victory. And if they had killed El, everyone that I . . ." He stopped, his eyes searching the shadows in the room's corners.

This time, Lystra saw right through his mask. Everyone connected to the curse would die.

Everyone that I love.

Elerek's tribe of cursed didn't only belong to him. They were Razhar's family also.

"Stars above." Razhar paced the length of the rug with anxious, jittery motions. He brushed a hand along his forearm, sending a shower of dust into the air, glittering like gold in the lamplight. "My actions were to save life—including yours."

A salvation built upon lies, like the shifting sands of the Sancen. Lystra rubbed her brow, her skull aching after so many sorrows. "Could you not have trusted him?"

Razhar's hands clenched, his amber eyes watching her without blinking.

"El told me that you found him the day he . . ." *Tried to kill himself.* A desperate act, a manifestation of the deepest, darkest pains festering in Elerek's tormented soul. But without it, they wouldn't have known that those who bore the curse also shared the danger. Lystra could hardly bear to think of it. "Myra said that you love him. Why would you even think to withhold this from him?"

"Do you trust him, Lystra?"

The question struck her like a thunderclap, rattling in her chest. Her mind returned to the night she took vows. When she'd handed the dagger over to the king it was meant to kill, their intentions aligning with the same precision as a constellation in the heavens.

But a pain far too recent moaned like mournful winds across her soul. Trust came with a steep cost, and her heart had paid.

"Yes." Lystra held firm. "I do trust him."

If only in the matter of saving Instanolde. He was still her king and, like it or not, the curse had given him the power to protect their kingdom. In this, they were still devoted.

Razhar looked away.

Drawing a shallow breath, she braced herself against the chill seeping into the room. A thick tension hung in the air, like a hidden knife in a bedchamber, meant to stab unawares.

In the short time that she'd known Razhar, she'd seen his kindness, his sympathy—towards Elerek more than anyone. This was a face she hadn't seen on him before, one that didn't possess a mask to complement it.

"What is it?" Lystra rose to her feet. "What's changed? Between you and El?"

Razhar's hands drew into fists. A small cloud of sand drifted from his clenched fingers, dusting finely over the table. Lystra stopped, her eyes fixated on the sand, those small, fine grains that, when grouped together, could prove just as deadly as a torrent of Elerek's waters.

They're total opposites.

There was so much she didn't understand.

"You've started calling him that . . ." An expression of complete defeat fell over Razhar's still shadowed face.

El. A nickname reserved for the closest of friends. Lystra wondered if she were worthy.

"You love him, don't you?"

Jealousy. It echoed loud and clear, like the territorial growls of cardants as they snapped their jaws at one another. Louder than any of Razhar's previous hints and suggestions.

The stranger who nearly kissed her in the market. The warrior of smiles and laughter, jokes and mirth. The man who called her lovely.

Their world lay on the edge of impending doom. Elerek had dreamed of a world he would never see, beyond his fragile life, scheming to ensure that Instanolde lasted. Mostly, these plans revolved around her. Perhaps Razhar had done the same.

Lystra looked away. For Razhar, she had nothing to offer. "I can't love him."

Razhar heaved a long sigh. Stepping past her, he settled onto the couch and shoved the loose swaths of his turban off his head. "Then I suppose we both have nothing to say." He tossed the verdant silk over the back of the couch. "I think they mean to keep me in here, and I'd like a few hours' sleep if we're to brave the Sancen."

Lystra wanted to protest. To grab him by the shoulders and shake all the answers from the folds of his flashy clothes. But she was tired. So, so tired.

"Why must we go?" She rubbed her forehead. "To the Sancen?"

"Leverage . . . on El."

Her fingertips brushed the bandage beneath her collar. The cuts—the *mark*—burned into her skin with the heat of a searing iron. A mark she carried for the sole reason of manipulating the king whom she loved, but who didn't love her.

Lystra sighed and turned away. This time, she moved toward her own chamber. A bit of heat burst on her face at the thought of Razhar watching her vanish into Elerek's chamber to sleep upon his bed.

She paused at the curtain, glancing over her shoulder. Razhar still sat hunched, staring into the lamp's tiny dancing flame. "One more thing." She summoned strength to her voice, a shard of the queen she'd tried so desperately to become. "Are you cursed?"

Razhar closed his eyes. "I feel cursed."

"That's not what I asked."

He huffed and hauled himself to his feet. Circling the couch, he approached her with deliberate footsteps. "I told you that El's curse was a monumental, horrendous thing. Well, the more powerful the curse, the greater the cost." He reached for her hand.

Lystra winced, backing away.

"Please." Such sorrow filled his voice. "Let me help."

Lystra relented. His skin felt warm, the first bit of warmth she'd felt since taking the curse. Black tendrils snaked up from their point of contact, stretching up their arms. She gasped as the numbness eased from her body. Rich, amber skin clothed her hands again, eradicating the curse's mark.

When they separated, sand fell from his fingertips. "I'm not cursed," he whispered. "I'm the cost—a consequence. A clear message to my baba that the deed he did was terrible. The curse was cast to cause suffering, to punish a bloody king, to doom his heir to death." Razhar rubbed his dusty fingers together. "And yet the curse's cost was the power to keep alive the very man cursed to die. El's utter opposite. Ironic."

She thought of Razhar standing between Elerek and

Gaudab, cursed water meeting cursed sand. The elements mingling, bringing the battle to an absolute standstill.

"But your sands, were you always like this?"

"It . . . it changed. It got worse."

"Like El?"

He nodded. "The same night that he drowned the Jarkin."

Both curse and consequence slowly unraveling. Lystra scoffed. "The same day we left for Kushan, and you chose to tell me all your secrets. It would seem that the truth only matters when it pertains to your own skin."

Razhar didn't speak nor look her in the eye.

Lystra turned away. Would the fate of her kingdom and the golden city she loved really be determined by the secrets of two men? Two men of vastly different backgrounds yet connected by a powerful curse? The king of Instanolde and the war orphan from the canyonlands?

And here, Lystra stood between them.

Preserving her kingdom had been her priority, to preserve the beautiful life they lived at the edge of the desert. The cursed were a part of her kingdom, a truth that Elerek had taken to heart, protecting those who shared in his suffering. He'd wanted her to cherish their lives too.

I wanted to save him.

Thanks to Razhar, she knew how to break the curse. But breaking the curse and saving Elerek were two different, impossible things. She'd made her choice. Her kingdom came first, and the lives she would save by sacrificing the king.

And now, she wondered if another threat had encroached on her kingdom. If Razhar would stand in her way, his secrets endangering not only Instanolde—but also her king.

Chapter 6

Razhar

Razhar watched as the curtains enveloped Lystra, the silk rippling like a gentle breeze over the river waters. Silence swept over the chamber, and a shudder crept along his arms, mingling with the sand clinging to his skin.

Neither of them will listen.

Rounding the couch, he tentatively seated himself, perched like another fluffy, decorative cushion. His eyes crept along the corners and the odd, angular edges of the ornate furniture. The room was too large, too lavish. Adorned for a king. How strange that he—a nobody, a child who'd come to this city with a dirty face and tattered clothes—should be here.

There were very few things that Razhar hated. An over-baked m'hanncha was one of them. But he *did* hate feeling inadequate. Even after all these years, the sting of distinction was as sharp as any scimitar.

He rubbed his face with both hands, drawing his fingers back through his shoulder-length hair. The bite of Lystra's voice echoed in his mind, calling him a coward. The fierce hatred in Elerek's eyes pierced his soul.

They didn't understand. How could they? He couldn't tell them the truth. Razhar pinched his eyes shut. No, not until he knew what they would do with it.

Meanwhile, Dalmah's words wormed in his mind and weighed down his heart. He'd seen the dagger, sheathed on Gaudab's belt. He needed that weapon. Then, no more friends had to die. He wouldn't have to spend his life trying to save them anymore. All at the cost of one death.

Stars above. Razhar wondered if he could live with himself, with Elerek's blood on his hands.

Would he live at all? When he'd told Lystra that his condition—his sands—were a recent development, it wasn't the whole truth.

No, he'd felt these sands before. His eyes, raw and itching worse than any insect's bite. His tongue swollen and dry, unable to taste. And his lungs, shallow and wheezing with every agonizing breath. At the time, a child bedridden, unable to rise and play, Razhar had thought he was dying.

His baba had done something. Something in the dark of night, with only the stars for company. Fahwal had claimed it was some great work, one that would stop the wars and their people from dying. But it came with a consequence, and consequences were to be paid, not undone.

Razhar clenched his eyes shut. One steady breath and then another. Even now, so many years later, he could still hear his baba's sobs. He prayed for forgiveness, for mercy.

Baba didn't give up. He found the way—the way for me to get better.

But now the sands had returned.

Lowering his gaze, his fingers brushed away a dusting of amber sand from his forearm, as fine as any swept from the mountain's clefts to accumulate in sloping dunes below. As quickly as Elerek and those he'd touched were turning to water, Razhar was turning to sand. Another sort of drowning.

He'd long suspected that the "aid" he gave the cursed held a beneficial effect upon himself. Hold back the water, the sand, and in the precarious ground between, they'd found a way to live. He wondered how long their survival might have lasted. Maybe they could have gone on forever. Maybe Elerek didn't have to die at all.

But still, he couldn't save everyone. No matter how hard he tried. The curse had played them all and won. Perhaps the king and queen would argue—loudly and vehemently—that no one had played more than him.

He slipped his boots from his feet, reclining back on the couch. With a wave of his hand, Razhar snuffed out the lamp, letting the darkness overtake him.

There was only one possible way where he—the cost and the consequence—could survive. By killing Elerek.

My best friend.

Razhar squirmed, pushing a tasseled cushion beneath his head. It seemed strange to think such thoughts in rooms like these. Then again, these rooms had belonged to a line of bloody Karim kings that had plotted plenty.

But Elerek wasn't like them.

Once the dagger lay in his possession, Razhar could decide his next course of action. A blade used to curse and destroy hardly seemed a comforting thing, but the settling of the matter allowed him to drift into slumber.

Chapter 7

Lystra

Leaving Razhar in the parlor, Lystra swept past the splendor of her chambers and onto the balcony, welcoming the cool kiss of night air on her skin. After the long hours of confinement between the palace walls, the openness touched her soul with the relief of a balm.

And up above, the constellations danced.

Lystra turned her gaze skyward, letting herself be lost in the sight of the swirling, spinning trails of stardust thousands upon thousands of miles away, and there, on the distant, eastern horizon, the wrathgiver lay small, positioned above the mountains.

And in between, the whole of the Sancen.

She knew the Sancen better than most. The taste of sweat and the grit of sand between her teeth. How the shadows could sink the narrow, slotted canyons into darkness even while last light burned the windswept crags a brilliant array of red, orange, and pinks. She'd charted its endless fields of dunes, rocky crags, and layered canyons from the back of a cardant.

Whether she trained for a race or simply took an outing for the thrill of it, there, she was free.

If I go out there again . . . could I survive a second time?

Tomorrow, at sunrise. Would they really take her away from her beloved Instanolde? Perhaps if she perished with Elerek in the wilderness everything would be resolved. Death was simple. An ending to the struggling, the striving, the surviving.

But can I die knowing that I failed my kingdom?

Would she have peace?

Gazing out over the kingdom, those lovely golden domes, the redstone structures that looked as if they'd grown from the land itself, and the sway of silk canopies, she set her jaw and clenched her hands into tight fists.

No, she would not.

There was nothing for her in the desert. Elerek certainly didn't need her. Her attempts at undermining the curse's power and seeking its breaking had only caused more disaster. She'd once sworn to never mourn a king again. A folly oath.

What of her people? She'd been Instanolde's beloved since her betrothal to Cormek. A unifying factor that even Elerek couldn't ignore, the foundation of their marriage alliance. Who would they follow when the king was taken away as a captive of the invading warlord? Lystra possessed the skills, taught by her poisonous grandmother. Perhaps, with the Jarkins crippled by the curse and Gaudab out of the city, she might lead a resistance. Take back what was theirs.

Lystra squared her shoulders, strength radiating through her muscles. Yes, she could do this. She just needed an escape plan.

Not here. Far too many guards and shadowed passageways where anything could go wrong. But if they were leaving, they'd take cardants. They were her domain. Surely the Jarkins wouldn't suspect her of attempting an escape *after* they were in the desert.

"Then I'll ride back," she whispered to the open air. "Back to save my kingdom."

Her eyes drifted down to her clenched hands. Though Razhar had pushed back her curse mark, she still felt its numbness. A cursed queen would lead her people. When her mark returned, it would stand in testimony that she still supported her king. And if, by some miracle, Elerek did break the curse, then their people would know his sacrifice.

You would leave him out in the desert?

She'd left him two days ago, hadn't she? Gone to Kushan without knowing if Instanolde would survive. She'd left him in the corridor with Myra, having seen them kiss, knowing for certain that he didn't love her.

"This is best," she whispered. For both their sakes. For the vows they'd made to their kingdom and the promises they'd made beneath the skies.

In the deepest darkness, just before the dawn, Lystra rose, ready.

She wore her riding boots, linen pants, and a favorite tunic of a soft, pale blue. A scarf sturdy enough to shield the sun covered her shoulders and she'd plaited her hair, biting her lip against the pain of her wound. To deflect the sun, she'd painted her eyes with kohl, as cardant racers did.

In her bag she'd tucked away the myrrh oil, more herbs for

her wound, and another bundle of bandages. She'd sought a knife, but the best she could find was a small razor in Elerek's room. Before she left his chamber, her gaze caught on the bookshelf. She stepped closer, withdrawing a rolled scroll. Pulling it back, an ornate chart of the heavens spread before her. She thought of that night, sitting across from Instanolde's king, and listening to his stories.

Starlight. Hope.

Lystra closed her eyes. In the darkness of her grief, Elerek had shown her starlight. He'd given it in support of her queenship, as an ally she hadn't expected, a partner in upholding their kingdom. She wondered if he still clung to starlight now, or if all had been blanketed in blackness.

She took one last look at the royal chambers. The space she was meant to share with Cormek and instead had formed an arrangement with Elerek. Regardless of their woes, and her intention to part ways by escaping, she would count these memories as precious.

Razhar waited in the parlor, dark circles beneath his eyes. The deep bronze of his skin lay hidden beneath swaths of traveling clothes, probably pilfered from among Elerek's things. The muted, neutral colors of the long robes diverted drastically from the bright shades he favored.

The sight of him made her insides seize.

The cost.

The punishment.

The opposite.

Lystra hardly knew what to think.

He stood near the window that looked east, the lattice pushed back. As she approached him, she saw that his eyes were full of tears.

"They're going to bury her," he whispered. "In the fields outside the north gate, where soldiers are buried."

Myra. Lystra's hardened heart softened, its callouses peeling at the edges. "Was her body retrieved?"

"Yes. I bribed some soldiers, made sure she was taken to our own. Ishtal, Cole, Bushra, Driss, they promised me that they'd see it done."

Our own. The cursed. The little family bonded together as they waited to die. They'd never needed a burial before. The thought brought tears to Lystra's eyes. The curse left nothing behind, only a shallow pool of spilled water. It seemed fitting that Myra would be buried among soldiers, a warrior who stood between life and death and defended it. Lystra sniffled, wishing she could be half as capable.

Razhar noticed her tears. "You would mourn her?"

Fingering the end of her braid, Lystra drew a deep breath. Death had a way of changing things, much the same way a taint of light could transform the varied colors of the desert. It gave depth, scope, a perspective that made even anger nothing more than bits of dust to be scattered upon the winds.

Myra had told her secrets. Some helpful, some not. In the end, she'd offered reconciliation, even if Lystra couldn't receive it. Elerek had done nothing.

Lystra lifted her gaze, pushing aside the storm brewing inside her. "I would honor her."

Closing his eyes, Razhar's tears fell, vanishing into his beard. He gave a small nod and asked no more questions.

Boots tromped down the hall, followed by the pounding of fists upon the oiled wood. Razhar retrieved his emerald turban and wound it atop his head.

Lystra's hands trembled. Now the battle began, and she prayed that she had the strength to fight it.

A company of Jarkin soldiers filed in. One bore two pairs of shackles.

Lystra stepped forward, feeling small and fragile, and mustered a glare. "No chains. We'll come willingly."

The soldier didn't press. Lystra forced her feet to move. One step. Another. The royal chambers fell behind, the rooms that marked her as a queen, as a bride, as all that she'd ever planned to be.

Traversing the palace corridors, cool in the pearly gray of the dawn, Jarkin soldiers behind and before, Lystra swallowed a sob rising in her throat. When Cormek ruled, laughter and color reigned in glory. A blessed time that now seemed a dream. When she and Elerek ruled, life burned in carefully tended candles, in stolen moments, shared meals among family, and cardant rides into the desert.

Would they be remembered as the last monarchs of Instanolde—if they were remembered at all?

No, she would make certain that they were remembered. Instanolde *had* to survive.

But when Lystra arrived at the top of the palace steps and drank in the scene before her, her courage ran as dry as the barren wilderness. She pinched her eyes shut.

Cardants. The great lizards of the Sancen, whose girth grew beyond a carriage and height towered nearly that of two men, had long been the companions of soldiers, merchants, and explorers. In peaceful times, races were held with festivals and celebration. But to Lystra, their sweeping tails, serpentine necks, and great horned heads were the epitome of might, power, and nobility. No one loved the reptiles as well as she.

Around twenty or so assembled in the palace courtyard, laden with heavy packs. Their taloned claws pawed the ground impatiently, wagging their great heads as men affixed saddles and harnesses. The men were dressed for travel. Long tunics, turbans, and scarves to protect them from the merciless sun. But they also bore weapons.

Panic elevated Lystra's heartbeat. She took steadying breaths, fighting the rise of memories assailing her mind, the anticipation of another journey into the desert. A terrible dream, one she never wanted to relive.

Cormek's body didn't haunt her this time. But the king who would ride with them might as well be dead.

"Move." The Jarkin grabbed her shoulder, shoving her down the steps.

Lystra gave a small yelp, her wound sparking pain.

Razhar's hands gently steadied her. "You hurt her, you'll have the king and Batu-Khasar to answer to." The soldiers backed away. Razhar met her gaze. "Are you all right?"

"Is that *actually* a question?" Lystra's hand moved to her bandaged shoulder.

He bristled, his eyes cast down.

Standing on tiptoe, Lystra scanned the mass of scales, leather, horned heads, and enemy soldiers. "Do you see El?"

"Be rather counterproductive to leave him behind, wouldn't it?"

While she promptly shot him a glare, her heart couldn't help but ache. She missed his humor, particularly the friendly, semi-aggressive banter shared between Razhar and Elerek. Mirth and laughter had given way to grief, and Lystra wondered if any sort of recovery was possible.

The blast of a ram's horn echoed over the courtyard. Immediately, the activity burst into something frantic as men stowed the last of their packs onto the cardants' backs and mounted into the saddles. Lystra eyed the reptiles. She'd have to pick the fastest of the lot for her return journey. These were strong, and some she thought she recognized from among those in the racing committee's possession.

"Water," she breathed, glancing back at Razhar. "No one's packed enough vessels. Not enough to go out *there*."

Razhar blinked; he'd certainly never prepared for an expedition across the desert.

"We're too many, we couldn't possibly carry—" A numbness crept down her arms, to hands that Razhar had clothed in skin. The sensation seemed both an answer and a reminder.

Somehow, their survival was tied to the curse—to Elerek, who'd declared it possible.

She closed her eyes. Why did everything always return to trusting him? Could she? After all they'd done? After what *he'd* done?

"Kushite."

Razhar stiffened. Lystra watched as a tall, rather slender Jarkin strode toward them. His beard was braided and upon his back he carried a lidded basket. The hand grasping the woven strap was streaked with the curse's watery mark. As he drew close, his eyes narrowed, reminding Lystra of the beady yet sharp eyes of a falcon.

"You'll ride with me." The man's words were laced with spite. He swung the basket down from his shoulder and heaved it at Razhar. "Carry the charts and parchments. Prove you're not useless."

Razhar caught the basket but made no reply.

Lystra eyed him from her peripherals. *They're not aware that he can push back the curse.* She wondered how long he intended to keep this secret, fully assured that it was within his capabilities. What would he do when his apparent "uselessness" ran its course?

The desert instinct to survive ran deep in their veins, perhaps deeper even than the curse. Lystra had felt its frenzied terror when she'd barely escaped Darcress, the feeling of fight or desperate, desperate flight. But never once had she let it cloud her judgment, her fierce desire to protect those whom she loved.

It had twisted Razhar to the point where he'd spent his life lying to his best friend. She hated to think what other catastrophes he might cause. While she remained with this party, she didn't intend to turn her back on him for even a moment.

The Jarkin turned on her, his lips twisting in a scowl. "*This* is her? The queen?"

Lystra narrowed her eyes. This Jarkin bore the curse but hadn't been in the battle or the throne room. How had he not yet seen her?

Not wasting a moment, the Jarkin looked to the nearest soldier. "Amak, she rides with you. See that nothing happens to her."

Leverage . . . on El.

Her insides knotted. She thought of Elerek and his guarded, calculated ways, the strategies working behind his eyes. *His eyes* . . . Lystra shook her head. She couldn't think of him, and he could not break, not even for her. Their kingdom needed liberation. Left without rulers, hope would evaporate quicker than water in the Sancen. Those who had fled would have nowhere to go. Their summer stores would deplete more quickly with the influx of refugees and the Jarkin army. Lystra had to hurry; Instanolde needed her.

"Yes, Datem Tangu." The soldier took her arm, this time more gently, and led her toward a waiting cardant.

Lystra glanced once more toward Razhar, but his eyes were hooded, shadowed beneath his turban.

The soldier took her bag from her shoulder and secured it to the saddle. Lystra studied the reptile. Its scales were darker than most, the color of the desert redstone, and its horns were striped with reddish streaks. Her fingertips brushed its scaled shoulder, sorry that the cardants were also being taken on a journey against their will.

Would this one be strong enough to carry her back home? It certainly looked of sturdy stock, but would it be fast enough?

She looked at the soldier, the Jarkin who had invaded her kingdom. Dark circles lay beneath his eyes too and his head was bowed as he checked the cardant's harness. For a moment, her mind hazed. The constant spiral of terror subsided. Maybe this soldier had no interest in pursuing this journey either? Perhaps he only followed the orders of his commander.

"Are you cursed?" How small her voice sounded.

The soldier's face transformed with a horrid sneer and Lystra saw again the monsters who'd stolen everything she loved. "We *all* are. Only cursed on this expedition." He uttered a sentence in his own language and Lystra didn't need a translation to know that it was full of obscenities. "Mount up."

Only cursed. Lystra gritted her teeth against her wound as she climbed into the saddle. It couldn't be a coincidence. One way or another, the curse was linked to their survival.

The Jarkin grabbed her wrist, yanking it back before binding her hands. Lystra couldn't hold in her whimper, her shoulder twisting with the movement. Her ropes were secured to the saddle, and then the Jarkin mounted in front of her, taking the reins. It felt foreign, sitting *behind* someone on a cardant. Control wrenched from her grasp.

She glanced over her shoulder, eyeing the thick ropes. The razor she'd taken would be useless against such bonds. Likely her Jarkin guard possessed some sort of knife, but could she procure one?

And the pain; her wound was getting worse. Could she fight through it? Would it hinder her? But she didn't have a choice. Instanolde needed her.

With a shout, the palace gates creaked open. The earth beneath seemed to shake as the cardants marched. And as their reptile lurched forward, eager to join its companions, Lystra hissed through her teeth. The familiar side-winding gait of a cardant usually brought comfort, but today, each bounce and jostle drew pain from her shoulder. Unable to hold tight, she lay wholly at the mercy of the reptile's movement, praying she'd not tumble into the thundering, clawed limbs below.

Within moments, the palace with its high walls and golden domes, her home, had vanished from sight. A lump rose in her throat.

"Make way. Make way. Make way!"

The ride through the city was chaos. Dust filled the air as the cardants hurled themselves through the narrow streets as one never-ending mass. Lystra's breaths were short and frantic, clenching her teeth against the pain in her shoulder. Nothing looked familiar in the frenzy. Had the markets been dismantled? The citizens and refugees shut up inside? Did they believe that they were doomed? That all was lost?

She shut her eyes. Such a failure was too monumental. It would break her.

They passed the city gates. Before them lay the desert. The sun streaked across the land in a wide band of light. Lystra blinked. Her scarf had fallen back, and she couldn't pull it back up. At her lips, she already tasted sand. Her eyes drew to the horizon, the mountains a dusty gray against the deep blue of the sky. The road stretched before them, farther than the eye could see, into the vast expanses of the Sancen. A road for the dead.

Lystra tried to crane her neck, to catch one last glimpse of the golden gates and pale walls of Instanolde, but her wound burned in protest. Already the distance seemed too great and she stifled a sob. If she returned a second time, *survived* a second time, it meant living more days grieving what was lost. Would she be strong enough? If her beloved Instanolde asked that of her?

They turned off from the main road, taking a reptile trail along a ridge of rising rock that forced them single file. Sparse, spiked plants somehow had taken root in the cracks, their stalks flapping in the hot breeze. A steep drop fell away to her left, a fall no human could survive. The trail afforded her a chance to survey the company. To the twenty cardants, more than thirty men had joined, many riders doubling up. She thought that she could make out Gaudab's immense form astride a cardant at the front of the caravan, but the heat hazed her vision. She still didn't see Elerek. The going slowed as they climbed, their packs heavy.

A foolish mission. Cardants could only run by day, and they sought the stars.

As they crested the ridge, the Sancen and all its miserable glory came into view. Windswept crags. Whistling canyons. Sun-bleached rock as far as the eye could see. A vast, lonely world. The landscape broke Lystra's heart.

And there, in the distance, the golden collection of Instanolde looked as if it were drawn for a map. Beside it, the Gungole's silver belt ran like the last strand of hope.

Beneath Lystra and her rider, the cardant gave a low rumble, pausing on the ridge's trail. The Jarkin, Amak, swore and urged it forward.

"We're going too fast," Lystra whispered.

The Jarkin scowled back at her.

"We've got to pace them." The words slipped out before she could consider holding them back. "Two riders and gear? This isn't sustainable."

Amak scoffed. "Speak to Khasar. Maybe he'll cut out your tongue."

From somewhere deep in her torn heart, a fire began to burn. Lystra basked in its heat. "Maybe my king will drown you."

The soldier growled, his hands tightening on the cardant's reins.

"Halt!" The call rang over the rock, echoing amid the emptiness.

The company slowed. The cardants smacked their jaws and lowered themselves to the rock, absorbing the heat. They turned away from the precipice, creating a circle congregating on the flat rise. Many of the men dismounted, adjusting packs and reaching for waterskins. Already, Lystra could feel the sun's scorch screwed down through her light clothes.

Amak dismounted. His eyes scanned the caravan from beneath his turban, his brow furrowing slightly, as if wondering what he should do. He loosed Lystra's bonds, freeing the arm that belonged to her wounded shoulder. The other remained firmly affixed to the saddle. He reached for the waterskins, secured in the saddlebags, and Lystra suddenly realized just how thirsty she was.

A growl erupted. The deep, guttural rumblings accompanied by a series of hisses. Lystra lifted her gaze. She knew that sound, the sound of a reptile that wasn't getting its way.

With a rear of its great head, a cardant burst from formation. Its ivory horns, striped with orange, flashed in the sunlight. Long, harsh talons scraped across the rock, digging ruts into the stone. The others shied away, averting their orb-like eyes. This great, majestic creature was one to dominate, to run wild. One that despised the rider upon its back.

Gaudab Batu-Khasar leaned low over the saddle, his twin battle-axes rising from their sheaths upon his back like projectiles. His dark eyes, set deep beneath his proud brow, were fixed on his mount like an alpha lion. He pulled at the reins, forcing the cardant into submission. The reptile wagged her head and flicked her orange-and-green-striped tail, an untamed force of tooth, claw, and scales.

Tiniah.

Lystra couldn't breathe. The fire in her heart flared, surging through her veins hotter than any forge. *Her* Tiniah.

A gift. An unexpected kindness. The hope of a future full of light and glory that Lystra had once craved with her whole soul. A freedom she now knew she would never find again.

"No!" Her shriek echoed over the rock.

All eyes turned on her. Sharp, leering eyes of the enemy.

"Don't do this. Don't do this. Don't . . ." Lystra felt her own sanity slip through her fingers. The air, even the wild, open air of the Sancen, seemed intent upon choking her.

Tiniah thrashed, as if she sensed the panic in Lystra's voice. Gaudab growled and pulled her head down. He withdrew a short whip with a tassel of leather lashes at its end.

"Stop!" Fighting the pain in her shoulder, Lystra slipped ungracefully from the cardant's back. She strained against her still-bound hand, feet slipping and skidding on the rock, fighting to free herself with the same tenacity as her cardant. "Let her go!"

Tiniah growled, stamping her limbs. Gaudab snarled. "Be quiet, girl. Amak! See that she's gagged."

But before her guard could act, Lystra's deft fingers had untied the rope from the saddle. Still with a loop coiled about her wrist, she dashed across the circle. Her breath came in pants as she drew closer, but she had none of the saddle soreness in her thighs. "I *said*, let her go."

"Lystra, what are you doing?" Razhar appeared in the corner of her gaze, terror in his eyes. He stood beside the slender, mapmaker Jarkin, the basket of scrolls in his arms.

Gaudab raised the whip. He struck Tiniah's flank. The reptile spun around, shrieking.

"You! You monster!" Lystra screamed. He killed Cormek,

he took her kingdom, but he would *not* have her cardant. Not her Tiniah.

Tiniah's tail cut through the air, sharp as the whip that lashed stripes against her scales. It sailed toward Lystra with enough strength to send her across the plateau—instead, she stumbled back, pulled away by Razhar.

Two more deafening *cracks* of the whip echoed over the desert before the reptile submitted, muttering and clicking. Gaudab dismounted, still holding the whip in one fist as he cinched the reins tighter in the other. He fixed his stare upon Lystra with her unbound hands, the heat in his eyes murderous.

"We haven't the time for this," he sneered.

Lystra glared. She wanted to pummel him, to feel her fists pounding on his flesh. To pay him back for all the wrongs he'd done to her, to them all. "She doesn't belong to you, you *murderer*."

Razhar's grip tightened on her arm. "Lystra," he hissed in her ear. "You've got to calm down."

She didn't. Instead, she burst into tears. The once bold and fierce queen of Instanolde now nothing more than a broken girl crying in the wilderness. If she could form thoughts, she might have been ashamed, the eyes of every enemy warrior fixed on her. But not now, not with the lashes in her soul matching those cutting into Tiniah's scales.

"He can't have her, Razhar. He *can't*."

"Who?" Razhar's face was pale.

"The cardant."

The tremors quaking through her body stilled. Lystra lifted her head, searching the circle.

The cardant.

Elerek's voice.

She found him.

The intensity of his eyes, the color of smooth-cut jade, cut straight to her core. He sat backwards behind the warrior who rode at Gaudab's right. They'd tied his legs together and affixed them to the saddle like another pack on the cardant's back. His shoulders were hunched, and thick ropes secured his hands behind his back. Despite his long tunic and the scarf wound about his head, the pale skin of his face had already flushed, and his beautiful, dark curls lay damp against his brow.

"It's *her* cardant," he repeated, his eyes shifting to Gaudab.

The cardant he'd bought for her. A wedding gift.

Lystra looked away, shame warming her cheeks. How could she weep over her cardant when he'd lost everything?

The girl he loved, Myra, was dead. His kingdom lay in shambles. This entire expedition into the harrows of the Sancen planned for the sole purpose of orchestrating his death.

Lystra sniffled, jerking her arm free of Razhar's grip and wiping the tears from her face. Her fingers came back black from the kohl she'd painted beneath her eyes. It looked like ash from a funeral pyre, like the mourning paint her grandmother had forced her to wear to Cormek's burning. That moment where grief and fate had met at the crossroads, carrying her on a collision course with the cursed prince who had taken the crown.

If she hadn't sought a way to break his curse, would they be out here?

Would she have fallen in love with him?

She wondered, in some twisted fashion, if all this had happened because of her. If she were responsible for all the sorrow that had befallen the king she'd wed.

"I'm sorry," she whispered.

But the one to whom it mattered couldn't hear her.

Chapter 8

Elerek

The moment that Lystra looked away, something pierced Elerek's heart and twisted—deeper than a dagger ever could.

I did this. He held no grudge against her passionate outburst or the tears cascading down her cheeks. He'd seen her as the perfect evell blossom adorning his brother's arm, as radiant as the life-giving sun itself. The girl who raced cardants, who had stood fierce for the kingdom she loved so much.

She had broken—and the guilt belonged to him.

He'd taken something beautiful and destroyed it—and it wasn't the first time. This was why his relationship with Cormek had fractured. This was why he'd given in to his own selfish desires and allowed Myra to take the curse. This was why his curse had become such a monstrous, vile thing.

The broken part of his kingdom, of Instanolde, was *him.*

"I don't care about the cardants," Gaudab growled, leveling his gaze at Elerek. "We'll need the meat on their bones before long. If the girl cares so much about the reptile, she can ride with me." A cruel sneer spread across his lips, taunting him.

Elerek's hands twisted against the coarse rope. He knew their game. They would hurt her to get at him and he couldn't let them—soon he would drown them all, but not until she was safe from them and his own cursed waters.

So he merely watched with a stone-cold countenance as Lystra wiped the tears from her kohl-lined eyes. The Jarkin behind her seized the length of rope dangling from her wrist, marching her forward. Elerek's gaze took her in. The whole of her—from the wisps of black hair flying from her braid to the dust coating her riding boots. She favored her shoulder, moving stiffly with the wound Gaudab had cut into her skin. Otherwise, she appeared uninjured.

There still burned a fire in her eyes.

Elerek ground his teeth. He needed the truth, craving it with the whole of his broken soul. Had she known about her grandmother binding his curse? Had she been sent to kill him on their wedding night?

And that bit of starlight, the illumination that began the night when the stories of the heavens spun in the air, had he only imagined it? The stars were real, even if they couldn't touch them—much like the love they weren't meant to share.

No, they'd been doomed from the very start.

Across the expanse, Razhar stood solitary, out of place with his beloved emerald turban shimmering in the Sancen sun.

Their eyes met.

Elerek sniffed and looked away. If they'd brought Lystra as leverage against him, why had they brought Razhar? It certainly wasn't Razhar's knowledge of the desert or the stars, nor could his sands even come *close* to subduing his waters. Not that Elerek cared what happened to him.

"Waterskins!" Gaudab barked. He approached Lystra's guard, snatching the rope with a disapproving sneer. The guard bowed his head and took a sulking step back.

Elerek narrowed his eyes. If there were any weaknesses in this caravan, any links about to break, he'd find them. Anything that might be useful.

The circle erupted with activity as the men rummaged through their packs, producing the stout pouches and a few jars. All of them empty.

A knot formed in his stomach.

The soldier behind him turned in the saddle and loosened the bindings on his hand. Elerek winced as the tension dispelled from his shoulders. He rubbed the raw and red skin encircling his wrists, prompting just the slightest bit of cursed moisture to his fingertips.

Before him, the Jarkins formed a line. The soldier at the front unscrewed his waterskin, lifting it toward him like a beggar asking for alms.

For a moment, Elerek wondered if he'd be sick. He'd known that this would be necessary. Perhaps the curse wasn't through having its way with him, but they were not invincible. The same curse that dwelt in their skin and doomed them to drown would also enable them to survive the unthinkable, the Sancen.

"Get to work," Gaudab growled. Beside him, Lystra stood as still as the lonely rock spires of the desert, staring.

Elerek lifted his hand, concentrated, and sent a trickle of water into the pouch. The cursed drinking cursed water. *I can drown, and I can give life.*

He tried not to watch their faces as he filled the vessels. The disgusting thought that the water dripping from his fingers would soon pour down their throats made him want to vomit. It was a pragmatic solution, one befitting a people that eternally took the route of survival in a world that could destroy them in a hundred different ways. The Sancen didn't need a hundred. It only needed one: no water.

He wondered what it would do with him.

The next pair of hands lingering in his peripherals didn't belong to the pale, sunburnt Jarkins. These weren't hardened or calloused, but smooth and colored a deep bronze.

Elerek stilled, the flow ceasing from his fingers. Fury plumed inside him, like the smoke of spent fields burning. Somehow, after all that had happened, he found it easier to grant water to the men who killed his brother—but not to his best friend.

The thought prompted a deep ache in his wretched soul. The Sancen air held a loneliness, a desolation that permeated everything it touched, but this void between them seemed to span up to the dancing heavens themselves. He and Razhar had always bickered over the years. Nothing too serious, nothing a few days' space wouldn't ease. But this was different. Something so agonizing that Elerek didn't even want to be healed of it.

But he swallowed, pushing his feelings deep, deep down, and filled the waterskin. "Isn't there enough sand out here?"

Razhar bristled, as if his words were cacti barbs. "El . . . is there anything I can do?"

Elerek lifted his gaze, watching as Gaudab led Lystra to the wild, monstrous cardant he'd gifted her. He permitted her to mount, pain twisting her face from her wound, before binding her hands behind her back again. "Get Lystra a waterskin."

"I'll do it." Razhar spoke in a whisper. "What else?"

Elerek looked at his former comrade just long enough to inflict a deep and terrible scowl. "Stay out of my way."

Dropping his gaze, Razhar capped his waterskins and turned away, giving space for the next man in line.

As the day wore on, each sway of the cardant sent another ache through Elerek's body. His bound legs had long since gone numb and there was no manageable way to get comfortable. Tied no better than a sack, more than once he'd felt himself teeter. As the trail they took wound higher and more perilous, his vision swam at the dizzying precipices.

Instanolde became a haze amid the desert, each step of the cardant only increasing the Sancen's immensity. Elerek swallowed, his throat parched in the sweltering heat, as his kingdom slipped beyond the horizon.

The only home he'd ever known—and he'd never return. The place where the ashes lay of his father and his brother, both kings before him. One had been king too long and one not long enough.

As for himself, he'd inherited a world too broken to fix. Even if he were whole, if he weren't cursed, could he have done any differently? Saved his people? Was there a way that he hadn't seen—one that didn't involve so much death?

The silence of the Sancen became his answer. The vast and lonely wilderness reminding him of his smallness. Once, the thought had brought him comfort. That smallness was enough in the chaotic world beneath the starry skies above.

Now, the windswept rocks were harsh. The layers of striped sandstone maddening, and the distant dunes of the deep valleys a mire in which to sink. Every bit of dust became a weapon formed against him, screaming with silent voices that it mattered not which crevice of earth claimed his feeble flesh.

Elerek tore his gaze away from the desert. Silent save for the jostle of gear and the scratch of claws along rock, the caravan kept a set, but determined pace. Purposeful in their intent to see his death. The sun gathered its strength, and unleashed the hellish heat they knew to expect. As hour after grueling hour passed, their discomfort became difficult to ignore. They tasted nothing but dust and the crystallized salt licks from their packs. The men held them like sugared candies, sustaining their shriveling bodies. The canyons provided some shelter, but the heat rose from the darkened rock, tormenting them still.

He found his gaze drawn to Lystra. At least, with her riding with Gaudab, he could keep an eye on her. Small compared to the mountain men, she sat hunched behind the warrior. Every so often, she looked his way.

Her face was a portrait of pain, sorrow swirling in her deep eyes. Her lips, chapped and cracked, moved as if to whisper. If they could speak, he wondered what they would say—what *he* would say.

Stars above, he didn't want to watch her die.

Countless cursed had already drowned. He'd watched his brother's pyre burn. Not even a full two days had passed since Myra bled out with a knife in her side. Once, he'd hoped she would flow away as peacefully as a river. Now, he hoped that she danced among the stars. He wondered if everyone he loved was doomed to die.

Did that mean that Lystra was next? Except Lystra wasn't his to love.

Shutting his eyes, a pair of tears slipped down his cheeks. Out here, haunted by nothing but death, who would mock him for tears?

The silence split as Gaudab called for another stop. Elerek blinked away his tears, steeling himself for another line of thirsty Jarkins waiting for their waterskins to be filled with expectant eyes.

But hers were the ones he noticed.

He stared back. *I'll save you.* He had to. He had failed her in every possible way, broken every vow they'd spoken before the altar with crowns upon their brows. In this, this fight for the hope they owed their kingdom of another sunrise, he could not —would not—fail.

At last, when the sun tipped toward the west, Gaudab called to camp. They chose a bone-dry gully, wide at its base but narrow at its top, worn from the rare and tumultuous floods. Pale lines ran through the rock, layered atop one another like the thinnest baklava dough.

Elerek's forehead split with pain, as if one of Gaudab's axes lay embedded between his eyes. He thanked the Starkindler for the shadows.

As the cardants settled, the warriors unpacked the gear and erected tents in a tight circle. A small bundle of kindling burned in the center, a candle in the wilderness. Tangu marched past, Razhar following with a basket of parchments swung over his shoulders. They didn't ask for water. Instead, the cartographer perched himself on a rocky ledge and sketched. Razhar stood nearby, his eyes downcast.

Elerek watched them wearily, wanting to see the maps, and wondering how much farther they must go. Would Razhar tell him, if given the chance? The thought of relying upon him for information made his stomach turn. Did Razhar gain anything from this situation? After all the lies, what would stop him from lying again?

Elerek hung his aching head, too tired to even think anymore.

Gaudab stalked through the camp, barking orders. "Four of you, go hunting. Be back before sundown or we'll leave your corpses for the night dwellers."

Elerek lifted his eyes. Before him, the walls of the gully extended into a haze the evening light couldn't pierce. How easily his mind conjured myths and legends from childhood stories. Wailing spirits that wandered the desolate canyons. Lions the size of shops. Vipers that could freeze a man's blood.

Shaking off a shudder, he pushed back the wilds of his imagination. Surely the curse that lurked in his body could rival the terrors of any specter or beast.

"Untie him." Lystra's voice, hoarse and dry, ricocheted off the stone walls. She still sat where Gaudab had left her, bound to her cardant's saddle. "Now."

Gaudab scoffed, approaching the cardant. His great height almost put him eye level with the queen. "I'd worry about your own skin, river lily." He released Lystra from her ropes, freeing her hands.

Elerek frowned. Her curse mark had vanished, the fingers that had touched him clothed in amber-hued skin.

Lystra glowered, as mighty as a lioness. Swinging down from the saddle, she withdrew a waterskin from the saddlebag. "He can't get very far, now can he?"

Elerek cast a glance over the barren rock and endless wilderness. He'd spent his life thinking so little of his disability, but out here, the terrain would prove yet another challenge he must conquer.

Gaudab gave a low growl and stalked toward the cardant where Elerek was tied.

Fatigue and the heat and the aches came to a crescendo in that moment, and Elerek found himself unable to bear it. As the bonds loosed from around his legs, a moan of relief slipped from his lips. Unable to steady himself on the cardant's back with his hands still bound, he toppled onto the sandy floor of the gully. His bones jolted. Sand caked on his dry lips, and he coughed.

Gaudab pulled the ropes from his wrists, looping them for another day. "Bring waterskins and whatever vessels we have. Some of us would fancy a wash." He loomed over Elerek, a monstrous shadow in the fading light. "And don't try anything. Amak, come stand guard."

Pushing himself up from the sand, Elerek blinked, suddenly aware of just how weak and weary he felt. He watched the warlord stalk away, replaced by the quiet Jarkin who had guarded Lystra earlier. The fierce rage, driven by the curse, still submerged his heart, but despite the wanting, he knew he hadn't the strength. Not now.

Before him, Lystra sank to her knees. So close he could hear her breathing, one steady breath after another.

Elerek maneuvered himself into a sitting position, stretching his sore legs out. The burning intensity in her eyes forced him to look away, to watch his plague-scarred hands as he massaged his knees.

Starkindler, what do I say? His heartbeat drummed in his ears. "Do you need water?"

Lystra slipped the strap of a waterskin from her shoulder. "Razhar got me this one."

"As I instructed him. For once, he obeys." He reached for it, and her fingertips brushed his. Panic thrashed in his chest. He'd lived his life afraid of touch, that one small brush would condemn someone to die. The air, that brief space between their nearness, suddenly turned suffocating.

"Where is your curse mark?"

"Razhar removed it."

"He *what?*"

Her shoulders fell. The kohl smeared beneath her eyes mingled with fatigue's shadows. "El . . . there's so much. So much you don't know or understand."

"Explain it to me." He ground his teeth. "Tell me what are truths and what are lies."

She called me El.

Lystra shook her head, stray wisps of hair floating about her face. "I've told you no lies. Not one."

"But the curse . . . its breaking . . ." A terrible weight settled over his chest, as if his lungs were full of water instead of air.

She was telling the truth.

An oath slipped beneath his breath, cursing his own idiocy. How quickly he'd dismissed her as a liar, a betrayer. Instead, she'd been clever, always a step ahead, weaving connections like the tapestries adorning the walls of their palace. If what she'd declared in the throne room was true—that the stars and the dagger and his death would break the curse—she had to have been intentionally investigating. Searching. The realization left his soul drenched in an ice far colder than the curse's numbness.

She wanted the curse broken.

She wanted him to live.

She wanted him . . .

Elerek snapped his gaze back to her, and it felt as if he were seeing her for the first time. They had come together as two forces of nature, like the oppressive heat and the towering thunderheads, with seemingly opposing intentions. Both collided upon the desert beneath the right conditions. And through the haze, the shadows, the shifting mirages, they had taken a path fraught with danger, the very one they were never meant to travel.

If she had fallen, her heart drawn toward his, then it was a forbidden desire that had led them here, into this wilderness, toward his death.

No, they weren't meant to fall in love, and these were the consequences.

"Everything I said was true." Lystra's expression didn't change. Regal and noble. "No one should die beneath the cruel judgment of a curse." Her voice dropped to a whisper. "I wanted to save you, El. I never expected that the truth would be . . . *this.*"

That the curse would demand his death all the same. Elerek turned toward her, her face only inches from his, and the nearness overwhelmed him. "Your grandmother cursed me. She wanted you to kill me, didn't she? On our wedding night?"

Lystra's breath shuddered, and he could see that she was trembling. "She manipulated me, El. At the time, I . . . I didn't know that she was a curse binder." She ran her fingers through the free wisps of hair. "And besides, I didn't kill you. El, you should know that that night is a precious memory to me."

As it was to him. A night that might have been perfect, when they'd sat across the bed from one another before the stars and found themselves broken and grieving, but whole. "No," he breathed. "You didn't."

Elerek unscrewed the cap on her waterskin, lifting his fingers to fill it. When he'd finished, he handed it back. This time, their fingers didn't touch, and it made his chest ache. Lystra took it, holding it between her hands as if it were her most precious possession. Of course, out here, it may as well be.

"I didn't want this, El." Lystra's voice turned hard and brittle. "Any of this. I'd hoped against hope for something more, something better. Maybe I was wrong. Perhaps the future we thought we could build was only made of dreams and sands, but this is reality. These are the truths that you asked for—and I gave them." This time, when Lystra lifted her eyes, they burned with a dark and furious fire. "I stood by you, El. I didn't betray you."

Elerek held his breath.

"But that night. You promised me no lies. No deceptions." Pain cut at the edge of her voice. She was a storm ready to break. "You lied to me."

The rumble of the judgment drums sounded in each syllable. The inevitable, haunting him down every palace hallway and had chased him out to the wilderness. Elerek clenched his jaw. He hadn't the words to answer. No, he deserved this.

Lystra's breath shuddered, a sob caught in her throat. "You owed me the truth." Her chest heaved. "Instead you . . ." She shut her eyes, tears falling.

Shame flowed in his veins, sure as a torrent. It didn't matter that he'd resolved to end his relationship with Myra or that he'd taken vows to be faithful to Lystra. His good intentions meant nothing in the unbroken light of his actions.

"You could have told me about her, you know." Lystra hastily wiped her tears. "I would have listened. I listened to Myra plenty, telling me exactly what she was to you and how unworthy I was of you." She closed her eyes. "I've been in love too. Cormek . . . he was everything to me."

Myra was dead. The fact slammed against his soul afresh. Grief, sharp and poignant. If only he hadn't felt this gaping emptiness so many times before—and the realization that nothing beneath the burning stars above could fix what was broken. Unless he died. Broke the curse and died.

"Unworthy . . ." No, that was wrong. Backwards. It was he who was unworthy. "She was wrong, Lystra."

Bowing her head, Lystra sniffled. "So was I, El. Wrong about so many things. And so were you."

Elerek's hands clenched. He had to speak. Lystra wasn't owed his silence. Not anymore. "Lystra, you're correct. On all accounts. I can ask nothing of you, not when you've given so much already."

She blinked, her eyes flashing with a cold resolve. "You have my loyalty, El, as your queen. My vows demand that you shan't lose that. You will always be my king." Her hands tightened around the waterskin, clenching it as if it were the dagger that was destined to pierce his heart. "But you're not my husband."

Up above, the light faded from the gully's stone walls as the sun slipped behind the mountains. The shadows grew longer, darker, and a chill swept through the air, tingling over Elerek's skin. Lystra still sat close, so close he could reach out and touch her, draw his fingers down her tear and kohl-stained cheek. But there was also a void, an impossible nothingness, that he knew he could not cross. Something in Lystra's soul had reached for his and found a handhold, but there was no reaching back.

It didn't matter that they were captives, adrift out in the Sancen's desolation. The rules of their court, of their political alliance disguised as a marriage, still applied.

Elerek swallowed. His heart, cold and numb, beat hollowly inside his chest. "Thank you, for your loyalty." How small his voice sounded against the rock and the sand. "I know my words are empty, but I *am* sorry."

As the Jarkins finished setting up camp, they gathered their waterskins, eyeing him like predators searching for a fresh kill.

"That's enough." Amak grabbed Lystra's arm, yanking her

from the sands. The shadows claimed her features and she turned away with her captor.

Elerek watched her go, feeling again the bitter, bitter sting of something lost. The cursed who had drowned, Cormek, Myra, and Lystra.

No world beneath the heavens existed for them. Only death. A sky without stars.

Chapter 9

Razhar

Razhar drifted through the camp like a bird seeking a place to land. He followed Tangu, hauling the cartographer's gear, including the parchments, a canvas tent, and two bedrolls, to a place near the cardants. Their bellies were pressed to the sand, soaking in the heat from the ground.

Razhar wrinkled his nose, the reptiles and the invaders equally smelly. He wondered how any of them would get any sleep. Not that he expected to sleep much anyways, with the towering rock walls feeling closer than they ought. Not with the expanse between him and the comforts of Instanolde. Not with the dancing stars above haunting him. Stars that he could not name.

"Tonight, you'll earn your keep." Tangu sifted through the rolled parchments, pulling out a map of the desert. "Since you river rats have different names for the stars, you'll identify which constellations are currently visible to us and their phases."

Razhar lowered the packs with a *thunk*, feeling no better than a pack mule. "I'm not a river rat."

Narrowing his eyes, Tangu sniffed. "Right. Condor scat. Then, we should be able to match our location and chart our course. Once we're through, we'll have some decent maps of this desert."

The only constellation Razhar knew was the one tattooed on his chest.

"I go to watch the stars." Fahwal had watched and waited. Spilled his blood with a cursed dagger beneath the wrathgiver constellation and cast something foul and evil. As a result, they'd never studied the skies together. Razhar had often envisioned it though, taking his baba's condor, flying into the open sky, finding a lonely cliff someplace where the skies were unbroken. His baba's voice would be soft and gentle, telling stories and pointing to the constellations to which they belonged. He'd ask Razhar to repeat them back, and he would learn.

Razhar shook his head. He'd had almost two decades to get over his loss. Why hadn't he?

While Tangu consulted his maps, Razhar busied himself with the tent. As he pounded one of the tent pegs into the ground, a sharp burning sensation ripped through his hand, stinging like a scorpion's poison.

He hissed through his teeth and stared at his palms. In the fading light of the hot, wretched day, sand glimmered like gold, fine and pure, covering his fingers and trailing up his arms.

His heart beat louder, stronger. Razhar clenched his hands, aware of each and every grain scraping against his skin. It made him want to scream for the injustice of it all, but instead he finished the tent and shoved his belongings inside. Everything he touched left a trail of sand. Memories of his illness—of *turning to sand*—made his head spin with terror. It was worse than his fear of the desert, the Jarkins, or the terrible truths the curse hid.

This isn't my curse. I didn't do this. I don't deserve this.

But neither had Elerek . . .

"Well?" Tangu glared at him.

Razhar blinked, glancing at the sky. "It's not dark—"

"The warmaker stars will be out. They're brighter than most and set far in the east. Tell me their position." He gestured to the cliffside with ink-stained fingers. "You ought to be able to see from there."

Rubbing his hands along his pants, shaking off the excess sand, Razhar approached the cliffside, noting a gash in its side packed with boulders. It would take some effort from his sore muscles, but he could do it.

"And try not to break my neck while I'm at it," he muttered beneath his breath. After all, his main objective was surviving this ordeal—even if he ended up sacrificing his best friend at the end of it.

"I ought to be trying to get that dagger." Razhar grunted, pulling himself up onto a boulder. He then planted his back against a sharp angle of rock, bracing himself as he moved up the narrow crack.

Was he so starved for attention that he'd taken to talking to himself?

Once he reached the top, he caught his breath. The desert blanketed about him in shadows, its colors deep as the sun set. How lonely it was, stretching for mile after barren mile.

Tangu was right. In the east, the wrathgiver stars shone cold and deadly. The lowest star, the point of the assassin's dagger, danced and spun just behind a nearby ridge. And between them, more rugged canyons, sloping valleys, and the imposing chain of the eastern mountains. Razhar gave a long sigh.

"Toward the mountains?" Tangu demanded once he'd climbed down.

Razhar shrugged. "The wrathgiver veers east."

"Back toward my homeland. Come, best tell Khasar." Tangu snatched up his parchments and trekked back toward the center of camp, gesturing for Razhar to follow.

There, a fire had been built, and the crackling of the dry brush burning brought a small notion of comfort. Except for Gaudab, looming like a terrible specter, dark against the orange glow of the flames.

"This will never work, Khasar," Tangu announced, joining him by the fire. "We ought to flee back to the city—while we still can."

Gaudab turned, scowling, and Razhar shriveled.

"The warmaker stars, what they call the wrathgiver, hang low in the east. Easily a three days' ride under normal conditions."

Three days? Razhar's heart sank. Would that be enough time? To steal the dagger? To break the curse before it was too late?

Too late for him. Too late for Elerek.

"I'd lose far more men to this curse if we waited for the turn of the heavens." Gaudab folded his massive arms.

"And if they're counting on that?" Tangu scoffed. "You've put far too much stock in the cripple's ability to keep us alive. Don't you see that?"

Then, a cruel smirk curled onto the warlord's face. He turned away from the fire, marching toward the place where his men assembled to have their waterskins filled. Razhar's eyes followed.

He'd never seen Elerek look so pale and weary. Sitting hunched in the sand, filling waterskin after waterskin, his bent figure looked as if it bore the weight of the world. It was strange to see him without his chair, and Razhar wondered if he'd accept his help if needed.

And . . . he missed him. These miserable, lonely days—had it only been days?—filled him with a strange emptiness. Had they ever gone this long without talking? Without a clash of their opposing personalities? His cheeky humor paired so well against Elerek's dry cynicism, a cheerful ray of sunshine to drive away every foul mood.

"I know that you care—deep down in that insensitive, disgruntled mess of yours."

Razhar desperately hoped that that was still true.

Lystra emerged from the line of waiting Jarkins, led by a guard. She cradled her waterskin and walked with her eyes downcast, such a contrast to the brave and bold queen.

Razhar cocked an eyebrow. Had they spoken? Was reconciliation possible? He wanted to hope so. Elerek and Lystra had been acquainted only a few short months and had achieved such a unique, layered relationship. If they could somehow find middle ground, then there was certainly hope for him.

Stepping into the queen's path, Gaudab grabbed her arm, yanking her free of the guard. Before Lystra had the chance to react, the warlord snatched the waterskin from her hands and threw it to the ground, its contents accepted by the sand. He shoved her after it, sending Lystra to fall in a heap.

"You've had your share," Gaudab growled.

Razhar clenched his hands. Fire burned in his chest—but his rage was nothing compared to the storm breaking upon Elerek's face.

Water squeezed between the king's fists. Assuming a threatening pose, he raised his hands, ready to unleash a torrent. He looked again as he had in the square, facing the entire army of Jarkins with nothing more than water and the will to save his kingdom.

"Leave. Her. Alone," Elerek growled with a voice that would have frightened away any of the desert's monsters.

A shiver crept up Razhar's spine.

Gaudab towered over the cursed king. "As long as you follow orders. Get to work." Then he turned, stalking back to the fire.

Razhar didn't miss the smirk he exchanged with Tangu, and the implications of their little "display."

Lystra rose, her lithe frame practically shaking. She glared after Gaudab, eyes burning.

Stars above. Razhar dashed across the camp, stooping to pick up her spilled waterskin. "I'll get you more, Your Highness."

In response, the queen of Instanolde turned her glare on him and wiped the dirt from her face with her sleeve. Her guard took her arm again, pulling her away from the circle.

Still holding the empty waterskin, Razhar then looked toward Elerek—only to meet a glower of equal proportions.

You two are perfect for each other. Razhar pulled his robe tighter, the Sancen's chilled air funneling through the gully and straight to the bone.

He waited as the Jarkins migrated toward the fire, keeping his distance, but close enough for the king not to ignore him. One warrior remained, standing watch over their captive.

Elerek's jade-colored eyes flashed. "Get out of my sight."

Rather, Razhar shuffled another couple steps closer. "I can't do that."

Elerek pulled himself up onto a shelf of rock with a grunt, his legs dragged out in front of him.

"Do you need help?" Razhar's voice was a whisper, wind lost in the canyons. Elerek rarely asked for help, but Razhar always gave it. An aiding hand, a kind word, a witty insult when the situation required it. And the greatest support he could offer—holding back the curse.

"Not from you," Elerek muttered.

"Reasonably speaking, I'm probably the best suited to the task." Small steps. Timid steps. If Elerek truly were to die, Razhar had to clear some of the haze.

Even if he had to be the one holding the dagger. Even if holding back Elerek's curse benefited himself as much as it did the king. Gaudab was right; he was a selfish bit of dust.

"Oh, now you're interested in being reasonable?"

Razhar wished he could manage a smile. That sounded like the Elerek he knew. He pushed up his sleeves, his forearms coated in sand. The same sands that had nearly killed him as a child. The sands that demanded that Razhar spend his days paying a cost, his entire life a punishment.

"Go away." Elerek's jaw clenched.

"No. I won't." Razhar knelt, leveling their eyes with one another. "Not after all we've been through."

He seized Elerek's wrist, the king's cursed skin cool to the touch. Tendrils, dark as tattoo ink, wound across their skin, streaming from their point of contact. Elerek startled, no doubt his knee-jerk reaction to touch of any sort. He drew a sharp breath, but didn't speak, watching with his shrewd, calculating gaze.

Razhar's insides twisted. After carrying the weight of this secret for *years*, he'd thought he'd feel different. Relieved. Maybe even proud. Sneaking through the shadows, into bedchambers, was no longer necessary. Using camche tea, a powerful sleeping draught from the canyonlands, to lull his friends to sleep was over.

When he drew back his hand, sand spilled from his palms, pale and as fine as sugar.

Elerek continued to scowl. His hand moved to the hem of

his tunic, lifting it to expose his side where the mark of transparent skin slashed across his ribs and chest.

Archers like Razhar's baba were called away to fight Lorkin's wars, and it was *Elerek* who received the curse. Razhar didn't expect fairness, least of all from kings and chiefs and rulers. Never once had he held Elerek accountable for the sins his father committed, just as he knew he wasn't responsible for his own baba's actions.

"It's shrunk . . ." Elerek whispered. "It was *you*."

Razhar gave a sober nod. He wondered who they would've been—if the curse had never happened.

Elerek would have been king and Razhar would have grown up in the Kushite canyons. They would've never met, never become friends. Maybe Razhar would have become an archer, like his baba, with a condor earned from his chief.

Yet would Elerek have also become like his father, a cruel, vengeful, warmongering king? Perhaps he too would've called Kushite archers to stir up strife and spill blood.

What's a lowly Kushite to the king of Instanolde?

"How?" Elerek demanded. "Why can you touch me? Can you be cursed?"

Razhar hesitated. In his mind, the words formed. They swirled in his mouth, bitter as the camche tea. Unfortunately, no one would be lulled to sleep by their implications. He didn't want to speak, to shame his baba. A man who only possessed value in his society for his skill with a bow and killing the king's enemies, driven into desperation.

"I won't drown . . ." Razhar croaked out.

"Neither will I, no thanks to you," Elerek spat. "Now I'm to be stabbed with the Arghan countess's dagger."

His heart lurched. "Lystra told you?" Had she said anything about him? About the writ of the curse's sale?

The expression that twisted the king's face was nothing

short of torment. "She told me a lot of things." A long sigh deflated his chest. "But I saw the countess myself, in the palace prisons. She told me to die. What does it matter if I can name the culprit? Can I bring them to justice? Can I do right by anyone in my kingdom? Can I save those whom I've cursed to die?"

Razhar said nothing. His own pleas echoed in Elerek's voice, in the desperation of his tone.

"And *you*." In a moment, the king transformed into the raging, vengeful man whose blood pulsed with a destroying curse—the man that made Razhar so terribly frightened. "You took the fate of *my* kingdom into your hands." Elerek growled deep in his throat. "How dare you."

How can I possibly tell you the truth? This was the same argument Razhar had made for years. Since he'd taken his first ship back to his homeland as a teenager, to glimpse the red and white sandstone cliffs with his own eyes. When he'd found the vault belonging to his poor baba and seen the writ for himself, confirming all that his heart knew to be true.

If Elerek knew, would he show compassion? Would he understand the war that waged in Fahwal's soul? Or would it only justify Lorkin's bloodlust? Razhar didn't want the truth to change Elerek. He just wanted his brother back.

The brother that I thought cared. If Elerek could care for the people who had only weeks to live, those who held no value to his kingdom otherwise, whom he made family, ought he to care for even the lowly Kushites?

"I did what I could, El." Razhar stared down at his hands, now clothed in smooth, bronze skin. Balance restored. "I kept you alive. I kept them all alive." He forced himself to stare into the dark fury consuming the king's face. "Driss, Bushra, Cole, Ishtal, Norbah . . . Myra."

Elerek's hands clenched. "What gives you the right to hold life and death in your hands, Razhar?"

Oh? Like you? Razhar could almost scoff.

"Does anyone else know?" Elerek demanded.

Heat burned in Razhar's cheeks. He looked away.

"Razhar . . ." *Drip. Drip. Drip.* The sound of water upon stone was warning enough.

"Myra. I needed her help. I could only manage the task while you slept." He should've stopped talking, even as Elerek's eyes burned dark, a fire cast from obsidian flint. But he kept going. "And Lystra, she—"

Bam! Darkness and light exploded across Razhar's vision. He stumbled back, his knees hitting the sand.

"You let them lie to me?" Elerek also landed in the sand. He raised the fist that had hit squarely in Razhar's eye, a stream of water pouring from his white knuckles. "Both of them? Give me one reason why you deserve to live? After everything you've done?"

Everything I've *done?* Pain pulsed across his face. Razhar clutched his eye, the surrounding skin swelling swiftly. He'd kept the cursed doomed to die alive. Time after time after time.

Even that horrible day, the only other time that the sands had returned. When he'd woken with a cough deep in his chest, his bed in the servants' quarters covered in sand. When he'd known that something had gone terribly wrong—and he'd found Elerek lying in a pool of his own blood, a knife in his hand.

He'd always saved Elerek. But now, holding his hand against his bruised and swollen face, he wondered if there would be anyone to save him.

"What is this?" Tangu's voice boomed as the warriors descended like a swarm of vultures to a fresh carcass. "Bind him at once!"

Two hulking Jarkins grabbed Elerek's shoulders. Without the use of his legs, he crumpled, wholly at their mercy as they bound his arms. Another pair of warriors dragged Razhar back with rough hands, out of reach from the king's wrath. Elerek looked away, ignoring Razhar as if he were another dune cast across the Sancen's wasteland.

Was this how Fahwal had felt? When he would press his back against the door and slide to his knees? When he would cover his face, marked with the archer's brilliant crimson battle paint, and sit in silence for hours? Helpless and small in a world where they didn't matter?

Tangu stood between them, disgust upon his face. "Idiotic plan," he muttered. "I knew he'd kill us out here." He shot a glare at Razhar. "Keep your distance." Then he barked a laugh. "Pity you've nothing for your face. It'll be black as ink by tomorrow."

Razhar ran his fingers along his eye again, the skin swollen like a ripe plum—probably a similar color too. Elerek had excellent form for a man who couldn't spar.

"Take him to the fire." Tangu spoke to the warriors holding Elerek. "Guard him at all times and keep him bound. If he tries anything, damage him." He spat, narrowly missing the king's face. "Your legs are already useless, right, cripple? You wouldn't mind if the bones were broken? And the curse will permit you to lose a few fingers, eh?" He straightened, standing tall. "If that doesn't work, see what Khasar will let us do to his queen."

Elerek made no reply, but his stone-cold exterior began to crumble, giving way to a deep exhaustion.

As Razhar's face pulsed in tandem with the furious pounding of his heart, he wondered if he'd begun to understand his baba in ways that he hadn't before. The helplessness turned to spiraling anger. The willingness to do terrible things, even consulting a curse binder, take a beautiful dagger and soil it and his soul with a dark ritual. To hear, with a weary relief, that the king would be preoccupied with a devastation. Not killed, for killing a king was no small task, but there would be no time for war and conquests.

He'd begun to follow in his baba's footsteps, willing to kill a king for some sense of security.

"And you." Tangu spun toward him, sneering with hawkish eyes. "Forget the stars tonight; I don't trust you not to deceive us."

A narrow escape that felt like a trap. "I—I can still go," he stammered. "R-read the stars."

At that, Elerek lifted his gaze, a scowl written over his face.

Razhar swallowed. If he wanted the chance to kill a king and break a curse, he needed to survive, and he could only see one way to keep up this charade. He needed Elerek's help.

Tangu stood over him. Though he wasn't as bulky as the rest of the Jarkins, he still held an intimidating stature. "As if you could see the stars clearly with your face like that." He glanced at the guards again. "Keep him near the fire till I return, then I'll deal with him."

As one of the guards took Elerek by the shoulders, dragging him across the sands, the other seized Razhar's arm and they marched toward the fire.

Razhar blinked his swollen eye, trying to meet Elerek's gaze. "El, the skies, you know—"

"Quiet." The guard smacked the back of Razhar's head.

Elerek looked at him as if he truly were an unsightly mass of condor scat. "You disgust me, Razhar. Your lies, schemes, and sands."

The grains crunched beneath his boots, gathered by the winds that had blown through this narrow slot of land in the middle of nothing. If Razhar did turn to sand, right here and now, he would be lost to the desert, indistinguishable from the rest of the landscape. Just another bit of dust.

Baba was right. About the consequences, about Razhar's life traded to pay the cost of someone else's sins. The cost Fahwal paid, unaware that he would lose that which he held more precious, even beyond that of his own life. Even about the secret, the terrible one that Razhar could never tell.

His desire to save his own skin meant nothing, but saving the king of Instanolde? That *mattered.* A life weighed in the balance, and it didn't matter that Razhar only wanted to live too—wanted it just as badly as Elerek did.

Chapter 10

Lystra

Lystra could barely keep up with Amak's strides, her boots skidding over the terrain as he pulled her along like a child. Her face radiated heat, both from the long hours in the sun and the humiliation Gaudab had caused, using her for the sake of a feeble taunt. Tears burned in her eyes and she hastily wiped them away.

She couldn't stay here any longer. She wouldn't. One day of travel lay behind her and she couldn't risk another separating her from Instanolde. She'd been gone too long already, and she ached with the time and the distance. What of her father? Did he hide refugees on House Arghan's estate with the help of Corsha, her benevolent cousin? Had Kimzi, Corsha's brother, been held prisoner with the rest of Elerek's newly trained archers?

Her grandmother, did she remain under lock and key—as Lystra had commanded?

No, she *had* to go back, to rise like the glorious sun and give her kingdom its best chance.

"I need my pack." She tried to wrench her arm free but Amak's grip seemed made of iron.

The Jarkin scowled.

"It's on your cardant. Please, I must rebandage my shoulder." A truth she shouldn't have ignored for so long. And her chances of escaping were dependent upon the cardants.

Amak didn't speak, but his boots changed their course. The cardants huddled just beyond the tents, clinging to the rock for the lingering warmth. Lystra stared down the gully. A haze of indigo dropped like a blanket across the desert. A wild loneliness spread across her soul, like the chill from the faintest of winds. No longer a captive only to the Jarkins and their cruel intentions to use her as leverage for a king who had betrayed her, but to the emptiness, the largeness of the Sancen.

"Ride hard. Don't look back."

The memory of Cormek's voice, of fleeing across the desert after his death, felt as if it belonged to someone else. A nightmarish haze of sand, heat, and sorrow. But she hadn't flown to safety, like a bird seeking a high perch. She'd returned as iron upon the smith's anvil, heated and ready to be forged anew. With resolve and grief both surging in her veins, she'd taken the crown, married Elerek, and ruled as queen.

She would do it again. Return to the role her grandmother said she was born to live. This plan certainly sounded like Grandmother, who knew only power and consequences. Take what belonged to her and leave behind another king to die.

Amak's cardant, the one with red scales, nearly blended into the gully walls. The saddle clasps had been released, freeing the reptile's belly to flatten against the sand, and the packs were still tied to its back. A large, orb-like eye blinked at them as they approached.

"Such good cardants," Lystra whispered, reaching to scratch the reptile's snout. She thought she knew this one, taken from the racing committee, perhaps House Yissal for whom several friends raced.

Amak released her and began untying the packs. Lystra reached for her own and slipped her hand into the tack bag tied to the saddle, where oil and extra straps were often stored and, yes, a small knife sharp enough for cutting the saddle's leathers. She slipped it into her pack.

A simple plan: cut her bonds before dawn and risk it all. Slip through the shadows and seize a cardant. The packs would have enough food for the journey. As for water . . . Lystra huffed, thinking of her spilled waterskin and the furious droplets clinging to Elerek's hands. He would've fought them all, she knew, drowned them for her.

"You will always be my king. But you are not my husband."

Her words had struck true. Elerek had eyes of ice most of the time, but she'd seen the fissures. How small those cracks had appeared in comparison to the cleave rending her own soul. But she didn't regret her words, no matter how deeply they'd also wounded her. The air was clear, and their positions set, like pieces on a gaming board. Now they could strategize, plan their sacrifices, and forge on toward their end.

Cold, callous thoughts. Lystra hated how it ached to steel her soul, a muscle stretched too far. She wished she didn't have to carry so many burdens. Here, at the edge of the desert, she felt completely and utterly alone.

Slinging her pack across her good shoulder, Lystra whistled softly. Across the gully, a great horned head rose. Tiniah watched her with large, inquisitive eyes.

That's my girl. Lystra moved toward her, holding out her hands. The reptile nestled its snout in her palm and blinked her large, yellow eyes. "I'm sorry they took you."

The cardant pawed at the sand and uttered a series of mutters deep in its throat, a restless response. But with the temperature dropping, their cooling blood would soon sink the mounts into a deep sleep. Lystra hoped they'd rest well and be ready to ride with the dawn.

"An impressive reptile." Amak followed her, keeping a close eye.

Lystra nodded. It would be risky, stealing Tiniah back. She'd only been working with her a few precious months, the same length of time as her strange, political marriage. But Gaudab deserved this revenge, and her heart burned fiercely at the thought. She swept her hand along the smooth scales of Tiniah's neck, imagining the ride. The sun on her shoulders. The wind in her hair.

What would Elerek think, she wondered, when she was gone?

A hand clamped down on her arm. Lystra startled, staring up into Gaudab's snarling face.

"Inspecting *my* cardant, little queen?" A cruel laugh rumbled in his chest.

Lystra sniffed. "I think we both know whose cardant she is."

"Ah, no arguing with either of you, is there? Whatever the disgraced king and queen of the river rat kingdom say." He narrowed his eyes. "I know you were there, at the kasbah. Your guards took your king's corpse back to your kingdom. You survived. The desert calls you back."

He spoke low and ominous, a warning of a destiny she could not escape. But as Lystra inhaled the desert air, a resolve knitted itself deep in her soul. The Jarkins called them river rats, but it wasn't true. They belonged to the canyons, the rocks, the sands. The desert flowed in her veins and she wouldn't let it conquer her any more than she'd let the Jarkins steal her kingdom.

Lystra raised her chin. "You made an enemy of me the day

that you killed Cormek. Even if you kill another king, know that I *will* hunt you down and destroy you. Instanolde will not bow to the likes of you—and neither will I."

She knew her words sounded like empty threats, but into them she poured her fortitude, her will, and the faintest shred of a hope she so desperately wanted to feel again.

Gaudab released her, taking a moment to size her up. Then, he lifted his hand, skeletal with the curse. "Where is your mark?"

Lystra stilled.

"You're cursed. Same as the rest of us." He leaned forward. "The Kushite has something to do with it, doesn't he? If I find that he is spinning lies with that snake-like tongue . . ."

Swallowing her fear, Lystra folded her arms. "If you believed they were lies, would we be out here?"

"Your king would be dead."

A threat hung in his voice. For now, they lived. But then what? If the curse was broken and Elerek dead, she and Razhar would hold no value. They'd be killed or made slaves anyways, just like the rest of her people.

As despair once again threatened to bury her in mire, she had to grasp on to hope, glimmering like distant starlight.

"I refer to hope as starlight."

In this she had no choice; she had to fight for her people—to give them starlight, as Elerek had done for her.

A cheer rose from the fire, announcing that hunters returned. Gaudab turned, the distant glow highlighting his features. Then he took her arm, forcing her to walk beside him back toward the circle. "Come, river lily. You'll eat with me."

Lystra made no reply. Even here, as a captive in the wilderness, their every move was a staged display. Subtle positioning and shows of power. These were skills her grandmother possessed in plenty, skills that had been honed into Lystra since childhood. But she was tired, and could hold so little in her cursed hands. Vulnerable didn't even begin to describe it.

The men appeared as dark hills about the fire, casting large shadows across the gully walls. The hunters had already begun work on their kill, a scanty brace of polecats. The smell of roasting meat overwhelmed Lystra with a hunger she hadn't felt since this terrible journey had begun.

Tangu sat closest to the fire, clutching a bit of charcoal as he continued sketching his map. He looked up with a sneer as Gaudab sat down, forcing Lystra to settle beside him.

"Worry not, Datem," the mapmaker muttered. "I broke them apart. Best you keep that *dog* leashed. No thanks to the useless Kushite."

Beside Tangu, Razhar sat cross-legged, staring into the flames. Lystra winced, turning her attention from his eye, miserably swollen and purple as a plum, to Elerek, hunched and bound with his face turned toward the shadows.

Stars. She shook her head, her appetite fleeing back into the desert.

The warlord made a low *humph* in his throat. "Not useless. Not yet." He narrowed his eyes at Razhar. "As long as our course holds." He gestured to one of the soldiers who roasted the meat from the polecats over the flames.

The Jarkin handed him a bone, a rib from the shape of its curve, bits of sinew still clinging to it. A hush fell over the men, all movement ceased.

Lystra drew her knees to her chest, a chill sweeping over her skin. A mealtime blessing. The Jarkins had committed terrible, heinous acts. Survival was often a path of bloodshed. But like her own, the mountain men bore a culture, a society.

Gaudab held the bone, his arm stretched toward the fire. "May the gods of the mountain find us here among the canyons of the desert. *Di karim baho di natu.*"

"Di natu," the men repeated.

Gaudab cracked the bone and tossed its two halves into the fire. Packs were opened and dried crusts of flatbread and hardtack circulated. The polecats didn't yield much meat, giving each a small portion. Lystra forced herself to swallow, her mouth dry. She reached for her waterskin, and then remembered it was empty.

"Here." Razhar handed her his own, moving to sit beside her.

"Thank you," she whispered, tilting it back to drink. She'd need at least two or three full ones if she were to reach Instanolde by sundown. A problem she'd need to remedy tonight. After taking only one sip, she tucked it into her pack and withdrew a blanket of *tui* wool and threw it about her shoulders. It smelled of home, of warmth and security.

"Razhar," she whispered. "Could you get me another waterskin?"

He frowned, confused. She held his stare, signaling that this was no mere request, but an order from his queen.

"Tell me." Though his hands had been untied, Elerek didn't touch the round of flatbread in his lap. "Your blessing. How does it translate into our tongue?"

Scoffing, Tangu shook his head. "Instan river rats don't know our tongue."

Elerek narrowed his eyes, and then spoke what sounded like a phrase in the Jarkins' language. His voice was smooth, eloquent, as if he were giving orders to the tribes and houses of the river delta. Lystra's heart pounded. Somehow, despite the fatigue and dirt clinging to his face, clothes, and hair, she still saw the proud, stern prince she'd met at the pyre of his brother. The man who stared death in the face with each new dawn.

"I have a text on languages. It claimed that yours bears similarities to that of the southern delta," Elerek said. "We also have the word *karim*. It means noble."

Karim. His house. Lystra blinked.

Tangu regarded the king with a scowl. "To power we give honor. That's as close as it translates. *Karim* means power to us, a power ascribed to predators and conquerors."

Elerek dipped his chin, acknowledging the response, but his eyes darkened.

Noble. Power. Conqueror. Lystra took a bite of her meat, chewing thoughtfully. She thought of Lorkin, Elerek's blood-thirsty father, and the terrible, bitter wars. Perhaps the Jarkins' use of the word held a more accurate meaning.

Gaudab cast a picked-clean bone into the fire. "Southern delta. Our people once lived there." He chuckled. "Your coloring . . . pale for a river rat. Maybe you're one of us."

Lystra dusted the crumbs from her lap. If they were to perish, and the desert claim their bones, would it matter if they were Instan, Jarkin, or Kushite? They died the same, flesh and soul cast together to blaze across the world with the glory of starfire. It was the cruelty, the bloodlust, and the destructive ways of the Jarkins that made her hate them. The children they'd killed, the women they'd taken, the murders they'd committed. These were choices that drew lines and stirred hearts to action.

But the king had also killed. She watched as Elerek's already pale skin grew paler, and she wondered if he contemplated much the same.

As the meal concluded and the embers began to lose their glow, the men stirred, taking their packs and moving toward their tents. Lystra glanced about the circle, and a cold terror shot right through her bones. One night. She just had to make it through one night.

The Jarkins formed a cluster, empty waterskins in hand.

Elerek lifted his head, exhaustion casting deep shadows across his face.

Lystra took her empty waterskin, handing it to Razhar. "I need this filled."

He raised his eyebrows. "Your Highness, I'm *not* interested in getting my other eye blackened."

Lystra tilted her head, pulling her fraying braid over one shoulder, slick with sand and oil. Absolutely grotesque. "He did that?" She didn't wait for a reply. "I'm sure you deserved it."

Razhar gave a deep sigh. "Probably." He scooted closer to her, his voice low. "You've got a full waterskin in your pack. What are you planning?"

Lystra watched the firelight dance on the gully's sandstone walls. She weighed her answer, measuring as the spice merchants measured saffron and cumin. Her voice was a whisper. "Gaudab suspects your abilities. He noticed that my curse mark is masked."

"Stars above."

"But wouldn't they . . . keep you alive?" Lystra stopped talking as Gaudab stalked across camp. His robe streaming behind him, the gold of the dagger caught in the dying embers. "If they knew?"

Razhar's eyes didn't leave the dagger. Something ignited in his gaze, a sense of strategy, of a challenge. Lystra remembered seeing something similar the night they danced in the market, where their footsteps found their match.

Razhar wanted the dagger. Why? When they reached the stars the weapon would be required. Plunged into Elerek's heart. The curse broken once and for all and the man for whom it was intended would be dead.

But Lystra didn't trust Razhar. "What are you planning?"

His throat worked with a swallow. After a moment, he

bowed his head. "They think I know the stars. That mapmaker expects me to track our course."

"You don't?" Lystra herself couldn't recite every story and fable associated with the constellations, but she couldn't imagine not recognizing the stars any more than she could imagine un-learning to read.

Razhar's voice turned flat. "My baba was executed before he could teach me."

She opened her mouth to reply but had nothing to say. The sorrow in his voice was familiar, a song her soul knew well. Razhar had also known grief; he'd been acquainted with it all his life.

Lystra rose, still clutching the blanket about her shoulders. Her body ached with the sudden movement, her head splitting from the long hours beneath the sun. She grabbed her pack, the empty waterskin poking out of the top. Then she joined the line of waiting Jarkins. Two waterskins wouldn't be enough, but it was a start.

When her turn came, she handed Elerek the waterskin. He avoided eye contact, the stream of water from his fingers weak. Lystra wondered what sort of toll this work took on him, and if it would provoke the curse to take him quicker.

"Razhar doesn't know the stars," she whispered.

Elerek scoffed. "I know he doesn't."

"You won't help him?"

"No."

Lystra took back the waterskin, screwing its cap tight to seal its contents. The storm between them billowed and thundered. Any moment and the air would crackle, the lightning strike, and she wondered what would happen next.

"Ah, river lily." The last of the firelight became eclipsed by a shadow worthy of the man's monstrous atrocities. "There you are. Arrangements must be made."

Thunk. Thunk. Thunk. The sound of tent pegs being hammered into the ground echoed up the gully. The walls suddenly felt too tight, and the thought of the canvas walls of a tent were too much to bear.

"You touch her," Elerek's voice growled, "you're a dead man."

Gaudab lifted his hand, the curse mark shimmering in the fading light. A cruel smile twisted his features. "I'm a dead man anyways, aren't I? What makes you any different?"

Lystra held her breath. Caught between them, she felt like the pieces of meat they'd picked through. She glanced at Elerek, whose eyes burned with a deep and vile hatred, and shuddered. The king's silence was more frightening than his words, but she didn't know if he possessed the strength to fight Gaudab. Not now, and not over her.

"Enough." Lystra stood, still clutching the wool blanket. "You've done enough to incite the king's wrath, haven't you? If you desire a prize, wait until you are the victor. Without the king, none of us will survive." She held her head high. Like a queen.

Gaudab edged closer, his boots shuffling in the sand. Lystra held her ground, her heart pounding, and didn't dare blink. She'd faced many perils, but this terrible warlord who'd carved his knife into her skin remained a frightening threat.

One night. She just had to survive one night.

Gaudab's eyes didn't leave hers. "Kesh, Jul, you heard the little queen. Without the abomination, none of us survive. Bind him—and keep his arms strung up. That way, if he tries to drown us in the night, he'll drown himself too."

Lystra's heels spun circles in the sand as the two Jarkins swept in to perform the warlord's bidding, grabbing Elerek's shoulders and dragging him across camp. Unable to help herself, she gasped. "Wait—"

Gaudab seized her shoulder, the one where he'd left the mark of his people, his claim on her. "It seems only fair, river lily, that you do your share in, as you said it, not 'inciting the king's wrath.'"

Pain spread across Lystra's back like a pair of broken wings. A cry escaped her lips as Gaudab towed her faster than her legs could keep up, like a puppet grasping at its strings.

In the center of camp, where the fire had nearly burned out, she realized the *thunk, thunk* that she'd heard hadn't been the tent pegs, but the pounding of a stake into the hard earth. They bound Elerek's wrists and lashed the rope to a notch in the top of the stake, stretching his arms above his head. Without the use of his legs to manage his weight, he simply hung. His muscles tightened, chest heaving for each breath; though he made no protest, agony burned in his eyes.

Lystra's eyes filled with tears, the horrible image blurring before her. No, Gaudab was wrong. None of this was *fair*.

Gaudab laughed as Lystra's hands were also bound. He forced her to her knees beside the stake, and there she was anchored. Hot drops of blood seeped through Lystra's tunic. They didn't string her up, her hands curling the loose sand. If water fell from Elerek's fingers, she too would drown.

She planted her forehead against the stake, tears streaming down her face.

"You can't protect me, Lystra," Elerek whispered between labored breaths. He turned his head, straining to look at her.

"And you can't save me." How bitter it sounded, coming from her. This was her fault, wasn't it? All of this misery?

"Maybe not," he whispered. "But that's all I can do. Even if you can only despise me, you have to survive."

Then, they gagged him. The embers were scattered, and darkness fell over the gully. The men turned toward the security of their tents. A pair of guards remained, and Gaudab gave them one last sneer before stalking away.

Lystra slumped in the sands, leaning against the stake and listening to the sound of Elerek's labored breaths through the gag. She didn't want to survive, striving for another breath, another sunrise. She wanted to *live*. See the dawn break over the mountains and turn her kingdom to glittering gold. But the only light came from the river of stars atop the gully. Tiny specks, too far to give comfort.

Once darkness claimed the desert, Lystra found herself shivering, her tears run dry. It seemed impossible now to imagine the oppressive heat. Now, a cold seeped up through the sands and into her bones. Her pack still lay looped through her arm, beyond her reach. As the blood dried on her shoulder, her bandages and tunic grew stiff but the wound beneath pulsed with a tender pain. Her heart was much the same.

Above her, Elerek's head tilted back against the stake, his eyes fixed heavenward, watching the starlight. Hope.

Lystra gritted her teeth, biting down on sand. She moved her bound wrists up the stake until they touched Elerek's back. "Can you move at all?" she whispered.

With a grunt of effort, he arched his back, allowing her hands to shimmy up to behind his neck. Her fingers, numb from the cold, pulled at the gag, loosening it until it fell around his neck.

Elerek gasped for air, drinking it in as if his lungs were

already full of water. His lips were chapped and the skin around his mouth raw from the tight gag. His head turned toward her, jade eyes meeting her own.

"Thank you," he whispered.

Lystra's fingers lingered on his cheek, and there, in the pale starlight, the skin peeled back from her fingers. His curse, the mark that she shared his fate, returned to her flesh. She drew them back, pale as bone, but a dark curl of his hair looped about her forefinger like a signet ring. She quickly looked away, her breath like ice between her teeth.

"You shouldn't have touched me." Elerek grimaced, muscled arms tightening as they bore his weight. "I . . . I never wanted you to be cursed."

Lystra stared into the darkness. The wind had picked up, whistling through the rocky crevices with a forlorn sound. She was cursed before she'd touched him. Cursed to lose Cormek. Cursed to marry a king who loved another. Cursed to fall for him anyways.

"You promised me that you wouldn't hurt me," she whispered. A promise made when the world was simpler. When they'd dared to seek a cool oasis but found only the heat's twisted mirages.

Elerek released a long, tormented breath. "Will my death be enough, Lystra? If the curse is broken, will I have paid enough? Will we have done what we set out to do?"

Lystra closed her eyes. "We have to save Instanolde, El. That's why . . . I have to—"

Then, the howling began.

A tingling, chilling drone, as if a thousand mourners sent their moans ravaging through their camp. Cries worthy of demons, wraiths, sirens. The air hit them with the force of a cardant at full speed and stole away their breath. Knocked to her knees again, the wind ripped at Lystra's hair and clothing. Her ropes felt as tethers, anchoring her to the earth.

Dear Starkindler . . . Lystra huddled against the stake, her shoulder touching Elerek's side. In this forsaken terrain, a storm only required one ingredient—wind. The narrow canyons. The rocky gully. This storm had a voice of its own, moaning like the desert wraiths she'd heard about in stories—the ones she prayed didn't haunt this storm.

Then came the sand.

It pelted the gully in droves, like rain but louder, denser, destructive. Closer and closer, it hung like a veil across the heavens, blotting out the starlight. Thick, deep darkness buried them.

The guards shouted. Roused from their posts, they ran against the wind, robes streaming behind them. The sands thundered closer. Elerek's ropes were released and his body fell slack. They seized his shoulders, dragging him away toward the nearest tent.

"No!" The shout tore from his throat, louder than the winds. "Lystra! Please, you can't leave her . . ."

Lystra looked into near-complete darkness. In the fading starlight, she saw the frantic, desperate gleam of Elerek's eyes. He raised his bound hands, but no droplets fell. They already knew that his waters were no match for the sands.

Then, the sandstorm enveloped them. Lystra doubled over, eyes shut fast. Sand and grit sliced across her skin, each jagged grain razor sharp. Dust burned in her eyes, her nose, and immediately made breathing impossible. She gasped and sputtered, grime filling her mouth. The noise swarmed in her skull like a thousand furious bees. She no longer feared imaginary wraiths, the constant sand frightful enough. The desert's distance had never felt so great—and death had never felt so near. No longer the queen of Instanolde, but feeble flesh and bone fighting for breath and overwhelmed by the storm's fury.

Hands yanked at her bonds and lifted her from the ground. The storm seemed to intensify, and Lystra found she could no longer bear to blink and her lungs lacked the strength to cough.

Then, all was still. The sounds of the storm muted, distanced by canvas walls. The coarse fibers of wool and soft tufts of sheepskin caressed her face and cradled her body. She coughed and sputtered, trying to rid the burn from her lungs and throat.

"Don't move, either of you."

Lystra didn't think that she could. She burrowed into the sheepskins, taking in their warmth. The blankets shifted beside her, a shoulder brushing her own.

"We cannot be close."

In that night of necessary distance, the stars had shone. Their great task lay before them and the impossible felt achievable. Now they lay beside each other, their hands bound, taking shelter from the storm.

Lystra turned, meaning to shift away, but the movement sent her coughing again.

"She needs water." Elerek's voice split the sandstorm.

Thunk. Not even the storm could disguise the sound of a waterskin. It fell near enough for Lystra to find with her bound hands, but her fingers also found his, cold and cursed. They laced into hers and didn't let go.

"I'm sorry." His whisper was a breath on her forehead.

The water soothed her throat and quieted her lungs. Lystra pulled it to her chest, suddenly aware of the significance. With the two in her pack, lying against her hip, she'd come into possession of three waterskins.

Enough to last the hard day's ride back to Instanolde.

Surely she could reach the knife in her pack, steal away

before morning, and take back her cardant. The pieces were here. She could do it.

She *had* to do it.

"No," she whispered into the darkness. "I'm sorry."

She wondered if it would be easier, once she was gone. Easier for him, to face what he must, and easier for her, wild and free as her cardant carried her back home.

"Poor things." She imagined the cardants, tucking their heads beneath their tails, coiled like great snakes, their scales suitable defenses against the elements. Still, these were reptiles raised from eggs, accustomed to their pens and their care.

"Hmm?" Elerek's voice came from near her ear.

"The cardants."

"They won't fit in here."

"Quiet!" the Jarkin snapped, his admonition louder than the wind and sand shaking the tent.

Lystra turned around, still clutching the waterskin, and shut her eyes. She wondered if the Jarkins felt the same terror that cleaved her chest. To live in Instanolde had always meant dwelling in death's shadow, the desert and its harrows, the shift of enemies and invaders at the door—and the curse dooming the man who lay beside her. So, so much death.

"Let's not grow weary of life."

Somewhere, in the nightmare, Razhar's words returned to her, comforting her mind even as the shift of Elerek beside her flooded her with not the cursed numbness, but a soft and gentle warmth.

Chapter 11

Elerek

Skies full of endless stars. White light, pure and shimmering, more pristine than anything upon the ground. More untainted than anything that fought for survival down below.

The wrathgiver constellation. The image of an assassin bearing a knife filled in between the stars, but his robes were white and his face obscured by starlight. Stories spoke of an assassin commissioned to seek out his mark. No one knew if he succeeded or if the mark were worthy of death. An unending hunt. Forever to wander. Forever to wonder.

Darcress, its red towers stretching to the sky. Blood stained the sand between them and the bones of cardants and men bleached white beneath the relentless summer sun. The wind kicked up, sending spirals of dust. Did Cormek's soul roam the sands, waiting for vengeance? Praying for peace?

Then, the land opened up, running the length of rock between Darcress's twin towers. From this great split, a canal emerged. Waters bursting from the depths of the earth, crashing and foaming, raging against the desert rock. The water flowed

between the two towers, spilling through the pass like an army.
An army no man could command.

And there, in the water, starlight shone. The light of the
wrathgiver constellation.

Elerek woke from the dream with a start. A dry heave retched
his stomach, the tight gag making it difficult to breathe. He
couldn't feel his jaw and his lips were cracked and bleeding. At
some point in the night, once the terrible sandstorm had passed,
they'd strung him up again, this time by way of the tent's
central pole. Mercifully, most of his joints had lost all feeling,
but pain knifed up his spine, sharp as a cardant's claws. The
gag had also been replaced and the coarse fabric tasted of dirt.

Heat already tinged the air, but the light seeping between
the tent's seams wasn't yet golden. The tent flap fluttered as the
two Jarkin guards stepped outside.

And there, nestled in the sheepskins and blankets beside
him, lay Lystra. Her braid had come undone and her long
tresses were streaked with sand. Eyes closed in slumber, her
chest rose with gentle breaths. Her bound hands still cradled
the waterskin, a reminder that this terrible desert would rage its
best to destroy them.

As for him and Lystra, he feared they were already
destroyed.

If she had ever loved him, she seemed resolved to stop. He
could hardly blame her, and he'd done his share to tear down
whatever they might have built. They had undertaken a political alliance, not a marriage, and now, in the shattering of their
world, they too had broken.

Their kingdom couldn't pay the consequences of their
doomed affections.

Elerek shifted, trying to work the blood back into his

limbs. Of all people, he should've known better. Instead, he'd been stupid enough to fall in love again. Lystra was right to draw lines in the sand, to distance herself. Her actions mirrored those he'd taken with Myra, to protect them from further pain.

Actions that had resulted in a spectacular failure. The lines that Elerek had drawn between himself and Myra came too late, far, far too late.

Stars, Elerek was so tried of feeling helpless. Against the curse, against the shifting sands of his kingdom, and against his own shortcomings.

His mind strayed to the dream, to the canal running through the desert. Only a flash flood could create such a thing. An impossible hope this time of year. But was he not also impossible? A man consumed by a curse with waters of death that flowed from his fingertips?

Lystra's eyes shot open. The appearance of peaceful sleep vanished, replaced by the fierce and fiery queen. Elerek blinked, finding the latter no less beautiful.

She reached for her pack, bound hands fumbling with the opening. A moment later she withdrew a small knife. Her curse-marked fingers twisted, the blade gleaming in the pale light, and within minutes she had the fibers weakened enough to sever.

Next, she stood, stooped against the tent's low roof, and pulled the gag free again.

"They'll know that you have a knife," he whispered.

Lystra stowed the blade back in her pack, along with the waterskin. "Only if . . ." Her voice trailed off, her eyes staring into the depths of her bag. A moment later, she withdrew a rolled scroll. Ornate inking, deep as midnight, adorned the edges, depictions of the heavens.

A star chart. *His* star chart. The one that they'd spread on the bed between them, the whole of the sky testifying to the void separating them.

"Why did you bring it?"

Lystra's eyes closed briefly. "A memory."

A place where their griefs had collided, and they'd found strength. An intimacy they might never share again.

"It ought to go to Razhar. He needs it more than we do."

Elerek scoffed, thinking of such a sacred token of their relationship being employed by Razhar's ever-shifting lies.

"You need him, El." Lystra's eyes flashed. "Especially after . . ."

What was it she was trying to say?

Footsteps pounded toward the tent. Lystra's eyes widened. She nestled down within the blankets again and pretended to sleep. Her hands were tucked beneath her, along with the cut rope.

The tent's flaps flew back. Gaudab bowed as he entered, his hulking figure somehow seeming larger. The warlord folded his arms, staring down with a triumphant expression. "No one has drowned this night." His eyes strayed toward Lystra's still form.

Elerek glared at him.

"We march within the hour. You will fill the waterskins." Gaudab approached him, setting to work on the knots.

Give life, not death. Elerek gritted his teeth. These Jarkins deserved a canal, not mere droplets.

The rope went slack. He crumpled, his muscles screaming with relief. Touching the ragged skin across his cheeks, where the gag had been, he washed the cuts with a bit of water from his fingertips. A small relief in comparison to all the horrors.

But he'd dreamed of starlight. Did that mean that there was hope? Would the Starkindler remember him?

"You do believe in the Starkindler?" Lystra's voice. On their wedding night.

"I have to believe in something good. Something greater."

Now, even the Maker of the stars seemed distant.

Gaudab lingered. Methodically, like the warrior he was, he checked his weapons. One by one. His axes. A long hunting knife. The dagger that bound his curse—that belonged to the countess of House Arghan.

Elerek rose from the sand, rolling his stiff shoulders. He was almost glad he'd never see that foul woman again. No, he didn't believe his father was right to force her from the throne, but such was the way of conquerors. He hoped she was satisfied with her revenge.

Glancing at Lystra, a heaviness compressed his heart. A revenge that threatened even her granddaughter.

"My men were whispering." Gaudab looked at him, his gaze hooded. "The stars bear different names in our culture. Our legends, told by elders around the fires in mountain caverns, are also different. But of all the tales, I've not heard of anything like *you* before."

Elerek stretched his legs out, wincing at the effort it took his sore muscles. Gaudab spoke as if the blame lay with him, but he knew of the curse he was innocent. His brokenness came as the result of his own choices.

"We too have curses and those who bind them. In our culture, they are given as a punishment, often to satisfy a vengeance."

Glancing up at the warlord, Elerek narrowed his eyes. "The cost of the curse is worth vengeance?"

What was the cost of his curse? Had Dalmah paid it?

Gaudab nodded slowly. "A cost is a little thing to suffer. Wrongs must be avenged. Debts satisfied. For this reason, we don't seek curses broken. They are left as markers, testaments to the wrongdoing."

"And if they are innocent?"

A sneer covered the warlord's face. "If proved innocent, we will break the curse, but the task is often difficult, which is why it is rarely done." He turned toward Elerek and folded his arms. "Slay you beneath the stars. Is that all?"

Heat burned in Elerek's chest. He met the warrior's stare and did not blink. "I know of nothing else."

"And the Kushite? His sands?"

Then, Elerek looked away. *That vile . . .*

Razhar had lied. His sands, his touch, had extended his life. The brother that he'd loved, who had kept him from despair, who had cast a patronizing ray of sunshine over the misery of his cursed existence. And he'd dragged Myra into his secrets. All those nights that she'd slept beside him, she'd carried the knowledge that Razhar had given them more time.

Lystra also knew.

Elerek shook his head. The star chart lay amid the sheepskins, once again between him and his queen. She wanted to give it to Razhar? Keep him safe from the Jarkins' wrath? No, this was just punishment and Elerek found himself without mercy. He couldn't forgive Razhar. Not now, maybe not ever.

"The Kushite is your opposite. How is he tied to your curse?"

"I don't know." Razhar hadn't given him an answer, like a perfect idiot.

"We have legends—of counter curses."

Counter curses? Elerek scowled. They didn't exist. Gaudab spoke of folklore, a fabrication of mythical proportions. Curses were evil. Curses ruined lives. Curses begot consequences.

Curses didn't have opposites.

And yet.

Was Razhar tied to his fate? If he had died on his wedding night by Lystra's hand, would Razhar have also perished?

When his blood finally spilled beneath the wrathgiver, would Razhar be set free?

"In our stories"—Gaudab lowered his voice—"a counter curse must first be killed, otherwise the curse will only grow stronger. Consuming."

"I . . ." Elerek blinked. "I've never heard or read of anything like that."

Gaudab huffed. "And that's why the Kushite still lives."

Razhar still lived while Elerek was doomed to die. But thanks to Razhar's mysterious "curse," Elerek had lived far longer than he ought to have, long enough to become king, even a poor one. He rolled his head back, stretching out his sore neck muscles. His days as king were numbered; he *had* to make them count.

Gaudab turned, his shadow falling across Lystra.

"Let her sleep," Elerek said. He didn't know Lystra's plans, but he didn't want to discover what might happen if Gaudab realized she'd cut her bonds and stolen a knife.

As for the star chart, Elerek slipped it inside his shirt, keeping it and its memories close.

The warlord called for the guards to gather their waterskins. Then he grabbed Elerek's shoulder, dragging him out into the morning light.

"Useless cripple," he muttered beneath his breath.

"Just let go. I'll manage."

He obliged, dropping him to the newly shifted sands. Elerek pitched forward, landing on his elbows. He coughed, inhaling a cloud of sand. Gaudab stalked away, barking orders to his warriors.

Hands that weren't rough helped him up. "Please, don't hit me."

Elerek shoved Razhar away. "I'm fine." He gripped a

nearby shard of sandstone rising from the gully floor, hoisting himself up on it. Then he straightened his tunic and brushed the sand from his hair.

Razhar hadn't yet bound his turban, his coffee-colored hair hanging free about his shoulders. His swollen face resembled fruit from the bottom of a seller's crate. Elerek inhaled. It had felt *so good* to hit something.

But a counter curse? How could this Kushite orphan become a page taken from the most obscure of myths?

Elerek looked away. The storm had long passed, the sands leaving the gully less deep and the sky a bit nearer.

"Where is Lystra?" Razhar took a self-preserving step back, putting himself out of range of Elerek's fist.

"Sleeping." Far too easily, the image of Lystra, bundled in the rustic wools and animal skins, her ebony hair pushed back from her amber skin filled his mind. Before they'd strung him up, they'd lain so close, closer than they ever had before. And still, a lonely wilderness ached between them. One he couldn't cross.

"You're not my husband."

No, and he would never be.

He thought of her touch, her lingering fingertips as she'd loosened the gag—and how quickly the curse mark had spread across her skin like a plague.

No, the rules hadn't changed. His touch would still kill her.

"They"—Razhar rubbed the back of his neck—"kept you together?"

Dealing with Razhar's rambles would be more tolerable if a hot cup of mint tea were available, but he also didn't think one would materialize.

"If you mean bound to a stake together, then yes. At least until the sandstorm hit."

Razhar made a face, one that might have been a smile if not for the atrocious swelling.

"What?" Elerek snapped.

He shrugged, the unbound swaths of his turban's green silk settling around his shoulders. "You two haven't slept together before."

Such a statement was practically an open invitation to another black eye. "It wasn't—why am I even talking to you?" Elerek ground his teeth, almost thankful for the Jarkins and their waterskins. The flow from his fingertips came effortlessly, the curse wholly a part of him.

But Razhar remained; arms folded, lanky figure casually leaning against the shelf of rock protruding from the gully's sands. He waited as Elerek filled the waterskins, for once, silent.

At least, until the task was done and most of the warriors busied with breaking camp. "El, you *do* know that Lystra's in love with you, yes?"

Elerek leaned back against the rock, fending off the weariness that followed using his strange powers. He rubbed his forehead, his skin clammy from the hours spent in the wilderness, exposed to the heat and the elements. "We're king and queen, nothing more," he scoffed. "And we're hardly that now, aren't we?"

Shaking his head, Razhar cast him an expression of utter hopelessness. The type that usually accompanied a lecture to "cheer him up" or "be encouraging" or some other nonsense.

With another scoff, Elerek closed his eyes. Razhar had spoken many lies, but this wasn't one of them. This was a truth Elerek knew as sure as the sun would rise in the east. A torch against the darkest of nights, Lystra's love had brought them to this moment, this tragic adventure to break the curse and save their kingdom.

It was he that brought ruination.

"She won't forgive me," he whispered.

And he refused to forgive Razhar. The irony tasted bitter on his tongue.

"I don't deserve it, anyways. I tried to be a better man. I tried to overcome my failings. I tried to uphold the vows I took. I failed." Perhaps his curse had been cast for the sins of another, but he'd committed plenty of his own.

Razhar sighed. "Answer me this—and I beg you, leave my face alone—but you're in love with her, yes?"

Even the width and wildness of the Sancen seemed too immense to house such words.

"I am," he whispered, his gaze focused on the thin strips of marbling running through the gully rocks. "But we also know how this story ends."

"We do?" Razhar shrugged his thick shoulders. "That's disappointing."

Elerek narrowed his eyes, regarding him with a sidelong glance. For a moment, it seemed the air had given a bit of clarity between them. *This* was the Razhar that Elerek remembered and, from this angle, the swollen half of his face was just barely visible. He thought of the star chart, secure in his shirt. Lystra wanted him to forgive Razhar. Did that mean—there was hope? Hope that she might forgive him?

"You, Kushite." Tangu stalked toward them, the sand seeming to quiver beneath his boots. He unslung his basket of parchments from his shoulders and unrolled a star chart. "When did the constellation we seek last dance over your city?"

The unmarred skin of Razhar's face turned purple, matching his swollen eye. He took the chart in shaky hands.

Elerek leaned in to look. Lacking the beautiful illustrations of most Instan charts, this one was more simplistic and lacked the connection between the heavens and any geographical location.

Razhar didn't know the stars. Elerek had tried. A tradition given by fathers to their sons, this rite of passage had cast the Kushite orphan and cursed prince upon common ground. Lorkin had never bothered to teach Elerek, occupied with Cormek's ascension as heir. Often enough, Elerek would ask his cursed attendants to carry his chair up to one of the palace towers where he could watch the skies and thus taught himself. Razhar would join him, lounging on the window's ledge, usually a bag of almonds in hand. Night after night, Elerek offered to share his lessons and, night after night, Razhar refused.

Razhar stared at the chart as if it were hiding all the answers he needed. "Uh, well, the wrathgiver was in the east . . ."

Tangu sneered. "No stalling."

Panic flashed through Razhar's eyes, matching the tension carried in his broad shoulders. Subtle hints, recognizable only by someone who'd known him for as long as Elerek had.

Stars. He couldn't let Razhar drown like this.

"The wrathgiver hung apex over Instanolde in early spring," Elerek said. "The beginning of our harvest season." He could have died then, broken the curse and none of this would have happened. He cast a cool eye on the cartographer. "Show me a map."

Tangu glared, the morning light burning on his weathered skin. "You'll just as soon spin lies, leading us in circles."

Elerek held his stare. "And why would I do that?" He lowered his voice. "I could drown you *right now* if I wanted."

Hatred flickered in the Jarkin's eyes, the same fire that burned in the invaders' lust for Instan blood. A fire that would consume his kingdom, his people—and *he* had the power to snuff it out.

Taking another scroll from his basket, Tangu unrolled a map and handed it over.

Drying his cursed hands on his tunic, Elerek traced his fingers over the roads and trails branching from Instanolde. Out here, the Sancen seemed a dizzying labyrinth, not at all like the ordered valleys and mountains inked on the map. The land couldn't be contained. It ravaged like an untamed cardant, thrashing and writhing beneath the skies.

Almost in tandem with his thoughts, the growls of a cardant echoed across the gully. All around them, heavy packs were lashed to saddles and the reptiles ambled restlessly. Tangu stood, sweeping his eyes over the camp.

Elerek swiftly rolled the star chart and shoved it toward Razhar. "His charts are rubbish. This one is accurate. If you want to get me killed faster, this'll get us to the wrathgiver."

Razhar's eyes widened. No doubt he recognized the chart as Elerek's favorite. He tucked it inside the folds of his robe.

The cardant growls grew louder, one in particular rising like a scream up the gully walls. Tangu swore while Elerek's heartbeat quickened, its rhythm pounding in his chest like a war drum. He didn't need to be told *which* cardant made the ruckus.

"You!" Gaudab stalked through the camp, his boots smashing the charcoal circle of ash from their fire last night. "Contain that cardant."

Tiniah, the boldly striped reptile that had only just been tamed, stood saddled and harnessed. Her reins were held by the hands of the bold and barely tamed queen herself.

Lystra. She stood free, unguarded and unbound. Her scarf was pulled up over her head, her riding boots on her feet, and her pack slung over her shoulder. Elerek stared, reminded of her early rising with the dawn, always with cardants on her mind. Then he looked down at the map in his hands. One cardant bearing a lithe rider. If anyone could do it, it was Lystra.

She's . . . she's leaving.

Chapter 12

Lystra

L ystra gripped Tiniah's reins as if they were her only chance.

Please, girl, please. The reptile thrashed and growled, raging against her harness, each sound shattering the air. The heat stirred her blood, restless energy ready for the desert. Her saddle, cinched far too tight, evidence of the Jarkins' haste and carelessness, proved another reason for protest. Lystra gritted her teeth, trying in vain to adjust the straps. Her stolen minutes working with the cardant between the hours that she ruled a kingdom weren't enough to quell her.

"What do you think you're doing?" Gaudab rumbled like a thunderstorm, lightning flashing in his eyes.

Lystra's heart sank straight to her boots. She gave Tiniah a bit of rein, letting her pull away. "I . . . the cardants need sunlight," she blurted. "If they're going to exert themselves as brutally as yesterday. And her saddle . . ."

The Jarkin towered over her, so close she could see the glint of murder in his eyes. He wrenched the reins from her hands. "The heat will be upon them soon enough." His gaze traveled from the saddled reptile to the pack slung over her shoulders, assembling the picture.

Lystra took a step back. She felt exposed, stripped. A foolish girl lost in the desert. She shouldn't have tried to take Tiniah. She'd meant to take Amak's red reptile, but then . . .

Then she'd seen *her* cardant. Her gift from Elerek—a gift she wanted to take back with her.

Gaudab released the reins from his vice-like hands and grabbed her pack and, one by one, dropped the trio of water-skins to the sands.

"Twice a thief, river lily?" he snarled. Then he seized her by the throat.

Blood pounded. Lungs burned. Lystra's limbs trembled, reaching to pull away, but such an act was akin to pushing back the eastern mountains. Black blurred across her vision, blocking out the sun, the sand, and the fury of Gaudab's eyes.

The next moment, all was water.

It swept over them both, loosening the sand beneath their boots. Lystra landed sprawled in the mud, the river of deep azure sky unobstructed above her, drenched from head to toe, and coughing cursed water from her lungs.

As her chest inflated, Lystra lifted her head, sweeping wet hair from her eyes. Gaudab rose beside her, stalking back across the camp, to where Elerek sat on a shelf of rock, surrounded by the maps his scholarly mind loved so dearly.

Lystra stared. He no longer looked like the king of Instanolde.

Raw skin, cracked and bleeding, stretched across his cheeks where the gag had been tied and dark trenches dug beneath his eyes. His scarred hands were raised, curled like condor claws, ready to release another onslaught of water. He was a creature of myth, built of water, filled with the vilest of curses, a force strong and fierce enough to take on the whole of the desert.

Gaudab towered over him, his eyes unblinking. Then, he signaled two brutes clad in leather with fists streaked with cursed skin. They grabbed Elerek, throwing him into the circle of ash—and began to beat him.

The sound of flesh upon flesh echoed down the gully, like the pounding of an agonized heart. Lystra opened her mouth to scream, but a lump swelled up in her throat. She wanted to rise, to run, to rush to his defense, but she couldn't move, transfixed by the sight of their fists as they pummeled Elerek's crumpled form.

They were punishing him. Not her. *Him.*

Razhar, even bearing his own bruises, shouted and tried to force his way between the Jarkins and the king, but there was always another pair of soldiers to hold him back.

Stop. Please. Tears streamed down Lystra's face.

After what seemed an age and a day, the Jarkins backed away. Elerek lay face down, stained with ash and sand darkened by his water. His shoulders arched, rising in a steady rhythm.

Gaudab's shadow consumed him, a conqueror come to claim what was his. He grabbed a fistful of Elerek's tunic, dragging him up from the earth.

Elerek's head lopped back, blood trickling from his nose and a gash above his eyebrow. His eyes were dull, but the anger hadn't fled. If anything, the blood and bruises meant nothing. Burning with all the fire of the constellations, he wore his fury like a crown, a vengeful king ready to execute justice.

Lystra caught her breath.

"We cannot kill you, cursed king . . ." Gaudab growled, low and terrible. "But perhaps now your little queen will think twice about her intentions."

A sob welled up in her throat. *I'm sorry, El. I'm sorry . . .*

Gaudab released him and Elerek crumpled. His hands

slowly clenched, sand squeezing between his fingers. He didn't look at her.

"Now." The Jarkin warlord's voice rose, addressing the entire company. "We've wasted enough daylight. I want the caravan out within the hour." He huffed, fingering the hilt of the curse binder's dagger at his belt as he scowled down at Elerek. "And I want the waterskins filled."

Elerek's body shuddered, his breathing ragged. He glared as Gaudab approached Lystra. She imagined she could feel the sand quaking beneath his boots. Before she could react, he took her shoulder—the one bearing the mark he'd carved—and yanked her to her feet.

The stiff bandages shifted and she yelped. Lystra felt skin pull from skin and hot blood dripped down her back.

"Next time," Gaudab growled as he bound her hands, pulling the rope tight. He leaned close, his breath hot on her neck. The pain made her lightheaded, the world spinning on a tormenting axis. "It will be *you*, river lily, whom I will punish."

Lystra rode in Tiniah's saddle, but not how she'd intended. Her shoulder continued to bleed, the blossom of red on her pale blue tunic hovering on her vision's horizon. They'd stretched a filthy gag between her teeth, cutting against her chapped lips. Between the heat and her inability to breathe, facing another day in the Sancen was almost too much to bear.

Gaudab had ordered haste, but the sands yielded protest. The cardants, sluggish from the cold of the night, blinked their orb-like eyes and kept their heads down. Tiniah growled as the cruel Jarkin mounted her, filling Lystra's gaze with the ridge of his shoulders.

She craned her neck, prompting another spasm of pain from her shoulder. Elerek faced backwards on the cardant behind them. His head was bowed, sweat glistening on his neck. He braced himself against every jolt and jostle, his legs and hands bound.

Did he blame her? Did he think her selfish for wanting to run away? Did he believe that she was abandoning him?

Not that it mattered now. Her chance to escape had slipped away. Every step took her farther from her Instanolde.

They traveled the gully for hours, chasing the shade cast by the sheer walls. By noonday, when the sun stood at its apex, the land sloped into a wide valley. Lystra marveled at the sight of the glittering, windswept dunes that boasted a height to rival the palace itself. They kept to the fringes, the cardants unable to manage the dunes with bulky riders and gear. Lystra could feel the lag in Tiniah's gait, and sorrow pierced her heart. Her fierce mount subdued by the wilds, by the Jarkins' cruel conditions.

Here, in the lower lands, completely exposed, the heat intensified. The air didn't move, settling thick and heavy, and Lystra prayed for even the smallest breath. The riders rode with their faces down, trudging forward. Flies and gnats thrived in swarms about their heads. Scorpions and lizards scurried across the sand, reminding them that not all was dead out on the Sancen.

"Waterskins!" Gaudab called, summoning the caravan to a grinding halt.

Lystra blinked against the blinding paleness of the sand. When Gaudab dismounted, she swayed as Tiniah adjusted her footing. Her muscles ached, stiffening to stone.

The cardants circled round and the men dismounted, reaching for their waterskins and forming a line behind Elerek.

Gaudab pulled the gag from her mouth, letting her breathe a bit easier, and pushed a waterskin into her untied hands. Nausea rolled in her stomach as the cool, cursed water ran down her throat. She despised drinking it, but she knew the rules of survival as well as anyone. Glancing over her shoulder, she watched as Elerek filled the waterskins. His cheeks were flushed and blood stained his tunic, badges earned by her recklessness.

Lystra shook her head. She couldn't let them punish him, not for her actions.

"Your Highness." Lystra hadn't heard Razhar approach. "Here." He pushed a small pouch into her hands.

Lystra opened it, finding a stash of hard sugar candies. Only Razhar. She sent him a grateful expression as she slipped one into her mouth, relishing the flavor of honey.

"You don't look well." Razhar stepped closer, concern swirling in his amber-colored eyes. He slipped a hand into his pocket and withdrew a cube-shaped salt lick. "Hang on to this —and keep the sweets."

She whispered a thank you.

Behind them, the sound of wretched gags echoed over the dunes. Lystra turned in time to see the Jarkin who rode with Elerek bow over the side of his cardant and vomit. Sweat shone on his brow, but he'd gone incredibly pale despite the scorching sun.

"Khasar." Tangu drew closer, his cardant wagging its head. "We're traveling too hard. This heat is dangerous."

Lystra would have agreed if she hadn't felt so weary—and dizzy.

Gaudab dismounted, letting Tiniah's reins drop. He approached Tangu. "How's our position?"

Reaching into his basket, Tangu withdrew his maps. "Not good. The sun sickness will take us before we reach the stars."

As they conferred with their parchments, Razhar rounded Tiniah, putting the cardant between him and the Jarkins. He leaned closer. "Your Highness, what you did this morning—"

"A mistake," she whispered.

"Is that what you want? To go back?"

Lystra braced herself, nausea tossing her stomach. Darkness fringed the edge of her vision. "What good can I accomplish out here? If I go back . . . Instanolde has a chance. They need me."

Elerek certainly didn't. She'd only made things worse for him.

"I can help you," Razhar whispered. "If you help me." He pulled a rolled parchment from his robe. The star chart. "I'm not sure Tangu will put up with me much longer. I need the dagger."

She blinked. Elerek *had* given him the star chart. "Why do you need it?" Razhar's proposition put her on edge. Thus far, his schemes hadn't turned out favorably for anyone but himself.

Raised voices traveled over the caravan. The Jarkin who'd vomited had dismounted, holding his head in his hands. Gaudab and Tangu were still locked in an argument, the heat stirring their irritation.

"This can't go on." Razhar unrolled the star chart. "Eventually, they'll snap. And what about El? It'd certainly be easier for him to drown Jarkins if we had the dagger. Wouldn't want it to wash away out here."

"We." Lystra huffed, struggling to keep her eyes open. "Will you stay with him? Until the end?"

"I have to." Razhar grimaced, as if he too felt sick. "I couldn't leave if I wanted to."

She frowned.

"The cost, the consequence . . . I was sent to Instanolde because I would've died otherwise. When my baba cast the curse, I turned ill, turning to sand. But when I arrived in Instanolde, at the palace, I recovered." He huffed, as if loath to give up his secrets. "It's El. I've got to stay close to him. Fortunately, he always made that quite easy, recluse that he is. If I'm separated from him, I'll die. Fade to sand."

Lystra blinked, struggling to understand. "But you . . . in the market . . . in Kushan."

"It takes time. If I vanish for a day or two, I won't notice."

"El doesn't know, right? Just like everything else you haven't told him."

Razhar looked away, his eyes tracing the sea of dunes about them. "We're even, Your Highness, because he doesn't know how deeply you're in love with him."

The waterskin tumbled from Lystra's hands. Around her, the desert spun until she forced her eyes closed. What was happening? Had the sun sickness come for her as well?

"Loving him will get us all killed." But maybe the Jarkins were right, and the elements would take them first. Lystra's breath shuddered in her lungs. "And he shouldn't have broken his vows."

Was it only this morning that she'd urged Elerek to forgive Razhar? Even while she hadn't yet forgiven him for his betrayal? Suddenly it wasn't just the desert that was spinning, but the hurt, the sorrow, and the horridness of their predicament swirling in her aching head.

She pitched forward, and the blinding desert faded to nothingness.

Chapter 13

Elerek

Elerek filled the waterskins as Gaudab and Tangu argued with voices far too loud for this desolate place. His body throbbed, and every jolt of the cardant reminded him of each bruise, cut, and blow dealt by his enemies. A punishment. A consequence.

And he would pay it. Again and again and again. Anything to keep them from hurting Lystra.

"We'll be safer in the canyons," Gaudab was saying, pointing to the afar off mountains and ridges. "Those are closest."

Tangu consulted his map. "Safer from the heat, but not cursed water. We're not moving fast enough. These dunes have put us off course. We're going north when we need to veer east." He huffed. "I won't know for sure until the stars are out."

"Where's that blasted Kushite? Shouldn't he know if the warmaker stars go east or north this time of year?" Gaudab growled. "Didn't I tell you to keep him bound?"

Throwing up his hands, the map waving like a flag of truce, Tangu scoffed. "If he goes far, he's a dead man."

"And so are we without him." Gaudab sneered. "So far, Tangu, you're not proving effective on this campaign."

"You call this a campaign? You won't even kill the cripple!"

Elerek gritted his teeth, their every word piercing his mind like a metal spike driven into his skull. Beside the cardant, his rider, Kesh, uttered a long groan and slumped forward. The heat. The sun sickness.

"Someone! Please!" A desperate cry carried over the dunes. A figure hurried between the cardants, sand kicking up from his boots. Razhar met his eyes, wide and terrified. "El, you've got to help!"

In his arms he carried a limp figure, long black hair draping over his arm. Lystra.

The scorching heat faded away. A creeping numbness spread over Elerek's skin, working inward. He no longer felt the heaviness of his clothes, the itch of sweat, or the dried blood from his wounds clinging to his skin. No heartbeat pounded in his chest, just a cold, dark void. The kind that drove him to do terrible things.

"What did you do?" he growled. Droplets ran down his arms, from his sleeves, and down the side of the saddle.

Razhar's eyes bulged. "Me? El, we're trapped in this heat, stars above, *in this desert!*"

Elerek opened his fists, and a cascade burst from his fingers. The cardant beneath him startled. Tangu swore and rushed to seize the reins, nearly tripping over Kesh's limp form.

"Khasar." Elerek glared at the warlord. "We stop here."

Gaudab took a decisive step toward him. "You do not command this expedition, river rat."

A flick of his wrist, and water swirled around the Jarkin's boots. It immediately sank into the sand, swallowed by the Sancen much the same way Elerek knew his torrent could destroy this man. How his rage wanted to do it—to consumed him.

"We both command kingdoms," he ground out. "But not here. Here we heed the desert." Elerek's hands shook, and as he pulled them back to keep his balance in the saddle, he felt as if he was holding back enough water to bury the Sancen.

His words were enough for Gaudab to give the order and the men wearily slipped from their saddles and began erecting tents and canopies. But not for him, no, if something happened to his wife, Elerek would see that even the desert paid.

They huddled in the shade, mere canvas between them and the sun.

Elerek ordered those with sun sickness to be taken to the first available tent. The flaps were tied back, like sails seeking the slightest breeze, anything to keep its occupants comfortable. Besides Lystra and Kesh, one other had fainted. They lay on blankets in the sand, lined up like the fallen after a battle.

Razhar helped him inside. Using the slope of the dune beneath them to brace himself, Elerek settled beside Lystra. Breath rose in her chest, but her amber skin had lost its depth, its richness. He brushed his fingers over her brow and then, and only then, feeling returned to his skin. How did the curse know when he touched someone that he ought not to?

At first, he felt the clamminess of the sun sickness, then only cold as curse mark spread across her forehead, removing her skin and leaving only water.

She tried to escape.

Gently lifting her head, he slid her scarf out from around her shoulders. Then he prompted water to his hands, soaking the fabric. Out here, his curse had become not death, but salvation. The waters were deathly cold; just like him.

"Razhar, remove their scarves and turbans."

He took the wet scarf and spread it across her forehead, down her cheeks, and across her chest. His fingers moved over her shoulders, down her arm, leaving water soaked into her tunic. Lingering at the bloodstains blooming on her shoulder, he swallowed, jaw clenched tight.

Could she do it? Return to Instanolde? Rally their people? Take advantage of Gaudab's absence and restore their kingdom?

Elerek closed his eyes. If anyone could, it was Lystra. Instanolde knew her as the queen who returned after the king was dead. He supposed then that he knew exactly what his queen thought of him.

"Here." Razhar dumped the garments beside him.

One by one, Elerek soaked them while Razhar spread them across the victims. The constant use of his abilities took its toll, and fatigue settled like a heavy pack across his shoulders. He reached for Lystra's hand, her fingers lacing into his. Her touch filled him with a warmth that burned as bright as the noonday sun, but without the scorch.

Lifting his eyes, he stared at the sun's white glow through the canvas. They tracked the sun much the same way they tracked the stars. Watching its trajectory and waiting for its march toward the horizon.

If Lystra wanted to escape, she didn't have much time left. A desperate chance, one that grew even as the miles wore on, but one he had to give her.

"El, I have a question." Razhar settled beside him, his back to the tent's entrance. "Please don't ruin my face any more than it already is."

"Purple suits you."

Razhar released a mournful sigh. "Alas, my colorful clothes, all abandoned at home."

Home. Images of the grand and gilded palace with its pillared courtyards filled his mind. But that wasn't where his heart dwelt. His soul craved late nights and warm hearths, surrounded by strong coffee and stronger laughter. The presence of people whose skin was marked for death, but life dwelt in their eyes.

He added Lystra to their number, though she'd only joined one such gathering with his cursed tribe. She belonged with them even when she wasn't cursed. She knew what it meant to be surrounded by death and grasping for hope, much the same way that he grasped her hand now.

Razhar pulled the star chart from his robe. "I . . . I've been looking at this, and Tangu's maps. I'm trying to make sense of it."

Razhar? Trying? Elerek raised an eyebrow. "You must fear for your skin."

"I saw the wrathgiver." Razhar rubbed the back of his neck. "It's in the east, like Tangu said. But . . . isn't Darcress also east?"

The mention of the desert fortress returned the cursed numbness to Elerek's spine. He looked past Razhar, beyond the folds of the tent, to the rocky crags on the distant edge of the dunes. Veins of pale stone ran through the mountains, reminding him of the layers of crisp pastry that Bushra would create for celebrations.

"If we have veered north, like Tangu said." Elerek leaned over the star chart. "The naeva girl constellation would be right above us."

Razhar's finger traced to the wrathgiver, his brow bent in concentration. "This would be easier if the stars didn't move so much."

"I tried to teach you," Elerek muttered.

Ignoring him, Razhar huffed and pushed his hair over his shoulder. "But I'm right, aren't I? The wrathgiver is moving toward Darcress?"

If that were true, their journey ought to be shorter, easier. They'd need only cut across the canyons and find the road—the same road that Cormek took to his death. Elerek again felt the void overtake him.

But more than the stars awaited them at Darcress. The whole other half of the Jarkin army remained there, waiting out summer's end on Instan sands.

"We won't know for sure until the stars come out," Elerek said softly.

A shadow fell across the tent's entrance, accompanied by Tangu's sneer. He surveyed the scene. "If they perish"—he gestured to the Jarkins taken by the sun sickness—"their blood is on your head."

Elerek lifted his chin. "And my brother's blood is on yours."

Tangu leaned forward, looming over him much the way those who sought to intimidate had stood over his chair. His eyes fell on the unrolled chart. "What is this?"

"I . . ." Razhar made no attempt to hide his panic. "The wrathgiver is moving toward Darcress. We need to adjust our course."

Snatching the star chart, Tangu scowled at the heavens inked across the parchment. "A road runs through the canyons, doesn't it?" He pointed out the tent, toward the east. "Straight to the fortress. Finally, a fortunate bit of news." Then he looked up, glancing between Razhar and Elerek. "The condor scat doesn't know the stars, does he?"

Elerek said nothing while the rest of Razhar's face turned purple, matching his bruises.

"If you're lying, I've no use for you." Tangu scoffed. "Judging by your battered face, your king doesn't either."

The mapmaker's eyes shifted toward Elerek with the countenance of a hawk watching its prey. Was he waiting for a reaction? For Elerek to rush to Razhar's defense? Didn't they realize that they couldn't use Razhar to threaten him?

"You'll know tonight if I'm lying or not." Razhar pointed to the chart. "If we stay north, we'll be under the naeva girl constellation. Use it to judge our position."

Tangu sniffed. "If you're wrong, I'll slit your throat." He grunted as he rose to his feet, taking the star chart with him. "I hope we end up at the Darcress Kasbah. Then your blood can darken the same sands where your brother bled."

"At least I'll die on Instan sands." Elerek lifted an eyebrow. "As for my brother, I'll avenge him right where he died."

Tapping the rolled chart against his shoulder, Tangu scoffed. "We'll see." Then he stalked away.

"You really ought not to taunt them," Razhar muttered. "And I'll get your chart back. Tangu sleeps heavily—and snores."

Elerek squared his shoulders, as if he were seated upon his throne rather than this nameless dune. The swirl of constellations inked on the chart filled his mind. Though they weren't the real stars, the light he loved so much, they still filled his dark soul with a bit of hope.

"I'm going to drown them all."

Razhar stared at him with an incredulous expression.

Reaching for Lystra's hand, he held her fingers tightly in his. At his touch, she stirred but didn't wake. The warmth spreading from their touch set a spark to ignite his resolve.

"I'm not letting them drive a blade into my heart. My death is my own. The Jarkins will not kill another Karim king."

Bowing his head, Razhar heaved a long sigh. The tail of his emerald turban flapped over his shoulder, a flag that hadn't caught the wind.

"What?"

"I knew it would be like this."

Elerek scowled. "Like what?"

"If you knew that your death would break the curse, you'd rush headlong into it without a moment's hesitation." Sorrow hung like a funeral shroud over his words. "I watched you die once before, El. One doesn't forget a thing like that."

Razhar had found him—in a pool of blood. Elerek's hand moved to his forearm, where, beneath his sleeve, his flesh lay ruined by the scar he'd dealt himself the hour he'd sought to end his days.

"I didn't know the consequences of my death then," he whispered. "Now I know better. The curse will be broken, our family set free, and Lystra will lead Instanolde into the light." He gave a small shrug. "Not too far off from our original plan."

Razhar scowled, gesturing to their surroundings. "Except the Sancen, smelly cardants, and terrible food."

The quip sounded so much like *him*, the Razhar that Elerek had known nearly his whole life. But something else resounded in his words, something Elerek hadn't heard before from him, but a tone he knew as well as his own heartbeat.

Grief. Not just sorrow, the soul-crushing, lung-stabbing grief that seemed to haunt their steps at every turn of the twisting desert canyons. Had Razhar shown him this part of himself before? Had he missed it? Elerek suddenly wondered if he truly was as insensitive as Razhar claimed him to be.

But Razhar still had his secrets; he hadn't shared everything.

"Is she going to be all right?" All mirth faded from Razhar's face as his eyes lowered, watching Lystra's still form.

"She will be," Elerek whispered.

She had to be. A journey awaited her. One that would take her away from the harrows of the Sancen to survive an Instan king—a second time.

Chapter 14

Lystra

When Lystra's eyelids cracked open, sand caught in her lashes, she watched as a body was hoisted between two Jarkins and carried away.

Heat still smothered the desert, but she no longer felt dizzy or nauseous. She lay inside a tent, a blanket between her and the soft sands, and she felt—cool. Her scarf caressed her cheek, its touch damp and refreshing.

She pushed herself up. Beyond the tent's open flaps, the Jarkins stood in a long line, their heads bowed as the body was taken beyond the next row of dunes.

The Sancen had made its claim from among their numbers.

A chill shot through her heart, followed by an ominous weight of dread. She looked down at her hands, her skin again replaced by water—and her fingers were interlaced with Elerek's.

He sat beside her, solemn and still. His brow lay shadowed as he too watched the funeral procession with an intensity to rival the sun itself. The bruises and cuts upon his face no longer appeared as the marks of a victim, but prizes won in a hard fight.

His eyes found hers.

Lystra looked away, pulling her hand back for good measure.

"Sun sickness," Elerek whispered.

She nodded. "I feel better, thank you."

"I couldn't save Kesh." A long exhale deflated his shoulders. She'd heard this sorrow lining his voice before. When a cursed died, drowned, all on account of having touched the king of Instanolde.

"It's the Sancen. At high summer. None of us should be out here."

Elerek pushed a hand through his hair, catching tiny droplets in his curls. "Yet here we are. Breaking a curse."

If they survived long enough to break it. Lystra surveyed the tent, noting the way the blankets were indented in the sand. Two must have had the sun sickness beside her and the other had recovered while Kesh perished. They were alone in the tent, well within sight of their captors, but more alone than they'd been since . . . before the Jarkin assassin climbed through the library window, before Elerek had kissed Myra, and before the invasion where everything had gone so horribly wrong.

Shifting in the sands, she turned toward him. "I'm sorry they punished you, El. I didn't mean for that to happen."

"You tried to escape." Afternoon light spilled into his eyes, casting them the color of the purest jade. The shimmer of springtime, where the river delta was bathed in life and greenery.

Lystra's breath caught. Was he angry? But surely he would want her to escape, wouldn't he? Their relationship stood solidified in their duty as king and queen and their honor demanded that they stand by their people.

"I thought I could do it," she whispered.

"I didn't say that it was wrong." Elerek leaned toward her, closer than he'd ever dared before. Hesitant fingers brushed her hair, pushing it back from her temple and caressing down her cheek. His touch didn't feel cold or numb as it had when she'd chosen to take the curse. No, instead it felt like coals stoked in the heart of the sun itself.

"This time, Lystra," he breathed, his lips hovering just above hers, "don't get caught."

The Sancen and its terrors faded, taking with it the heat and the Jarkins and the death hanging over them all. Lystra found herself trapped, the walls of her own resolve closing her in. Her hurt, her anger, her quest to fight for her people, and the highest wall of all, her determination not to fall in love.

How she wished that, just this once, she could be wrong.

"Go back to Instanolde," he whispered, the fierceness in his voice rivaling the stars. "Ride hard. Save our kingdom. Reign like the queen you are."

His heartbeat pounded in her ears.

Ride hard.

"The first chance I get"—his breath turned ragged—"I'm going to drown them all, and you cannot be here when I do it."

Lystra drew back, retreating behind the lines that she had drawn and watched the war waging in Elerek's eyes. She saw the king of Instanolde desiring so desperately to save his people, the task that had always lain just beyond his reach, and she saw the cursed man living out his last moments with all the radiance of a dying star.

But dying stars were also destructive, swallowing everything that their light could reach.

"And, after?" she whispered, almost afraid to know.

Elerek's jaw tightened. "Once Cormek is avenged, I'll go on alone. Break the curse." His gaze dropped to her hands, where the silver thread of the curse unraveled her skin. He reached for her fingers again. "I'll break it for you, for all of them."

Lystra stared down at his hands, his fingers, as they caressed her wrists, her palms. "I didn't take the curse so you could save me, El."

"I know you didn't."

The air bristled with a chill unbecoming of the desert. Lystra wrapped her arms around herself, the distance becoming a canyon. She glanced outside the tent, the Jarkins moving down to the lower dunes to see to their dead. Battlements rose about her soul again, and she wondered if he indeed knew. She took it because she loved him.

"Lystra." He spoke her name with a resolve stronger than death, stronger than the curse itself. Stretching out his hand, he touched her cheek, gently turning her face toward him again. "I . . ." Words seemed to fail him. "I wish there was another way."

Lystra didn't blink, didn't move. Her heart thundered in her chest, raging like a sea swiftly rising. Depths that could swallow the stars themselves. "We don't always get what we want."

Elerek cupped her chin, the numbness fleeing his touch, and he kissed her. Deeply. Longingly.

A warmth that the curse could not touch ignited, burning away the distance and consuming the canyon between them. Lystra pushed her hand against his shoulder, seeking shelter from the heat as one would a roaring fire, but he held her tighter, as if he wouldn't let go.

A gasp shuddered on her lips as they separated. The moment over almost as soon as it had begun, a fleeting, stolen moment that should never have existed.

Yet it did.

Lystra bowed her head, tears blurring her vision. This wasn't the beginning of new love blossoming like the summer evells as her relationship with Cormek had. She hadn't the words to shape what had become of their political alliance, tainted by their sorrow, their desperation, and even their anger.

No, this was an ending. This was goodbye.

She wiped away her tears, the droplets blending with the water that had replaced her skin. Then she looked up into his eyes. Perfect and tragic, filled with strength. "Starkindler keep you, Elerek." She turned away, taking her scarf as she slowly rose to her feet. "I won't forget you, El. For as long as I live."

"You will live," Elerek whispered. "Gem of the Gungole. Fire of the Sancen. Fierce as the dawn."

Lystra took one step, her foot sliding in the dune's slope, and then another. Into the sunlight. Away from him. "Mighty as the constellations."

The tears ran down her face unchecked. A waste of water here in the desert. Around her, the Jarkins dismantled their makeshift shelters and prepared to continue their journey. Lystra marched forward, seeking out her cardant.

Tiniah waited in the cracked clay at the base of the dune. Lystra leaned against her snout, the reptile nestling against her chest. The cardant's scales were warm, but not hot, and comforting in their own way. Large, orb-like eyes blinked at her.

"With the dawn," Lystra whispered. "You'll take me home."

She wondered if Instanolde would still feel like home.

"There you are." The rumbling voice of Gaudab thundered

over the sand. He swept past her, checking the straps on Tiniah's harness.

Lystra climbed into the saddle without a word. She glanced over her shoulder, ignoring the pain of her messy wound and the stiff pull of dried blood against her tunic, checking for her pack, still tied to the rest of the gear. She reached for a waterskin, hoping that perhaps he might leave her unbound if she needed to drink to not fall prey to the sun sickness again.

On the cardant beside Tiniah, a new rider had replaced Kesh, and Elerek had already been tied facing backwards, his legs tightly bound. Their eyes found each other, but Lystra swiftly looked away.

Gaudab stepped around Tiniah's head, standing between the two cardants. "Tangu tells me that we're to go east, towards your occupied fortress."

"Even if the route is wrong," Elerek said flatly. "We'll be out of these dunes and within the canyon's safety. I trust you don't want to lose any more men."

"No, but your Kushite dies tonight if you're wrong. More rations to go around."

Razhar. The dagger. Lystra looked up, her gaze roving over the warlord's figure. He'd removed his battle-axes, cloak, and traveling robe. His scimitar and array of knives were still strapped to his belt—but not her grandmother's dagger.

Her heart dropped. Had Razhar already snagged it somehow? Why would he ask such a quest of her? Could he truly deliver on his promise to help her escape?

He'd swept her into his schemes before and she'd tumbled headlong into the intrigues of her grandmother's quest for revenge, the plight of a Kushite archer, and this harrowing journey to slay her husband.

But she needed help—and was indeed running out of time if she were to attempt escape a second time. But where would

Gaudab have stowed it? He wouldn't have entrusted it to any of his men.

That left Tiniah's saddlebags.

"We'll see," Elerek replied, his tone cold and indifferent. He looked as if he were carved from stone, as mighty as the mountains looming in the east.

Lystra slid the waterskin into one of Gaudab's bags and began checking each pack—and found nothing.

The last bag held crumpled up clothing. She plunged her hand inside, digging beneath—and lost all feeling in her hand. A chill shot up her arm, straight to her heart, numbing her soul. It came with a detachment, sealing her in a void, almost as if she no longer were physically present here in the desert.

The curse.

Lystra caught her breath. She'd felt this before—the moment she'd touched Elerek. His daily struggle, it tormented his mind and left his body numb and inhuman. It signified the depths of the battles Elerek fought, but also stood testament to his strength.

What had he felt when he'd kissed her? Did he feel the heat and desire as she had? Had she helped him remember his humanity even as he set his course to commit this monstrous act of destruction?

Lystra sighed. Maybe he'd felt nothing at all. Hadn't Myra continually reminded her that she couldn't help her king? That she could offer him nothing? But maybe Myra had been right, and Lystra had underestimated Elerek's struggles. Maybe he also needed starlight.

Enough. None of this mattered. Not even that kiss—that glorious kiss. Lystra plunged her hand deeper. Her confidence rose like a golden loaf of bread. If the curse had chosen to intensify, that meant the dagger was near.

"What are you doing?" Gaudab growled. He seized hold of the saddle, ready to swing himself up.

Lystra blinked. "Um, I lost my waterskin. I'd rather not faint again."

It didn't take long for him to notice the long neck of the vessel draping out of the pack—exactly where Lystra had left it. He handed it to her and climbed into the saddle, her hands unbound in accordance with her plan. Tiniah shuffled, adjusting to the added weight upon her back. The feel of the cardant's muscles beneath her spoke of an anticipation, a strength great enough to combat the dangers of the desert—to survive.

As the caravan set out through the glittering sands, Lystra found her gaze wandering once more toward Elerek. His shoulders, broad and gleaming with sweat, were bent and his head hung wearily.

Here, in the Sancen, surrounded by death, survival was a cheap trick, a gaudy jewel too large and too polished to be real. Because even if she survived and outran death a second time while leaving another Karim king to face his death, not even the fastest cardant could outrun grief.

Chapter 15

Razhar

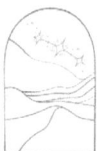

Razhar released the tight grip he'd kept on the cardant's—impossible creatures—saddle to rub his temple as he nursed a headache. The sunlight had stolen his vigor and the heat his appetite. Each swallow of cursed water nearly gagged him. He wanted sleep.

That is, if the Jarkins didn't cut his throat when they made camp. His information regarding the stars was correct, of course. Elerek wouldn't have wasted such an opportunity to be right and prove him wrong. But their captors' mood had soured since the sun sickness took one of their own and Razhar wasn't too trusting of their word.

"I'm going to drown them all."

Razhar shuddered at the memory of Elerek's voice. Cold, calculated, and callous. A king's declaration of battle, but he would assemble no soldiers or captains. No archers would be summoned away from their homes with scrolls tied with Karim orange ribbons.

The cursed king of Instanolde himself was justice, vengeance, and destruction.

A deep sigh deflated Razhar's lungs. He longed for simplicity, the life they'd lived in the palace. He missed the man that Elerek had been and feared the one he was becoming.

The man who would die—by his own hand.

When the dunes faded and the land sloped upward, they ventured into the mountain's roots again. Canyons broke passages through the rock, places carved and hollowed out. Gaudab called a halt to take refuge within the blessed shadows.

Razhar slid off the cardant and nearly lost his footing. Nobody had bothered to tell him how uncomfortably sore cardant riding was, and he grimaced. His gaze wandered down the canyon where the sands of the weary valley had turned pale blue in the fading light. He'd never been so far from home.

"My son, I need you to be brave."

"Are we going somewhere, Baba?"

"Yes, we are. Both of us. Just not together."

None of it had made any sense back then. He'd been a terrified child. But since the day he'd left the canyonlands of Kushan and journeyed to the golden city of Instanolde, his home was standing at Elerek's side.

Razhar glanced over his shoulder. Tangu showed no interest in him, taking long gulps from his waterskin.

"I can get that filled for you."

The mapmaker scowled, shoving the waterskin into his hands. "Be prompt, condor scat. As soon as the stars appear, we'll see if we slit your throat or not." He cackled. "I'm sure a swift death is preferable to a slow one if you choose to run. Think you'd survive out here?"

He made a fair point. Things were bleak enough with their food offerings and he'd given away the last of his candy to Lystra.

Gathering the rest of their waterskins, he trekked through camp. Passing the fire, the Jarkins took no notice of him. Their shoulders were hunched and their faces flushed from the heat. Mere men, broken by a grueling day in the desert.

Only a few Jarkins remained waiting for water. When Razhar reached the front of the line, he found Elerek still tied to the back of the cardant, his hands shaky, and barely able to keep his eyes open.

Razhar dropped the waterskins and set to work prying the knots free. Elerek all but fell off the cardant, Razhar catching him and lowering him to the sand.

"My legs . . ." Elerek whispered.

"They haven't been working for some time, El."

That earned him a glare. Razhar grabbed a blanket from the cardant's packs and tossed it at Elerek, who slipped it between his shoulders and the rocks. He took the king's silence as a thank you, familiar ground found in the wilderness.

Just not together. Razhar shut his eyes. It was happening again. A loss that would define his existence. Something he didn't know how to get over. Losing Elerek would hurt just as much as losing his baba had.

His baba had died to satisfy a wrong. Razhar had lived to serve a punishment. Fahwal's last command, a dying soldier's charge to his son, had been to find the king of Instanolde.

Well, he had.

An Instan soldier had smuggled him out of Kushan. Taken him by river vessel to Instanolde, that golden city steeped in legend and myth. That soldier transferred to the ranks of the palace guards and talked a kitchen girl into giving Razhar a bed in the servants' quarters and, just like that, a Kushite orphan had a home in the palace of Instanolde. Legendary indeed.

Almost as legendary as his baba's mad theory.

"You're a counter curse, Razhar. I'm sure of it."

"Um, when . . .?" Razhar cleared his throat. "Will you attempt your grand scheme?"

Elerek tilted his head back, dark shadows beneath his eyes. "As soon as Lystra gets away."

Perfect, it seemed that Elerek's plan would coincide with Razhar's. Picking up the fallen waterskins, Razhar placed them in a neat line at the king's side. "Could you?"

With weak, fatigued motions, Elerek summoned water. When he finished filling the skins, he slumped back against the rock, eyelids drooping.

Razhar seized his shoulder in an expression of camaraderie. "Try to stay awake, things might get tense."

He crept away before Elerek could respond.

The Jarkins made no attempt to organize their camp, their cardants and tents intermingled. Some were already forsaking the fire and ambling away to sleep. The desert had won, again.

Razhar found Lystra seated with her back against her cardant's great girth, her hands bound in front of her. Her long black hair fell over her eyes, obscuring her face. She'd discarded her scarf, revealing dark blood against her blue tunic.

Stars. "Your shoulder . . ."

"It reopened," Lystra whispered. "I can't do much to treat it."

He knelt and untied her hands. She turned away, procuring a small bottle of ointment. As she removed the cap, Razhar noted the sharp scent of myrrh. "Did you succeed?"

Lowering the bottle, Lystra reached into her pack again— and withdrew the dagger. The curse mark shimmered, each pale bone of her slender fingers visible beneath a sheen of transparent, wet skin.

"I need to know what you're going to do with this." She lifted her eyes, the dying light exposing her face.

The curse mark streaked across her cheek like the stroke of a painter's brush. It spread across her mouth, her lips, and down her chin, revealing the white bone of skull beneath.

Razhar lifted his hand, reaching toward the dagger's hilt.

Lystra pulled it back. "Answer the question."

Unable to meet the burning starfire in her gaze, Razhar stared down at the sand beneath them. His future—if he didn't take matters into his own hands. "You know what El's planning?"

"Yes." She nodded slowly. "And I'm to believe you'll just hand this over?"

His stomach turned, either from this predicament or lack of any sort of real food. "When the time is right." A long sigh escaped his lips. "When El tried to die before, he was alone. There was nobody to stop him. This time, I don't want him to be alone."

To make sure that the king of Instanolde died, that the job was finished. The exact opposite of Razhar's lifelong pursuit of ensuring that Elerek and his loved ones lived.

Always opposite Elerek, but never equal.

Lystra wilted, a desert flower succumbed to the heat. She placed the dagger in the sands between them and sniffled softly.

Razhar went still. How strange it was to kneel here before the fierce queen as she shed tears like any ordinary girl. Oh, but he knew that she—the infamous Lystra of House Arghan who survived the desert, and wedded a cursed king—was anything but ordinary.

Besides, he'd seen her shed tears before. Razhar thought

back to the morning they'd taken the river vessel to Kushan, hoping against hope that his people would answer their call and stand against the Jarkins. Lystra had shed tears because of Elerek . . . and Myra.

"Did you . . ." He trod carefully, wondering if this act of balance was similar to the way acrobats walked across ropes. Without finesse or flourish, he tiptoed between king and queen, trying not to make them angry. "Speak with El?"

Lystra wiped her eyes, but it did no good, her fingers nearly made of water themselves. "Yes, I said goodbye."

Reaching for her hand, Razhar's touch banished the water and restored her rich, amber skin. Eyeing her face and the tell-tale trace along her cheek, realization caused his lips to curl into a smirk. "Hold still now." He brushed a finger across her lip and jaw. "So, he knows, yes? On account of the kissing?"

The look the queen gave him could stop a starved lion in its path.

Unafraid, Razhar grinned. The quip made him feel giddy, a bit more like his mischievous self. He had to tease Elerek tomorrow—without getting another bruise on his face.

Stars. He missed "himself" nearly as much as he missed Elerek.

Lystra reached for her bag, withdrawing a familiar pouch bearing the sweet fragrance of honey and caramel. She returned it to him, like an offering of peace. "You said that if I got you the dagger, you'd help me escape."

Razhar took the bag. The candies had molded together with the heat, but he broke off a piece and popped it in his mouth. "I wasn't lying, Your Highness."

She frowned. "Forgive me for not believing you, after such an abundance of lies."

She sounded too much like Elerek. Razhar folded his arms. "I'm going to cause a distraction, one where you can escape, and El will have the opportunity to drown them." He forced a smile. "Please, I hope you can believe that I *can* be distracting."

He chose that moment to take the dagger, concealing it within the folds of his robe. That way, Lystra wouldn't have the chance to stab him.

"If you can, stay close to your cardant." He lowered his voice. "I hope you make it."

Lystra wrapped her arms around herself. "Me too. I . . . I miss home."

For a moment, Razhar tasted only the candy and thought only of the golden city—and what it would be like to go back. He reached for his turban, unraveling it. The sun had begun to leach the verdant hues from its cloth, destroying its vibrancy. If he returned to Instanolde, his entire world would be leached of its color. His closest friends were the cursed, the outcasts, the untouchable. Were any of them still alive? Separated from him and his abilities?

And Elerek would be dead.

He thought of the mountains. Strong and solid, like the life he might have lived and the man he might have become. Instead, the curse blew into his world, carrying off bits of him to form useless piles of sand. But the true element that shaped the desert was water. In flashes of flood and rainy seasons, canyons were carved and valleys formed. The curse had shaped both their lives.

He hoped that, in the end, Elerek would forgive him. He broke off another piece of candy, by far the best thing he'd eaten in days. "Have you forgiven him?"

Lystra watched the horizon, that great expanse beyond the canyon's mouth, her gaze filled with the whole of the sky. "I ought to, especially now."

Razhar couldn't look away. Her matted hair and bloody clothes didn't matter. She still looked like a queen. "Back . . .

before, it seemed that I'd have to tell El daily that he wasn't defined by his curse. Well, I'm not sure any of us should be defined by our mistakes either."

"He could have told me. Myra did—blatantly, boldly."

Another sorrow twisted Razhar's heart as he remembered that Myra was dead. "El wasn't with her that night."

Lystra looked at him.

"After the prison—when he drowned the assassin—the curse changed. For both of us." Razhar sighed. "I was frightened, and he was a mess, completely unreasonable. I did what I've done before. I've a draught made in my homeland, works quite well when trying to keep a secret like reversing a curse."

"You *drugged* him? I ought to have you thrown in prison."

Razhar wasn't proud of the fact and admitting it to Elerek's queen wasn't clearing his conscience. "He didn't want you to be disturbed, ashamed of the violence he'd done and afraid of what you would think, so we took him to his old rooms. Myra kept an eye on him, but that was all."

"Afraid?" Lystra's face twisted with sorrow. "Stars, we've both been foolish, so far from what we ought to be."

Razhar shrugged, supposing that he sympathized. He tucked the candies back into Lystra's bag. "Well, at the end, we are what we are and striving to be all we can be."

If only it all wasn't so, so hard.

"I wish you a swift journey, Lystra, and that you save Instanolde." He sighed. "I'll have to bind your hands again."

She reached for his arm, her fingers now clothed in sun-kissed skin. "I *will* save Instanolde—and Kushan too if I can. But if you go with him, keep him alive, Razhar. Hold back the curse for as long as you can. Swear it." Then she offered up her wrists for him to bind.

Razhar's insides churned, knotting the ropes to only be tight, not cruel. She had no idea. The impossible task of keeping a cursed king alive. Yet this was the task he'd begun the moment he'd entered the palace and, a child himself, met a little boy who couldn't walk. The task he intended to fail, his own hands gripping the dagger's hilt as the blade sank into Elerek's heart.

Chapter 16

Razhar

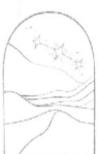

R azhar dropped the star-cast dagger into Tangu's basket of parchments. Then he turned on his heels and put as much distance as he could between himself and the mapmaker's tent.

Only the slightest tinges of nerves danced in his stomach.

He approached the fire and sat down. A few of the Jarkins remained, chewing hardtack and staring vacantly into the meager flames.

Tangu sat among them, sketching his map. Elerek's star chart lay in the sand, the deep ink gleaming in the dying light.

He acknowledged Razhar with a sneer and then glanced at the sky, still a few minutes away from first starlight. "Not long now, condor scat."

Gaudab entered the circle, his enormity eclipsing the sky. With him came Elerek, his legs dragging in the sand. Razhar winced as Elerek was dropped beside the stake, once again hammered into the ground. Dirt and shadows darkened the king's face, and he appeared far too fatigued to be drowning anyone.

But he would. He *had* to. Razhar met his gaze, hoping to convey this vital requirement to the plan.

Elerek only scowled back at him.

"Where's the girl?" Tangu asked, not looking up from his map. The *scritch scratch* of his charcoal held a rhythm of its own, beating in tandem with the crackling flames.

Gaudab grabbed the ropes binding Elerek's hands and yanked them against the stake. Elerek grunted, a grimace twisting his face.

"Left her tied up with that reptile she seems to love so much."

"You think that's wise?" Tangu asked. "After her escape attempt?"

Rising to his full height, as towering as the mountains themselves, Gaudab gave a cruel smile. "I'll fetch her when I've need of her."

Elerek's eyes shot wide, his face white with rage as his intensity turned upon Razhar.

He kept still, his features passive. The plan *would* work. How he wished that his friends could trust him—though he did suppose that he'd earned their skepticism.

Was he wrong to prolong their lives? He claimed that he'd done it for Elerek, but he also had done it for himself—just like this plan birthed of insanity.

But he'd promised that Lystra would escape. Safely. No Jarkin would touch her.

Huffing, Tangu rolled up his map and snatched the star chart. He rose to his feet, dusting the sand from his robe, the curse mark on his hand writhing like snake coils. "Get up. The stars are coming out."

Razhar lifted his gaze. Spinning and dancing in their orbits, the constellations' glow broke through the darkness. Tonight, their light seemed almost harsh, certainly too pure for the likes of him. His soul ached with a lonely, lost feeling he hadn't felt since he was a child. The knowing that most every child in the kingdom could read the stars as one would read a scroll, while his soul felt as if it would burst with the unknowing.

Maybe he ought to have let Elerek teach him.

"Just a bit farther up, those boulders will give us a better view." Tangu pointed to the rocks, now highlighted in silver starlight.

Razhar nodded, unfolding his lanky figure. "We need to bring the dagger."

Tangu narrowed his eyes. Elerek scowled. Gaudab glared.

Shrugging, Razhar huffed and tossed the green silk of his unraveled turban over his shoulder. "The wrathgiver constellation is on the blade. We need to see what position it's in. That'll tell us how long we have. The stars must match up to break the curse."

A long, low growl rumbled in Gaudab's chest. "You might have mentioned that sooner."

"Useless condor scat!" Tangu cursed. "You *have* been playing us!"

Razhar sighed and rolled his neck back on his shoulders. "Get the dagger and see for yourself. Either way, we're chasing the stars, and you'll see that I'm right. We go east, towards Darcress." He sighed. "Right back where it all began."

Gaudab folded his arms, contemplative.

With another curse, Tangu turned an exasperated expression upon his captain. "Enough of this, Khasar. Let me kill him." He withdrew a knife from his belt. The sharp, jagged kind, the likes of which Razhar didn't wish stabbing through his heart.

Of course, crumbling to dust was no better future. If such a thing were to happen right here, right now, he'd become a memory long forgotten. Another mystery haunting the desert. But he'd rather not. No, he insisted. He would not fade to dust.

He would live.

"Wait a moment." Gaudab turned away from the fire, stalking through the darkness. "It takes no effort to prove his words—or his lies."

Razhar released a long breath and waited. He ignored Tangu's muttering and Elerek's scowl, the air electric, like the moment just before a storm broke. It seemed nobody in this camp possessed an ounce of patience.

Gaudab returned, the pounding of his boots as a tempest. Fury flashed in his eyes and a snarl curled over his lips. He grabbed Razhar by his robe's collar, nearly dragging him off his feet.

"Where is it?"

Razhar's eyes widened. "Where's what—the dagger?"

Gaudab dropped him and he hit the sand hard. Wincing, Razhar wondered if this was how Elerek felt *all* the time being hauled about like a sack of rice.

"It's missing!" the warlord hissed, his eyes circling the fire.

Missing. Missing. Missing. Gaudab's voice shattered over the canyon walls. The remaining Jarkins rose to their feet, postures bristling as they shook off their fatigue. Razhar felt sand squeezing between the pores on his fingertips, an anxious reaction. Another deep breath and he reminded himself that everything was going according to plan.

Tangu swore another string of oaths. "Search them! Don't forget the girl."

Razhar let their hands rove through his clothing, finding nothing but piles of sand in his pockets. "Why would she want to kill her husband?"

Shooting him a glare, Tangu stalked towards the place

where Lystra and Tiniah huddled in the shadows, far from the fire's glow.

Gaudab finished his inspection of Elerek and motioned to his men. "Search the camp. From top to bottom. Leave no stone unturned. If we don't find that dagger—*we're dead.*"

They set to work, activity stirring the camp with the frenzy of a sandstorm. Razhar didn't move, wringing his sand-covered hands. Across the coals, the king watched him warily.

I know what I'm doing. Razhar swallowed.

"Datem!" Amak shouted. "I found it!"

Impressive, they'd completed that task in record time. Razhar began to sweat.

"Where?" Gaudab demanded.

Amak returned to the circle, bearing the beautiful dagger with its ornate hilt and sheath that bound the curse—and belonged to the woman who had deceived Razhar's baba into a crime worthy of death. He startled, dropping the weapon as he noticed the spread of his curse mark enveloping his elbows and climbing up to his shoulders.

"*Where?*" Gaudab growled, snatching it up.

Paling, Amak looked at his superior with wide eyes. "The basket . . . of maps. Datem Tangu's maps."

A silence as deep as the desert itself fell over the camp. Razhar inhaled, his lungs expanding. Now, it began.

Gaudab did not rage. No, he became still, as if he were some fixture of rock, a monument of the rugged canyon that had stood for eons. He watched the darkness with a calculated stare, waiting until the return of Tangu's footsteps broke the silence.

"Datem." Tangu's face was carved with a harsh frown. "The girl's curse mark is gone."

Still, Gaudab did not speak. He only watched. A predator of the mountains.

"It makes no sense. She's drinking the cursed waters, same as us. She ought to have marks like ours." Tangu's eyes turned to Razhar. "Unless our theories are correct—about him."

Theories? *Stars. Stars. Stars.* Razhar felt ill, like he ought to vomit and flee for the mountains, the anxiety plastering his face becoming authentic. The Jarkins couldn't know, could they? At least, not everything.

"The sand . . ." Amak spoke quietly, still staring down at the curse ravaging his body. "His sands are the . . . opposite. C-can he heal me?"

Oi. This was getting out of hand. Razhar's hand moved to his chest, to the silk of his scarf that covered his tattoo. The only stars he truly knew. The Jarkins were supposed to be pointing fingers at each other, not staring at him.

Worst of all were Elerek's eyes. Cold and severe, the eyes of a king. Razhar held no fear of the king of Instanolde, but he did fear the criticisms of a friend, of the brother who had remained by his side for most of his life. Why did he fear? Shouldn't he have been able to tell Elerek anything? Even the darkest parts of his broken soul?

"It's no coincidence that we all bear the mark of this curse while the queen has none," Tangu declared, folding his arms.

Gaudab stepped closer, the last of the embers casting his skin a deep, terrible red. He tapped the dagger's sheath against his palm, watching Razhar.

Razhar drew a shuddered breath. Again, grains of sand emerged from his skin, coating his hands and arms. Perhaps the curse within him knew that he stood before the article of the binding—and the undoing.

If he did nothing—would he die? If the curse was broken, would he break with it? If Elerek was dead, would he also perish?

Except the Jarkins would kill him far, far sooner. "The stars are out," he stuttered, pointing to the shimmering expanse above them.

"So they are," Tangu said. "High time to slit your throat. Come along." He glanced at Gaudab. "Good, you've located the dagger."

Tension rippled through the company. The Jarkins all bowed their heads, standing as they had earlier during their funeral rites. Gaudab said nothing, only watching Tangu with bloodlust in his eyes.

They didn't venture far, but the darkness made the distance seem so much greater. Tangu lit a candle, creating a small halo of light to guide their footsteps. Its glow reminded Razhar of sneaking through the palace, following Myra's footsteps as he made his rounds holding back the curse and keeping his friends alive.

Tonight, his mission remained the same, only he'd counted himself also in need of saving.

Gaudab hadn't spoken a word, walking behind Razhar and Tangu, still clutching the dagger. Maybe Elerek wouldn't be the first one to feel the star-etched blade stab his heart.

Cresting a rise of boulders, Razhar scrambling to keep up with the taller Jarkins, their view of the sky opened. The desert lay deep and dark, but the skies teemed with light. Razhar tilted his head back, letting the heavens illuminate him. He lifted a finger, tracing the constellations as they spun and danced.

Naeva girl, north. Wrathgiver, east.

Darcress, east.

His finger moved toward the horizon's jagged line of mountains. The wrathgiver's lonely assassin stalked its mark, his steps almost touching the mountains. Had Elerek become the victim the wrathgiver sought? The thought made Razhar's heart slip down to the soles of his feet.

Beside him, Tangu cursed. "Loss of time and loss of life. This ludicrous expedition has a destination now." He huffed. "Back to the reeking kasbah."

Gaudab unsheathed the dagger, the pale, silver light highlighting the stars upon the blade. He raised it, lining it up with the wrathgiver. Razhar resisted the urge to smile, rather impressed by how nicely blade and stars matched—especially since he made up that bit.

"This ought to have been predicted," the warlord growled.

"Indeed." Tangu looked at Razhar. "But now that we have this information—we do *not* need you." He withdrew a knife from his belt.

Razhar's hands shook, a dusting of sand catching in the starlight. Was this the moment he revealed his abilities? That he could prolong their lives? Grant them more hours to threaten all that he held dear? The secret clogged his throat, making his head swim.

"Tangu, why was the dagger among your maps?" Gaudab's low rumble echoed over the canyon.

Razhar swallowed his secret, relief expelled from his lungs.

As for Tangu, he stared at his captain with bulging eyes. "Khasar . . . how dare you accuse me!"

"It was found in your basket." Gaudab stood chest to chest with the mapmaker, but still towering head and shoulders over him. "You've opposed this expedition from the beginning."

Tangu sputtered.

Gaudab seized his tunic. "I've killed men for less, Tangu. You know this."

A cold sweat beaded between Razhar's shoulder blades. He took a step back, closer to the darkness. Away from the starlight.

"I didn't *touch* the dagger, Khasar! If you think you're going to kill me—"

Releasing the man's tunic, Gaudab grabbed his throat instead. "You dare oppose me?" His massive hand, clothed in the curse mark, squeezed. A moment passed, long and terrible. Then he released, sending Tangu to his knees, coughing.

Razhar slinked deeper into the shadows. With the constellation inked on his chest, he became a wraith that belonged to both darkness and starlight.

"Maybe . . ." Tangu wheezed, coughing. "Someone ought to. You believe the lies of these river rats and doubt your own men?"

Gaudab slid the dagger onto his belt. "Prove your words, then. Challenge me. I'll kill you and leave your bones for the jackals."

"Better than a drowning," Tangu spat. "At first light."

"So be it."

Razhar turned away and ran.

First, he ran to Lystra. The queen huddled against her cardant's belly, her eyes softly closed. The reptile lifted its head, watching Razhar with defensive eyes, protective of her ward.

He touched her shoulder. Lystra woke with a start.

"It's time," he whispered, loosening her bonds. "You must leave. *Now*."

Lystra stared at him, fear encroaching on the starlight in her eyes.

"Can your cardant walk? At all?" Razhar had to confess he hadn't thought of this angle. The reptiles required warmth to move. "You don't need to get far, just enough for the darkness to hide you until morning."

Lystra thrust off the ropes and grabbed the cardant's harness, whispering to the reptile. Watching in awe, Razhar wondered if perhaps the massive creature sensed their urgency. The cardant rose, padding its giant claws softly in the sand. She still wore the saddle, and several packs were tied to her back, hopefully providing the queen with all that she'd need.

"We'll do our best; it's cool enough to keep her from making too much of a racket," Lystra whispered. Her gaze met his. "Thank you."

Razhar nodded as they vanished down the canyon, into the night.

Next, he returned to the center of camp. The fire's embers had burnt out to cold ash. There, starlight illuminated the form of the Karim king, Elerek's body slack as he hung against the stake. His head drooped forward, the gag tied taut between his teeth.

No guard? Razhar rushed to pull the gag free and loose Elerek's bonds. He slipped his arm beneath the king's shoulders, gently lowering him back to the sand.

Elerek woke in a panic, jade-colored eyes flashing. He raised tight fists, ready to fight.

"Shh, it's me." Razhar glanced around. "Is there a guard that's supposed to be watching you?"

Breathing heavy, Elerek closed his eyes. "The curse claimed him," he whispered. "Amak, the one who found the dagger."

Razhar's insides twisted. Had the dagger done it? Spurred the curse to take him so swiftly? Reality struck deeper than any violence the Jarkins could level against him. The curse had been wrought to be an untamed force of destruction, designed to drown souls far quicker than any river.

Now, the monster had awoken, ready to ravage, and it was growing stronger.

Am I enough? Enough to keep them alive until it was time to slay the curse?

He hadn't time for such melancholy thoughts. "We should hurry. Come with me." Without waiting for approval, he reached beneath Elerek's arms and around his chest and lifted. He grunted, wishing that he had the strength of the Jarkins who dragged the king around with ease.

"Why?" Elerek's voice sounded strangled.

"No talk." Razhar hadn't the breath. He managed to get them to Tangu's tent, where he dropped Elerek and lifted the flap. They crawled inside, Elerek using his arms to heave himself into the darkness.

"How much of this is plan and how much is you simply making this up?" Somehow, Elerek's words sounded just as harsh in the darkness with his scowls obscured.

Please, shut up. Razhar wasn't quite brave enough to address the king so, even if the man had been his insensitive friend long before he'd taken the crown.

Any minute now. Razhar drew the tent closed and sat down.

"Is Lystra—?"

"She got away."

Elerek blew a long exhale and made no reply. Razhar let his shoulders drop. Here, the tragic story that had begun in the golden palace of Instanolde ended. A wedding meant for a political alliance closed with a cursed kiss in the wilderness. He felt sorry for them both.

Footsteps pounded outside the tent. Razhar stiffened, bracing himself for what would come next.

"I can hear you breathing, Kushite. You ought to have run away." The sound of a knife being drawn from its sheath shrilled in the darkness.

Canvas thrust back, revealing a sky full of starlight, framing the dark form of Tangu, holding a knife.

"I know you planted the dagger in my possessions," he growled. "Thinking you'd have some fun before your usefulness ran dry? You'll pay for that. Your body will rot out here in the stones."

Razhar swallowed and held out his palm. With a deep inhale, a moment's concentration, and a bit of dramatic inspiration, sand gathered along his fingers and trailed up his wrist. "Sand and stone aren't so unfamiliar with each other."

Tangu narrowed his eyes. "Nor are you from your crippled king. If a curse is to be undone, first you, disgusting wretch, must be destroyed—the *counter curse*."

Must be destroyed. Another piece of destruction in a shattered world. But after watching countless lives end on account of a curse bound by a single woman, Razhar understood. Brokenness continued to break and corruption continued to corrupt. And curses, curses would always curse. How did one become noble in a world torn by curses? Bravery and nobility didn't suit him, like armor that he had no idea how to wear or wield. Perhaps he really was the lying coward Lystra and Elerek thought he was—and liars continued to lie.

"I'm *not* a counter curse." Razhar spoke through clenched teeth.

A sneer tugged at Tangu's lips, his eyes dark and hollow, like the sockets of a skull. "That, condor scat, is what makes you —and your king—weak, and why your kingdom will fall."

Tangu lunged, his dagger raised. Razhar lifted his arms, a pathetic attempt to defend himself, but the Jarkin crashed into him, slamming him down against the earth. Tangu lifted the dagger, aiming to strike, but Razhar caught his wrist, pushing it back with all his might. His fingers slipped, sand covering his hands, and the blade grazed his bicep.

With a sputtered gasp, Razhar attempted to roll, to knock Tangu off him, but he was no warrior and certainly not strong enough to match one of the mountain men.

Tangu drove his knee into his chest and Razhar felt the air leave his lungs. Bloodlust glimmered in the Jarkin's eye as he raised the dagger once more.

Razhar didn't need to be stronger than the Jarkins—he knew of something, *someone*, who was far more powerful.

"El . . . now!" Razhar croaked.

Water shot through the darkness, the stream enveloping Tangu's neck and head. The force of it knocked him off Razhar, pinning him to the earth. Subdued by the torrent, the man could only writhe helplessly.

"Razhar . . . hurry." Elerek spoke through clenched teeth.

Razhar scrambled for the dagger. As he stared at the drowning man, a fierce wrath welled up in his chest. Was this how Elerek felt, hour by hour, as their world crumbled to pieces?

He would not die on account of this curse. All his life, he'd lived while death stalked the shadows. Playing his secrets as he played games of *barjee* with the cursed king of Instanolde who held death in his hands.

Tangu convulsed, fighting for oxygen. But the waters were slowing, growing weaker and less potent. Razhar's sand-coated hand clenched the dagger. *This is my battle too.* Elerek and Lystra fought for their kingdom with each breath in their lungs. Razhar had no goals so lofty. He only knew that the Jarkins deserved justice. They'd destroyed the world he'd stolen for his own, that beautiful bit of life he'd found amid the harsh desert sands. *And my secrets belong to me.*

With one swift motion, he heaved Tangu onto his side—and drove the knife between his shoulder blades. The Jarkin went still. The darkness masked the blood, sand, and water.

Razhar fell back, catching himself on shaky limbs, and dropped the bloody dagger as if it were covered in scorpions. He'd seen plenty of death, of cursed victims drowned from the inside out. This was different. Tangu didn't drown, no he, the Kushite who lived in the palace of Instanolde, the dancer who haunted the markets—the patronizing ray of sunshine, had murdered a man with a knife.

He covered his face with his hands, tears falling between his sandy fingers.

Breathing heavily, Elerek lowered his hands. Outlined in the scant starlight, deep, fatigued lines ran across his noble face. "Was that the plan?"

Razhar swallowed, his stomach churning with bile. "One less Jarkin in your way, Your Highness."

"Razhar, I'm exhausted. Just tell me next time." Elerek shook his head. "Of course, asking *you* to follow your king's orders is far too large a request."

"Well, it didn't go quite as planned, Tangu challenged Gaudab's authority and they were supposed to fight it out in the morning. I figured you could step in." He winced at his own phrasing. "I mean, you know. You were going to take care of them all tomorrow anyways."

Elerek heaved another long sigh. Razhar lifted his eyes, risking a glance at the king, and met a glower worthy of shriveling the most formidable cardant.

Shaking his head, Elerek snatched one of the dry blankets, casting it over his legs. "Get rid of the body."

This time, Razhar supposed he ought to follow orders. Rising on shaky legs, he dragged Tangu's body outside the tent and into the starlit camp. With Amak dead, no guards stood watch. He had to look away, unable to bear the sight of the man's face and his cold, stilled eyes. Never in a million years beneath the dancing constellations had he thought that he would take a life, and it frightened him how quickly it had ended.

How did he expect to wield the dagger against Elerek—his best friend? Would he die as quickly as Tangu had? Heart pierced, each fiber of flesh, fragile and delicate, severed by blade. Would Elerek's soul, one forged by fire and accustomed to fighting, rage as it unanchored from his cursed body?

Razhar only managed to drag Tangu a few paces. He fell to his knees, staring down at his hands, covered in blood and starlight. Two things their world held as precious, sacred. Two things that had been manipulated and twisted into something terrible—exactly like him.

When he opened his eyes, the dead Jarkin remained. As he'd been dragged, something fell out of his robe—the star chart. Razhar slipped it inside his shirt. Then, swallowing, he held out his hand, closed his eyes, and concentrated. It came easily, as if prompted by the stars the same way Elerek's waters increased. Grain by amber grain, the mighty Sancen grew, burying the Jarkin until he was covered in cursed sand. Razhar wished he didn't know what that felt like.

At the end, the mound stood in the center of camp. A dune

of another kind. Then, Razhar turned his back and marched back to the tent.

"No one saw you?" Elerek whispered.

Shaking his head, Razhar settled down, wiping his hands on one of the blankets that had been soaked in the cursed water.

"Are you all right?"

Razhar couldn't look at him. The curse had consumed his entire life—and if he didn't act quickly, it would steal the future too. That meant that Elerek was only another body built of blood and flesh and destined to die.

Meanwhile, Lystra had instructed him to keep her husband alive. Razhar closed his eyes, bracing himself against the storm swirling inside. A storm of chaos, of terror, and of sand.

Chapter 17

Elerek

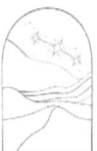

The tent's canvas fell back into place, obscuring the heavens and banishing the starlight. Elerek could only see the faint outline of Razhar as he sat hunched, head hanging. The weight of the deed committed felt as heavy as the darkness.

Don't trust him. No. Not even for a moment. This man, the one he once called closer than a brother, had crippled him worse than the skeetos plague had, wounding him with lies and deceit.

Yet, in *this* moment, Elerek saw a sliver of his own soul, bleeding and raw, in Razhar. He knew the deep spiral of horror, the aftermath of a murder. The desperate need to kill someone and the frantic terror of following the impulse through. And who had stood by him that night, when he'd drowned the Jarkin in the prison cell? Razhar had been there; the friend he needed.

Well, mostly. Elerek had several suspicions about that night, and he wondered how much heartache might have been avoided. He wondered what he'd do with Razhar after tomorrow—after *all* the Jarkins were dead.

"Does Gaudab still have the dagger?"

Razhar sighed. "Sorry, I couldn't figure that one out."

"A problem for tomorrow." Elerek rubbed his wrists, the skin ragged from the rope. "You do realize that I must see this journey through? Once my business here is complete, I go to the wrathgiver."

"I understand."

"You intend to come with me?"

"Yes."

Elerek's shoulders dropped. That would be better, wouldn't it? He didn't have his wheelchair and still hardly knew anything about cardants. Someone had to help him. And . . . this way he wouldn't die alone.

Maybe they could pretend that things were fixed between them, at least for now.

Razhar shifted in the blackness. "Here." He leaned across the tent. "This is yours."

The rough texture of parchment meeting his fingers. Elerek's heart rose in his throat. If only he could return the star chart to Lystra, a gift for her to remember him by, even as she swore she would never forget.

We didn't have long.

Thoughts of her filled his mind. The way she'd looked at him, her countenance crafted of the purest marble. All the regality she'd worn to their coronation, a noble purpose as grand as any crown or polished fire opals. His last words to his brother had been full of wrath. He couldn't end that way with Lystra; his queen deserved better.

And so, he'd kissed her. After all the time they'd spent at arm's length, her nearness had assailed his senses. The warmth ebbing from her sun-kissed skin. The scent of wildness clinging to her hair. Wonder and starfire and perfect, and yet she could not be his. Even now, he felt the emptiness, the expanse between them. A bitter, bitter ache that all the bruises, cuts, and beatings couldn't match.

When she'd pulled back, astonishment washing away her severity the same way his cursed touch evaporated her skin, she again became the girl who'd come to his chamber with the dagger, her every mask shredded like silk. She'd brought her grief, her fear, and had given him hope where none dared burn before. A *queen*, one that had thundered into his world with the fury of an untamed cardant.

He hoped that she knew the truth—that he loved her.

"So . . . how was it?"

Elerek woke from his thoughts. "What?"

"Kissing your queen?"

Shaking his head, Elerek muttered a string of choice words. Razhar was not worthy of such a conversation. "I'm going to sleep. I suggest you shut up."

Before he could lie down, a sodden wet blanket slapped his shoulder, a reminder that Razhar didn't always need words to get his point across. Elerek supposed it was appropriate, considering the dismal destination of their miserable journey. He shoved the blanket aside, reclining on the sheepskins.

The Sancen's silence deepened, broken only by the slightest gust of air channeled through the narrow crevices of the rock. Elerek closed his eyes and exhaled air that wasn't crowded with enemies. Its taste reminded him of the first day he'd ridden a cardant into the desert, Lystra at his side. The day he'd seen the Sancen as beautiful and not deadly.

Lystra.

"We'll never know . . ." he whispered.

"Hmm?" Razhar's voice was muffled.

In the darkness, Elerek almost wished for the curse. That its numbing void would envelop him in nothingness. Then maybe his heart wouldn't hurt so much. "If Lystra returns to Instanolde."

"She will," Razhar replied.

He would never see her again. Her fierce eyes, severe beauty, the set of her proud shoulders, the boldness that could never be taken from her—this loss hit his soul with a different sort of grief than those he'd lost before. Cormek and Myra he had lost to death.

At the end, he hoped to lose Lystra to life.

Starkindler, let that be enough.

Endless skies lit with brilliant lights, purer than anything. The horizon beneath the heavens lay flat, no sign of jagged mountain or sloped dune. It rippled, a sea of glistening waves and no sign of the desert he called home. Only water, sky, and stars.

When Elerek opened his eyes, the light belonged not to the stars, but the blazing sun. Dawn had broken upon the day that he would drown them all.

At least the veiled stars wouldn't watch as he turned the curse upon his enemies. In his tarnished soul, he could already imagine the torrent, white-capped and foaming as it crashed against the canyon walls.

Pushing himself up from the blankets, Elerek blinked. His wrists stung, raw and red, but they weren't bound. His back ached, but it wasn't the agony of being strung up. He didn't feel rested, but what hours of sleep he managed were an unexpected blessing.

Starkindler, please, help us survive. Just a bit longer.

He wondered if the Maker of the stars heard such prayers, wrought with fury and anger. The ooze from the wound grief had dealt these cruel, short days. His dreams gave him some comfort. If starlight could visit him in darkness perhaps there was still hope. Hope that he wasn't completely broken by his cursed days.

Across the tent, Razhar slept with his arm tucked under his head. Beside him, the dark stain of blood marred the dirt, where Razhar had killed a man.

Elerek knew what death looked like, well acquainted with its visage. It held a value of its own thieving sort and the sight of it didn't frighten him. After all, could one truly esteem life without understanding the consequences of death?

But it seemed a profane thing to see Razhar's soul stained with it; at least, the Razhar that Elerek had known. Clothed in his questionable fashions, bursting with laughter and equally questionable jokes, with a smile that one could die of jealousy over. A mischievous troublemaker who was both innocent and guilty.

All a guise. The Razhar that truly existed Elerek hardly knew at all.

Elerek's stomach tightened, distrust a knot he couldn't dislodge. They had a long day's ride ahead of them. Plenty of time to discuss everything Razhar hadn't told him.

The tent flap fluttered in the morning breeze, revealing a patch of pure, blue sky.

"Razhar."

He didn't stir.

Elerek glanced about the tent. An extra pair of leather gauntlets lay in the corner. He hurled one at Razhar.

Starting awake, Razhar grumbled. "Oh, so you *are* still hitting me?"

"It's morning. Gaudab will come to meet Tangu's challenge. We'll have to act quickly." He reached for one of the packs left behind by the mapmaker, finding a bundle of traveling clothes, and withdrew a pale, sand-colored tunic which replaced his bloodstained one. "You need to get us a cardant. There'll be a spare, since Amak is dead. And get to higher ground."

Razhar sat up, pushing his hair from his eyes. "Anything else?" Sleep lulled in his voice.

The second gauntlet hit him. "Whatever supplies and gear you can find." He slid one boot onto his foot and froze.

Shouting erupted outside the tent.

Drawing himself to his feet, Razhar brushed the sand from his clothing. "You're sure about this?" A darkness lingered in his eyes, a darkness that shouldn't have been there.

A bit of the ice melted from Elerek's heart. Even if he couldn't trust Razhar, he found himself glad to not be alone. "It's far too late to turn back now."

Razhar nodded, a shadow like shame spreading across his face. Elerek watched him, the moment still despite the chaos outside. How had they gotten here—where the king of Instanolde and a Kushite orphan on opposite sides of a curse expected to take on the might of the Sancen and the threat of invaders?

"Well, Your Highness." As quickly as the shadow appeared, Razhar banished it from his features. "I'll go consult with an enormous lizard and use my wiles to charm it into carrying us to the end of the Sancen."

"Watch yourself." Elerek took his scarf and wound it about his head.

Razhar's eyes met his once before he stepped toward the canvas flap—and directly into Gaudab Batu Khasar. His cursed hands were clenched in massive fists and the heat and rage turned his face a deep purple. He seized the front of Razhar's shirt, nearly lifting him off his feet. "Worthless cur. Did you think that by killing Tangu, you'd spare your own skin?"

Elerek lifted his hands, vengeful waters waiting. "Leave him. If there is any challenge to authority, *I* will satisfy it." He set his jaw, meeting the invader's gaze. "This desert belongs to *my* kingdom."

Gaudab released Razhar, his cursed fingers rippling. He glared down at Elerek. "You want what's yours, river rat?" He lunged, grabbing Elerek by the shoulders and throwing him outside the tent's entrance.

Flung across the sand, pain shot up his legs. Beside him, Razhar had also been shoved to the sand with a loud groan. Wincing, Elerek pushed himself up—and stared into the dark sockets of a leering skull.

A Jarkin lay panting for air, coughing and sputtering. No skin clung to his body. Only water, bones, muscle, and blood. The curse on full display, the end desire of one touch of his fingertips.

Perhaps the stories were only legends, myths of demons and wraiths and lions suited to campfires and the bedsides of children. But here, in the grit and the sand of the blazing Sancen, the greatest monster of them all—was *him.*

Elerek had seen this face before. Just last night, in Amak. Time after time, skull after skull. The empty eyes bore little resemblance to the person they were before he had touched them, dooming them to drown.

Gaudab slowly circled his dying warrior, terror in his eyes.

He hadn't yet watched a man burst into a thousand droplets to be absorbed by the sand or heard their final cries, or felt the terrible weight of guilt and agony that the curse so desperately craved from Elerek's doomed soul.

"*This* is yours." Gaudab pointed, his whole frame shaking with fury. "Your curse. An omen that Instan kings must die." He withdrew a knife from his belt. "How do we stop this?"

Elerek shook his head, casting his soul in iron. "It's too late."

A wheezed growl escaped the dying—drowning, man.

"How is this stopped?" Spittle flew from the warlord's lips.

Whispers passed among the circle, warriors standing without armor, their faces pale with horror. Razhar visibly shuddered, watching and waiting for his next move. Elerek thought again of the myths inked in old scrolls, stories meant to terrify. Well, such tales worked on even the most formidable.

"It *can't*." Elerek commanded power to his voice, whatever power a captive king on his own death march could. The curse was his, and its destruction and doom would be wielded in his hands like a weapon. "This is what the curse does."

Azraa. Fin. Norbah. Bushra. Driss. Cole. Ishtal. Myra.

Lystra.

There would come an end. He would hasten it. He would be the ending.

Wrath billowed from somewhere deep within him, somewhere dark and vile. This nameless crevice in the earth held no significance, but it had walls and a narrow girth. Those who still breathed fixated on his death, but Elerek became only aware that he was *alive*.

Perhaps more alive than he'd ever dared to be before.

Now, brother, your blood will be avenged.

Water poured from his hands. It gushed in torrents, splashing against the gully walls and knocking several off their feet. Gaudab among them. Elerek concentrated, the water focused on the warlord. Pinning him down.

"Razhar! The dagger!"

Moving like a phantom, verdant silk flying behind him, Razhar ran through the chaos. As water swirled around him, he reached for the dagger on Gaudab's belt.

Two Jarkins sprang on him, scimitars drawn. Razhar ducked, clutching the dagger against his chest.

Elerek spread his hands wide, diverting the streams, sweeping the two warriors off their feet. Within seconds, the water was waist deep, centralized to their encampment. Cardants hissed, leaping and fleeing down the way they'd come. Elerek lost sight of Razhar among the fray, his mind filled with the curse, the insatiable demand to drown, drown, drown. Swirling whirlpools honed on each Jarkin, dragging them down. Seeing them gasping, struggling, and flailing awakened something terrible within Elerek's soul.

He wanted their fear and craved their screams. He wanted every one of them to die in this gully, to be forgotten. They were frail. Fragile. Easily snuffed out forever. He screamed, straining with the effort, and pushed himself harder. Further then he'd ever gone before.

And the curse reached back.

Suddenly, Elerek was underwater. The world turned murky as sand and silt shifted through the depths. Cursed water filled his lungs. His body seemed to possess no weight at all.

He could see everything. *Feel* everything. Every drop of cursed water coursing down the canyon, surging into the Jarkins' throats, tumbling packs, tents, and gear to the lower lands. He no longer held any grasp of his physical body—his broken legs, his sore back, and broad shoulders that had matched his brother's. No distinction between himself and the deluge. The water didn't come from him, a byproduct of the curse. It was all *him*.

One Jarkin ceased to breathe. Sinking to the mire, his body crashed against a boulder. One less enemy to threaten Instanolde. Regret or remorse had no place here.

But fear could manifest anywhere. Elerek felt as if he were drowning in it.

Water cannot drown.

Control slipped from his consciousness. Everything was dark, filthy water. Tumbling. Frothing. Churning.

Water cannot die.

And that filled him with fear most of all.

The curse hadn't killed him.

Instead, the curse had turned him to water.

Chapter 18

Lystra

"*Questa.*"

The sun hadn't yet crested the mountains and the sky shone pale, illuminated by a light that Lystra couldn't yet see as she leaned forward in Tiniah's saddle, but one she knew was coming. A light that reached for Instanolde. Her home.

Tiniah's side-winding gait didn't possess its full speed, her blood still slow with the clinging chill of a long night. Lystra had spent the night curled up against Tiniah's girth, startling at every sound in the canyon. They hadn't crept far from the Jarkins' camp, but the darkness became their shield, and they nestled behind an outcropping of rock.

At the first sign of fading stars, Lystra blinked the sleep from her eyes and steeled her soul for the journey ahead. Tiniah watched her with expectant eyes. Prayers for peace and stillness breathed on Lystra's lips as she checked the saddle straps. This time, the reptile listened, as if sensing the urgency of this, Lystra's last chance to escape the desert.

"She's meant for you."

As her fingers traced the bright green stripe along the reptile's shoulder, Lystra's heart lodged in her throat. She remembered how the cardant had growled and pawed the sands of her pen. A terror of teeth and scales, begging for the wilds.

Elerek had understood. He'd understood *her*.

Lystra pinched her eyes shut at the memory.

When she'd mounted, Lystra bit her lip, suppressing a cry against her wound. She'd bound it as best she could, but she could feel the wrappings working their way free again. There was no time for pain. It would be a hard ride, perhaps the hardest of her life. But she wouldn't stop, not until the golden spires of her city rose to pierce the depths of the skies.

Anticipation wound tight in Tiniah's muscles as Lystra steered her down the canyon. The wide valley stretched before them, the flatland shimmering with cracking earth, baked like bread beneath the radiant sun. A smattering of dunes rose in the distance, ghostly pale in the morning light while the mountains stood dark, sentinels of the horizon. Lystra caught her breath at the Sancen's beautiful, stark desolation. A world no one should survive.

And yet. She had.

Twice.

Why? Why her? An Instan girl who had lived as thousands of Instan girls had before. Girls who learned to dance, loved the intricate beadwork on their colorful kaftans, and memorized rules of etiquette and custom. Torras of noble houses who wore veils to the market and silks to the galas. She loved the smell of flatbread baking in the morning, bitter, spiced coffee served in silver samovars, and the sharpness of mint tea chilled with a hint of sweetness. She'd learned the stars from the skies and their stories in the temple.

But she'd been different—*more*. Grandmother's lessons

were long, wrought with visions of grandeur. The palace marked her destiny. Hours in politics, in diplomacy, in heraldry. A queen forged. A queen who wore no crown.

For all Dalmah's scheming, she'd done nothing to orchestrate her meeting with Cormek. Lystra had caught his eyes of her own accord, drawn to the soul of the king bursting with light, laughter, and love. How he would've ruled, but not in times like these.

Lystra blinked, her eyes stinging with tears. She tried to remember. Walking in the torch-lit gardens, the scent of evell blossoms, the touch of the king's fingers along her jaw, tilting her chin towards him. The touch of his lips against hers.

Before her, the last star faded on the darkened horizon.

The memories turned bitter, Darcress and its two red towers. Cormek sat tall and proud, mounted on a cardant, rallying his men to meet their attackers. His eyes had looked to hers that one, last time. In a flash, everything had ended. Black arrows protruded from Cormek's back. Gaudab's axe shattered his chest. Instanolde's king crumbled to the sand.

She'd screamed and fought with all the helplessness of her small, fragile soul. But she had obeyed her king.

"Ride hard. Don't look back."

A sob rose in Lystra's throat. She jerked on Tiniah's reins. The cardant slowed to a halt among the dunes, her long tail flicking behind her. Lystra drew a shuddered breath, hunched over the saddle. Her shoulder throbbed, but it was nothing against the agony in her soul. The weight of all that she had loved, all that she had lost.

This scene was familiar. The wilds of the Sancen. A fast cardant. The ache of a king's love twisting her heart. When the Jarkins ambushed Darcress, there had been no moment of goodbyes, no chance to embrace, to weep, or share a kiss.

Lystra pinched her eyes shut. Elerek had kissed her.

Because he loved her.

It pulsed in his touch as he had drawn her close. It burned in his eyes with a fierce and coveted desire. Its desperation scorched her lips with a yearning that even the curse couldn't quench. Maybe they had shattered, failed to be all they ought to. Nothing could undo what had happened, but perhaps they might forge a road through the wilderness ahead, a path of forgiveness where they might seek starlight.

"Don't look back."

Lystra lifted her head, shifted in the saddle, and looked over her shoulder. The canyon lay afar off, veined with pale stone and layers of clay. A lonely crevice in the bleak mountains. Its walls were another sort of Darcress, two red towers rising from the desert.

"Ride hard. Save our kingdom. Reign like the queen you are."

I can't.

She couldn't save Cormek, and probably couldn't save Elerek either. Lystra, the grieving queen, didn't fear death. Life frightened her far more, living a life that she would regret.

It began in the desert.

It would end in the desert. She would not leave another king to die. Not this king. The man that she loved now.

Tugging on Tiniah's reins, she wheeled the reptile about just as the first golden shafts of sunlight broke over the mountains.

"Faster!" she screamed to the wind.

All the world faded away, obliterated by the blinding light of the Sancen sunlight. Tiniah held her head higher, welcoming the sun's warmth. Lystra marveled at the cardant's power, the rush of thrill striking her blood like the strongest wine. The terrors and burdens of this last journey into the desert lifted from her shoulders, pulling her heart like a compass's needle to the path before her.

Maybe she would never see her beloved Instanolde again, but its fate would be decided here, side by side with her king.

With the light and heat on her side, the return journey took no time at all. The mountain's roots rose, crafting canyons of stone.

Growls and hisses echoed across the rock. Tiniah raised her head, her front limbs spread apart. Her teeth bared in a deadly snarl. Two cardants appeared, running at full speed. One bore a saddle, dragging a lifeless body by its stirrup. Its dark red scales were familiar; Amak's cardant.

Lystra leapt from Tiniah's back, holding her hands aloft. "Halt!"

The reptiles skidded to a stop, watching her with questioning eyes. Tiniah wagged her head, making low clicking sounds in her throat. The cardant without a saddle snapped its jaws.

"Peace, *gonia*." Lystra's voice rebounded back at her. She stepped toward the saddled reptile, her steps slow and deliberate. The air tensed with the panic ebbing from the cardant's tight muscles and poised claws. Lystra gave a short exhale, marveling that these desert lizards, with their might and prowess, might know fear.

And she knew exactly what had terrorized them.

The rider dangling from the saddle was Jarkin. The mark of the curse consumed his hands and striped across his face, but there was no breath in his lungs. Lystra tried not to look as she freed the dead man's boot from the stirrup. She eyed the full saddle bags, and then looked the red cardant in the eye.

"You'll come with me." She looked at the second cardant as it pawed the earth. "You go, be free," she whispered. *You belong in the wilds.* Lystra wondered if a bit of their strength and tenacity resided in her bones as well.

Tiniah and the red cardant watched as the reptile streaked for the lowlands, uttering low growls.

"I need you two." She clenched her jaw as she mounted again, her shoulder painful. "Follow along, Red." The cardant obediently fell in line behind Tiniah.

She left the dead Jarkin behind—only to find another around the next bend, this one soaked to the bone.

A knot lodged itself in her stomach. She lifted her gaze to the steep sides of the canyon. Streaks of color brightened the rock in places where water drenched its stone. Hues of red, burnt umber, and an orange as bright as the royal color of Instanolde. The king had left his mark.

If the water had reached this high, the passage ahead would be impassible.

Guiding Tiniah to the side, she gripped the saddle with her knees. The cardant knew her work, using claws to climb a narrow gorge where a flood had once broken down the canyon. Red followed nimbly. Atop the walls, a sweeping view of rippling rock, distant sands, and jagged mountains spread about her. A hot wind whipped with her hair, undoing her braid. A labyrinth of canyons lay ahead, each a varied shade of yellow, red, and beige. She wondered at the colors, at the patterns, and if the Maker of the stars had also fashioned the mountains and sands too.

Here, she let the cardants lead. Tiniah knew how to balance herself on the rocky precipices, winding along the high places and finding footing in the cracks and crevices. Lystra scanned the canyon below.

Perhaps the deed was done, Elerek and Razhar well on their way to the wrathgiver. Maybe she would see only the dead, Jarkins laid to waste and rot beneath the hot sun.

Then, her heart nearly stopped. Even Tiniah perked her head up, growling softly.

A wall of water, perfectly straight, reaching from the canyon floor up nearly to the top. It swirled and foamed, dark with silt, mud—and bodies. Several Jarkins lived, pulling themselves from the torrent, their cardants and what was left of the camp assembled before the water. And among them, shouting curses, and soaked from head to toe, stood Gaudab Batu-Khasar.

No sign of Elerek, or Razhar.

"Quiet now." She rode low across Tiniah's back. The last thing she needed was for the Jarkins to see her.

The water leapt in ravenous waves against the cliffside, catching Lystra in its spray. Tiniah steered away from the edge. Lystra scanned the dark waters, searching. Every moment it seemed her heart beat faster.

Up ahead, the canyon met a fork, and here, the waters receded, lapping down either branch like the steady, rhythmic waves of the Gungole. More bodies lay strewn in the water.

"Lystra? Stars above . . ." More swearing.

Razhar stood on a ledge, a shelf cut into the rock several feet lower from Lystra and the cardants. A wild, frenzied look inhabited his eyes, mimicking the panic in Lystra's heart.

"Where is he?" she shouted above the water's din.

Razhar looked back out at the water, his eyes searching.

No, death couldn't have him yet. Lystra remembered the surge of the Kushite canals, harsh water cutting through narrow gorges. Downriver, the canals formed the Gungole River, the clear, beautiful strip of water that gave life to their fields and sustained their city.

What she saw before her—this frothing mass of furious water and mud—was nothing like either of those.

This was Elerek. The rage in his soul. The war cry for

vengeance for his brother. The desperate hope of salvation for Instanolde.

"There!" Razhar pointed.

Lystra followed the aim of his arm.

A hand rose from the swirling water, pale against the foaming waves, followed by a head of dark hair.

Razhar tossed his pack up over the edge and jumped to a lower shelf in the rock. The water splashed against his knees. He strung himself against the rock, muscles taut, reaching for Elerek's hand.

"El! Just a bit farther!"

Elerek nearly blended into the fray, his clothes torn and stained with mud. As his hand found purchase in Razhar's, skin again clothed his limb.

He needed Razhar. To keep him human. Alone, Elerek wasn't enough. Lystra caught her breath. Was it only a few short weeks ago that she'd come to the same conclusion—about herself?

Lystra ran along the cliff. She dropped to her knees, gripping the ledge with shaky hands. Beneath, the water rolled and swelled. It reached for Elerek, tearing him away from Razhar and threatening to drag him back into the fray.

With a shout, Razhar leaned out over the water, bracing his feet against the wall, stretching his arm as far as it would go. Lystra couldn't breathe, focusing on his hand, his knuckles nearly white as he grasped the rock. What would happen if he fell? Submerged by Elerek's cursed water while his own limbs turned to sand?

Elerek reached for Razhar again. Their hands touched just as a large wave rolled over Elerek's head, pulling him under. But this time, Razhar held on.

"Lystra!" Razhar looked up. "Help him."

She lowered herself to her stomach, leaning out over the

abyss. Her shoulder groaned. Razhar wasn't too far beneath her, but Elerek lay completely out of reach.

"I can't," she whimpered.

Razhar grunted. "Hold on."

With the next swell of cursed water, he pushed himself against the wall, using the momentum of the wave to bolster Elerek up. The king found a handhold, clinging for dear life.

Lystra leaned farther. She couldn't breathe, her lungs pressed against the rock beneath her. Everything within her willed her arm to reach just a bit farther.

Elerek looked up. The curse mark stretched up from his ripped collar, wrapping about his neck like a noose. Their eyes met, and something in his eyes sparked with a light that couldn't be extinguished.

I came back, El. Lystra wished she could smile. And by the light of all the dancing constellations, she would never leave his side again.

Chapter 19

Elerek

The din of the raging water faded. The swirl of mud and blood and broken bodies fell away.

Lystra.

The morning sun caught in her hair. Her hand reached for him and he held on as if his very humanity depended on it. As soon as her skin touched his, it fled away, spreading its mark up to her forearm. Even so, the ghost of a smile swept across Lystra's lips. Her fierce eyes blazed with the same tenacity with which she trained wild cardants and fought for the future of Instanolde.

She was life itself, and she had chosen to invade his heart, territory claimed by death and destruction long ago. And in that moment, faced with the monstrosity of his curse—capable of reshaping mountains, shifting sands, and consuming flesh—Elerek knew he never wanted to be parted from her again.

He gripped the rock with his free hand, reaching as high as he could. Fortunately, his arms were strong, toned from years of lifting his weight. Razhar clambered up the cliff alongside him and vanished over the top. Together, he and Lystra heaved

Elerek onto the cliff top. As soon as the mass of furious water severed from Elerek, the waves receded and poured down the canyon with the strength of a flash flood, leaving only thin ribbons of water running in rivulets in the soaked sands.

Air filled Elerek's lungs with all the desperation of a drowning man. Hunching his shoulders, he braced himself against the rock on shaky arms. Then, he lifted his face—and a blast of hot, dry sand pummeled him.

Knocked off-kilter, he sputtered, sand clinging to his lips. "You idiot! What—?"

Sand. Slamming against his skin, irritating his eyes, grinding in his teeth. He coughed. "What?" He spat a mouthful of sand.

Lystra and Razhar looked at him as if they'd never seen anyone cursed before.

"You . . ." Lystra's hands trembled.

Elerek glanced down at himself. His hands, his forearms— had turned to water.

No bones. No muscle. No veins. Just water, perfectly shaped and sculpted to his body's form.

His mind plummeted into numbness, a deepness that turned the warmth of what blood he still possessed against him. Whatever happened down there had never happened before. But he'd also never attempted to flood a canyon and drown a whole contingent of enemies before. Somehow, he'd pushed harder, gone farther—too far.

What if he *couldn't* die? Would he only turn to water and live—no, *exist*—as foreign, vengeful, drowning depths? Humanity ripped from him as the curse ripped away his victim's skin. Elerek could fathom no worse hell.

Dear Starkindler, please, please just let me die instead.

Razhar edged closer. He touched Elerek's hand-turned-water with his hand-turned-sand. "You know." He huffed. "All these years, I thought we knew how this curse worked. Now . . ."

His touch restored them both. Still cursed, but human.

"That's twice . . ." Elerek whispered. "Twice that it's changed."

"Either time, were you in control?"

Elerek shut his eyes, blocking out the desert and its warmth and its light. Inside, a void opened. An emptiness, as if he'd poured himself entirely into the canyon behind.

"El . . .?" Razhar spoke as if he addressed a child caught stealing sweets.

His hands clenched, wishing that his fists could hold back the torrents lurking beneath his skin. "No," he whispered. "I was not."

These cursed waters were no longer his to command. The curse, his greatest and only weapon with which to save his kingdom, had turned against him.

Lystra exhaled a soft gasp. Razhar swore beneath his breath.

Opening his eyes, Elerek glanced between them. He wasn't alone in the wilds. One could keep his body grounded, securely planted in the gift of his own humanity. The other had become one with him in his grief and pulled his soul out of the shadows and into the light.

He needed them. By all the dancing constellations above, he *needed* them. Needing felt like weakness. But it also felt like strength.

Shouts echoed off the canyon walls. Furious voices seeking blood.

His breath quivered. "They survived?"

Lystra's features bent into a dark frown. "I saw them. Khasar is still alive."

Elerek swore. They'd be desperate. Without him, they

wouldn't last long. If the Sancen took Gaudab Batu-Khasar, so be it, but he wished he could've sent the Jarkin to his death himself.

Razhar stood, brushing dust from his clothing. "I see you've rescued your cardant, Your Highness."

Her cardant. Elerek glanced at the reptile, standing poised and tense several paces away. The one he'd given her as a wedding gift.

"I've got two." Lystra rose to her feet, her movements stilted. She whistled, summoning the enormous cardant, followed by a second reptile of dark red. Elerek's gaze followed her hand, still wrapped in the curse's mark, as she clutched her shoulder. A dark stain of red marred her tunic.

"Can you ride?" he asked, his voice soft.

Lystra's gaze skirted his. "For now."

Where did they go from here? He never thought he'd see her again, and the memory of their kiss burned in his mind, a warm hearth he'd like nothing more than to return to.

But did she feel the same way? Had she forgiven him?

Did she love him?

A reptilian growl echoed over the rock, and Elerek thought he could feel the earth tremble beneath him. Lystra's cardant raised its mighty head, snapping its jaws at the other and exuding its dominance.

Elerek glanced over his shoulder. Had the Jarkins heard that?

"Easy, girl, easy." Lystra reached for the reins, pulling the cardant's head low enough for her to take the reptile's snout in her small hands. "Did you get the dagger?"

"Yes, I have it." Razhar secured his pack to the red cardant's saddle. "Well, with the options presented to us, Your Highness, I'd rather not ride that one." He eyed Lystra's cardant skeptically.

"Do you know how to ride?" Lystra asked.

"Um, no."

With a short huff, the queen stepped toward the red reptile, still holding the reins to her own. "I think this one belonged to one of the houses associated with the racing committee. He's had more training."

As if to punctuate this statement, the red cardant barred its teeth and Lystra's cardant gave another shriek.

This time, amid the echoes of the reptile's voices, Elerek heard a response. More cardants, down in the canyon where the sands were still damp. Numbness crept up his spine, slowly spreading over his skin. The void sealed him again, robbing from him the touch of the wind, the heat, and the sand beneath his crippled legs.

Drip. Drip. Drip. This time, the droplets didn't fall from his fingers, but from sandstone clefts and boulders, seeping into the thirsty ground back in the canyon. Blackness fringed Elerek's vision, and he suddenly gained a strange awareness, as if a part of him still had a connection to the water he'd left behind.

Thrust back to the physical, the here and now, his heart pounded in terror. "We need to leave. *Now.* Razhar, will you help me?"

Nodding, Razhar slid his arm beneath Elerek's shoulder, lifting him from the ground. They moved toward Lystra's cardant, and Elerek had to swallow his anxiety as he climbed into the saddle. It was a relief to sit on the reptile's back, not tied like a sack of grain. The cardant turned its head, eyeing him with a scrutinizing gaze.

"I don't like you much either." Even after three days of the cardants, he still hadn't adjusted to their side-winding gait and the raw power that could choose at any moment to toss and trample him.

"I figured you'd want to ride with your queen," Razhar whispered with a wink.

Yes, but he pretended not to hear him, occupying his gaze with the eastern horizon. Somewhere, amid the canyons and valleys, the Darcress Kasbah lay. He'd never been there, only seen maps and sketches. Where it began with his brother's death, it would end with the curse's breaking.

Maps. Elerek started, reaching a hand inside his shirt. His fingers felt only the numb void of the curse. Somewhere in the deluge of his own making, the star chart had been swept away.

He closed his eyes. They no longer needed it, and a thousand copies resided back within his kingdom, but still, he was sorry to lose it.

"Let's get away from the Jarkins." Elerek pushed his hair, oily and caked with sand, off his forehead. His turban had also gone missing. "Then we'll set course—to Darcress."

He spoke it like a decree, an ordinance from the throne itself.

Behind him, Razhar exhaled a long sigh.

Lystra lifted her eyes, the light catching in her amber irises. They held no questions, only a determination to rival the strength of the cardants'. "And we will go with you."

She came back . . . for me.

She climbed into the saddle, and only Elerek heard the pain hissing through her teeth as she settled in front him. Her hair, free from its confines, brushed his arm, and he suddenly realized how *near* she was.

The cardant thrashed, stamping her limbs. Elerek drew a sharp breath—instinctively wrapping his arm around Lystra, thoughts of being trampled and beaten into the rock beneath the reptile's claws filling his mind. Lystra gave a series of commands, reining her in.

"Any living thing for miles heard that, I'm sure," Razhar muttered.

As his panic settled, Elerek exhaled—and realized that his arm was still around Lystra's waist. Heat flooded his face, and he slowly drew it back, gripping the saddle's edge near his knee instead.

"It's all right, girl," Lystra whispered to the reptile. "Now, *questa!*"

With another mutter, the cardant set off. She kept a fast pace, faster than their previous days of travel. Razhar followed on the red cardant, doing his best to keep his seat, and Lystra continually shouted commands to the cardants to keep them in line. Grasping the saddle was no longer possible, and Elerek realized he *had* to hold on to Lystra as every jolt threatened to send him careening headlong into the canyons.

When they reached a wide gap in the land, cut from a dark, blackish rock, they slowed. Lystra's cardant stamped and tossed her head regardless of her mistress's soft words.

"We'll pace ourselves, especially in this heat." She patted the reptile's sleek neck.

Razhar dismounted, glancing back the way they'd come. "I'd prefer to walk then. Do you think they'll follow us?"

Elerek huffed. "Without water, they'll either push themselves to catch us or turn back."

Lystra slipped over the side of the cardant. "I hope they perish. But if we keep to rock, we won't leave tracks." She handed him the reins. "Remember what to do?"

Gripping the leather between his fingers, Elerek sat a little taller in the saddle. "If I don't, you're here to help me."

Perhaps he ought to give the heat the credit, but a hint of color flushed on her cheeks. She took the reins of the red cardant, leading the way deeper into the canyon.

"Now that conversation is possible." Razhar attempted to

straighten his turban, but it only sat more lopsided atop his head. "We *are* going onward? To Darcress?"

Elerek's stomach knotted. "As we decided, yes?"

"Ah, yes, but now that we're all together." His eyes darted toward Lystra. "I can hold back the curse. I can keep you—all of you—alive. Shouldn't we go back? Without Khasar's influence in the city, we could liberate Norbah and muster your armies."

His heart sank. "You really believe that I'd last that long, Razhar? After what you saw back there?" After he'd turned to water—and didn't drown.

A pained expression filled Razhar's eyes. "I can try, El. I know my abilities are new to you, but I've been keeping you alive for years. Surely we can hold on a bit longer—together."

That *together* hung in the air, a note Elerek hadn't heard before. It rang with a dissonance, like an oud string in need of tightening. A piece out of place amid the melody, and Elerek thought he understood.

How many days could Razhar buy them? How many nights of dancing constellations till the wrathgiver returned? Could they live as they once had? Return to those simple meals shared among those doomed to drown? Burn bright with what time they could steal from the heavens?

And Lystra, would she share those days with him? Those nights?

He heaved a deep sigh. "We can't, Razhar. Even with your abilities, I could still perish, and if I die, everyone dies with me. Those who bear the curse—my devotion to them cannot be sacrificed on the pyre of my own self interests. Breaking the curse is the best way to save them—and to save Instanolde."

To save Lystra.

Razhar didn't reply, and silence fell over the canyon, broken only by the sound of the reptiles' immense breaths, the rattle of tack, and the scrape of their boots upon stone. Despite the heat, Elerek shivered. Without the caravan of cardants and warriors, the desolation deepened, and he felt as if they were the last bit of life left in the world.

His kingdom waited for him—for him to die. Elerek didn't like this answer. In fact, he almost preferred it when he suspected that the story had been a fabrication. But death had always been his destiny. If anything, the thought of saving Instanolde and losing the host of Jarkins to the desert, gave meaning to his demise. If he could redeem some good from the evil the curse intended, would there be atonement for his follies?

But the unrest in Razhar's face gave him pause. Tension lingered in the air between them, and Elerek hadn't forgotten how easily the deceptions flowed from his so-called friend. How even, last night, Elerek had helped kill a man because Razhar needed it done.

Elerek cleared his throat. "Now, Razhar, I demand answers."

"About?"

"Everything."

"Oh." Razhar tilted his head back, watching the sky. "Is that all?"

"Last night. Your grand plan." Elerek's hands clenched about the reins, and his rage billowed hot and deadly. "You're quite adept at late night sneaking, aren't you?"

Razhar scowled. "Are we really going to latch on to that again?"

That, and so much more. "I don't understand why you would lie to me."

Spinning on his heels, Razhar faced forward again, hiding his features. "I don't understand what it would change. If you knew, would you have made me stop?" He glanced over his shoulder, meeting Elerek's eyes. "Let them die quicker? Norbah? Myra?"

Elerek ground his teeth. Perhaps he asked questions that he shouldn't. Scenarios that would never be. "Then tell me how you're connected to my curse when the countess of House Arghan bound it. What does it have to do with you?"

Lystra snapped to her full height and stopped dead in her tracks. Her eyes smoldered with a fire hot enough to make the entire Sancen a funeral pyre. "You . . ." She hissed through her teeth. "Show him the writ."

For a moment, Razhar appeared to cower. "But—"

"Razhar Emblino, show him the writ." Lystra folded her arms. "Tell him everything you should have told him *years* ago."

Razhar bowed his head, anguish swirling in his eyes. With trembling hands, he reached into his shirt and withdrew a rolled parchment tied with a dirty, stained orange ribbon.

Elerek felt as if he waited on the edge of that canyon again, staring down into the swirls of cursed waters. The waters that had betrayed him, and he wondered if he were about to be betrayed again.

Chapter 20

Razhar

After so many years of sneaking, hiding his past and the truths he carried, handing the curse's writ of sale over to the king of Instanolde felt like a betrayal. Razhar looked away, unable to meet Elerek's eyes.

True to his baba's word, he'd never spoken of the star-etched dagger, the curse binder woman who convinced his baba to commit the deed, and the mysterious sands that had plagued him. But when he'd arrived in Instanolde—that city steeped in magic like the purest tea—he'd found all sorts of stories. Particularly among the palace servants, where the curse permeated all the talk and gossip in the shadows and corridors, easy pickings for the orphan who roamed at his leisure.

But one bit of information stuck out, sore as a stubbed toe— the fact that the king of Instanolde was *not* cursed.

No, instead it was the prince. The one he'd found in the palace gardens so, so long ago. Razhar had pushed him into a fountain. He wondered if Elerek remembered that?

His most beloved friend. The brother he never had. Someone Razhar ought to have been able to trust.

Elerek pulled the orange ribbon free and began to read. His intense, jade-colored stare pierced the parchment as if to burn the words that Razhar knew so well—and despised with his whole soul.

A curse for a legacy, for kings . . .
Wrought beneath a wrathful star . . .
By blade and starlight . . .
Let its cost be death . . .

Razhar glanced at Lystra, standing statue still between the two cardants. He marveled that here, in this forsaken desert, the heirs of the two families responsible for the curse would face the wrath of the king who bore it.

Elerek's fingers trembled, and his face turned the same greenish pallor as Razhar's faded turban. "This . . ." His voice sounded strangled, stolen. "Sworn in blood . . . House Arghan and . . . *Emblino?*"

Razhar folded his arms, bracing himself for the fury of the king capable of filling a canyon with enough water to drown an army.

Instead, Elerek looked broken. His shoulders hunched, agony filling his eyes with tears. "You . . ."

Razhar lifted his chin. "Not me. My baba. A Kushite archer tired of fighting endless wars and watching his tribe suffer. He hoped for a better world, one of peace and no more bloodshed. These weren't wrong things to want, El. But his desperation made him easy prey to a manipulative curse binder. The countess bound the curse—and talked my baba into casting it."

Lystra bowed her head, a crease marring her lovely brow.

"No one ever connected my baba to your curse, but Kushan executed him anyways, dishonoring his name." Razhar stared at his boots, resisting the emotions surging in his soul. Emotions he didn't want to feel. "El, my father never would've done this if he'd known."

"Known *what*?" Elerek bit back. "That the curse would cause suffering? That it would destroy and ravage? As curses do?"

Razhar drew a steadying breath. This was a storm he must weather. Let him be angry. "My baba cast a curse against the king of Instanolde. He didn't have the slightest idea that it would fall upon an innocent child." A son so much like his own.

"And that's supposed to excuse what he did?" Droplets of water beaded about Elerek's tight knuckles.

Razhar marched back to the cardant, taking the writ back before the curse could ruin one last remnant of his baba. "No, but he paid for his mistake. With his life."

"Elerek." Lystra's gaze softened as she turned to the king. Her hand touched the saddle, her skin rippling with the curse's mark. "My grandmother's skills with smooth words and empty promises know no end. I've lived my whole life at the mercies of her schemes. She's to blame and deserves every judgment."

"Please." Razhar made a grand gesture toward the queen. "Listen to your wife."

But even as the words left his mouth, he knew he'd made a mistake. He knew Elerek too well and could only watch as the king's expression turned raw with a pain too deep for fury. "The countess arranged our marriage. Another scheme in which we are all nothing but pawns—and how many are dead because of it?"

Too many. Myra, Fin, Azraa, and the rest. Razhar carefully rolled the writ into a tight scroll and slipped it inside his shirt, beside the dagger.

"No one held Cormek responsible for your father's sins. Would you hold us so responsible?" A heat laced Lystra's voice.

The aim of Elerek's rage struck true, like the most effective condor-mounted archer.

Razhar ground his teeth. Elerek couldn't push them away now, especially not Lystra. Not when they had only days left to live.

Elerek's eyes flashed. "He *is* responsible!" He pointed a finger, dripping with water, toward Razhar. "You knew, Razhar. You knew about your father, about me, before you'd fled Kushan. You knew how to break the curse before we'd even become friends."

How shameful it sounded, worded like that. Razhar wished that they weren't trapped out here. If they were back in the palace, he could walk away. Venture out into the city and visit every bakery south of the merchant sector. Let Elerek smolder in his anger for a few hours—or days. Then maybe, he'd saunter into the kitchens, join the rest of the cursed around a low table to share a lavish breakfast. He'd catch Elerek's eye, glaring at him over the rim of a bitter cup of coffee. They wouldn't speak, the laughter and good nature of their tribe enough to hold back an outburst. Then, maybe, after another hour or so, they'd forget the argument ever happened.

Not this time.

"I didn't know everything." Razhar chose his words carefully. "My baba didn't tell me to break the curse. He didn't speak of more death, more violence, or more destruction. He told me to find you." He lifted a palm, coated with unnatural sand. "I'm the cost of your curse, El, the punishment for my baba's actions. One son received a curse, the other the consequence. If I hadn't found you, hadn't spent my days holding back the curse, I would've died. Turned to sand."

"A means to an end."

Razhar clenched his hands, a cloud of sand bursting from his knuckles. "Stars above, El!" A growl rumbled in his throat.

So much for treading lightly. "Stop being an idiot for two seconds and listen! He told me to find you so we'd be able to *help each other*. By all the dancing constellations in the heavens, don't you see? Your burden isn't yours alone."

But Elerek snarled, his features vicious. "Is *that* what you think? That we're the same? That you know what it's like to be cursed? Well, you don't know."

Stars. Razhar took a step back, but it wasn't enough. A wave of water slapped against him, beating his body with the force of a blunt object. He toppled across the rock, skin scraping and tearing. As soon as he could, he jumped to his feet, a spray of sand at his fingertips. The only thing capable of stemming the flow of cursed water.

Well, not the only thing.

Chapter 21

Lystra

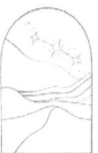

"**S**top it! Both of you!" Lystra planted herself between them. The spray of water ceased, misting her face and pooling beneath her boots. "We haven't the time for this."

Time, a curse unto itself. Twisting about her hand, her own curse mark exposed slender bones and reached up her wrist. She marveled that some who walked the palace's golden halls had borne it for years—thanks to Razhar.

She glared first at him. He looked away, his expression mirroring that of a broken warrior who hadn't the strength to fight any longer. Perhaps the man deserved pity, but her patience had run as thin as her scarf, compounded by the agony searing her shoulder.

Then she looked at Elerek, whose fists still dripped with water. His eyes moved to the horizon, filled with the deep blue reflection of the sky and enough pain to envelop the Sancen.

They didn't bear simple pains. Nor were they wounds that could be healed with a word. Her authority as queen couldn't serve them, and no matter how much she wished that she could make these two men understand each other, the duty before them took precedent.

"Razhar." She looked at him again. "What happens to you if we break the curse?"

Tugging the end of his turban, Razhar let it fall in swaths about his shoulders. He didn't meet her eye. "Your grandmother told me that I would die—same as him." He gestured toward Elerek. "Consequences are to be paid, not broken."

The thought turned her heart cold. "My grandmother has lied before."

"Maybe." Razhar's broad shoulders shrugged. "Don't blame me for wanting to go back and salvage what days I have left. I have family within the palace walls too. I've lost people I love." His voice cracked. "I didn't reach Azraa in time when she died. I couldn't keep Fin from drowning. I bribed soldiers to retrieve Myra's body so she could be buried."

Elerek clenched his eyes shut.

"But I know how it is." Razhar gestured toward the king. "The value of his life over mine."

Lystra stared at him, at the ache in his face. Did he truly believe that?

"Anyways, I'll go to the wrathgiver." Stepping closer, he reached for her hand. The curse mark fled and sand expelled from his palm. "And I'll never stop holding back the curse. Stars, I'm just as weary of death as you are."

What if they did go back? How long might life be held in stasis, suspended over the curse's impending doom? Would they live long enough to save Instanolde? To establish peace? Would it be better to have days that were less—but full?

Her gaze skirted toward Elerek once more. *"The countess arranged our marriage."* The bitterness in his voice had pierced her heart. An alliance arranged for death, but they'd still taken vows meant for life, no matter how short. Did he see that by choosing to come back, that she'd chosen to uphold those vows?

Vows that he had already broken. Elerek lived in moments, not days. He'd loved Myra in such moments, blind to how the choices might impact his days.

Lystra wondered if their kiss had been the same. A stolen moment, a bit of passion stirred by the quickening of the ending. Maybe he didn't love her, not in the way that she wanted him to.

"We cannot grow weary of life," Lystra murmured.

Razhar nodded.

"Then we ought to keep walking." She reached for the red cardant's reins, leading him forward. Tiniah followed.

They kept a slow pace to mitigate the heat, sometimes riding and sometimes walking. Though they kept to the shade, the heat, trapped between the rock walls, felt as thick and as smothering as wool. Lystra wished she could urge Tiniah into another full-out run and feel nothing but the wind in her face.

"Do you two need water?" Seated behind her on Tiniah, Elerek's voice was a breath on her shoulder. She tried not to think about it, his warmth different from the heat of the desert, and the feel of his arm against her waist holding them both steady.

She beckoned both cardants to halt, slipping from the saddle—and from his touch. Elerek's face was set like stone, hewn from the eastern mountains themselves, but his eyes betrayed him. Lystra remembered well the first time his guise had fallen, the day they'd become betrothed to one another. She'd thought his eyes a mirror in which she'd seen her own shattered soul.

This time, she saw into his soul—and he was in anguish.

"Thank you," she whispered.

He filled the waterskins and handed them down. Lystra

closed her eyes as she drank, barely able to stomach the thought that the water flowed with the curse.

When she opened them again, Elerek had cast aside his thobe, darkened by mud from the torrent he'd created in the canyon. The collar of his tunic shifted, exposing bruises along his shoulder from the beating he'd taken. A few more lined his face, and several cuts glistened red.

"Are you injured?" She slipped the waterskin into the saddlebag. If she could make the Jarkins pay, she would.

"I'm fine." But he grimaced as he twisted in the saddle, stowing the ruined garment away. "You?"

Lystra wished she could lie just as easily, but the truth hurt too much to speak.

A soft growl vibrated deep in Tiniah's throat. Lystra turned. The reptile had gone still, her every muscle stiff and coiled. Her eyes were alert, pupils constricted, and she flicked her long tongue, tasting the air. The red cardant also tensed, still bearing Razhar on his back. They sensed something . . .

Then, the silence shattered with a series of hisses.

Movement shifted among the landscape as dark shapes rose upon pale shards of stone, black silhouettes simmering in the heat mirages. Arched backs studded with coarse hair. Unnaturally long limbs with large paws. And rows upon rows of snarling teeth.

Lystra's blood ran cold at the red glint of feral eyes. Tungin.

"Stars." Razhar swore.

Leaping into the saddle, Lystra grabbed the reins. *"Questa!"*

But Tiniah needed no urging, lurching with a speed that almost defied reason. She flew down the canyon, coming out on a long ridge that sloped back down into sand. Lystra glanced behind her. The red cardant may have belonged to the races, but his speed didn't compare to Tiniah's, Razhar fumbling with the reins with one hand and holding desperately to the saddle with the other.

The tungin barked a sound between that of a dog and the cackle of a hyena. Their paws kicked up sand, but the terrain didn't hinder them—unlike the cardants, who began to struggle and slide on the loose earth of the valley before them.

"Starkindler, preserve us," Elerek prayed. His arms wrapped tight around Lystra's waist, her shoulders pressed back against his chest.

Lystra drew a sharp breath, the terror of being ripped to shreds and their bones scattered across the Sancen consuming her. They had no weapons; the curse would remain unbroken.

The curse . . . the raging waters of the canyon filled her mind.

A full-sized tungin rivaled the height of a horse and could match its speed. Its grinning, hyena face populated many night-marish tales of the Sancen's brutality. Their limbs, studded with hair at the joints, almost appeared like that of a starved man, which led to the story that if one were to be lost to the desert, their mind would be given over to that of a wild beast, forced to prey upon other unlucky victims.

Lystra didn't care about the stories now, not with their jaws snapping at Tiniah's heels. But these creatures weren't the only force of power in this desert.

"El . . . your waters . . ."

Behind her, he turned in the saddle. "I haven't a clear shot. I might startle Razhar's cardant."

Who was falling woefully behind.

Lystra drew back on the reins, attempting to slow Tiniah, but the cardant roared and thrashed. The racket seemed to spur the red cardant on, placing them side by side in a deadly race that they couldn't afford to lose.

"Loosen the reins!" Lystra shouted. *"Questa!"*

Razhar let go of the reins entirely, drawing a short knife from his belt and slashed as a tungin lunged. It barely dissuaded the beast as it growled and bared its horrid, canine teeth. On the second slash, Razhar's knife flicked flesh. The tungin yelped and fell out of line.

"We can't keep this up," Razhar shouted.

Lystra scanned their surroundings, heart pounding. Bits of dust caught in her teeth, grinding beneath her tense jaw. Up ahead, a sharp ridge of rock rose to their right, its side sheer and straight. Lystra doubted that Tiniah, even without riders, could scale such a cliff, and she didn't know about the red's climbing abilities.

They could only fly, maneuvering with a speed and agility that would've won any competition. Except it wasn't other reptiles snapping at their heels, but a pack of hunters, pressing their advantage. Lystra didn't just hold the reins in her hands, but their lives.

Tiniah hissed as a tungin's teeth found its mark in her leg and stumbled. Lystra yelped as she and Elerek were jerked to the side, nearly cast into the sand.

Elerek swore. "Lystra, take us closer to the cliff." He whipped his head around. "Razhar, this way!"

Lystra pulled on the reins, Tiniah straining as the land sloped downward into a wash filled with loose stones and boulders alongside the cliff. The terrain caused Tiniah to slow. She watched a trio of tungin on the higher ground beside them, their eyes, flashing and bloodthirsty, level with her own. One leap and the jackal-like monster would knock her from the saddle and tear out her throat.

A roar from the red cardant pierced the air, followed by a great crash as the reptile barreled down the slope, losing its footing. Razhar barely managed to keep his seat, clutching the saddle. His cardant righted itself, but fell behind. Lystra was about to pull Tiniah in again when, above them, a tungin running parallel with them leapt with a howl. All four claw-studded paws in the air.

Everything seemed to happen in slow motion for Lystra. She saw the gleam of the Sancen's relentless sun in the creature's blood-red eyes. Its lips curled back, revealing row after row of deadly teeth. She could do nothing.

A blast of water surged from Elerek's hands. The tungin shrieked, briefly blinded, and toppled back in a puddle. Out of reach of Lystra's flesh.

She whipped her head back, pushing her hair out of her eyes. She caught her breath.

Cormek's eyes. But it wasn't. Cormek had lived in lavish glory while his brother had known pain and torment. Elerek's gaze burned with strength and determination. More than his pain, than his curse, he was dauntless.

Instanolde needed *him*. He was its king—a king of curses and star-cast skies.

Chapter 22

Elerek

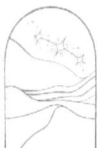

The desert blurred across Elerek's vision. A lonely, desolate world filled with death—his death.

The cardants' limbs thundered as they carried them across the dreary landscape with a swiftness that left Elerek breathless. But it wouldn't be enough to outrun the doom biting at their ankles. Not to escape the torment ripping at his soul like flesh between a predator's teeth or to subdue the numbness in his skin, robbing away his humanity.

He'd read of the tungin, seated comfortably in his library surrounded by soft pillows, candles, and cooling cups of mint tea. The murderous scavengers were certainly preferable in ink than flesh, bone, and ravenous teeth.

But they weren't the only monster in the desert.

The onslaught of water that had knocked the tungin back had also made quick work of him. His hands again turned to perfectly sculpted water. His heart beat wildly, fueled by terror and the curse's insatiable rage creeping up inside him.

No, this time, the curse would not control him.

Elerek clenched his teeth, watching the feral eyes of the tungin as the pack edged closer.

The curse was his. A part of him. And he needed it.

To destroy.

To drown.

To *defend*.

They weren't going to die. Not here and not like this.

He kept one arm around Lystra, bracing himself in the saddle, and stretched out the other. Elerek's fingers felt like ice, releasing another spout of water to deter the pack as they drew closer to Razhar's cardant.

"Oi, I could use a bit more help, El," Razhar growled.

Elerek surveyed the landscape. The rut they followed deepened, running flush with the cliff. Perfect for channeling a torrent. He leaned over Lystra's shoulder. "I need you to guide the cardant as close to the cliff as you can manage."

Her amber eyes flashed toward him, then she gave a swift nod.

Air fled his lungs. Had she always been so beautiful?

Twisting in the saddle, every bruise and strain in his shoulders groaned. "Razhar, get your cardant closer."

Terror mingled with panic in Razhar's eyes. The knife in his hands was better suited to spreading jam, not defending oneself in this horrid wilderness. "My cardant isn't as fast as yours!"

Elerek wished he'd just shut up and listen. "I need a clear shot."

They were running out of time. He felt the breath shudder from Lystra's lungs as she bent forward. "Come on, girl."

The pack of tungin converged, forming a tight cluster about the cardants like an army strangling a cornered foe. Elerek blasted another stream of water, but this time, the tungin knew what to expect and dodged. Infuriated, they seemed to increase their speed—or had the cardants begun to slow?

Elerek glanced over his shoulder. The red cardant strained, head extended. The space between the two cardants grew, and Razhar faded farther back.

The shrill shriek of the tungin pierced the air. A large creature gained on the red cardant's neck, its ears flat against its skull. Muscles coiled. Teeth bared, gleaming with foam. Then, in a blur of dark fur, the tungin pounced, sinking its teeth into the cardant's neck. Blood gushed over its scales and the cardant lurched. As the pack surrounded the disadvantaged lizard, one tungin mounted its back—and its jaw bore down on Razhar's arm, drawing blood.

For one terrible, agonizing moment, their eyes met.

Razhar . . . Elerek couldn't breathe, couldn't summon water.

The cardant crumpled in a mass of muscle and scales. The tungin pack assailed it, ripping flesh with bloodstained teeth. A swirl of dust rose through the fray, and Razhar vanished amid the bloody heap.

"*No!*" Elerek roared. He raised both arms, summoning water, but the stream sputtered as he swayed, forced to grab the saddle for stability. "Lystra, turn the cardant around. Can you ride one-handed?"

Lystra yanked the reins. The cardant skidded in the gravel. Her face was set like flint. "Yes."

"I need you to hold on to me."

She leaned back, grasping the reins in one hand while slipping her other arm around his waist. "I won't let you fall."

Their eyes met. The world—from the turn of the heavens to the march of the seasons—stalled. One breath. One heartbeat. A promise. A vow. Perhaps the strongest they'd given to one another yet.

I don't want to die. Dying for her was easy, the best and most responsible thing he could do. No, he wanted to live. To give her each glorious sunrise filled with the splendor of a thousand possibilities. To chase horizons and discover what they might have become. To see what might grow from the barren soil of their grief and to rise from the ashes of every ravaging fire.

He wanted to live—and love her.

Lystra shouted orders and the cardant wheeled around. Elerek pitched in the saddle, but she held him steady, his tether.

"Charge toward them, as close to the cliff as you can."

The cardant growled, but obeyed her mistress. Ahead, the pack and its prey loomed closer. Elerek raised his arms, narrowed his eyes, watched, and waited.

Now.

Water appeared, and then a wave taller than a building and as wide as a road. It arched over their heads and toward the cliff, hitting at the perfect angle to ricochet off the rock and rain down upon the pack. The roar of raging water filled their ears. The tungin and their hideous faces vanished beneath the wall of water, washed down the rut.

Lungs heaving, Elerek slumped forward and collapsed against Lystra. His vision swam, frayed black at the edges.

"Razhar? Where are you?" Lystra's voice sounded afar off, drowned out by the ringing in his ears.

Forcing his eyes open, Elerek watched the cursed water run over stones. The cardant lay dead, a crumpled carcass that oozed blood to mingle with the cursed water. Beneath the ridge of its back, twisted on its side, Razhar huddled soaked and coughing, his bloody arm pinned against his ribs. His other arm reached skyward, prickled with golden sand. He'd used his own powers to combat the flow. Lystra bent low over the cardant's neck, a hand outstretched.

"I am the cost of your curse, El, the punishment for my baba's actions."

After a lifetime of wondering, imagining foul and vengeful villains, Elerek had been given the story of a broken Kushite father corrupted by desperation and manipulated into reacting against a despised king.

A despised king who also knew desperation. Elerek remembered well his father's temper, hunting all over the desert for the curse binder that had wreaked havoc upon his family. The pain and shame as the curse tallied its deaths—his mother among them. Finally, Lorkin gave up, throwing his devotion to Cormek, and confining Elerek to the shadows. As if he'd never existed.

Both the desperate Kushite and the hated king were dead, their deeds with them.

Meanwhile, he and Razhar lived.

He'd been cruel, insensitive. He'd wielded his pain as he wielded the curse, like a weapon. Razhar had made mistakes, plenty of them, but so had he, and now wasn't the time to push him away. Especially if Razhar was destined to die with him, with the curse's breaking.

Taking Lystra's hand, Razhar pulled himself to his feet and climbed into the saddle behind Elerek.

"El?" He grabbed his shoulder. "You still with us?"

His eyelids dropped, darkness consuming him. But there would be no more rest, not for him. Not until the curse was broken.

Razhar swore. "Stars above. Get us away from here."

Lystra coaxed the cardant with gentle words, but the reptile growled and stamped its feet, unpleased to carry three riders. Eventually, they started moving again. Elerek didn't know how he stayed on the cardant, but he felt Razhar's steady hand on his shoulder.

Something in their frailty, their brokenness, knew to rage against the odds and survive, as his people had been doing for centuries. To fight for another, even to the point of death, that was something that burned brighter than all the stars in the heavens. And since the moment Razhar had set foot in the golden palace, he'd been fighting for the life of the king of Instanolde.

Blinking, Elerek lifted his head as they entered a narrow canyon. Sheer, rock walls colored a dark red rose on either side of them. Lystra directed their mount into a shaded alcove. Releasing a long exhale, the reptile settled onto the sandy floor.

Razhar gave a low moan as he clambered down, leaning against the cardant for support.

Elerek grimaced at the sight of blood covering his forearm and splattered across his tunic. "You're a mess."

Scoffing, Razhar held out his arm, the bite marks cruel. "I may never wear red again."

"Far too flashy." Elerek extended a shaky hand. "Let me see."

Summoning water, he washed away the blood. Though only a trickle compared to the river he'd conjured earlier, his vision spun and he pitched forward.

Razhar caught his shoulders. "Steady. Here, let me help."

Elerek pulled his leg over the cardant and allowed Razhar to ease him down from the saddle. Even after everything he'd said—and hadn't said—Razhar was still here.

If Razhar hadn't found him, remaining in Kushan to face his fate, would either of them be alive today? How swiftly would the curse's currents have taken him? Would Elerek have lived long enough to attempt death by his own hand?

"I'll try, Cormek. I'll try to live." That "trying" had become

one of the hardest endeavors he'd ever undertaken, a challenge as indomitable as the Sancen itself.

But the trying hadn't been entirely of his own doing.

"Just let me rest here." Down in the sands, he scooted back against the cardant, planting his spine against her warm scales. The reptile made no response. "I'll be fine."

Razhar took a strip of bandages from the packs and wrapped his arm. "For someone with a disagreeable attitude towards reptiles, you and the cardant seem to be getting along."

"It's not 'the cardant.'" One by one, Lystra took their packs down from the saddle and tossed them into the sand. "*Tiniah* keeps me from being outnumbered by you lot."

Once the queen had finished with the packs, she moved to the saddle, unhitching each clasp and meticulously rolling each strap. Elerek watched her hands, her skin again marked by the curse. Her movements were anxious, and her eyes kept darting back down the canyon they'd come, watching for the tungin's return.

Elerek drew a shallow breath. No, they were safe now, they had to be. As safe as three cursed could be fighting their way across the Sancen at high summer to break an impossible evil.

"Razhar." He craned his neck as his friend heaved the roll of tent poles beneath his arm like a pile of kindling. He couldn't waste a moment, not when he had so few moments left.

Razhar stilled, waiting.

"Will you . . ." It ached to breathe. "Will you really perish if we break the curse?"

Setting aside the poles, Razhar crouched beside him. The shadows seemed to gather in his eyes. "Don't worry about me, El. It's the kingdom that matters. That's your responsibility."

"You're part of my kingdom, Razhar."

A smile laced with sorrow spread across his face. The man

couldn't help but smile. "I contribute very little; it's a wonder I haven't been thrown out yet."

Elerek shook his head. Suddenly his mouth felt dry as cotton. Pushing his back off the cardant, he hunched forward, his head hanging. "Will you forgive me?"

What a marvel that those four words amassed such difficulty on his tongue.

Razhar didn't speak.

"My rage was unjustified, and I'm sorry."

Dropping his shoulders, Razhar gave a short sigh. "I deserved it, El." He slapped Elerek's shoulder with a sand-clad hand. "Let's put it behind us."

Elerek's insides twisted. "But—"

"For once, please don't argue." Razhar shook his head. "As I said, I'll go to the wrathgiver." Without another word, he stood and gathered the rest of the packs from the cardant's back.

And then what? Doubt assailed Elerek's mind like enemy arrows. It sounded so simple. Break the curse and then be broken himself. Years of anguish over in an instant. He wouldn't even drown.

His blood would save them—his tribe, his loyal family, his queen. They'd never had a chance to escape their cruel fate before. Such an opportunity couldn't be ignored.

But if Dalmah's words were true, he couldn't save Razhar. The thought broke his heart.

Elerek glanced across the canyon to where Lystra knelt rummaging through their gear. His eyes strayed to the bloodstain covering her shoulder, and the image of Myra bleeding out filled his mind. Another who paid for his mistakes.

"Razhar." He lowered his voice. "Did you really ensure that Myra was buried?"

Grief twisted his friend's face. "I wasn't there, the Jarkins kept me under watch. But our family promised that they'd do it."

Elerek leaned back against the cardant. "Thank you." He'd sent her to the far recesses of his mind, refusing to believe that she was dead. The memory hurt, as did every memory of every one of his tribe who had perished because of him. But Myra hadn't died because she was cursed; she'd died because she'd loved him.

Elerek's gaze turned to Lystra again. She'd loosened her hair, and it fluttered like an ebony wave against her back. It still felt strange, terrible even, that he loved her.

Was there hope? That perhaps their souls might bind themselves to one another, beyond the arrangements of their political marriage? Could they belong to each other?

Would Lystra be more than his partner, his queen, but his wife?

What of my vows? Elerek had taken them before his kingdom, before her, and while he'd shamelessly broken them, that hadn't set him free from them.

A vow is a choice, and they were his to commit himself to with his whole being.

Chapter 23

Lystra

Each time Lystra blinked, the darkness erupted with images of the tungin, jaws snapping and bloodlust glinting in their red eyes. Red like the blood covering Razhar's clothes, and the scales of the mangled cardant. The sight had made her want to weep.

Desperate for movement, a distraction, she combed through their pile of packs. With Razhar's help, the tent was pitched and their waterskins, empty by now, lined up.

She glanced to where Tiniah lay with her girth spread across the warm sand, her head nestled among the gravel. Elerek sagged against the reptile's belly, his chin dropped to his chest. His eyes were softly closed, lashes dark against his pale skin. In the fading light, with his hair damp and pressed against his scalp, he looked pitiably like a corpse.

"Razhar," she whispered, though she doubted that her voice would wake him. "Can we let him rest more comfortably?"

He nodded and rose to his feet. "I think our travels for the day are done."

Lystra released a slow exhale, thankful for a few hours' respite after their three days of sun and heat. To let her thoughts collect and muster what rest she could to her bones before . . .

Before the end, when the curse would take them both—and she'd be left alone.

Not alone. She'd have Tiniah. But alone across the Sancen, without water or passage back home until the summer's end. The Darcress Kasbah was equipped for such journeys, but it still lay beneath Jarkin occupation.

She closed her eyes, quelling the terror. She hadn't yet come to that mountain and there was no guarantee that she would survive that long.

Could Elerek do it? Destroy the entire army with his curse? After what she had seen today, she believed it—almost. Doubt crept into her heart as she watched Razhar kneel beside the king's sleeping form. Using his abilities had drained him, and they couldn't afford to let him lose control again.

Unbidden, tears misted her vision. She glanced down at her hands. Skinless. Cursed. Should she have come back? She'd complicated things, and Elerek certainly didn't need that.

The thought of his arms encircling her as Tiniah pounded across the desert filled her mind. His nearness, and the comfort it brought her, all entangled with the heat of that kiss—*his* kiss.

No, she chose this. She chose him.

Elerek woke with a start, drawing a sharp breath.

"Sorry."

Leaning forward, the king pushed a hand through his curls. The action made Lystra smile. "No, no, I . . . I was dreaming."

"A good one, I hope?" Razhar smiled one of his wining smiles. "Not that you and the cardant—" He looked at Lystra. "Beg pardon, Your Highness, *Tiniah*, don't look comfortable together." He shot a rude expression at the reptile. "Oi, don't make your queen jealous."

Stars, Lystra could kill him—and the face Elerek made told her that he perhaps thought the same. Her eyes moved toward the tent—the single tent they'd taken. Come nightfall, it would be tight—and very strange.

"It's still daylight." Elerek looked skyward, the reflection of blue eclipsing his gaze.

"You're many things, El. Stubborn, insensitive, endowed with the incredible abilities of an evil curse, and the powerful king of Instanolde, but you're not up for any more travel today."

Elerek gave him a look that could sour milk. "For the last time, I'm *not* insensitive."

"Come on." Razhar slipped an arm beneath his shoulders and winced. "A hand, Your Highness?"

Lystra rose, her steps a bit lighter with their much-missed levity. Razhar heaved Elerek up, an arm draped across his shoulder, and she came alongside the king, her movements mirroring those she had made the night she'd taken the curse. An arm around his waist. A hand planted against his chest. *Him.* Solid beneath her touch. Warmth bloomed on her cheeks.

Elerek's arm rested on her shoulder, but he immediately withdrew it. "Your wound."

"I'll be all right." Quite the opposite. Lystra knew she'd gone too long without treating it or changing the bandages. "Let's get you inside."

Moving as one, the three of them stumbled and hobbled into the circle of their tiny camp.

"I miss my chair," Elerek grumbled.

Razhar immediately followed with a dramatic sigh. "I miss food. Any sort of food that isn't stale or dried."

There were many things Lystra missed in Instanolde. Corsha and Kimzi. Her father. Chilled tea. Cardant races. Hot baths. Lystra's mind stalled on that last one, and she nearly began to weep.

Inside the tent, she knelt to spread the furs and blankets, covering the sand in the meager space.

"Actually, El, I also miss your chair." Razhar grunted as he, as gently as possible, lowered Elerek back to the ground.

Elerek's face twisted in a grimace as he straightened his legs. "I despise being so . . . hindered. I'm not used to feeling like this."

Lystra pitied him. Never had she seen him act restricted by his disability. Amid the palace corridors, his chair had seemed a part of him. As king, he'd made it his throne, and his steadfast devotion to his purpose had given him everything he needed to rule.

Yes, he was meant to be king. Born for it. The thought agonized her heart, and she wished so desperately that she could give him the kingdom.

"It's hardly your fault." Razhar checked the makeshift bandage on his arm. "Are you hungry?"

Lystra's hand moved to her stomach, as if its emptiness was something she could feel. Now that the thrill and terror of the chase had subsided, hunger wielded its claws.

"I need to sleep." Elerek gathered one of the blankets into a bundle. "It seems pointless, with so little time . . ."

So little time, and such a challenge before them.

"You need your strength." Her eyes met his. "And Instanolde may need your abilities."

Elerek's gaze held hers and she watched as the light sparked and burst into a steady and fervent flame. A fire that she knew passed from her; this had been their story. When one came to the end of their strength, the other carried them both. How was it possible that the short time that she'd known this man could seem like a lifetime?

How would she endure without him?

Managing a small smile, she brushed her fingers along his shoulder. "Rest well."

Wild, desert air filled her lungs as she left the tent. A slight wind blew up the canyon, tossing her hair and clothing. She turned her eyes to the sky, shining a deep blue against the canyon's stark red. Tonight, it would glow with starlight. How much closer would the wrathgiver hang in the eastern sky?

Starkindler, if you hear our prayers, even in this forsaken place, please, I cannot go on without him.

But she'd gone on without Cormek. Learned to walk and hold grief in her heart. Would this be a path that she would traverse again? Return to her kingdom alone, her heart shattered?

Lystra's hands drew into tight fists. She'd already chosen not to go back, a choice that very well meant dying, regardless of whether the curse was broken. The truth of it slammed against her soul with the weight of the eastern mountains themselves. The moment she'd chosen to turn back—chosen *Elerek* —she'd hastened the end.

Perhaps Cormek had been wrong when he'd told her to flee. He'd tried to spare her, much the same way Elerek fought to ensure that she'd outlive him. Instead, it was Gaudab Batu-Khasar, the murderer of Instan kings, who had spoken truly.

"The desert calls you back."

Tears teased at her eyes, causing the desert colors to swirl like paints upon an artist's brush. How did she make peace with it?

Chapter 24

Razhar

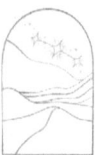

For the tenth time, Razhar checked the small bag that smelled of caramel. It was still empty.

His chest deflated in a long sigh. Digging into the packs, he withdrew a round of flatbread. He grimaced as he tore a piece and shoved it in his mouth. Hard as rock. An insult to "bread." Still, he swallowed, knowing a decent meal wasn't about to present itself anytime soon.

At least *he* hadn't provided the tungin with a decent meal.

His eyes swept over the bandage, taut against his forearm and still damp with the water Elerek had used to wash his wound clean. The entirety of the experience was one he'd rather not endure again, but . . . they'd come back for him.

"Have we much food left?"

Razhar looked up. He hadn't heard Lystra emerge from the tent. The queen stood with her hair seized in her hand, the wind having its way with it, and the last of the sunlight turned her eyes to gold.

"Enough." He withdrew another flatbread, handing it to

her. "I can't guarantee its freshness. Certainly nothing like those honey cream pastries they sell at the night market."

Good memories. The night market. Dancing. Pastries. Anything to block out the tungin teeth—and the fact that Elerek had saved his life while he carried the dagger with which to kill him. Bile rose in his throat as he glanced down at himself, his traveling clothes splattered with his own blood. How much worse would he feel if the blood belonged to the king of Instanolde? His best friend?

Lystra took the bread and seated herself beside him. "Oh, those were my favorite." Her nose wrinkled at the first bite. "Nothing like them at all."

Razhar managed a smile, but it only went skin-deep. Inside his chest, his heart quivered.

"Are you all right?" Lystra's eyes grew as large as her query. Razhar wondered if he possessed time enough to unpack such a question.

Rubbing his face, Razhar felt the sharp sting of sand scrape through his beard. "I think my arm will recover." *Speak, you idiot.* "I . . . well, you and El saved me. It could've just as easily been El dragged off the cardant, or you . . ."

Lystra blinked, the aloof expression of a queen filling her face. "Razhar, surely you didn't think we'd leave you to die?"

"Ah, well." He shifted, letting some of the tension from his sore muscles, but the rocky ground remained uncomfortable. "El made it abundantly clear what he thinks of me, now didn't he? But I have my uses."

And now, Elerek offered forgiveness. His stomach twisted with a weight far too queasy for their meager diet of rations. He hung his head. *I don't deserve his forgiveness.*

Not now, not with one more miserable secret molding in his heart. Maybe they ought to have left him behind.

"Uses?" Lystra's eyes caught fire, her words sizzling.

"Razhar, do you hear yourself? El has never loved you for your *uses*." She huffed. "Though you *have* been an idiot and ought to have told him about your abilities."

Razhar clenched his hands. Anger burned across his skin, prompting a fresh coat of sand to spring from between his pores. If he told him everything, then Elerek *would* only love him for his uses. Rage was an irregular emotion, it felt too akin to helplessness.

Why should I have to die? Stab my heart with the star-cast blade?

Nowhere was safe. Not even within the walls of Instanolde, where every direction painted a picture of perfect peace and prosperity. Death always lay one breath away. A sober fact buried beneath enough lies until one could nearly forget it.

"And if I can't do it?" Razhar forced himself to meet her stare head-on. "If the curse proves more than I can hold back? If I can't keep him human?"

What would happen to the curse if Elerek didn't—couldn't —break it?

Then, like water in the desert, the ferocity left Lystra's face. She reached for his hand, enveloping his fingers in hers. The curse swept back from her skin and his sands receded.

"Razhar," she whispered. Her eyes radiated kindness. Her touch warmth. Her voice held no scorn, no commanding air or aloof authority. Even the air she breathed seemed crafted of sincerity. "Your abilities have saved us, but so have your smiles. I think El knows that—and that he needs *you*."

Such a small thing, to smile, like amber grains of sand scattered to the wind. But even bits of dust could amass together and form deserts.

Razhar squeezed her hand, turning his gaze back to the

canyon's long shadows. "I'll try, Your Highness." Even Elerek learned to smile when the days were dark.

But Elerek didn't know all the things that he did.

Finishing her bread, Lystra stifled a yawn. "Will you keep watch? I'd like to rest."

Razhar nodded. "I'll wake you both when the stars dance."

The queen rose, her movements weary and stiff. "Thank you."

"Of course, Your Highness."

Once Lystra vanished inside the tent, the Sancen's silence filled his ears with a desolation somehow louder than screams. He hated it. Give him the sound of movement, of dish washing, food sizzling, sword drills, brooms sweeping. Laughter and chatter. Music and life.

Razhar yearned for it with his whole soul.

Reaching into his shirt, he removed the dagger. It was a relief that he hadn't lost it in the tungin attack. He set it in the sand beside him. He didn't doubt Lystra's sincerity, but surely the king and queen realized that they *had* to rescue the dagger as well as him.

He huffed. Perhaps he ought to settle for simple gratitude, that he still possessed that which he wanted most—to live.

Next, he withdrew the rolled scroll. Damp with Elerek's water, bits of parchment dissolved into soppy fragments. The word *Emblino* ran in tiny black tendrils. Damning evidence, only this tied his family to the curse at all, but it also condemned House Arghan. Razhar laid the writ on a rock, hoping it would dry. His baba's name, written in his own hand, was something he didn't want to lose.

His fingers moved to his open shirt, to the stars inked across his chest. He thought of the day he'd set foot inside the tattoo parlor, spreading a wrinkled parchment on the counter with the stars drawn by his baba's shaky hands mere hours before his execution.

A constellation that the tattooist called "fell stars."

"One can hardly help the stars beneath which they are born." It sounded like something Elerek would say, a dramatic quotation resulting from the copious hours the prince spent reading.

Really, he'd no idea which stars danced the night of his birth. He never knew his mother, who'd decided to find something better to do than remain at her husband's side and raise his child. But his baba had made him promise to remember these stars, the stars that knew the curse.

A tattoo seemed fitting. Not only would it make an interesting conversation piece, but he put a high value on his skin. Skin that hadn't turned to sand.

He'd burned that parchment even as the ink on his chest dried. Choosing to forever seal the truth within his soul. His visit to the tattoo parlor hadn't been long after his trip to Kushan, the first since his flight as a child.

A trip he wished he didn't have to make.

His stolen world had begun to change, like a constellation veering off dance. The curse behaved as it always had, but each death grated on Elerek's conscience like an herb crushed between a mortar and pestle, darkening his moods at a terrifying rate. It hadn't helped that Cormek had begun his public duties as prince-heir and that King Lorkin's adoration for Cormek continued to increase despite his failing health. Razhar also bore the burden of keeping Myra alive as their attachment grew.

Razhar had always known that the writ of the curse's sale lay deep in the archives, among his baba's records. Such things were best hidden. As long as Razhar had his abilities and stayed near Elerek, perhaps they'd pull through.

Then, Elerek tried to kill himself—and had nearly killed them *all*.

Sometimes the evil things could no longer be ignored.

When Razhar left for Kushan, a stranger among the red canyons, he sought the truth that he never wanted to find, but he'd never imagined that the burden of knowing that the curse could be broken would be *so heavy*.

He fought for life, for stolen days. And he wanted to live, to burn with the light of a thousand constellations. If Dalmah's words were true, he could have all that—if he only drove the cursed dagger into Elerek's chest.

But what about after? Could he move on? Forget that the whole thing ever happened? Perhaps he'd leave Instanolde, settle in a remote village of some tribe to which he had no connection. Find an occupation to busy his arms. Find a girl of his own to love. Watch the stars. Live.

It sounded impossible. If Elerek was destined to die, how could Razhar be destined to live?

Groaning, he pulled himself to his feet. Why did boots that were made for the wilderness do his feet such a disservice with this soreness? All this talk of destiny didn't sit well with him, like undercooked pastry dough. If not for the curse, that dark force of twisted human will, he'd argue that it didn't exist at all.

He didn't want to be destined. Not to anything.

"It's not my responsibility," he growled. "Why should I have to give my life? I'm no king and Instanolde isn't my kingdom."

But he would keep his word. He would go to the wrath-giver. Their world would tilt on the actions of the king of Instanolde—not that of a lowly Kushite.

You do see, that they—El and Lystra—have never treated you lowly? Razhar stilled. The admonition sitting heavy upon his shoulders. That was more than he could say for himself. He wondered why believing it came with such difficulty, almost as difficult as giving up his own life to break the curse.

Out of nowhere, a gust caused the entire canyon to shudder. The wind pulled his scarf over his shoulder—and swept away the curse's writ.

Razhar bolted after it. The writ caught in a swirl of dust, spiraling up into the sky. Beyond his reach. The last bit of his baba vanished into the rock. Claimed by the desert.

Just as it would claim him. A gaping void opened where his heart—his heart that only wanted to live—should have beat.

Chapter 25

Lystra

Inside the tent, the shadows deepened. Lystra held her breath as she crept inside, the tent's flaps shifting in an unfelt breeze. Elerek lay still, his back toward her.

She moved with the silence of a jerboa mouse. Her small pouch of medical supplies lay in the corner, and she took a fresh roll of bandages and the bottle of myrrh. Biting her lip, she stretched her arm over her shoulder, fingering the ends of the stiff bandages, plastered against skin and scabs. The thought of peeling it back made her want to cry.

Binding her hair with a huff, she loosened the fastenings of her tunic and drew it up over her head. She swallowed against the dried blood caked along her side and staining the wrap about her chest. Then, she gritted her teeth and slowly, painfully, pulled the bandage free.

Hot blood poured from the wound, its metallic scent burning her nostrils. Pain sent spasms of light across her vision. She bit back a whimper, pushing fresh bandages against her shoulder. Amid the blood and the broken scabs, she wondered, was the Jarkins' emblem still intact?

"Here, let me help you." Gentle hands covered hers, holding the bandage, and stemming the flow.

Her heart dropped as her stomach leapt. Lystra looked over her shoulder—and into Elerek's jade-colored eyes. The tent and its closeness, their nearness, seemed to lose its capacity for breathable air.

"I . . ." Her face burned.

Elerek drew the bandage back, his fingers immediately soaking it. The stains bled out against the white cloth like a burst of starlight. His eyes dropped to her shoulder, her skin prickling with heat beneath his incinerating gaze.

"I'm sorry," he whispered, his voice low and thick. "That he did this to you."

She heard it, the undercurrent of rage, flowing as easily as the cursed water from his fingers.

"It couldn't be helped." Lystra's hands clenched about her tunic, discarded in her lap. By all standards, she was covered enough, but still, she wished she could don it again.

Why? She had nothing to hide; she was married. She faced forward again. If she were to be so exposed, she might as well avert her gaze and not let him see the questions, the desires, forming in her own mind.

Cool droplets fell over her shoulder, along with the barest touches of his fingertips. She flinched.

"Hold still." Taking the damp bandage, Elerek cleaned the wound. "I'm not versed in anything like this."

Healing from the hands that had destroyed, drowned, and cursed. The thought filled Lystra with a hope that made her soul soar like the great condors of Kushan. Despite grief's haunting and the harrows of their journey, Elerek could still choose an act of generosity, of kindness.

She'd seen it, she knew it—that was *him*. Beyond the vengeful, cursed king able to drown armies, she'd glimpsed his heart in the small, the simple. His griefs had broken him, yes, but not shattered him.

"Is . . . is the emblem still visible?" Lystra held her breath.

A sigh escaped Elerek. "No, I think you've reopened it too many times." A trail of water ran down her shoulder and across her ribs and side, followed by the touch of his fingers, washing away the blood. Little rivulets of curse mark wound across her skin, a reminder that drawing near to this king was dangerous. The droplets were cool, but his touch was not. "It'll still scar."

"I can handle scars." Lystra closed her eyes. "But I'll not wear their disgusting mark on my skin."

"We all carry them," Elerek replied softly. After generously applying the myrrh oil, he took the roll of fresh bandages. With hands as careful as a physician's, he rebound her shoulder, tying it off just tight enough to not slip free.

Lystra lifted a hand to the soft gauze, the scent of the oil seducing her senses. "Thank you."

Elerek didn't speak. At least, not with words. His fingers lingered on the bandage, and then traced along her back, just above the band of her wrap. Leaning forward, his breath hot on her collar, his lips planted beneath her ear. A question. An invitation.

"We don't always get what we want." Lystra wanted him. To rid the curse from his skin. To save him from the cruel death beneath the stars. To give him the dawn and the sun. To honor the vows she had taken with a promise. To love him to the end of her days.

She turned, facing him. Beneath the intensity of his gaze, she basked in its glow, in the same desire she saw there, and did not hesitate to answer its call, wrapping her arms about his neck and drinking deep of his lips.

His arms enveloped her in their warmth, pulling her against his chest. Even through his tunic, the skin that stretched across taut muscles seemed set aflame. As his hands traveled down her back, fierce against her waist, it consumed them as the Sancen consumed flesh. No longer the numb deadness she'd felt the first time she'd touched him.

Lystra opened her eyes. "Can you—" His mouth was on hers again. "Can you feel me? Am I real, another warm body? Or do I feel . . . cursed?"

The fire doused in Elerek's eyes, turning them to polished stone. The hesitation, the tension, the wall they'd built between them suddenly manifested again. He was a fortress, beyond siege or ambush.

"I . . ." His breath hitched. "No, not cursed. Not now. It— the curse—knows well how to torment me."

With me. The curse is using me. Even now, as the mark moved with his hands, with his touch. Hopeless helplessness submerged her, as if Elerek still dangled from the cliffside, the deluge below, and Lystra could not reach him.

"What am I to you?" Lystra lifted her chin, set her shoulders, and became the queen he needed her to be.

Fear flickered across the hard surface of Elerek's gaze. Did he fear for himself? For her? For another loss? "How would you have me answer?"

"As you did on our wedding night." She drew close, her lips hovering just below his. "With nothing but the truth."

But he didn't kiss her. Instead, he bowed his head, his forehead touching hers. "You're real, Lystra. Real and wonderful. But the truth is that I am wretched and unworthy. That I take beautiful things and tarnish them. That I lose myself in my own darkness and drag others down with me." His eyes clenched shut. "If I tell you that I knew that I'd dishonored Myra and myself by taking her to my bed, it wouldn't matter, because I did it anyways. She was kind and beautiful and I loved her—but wrongly. When Cormek died, I swore to be a better man. To my kingdom, to the throne, and to myself. I made vows to you and . . ." A tear escaped out the corner of his eyelid. "I broke them. If I tell you how sorry I am, it doesn't change anything."

No, their past was written, including all their mistakes. But here, now, their moments were new. The promises they'd made to each other didn't have to die but could breathe and live.

"Vows can be rebound," Lystra whispered. "A vow is also a choice."

"Then have you chosen to forgive me?" A longing filled Elerek's voice and solidified the touch of his hands on her waist. "You know all my faults and failures. You've seen me for the broken man that I am."

Lifting her gaze, she watched him without blinking, studying each jade shard glimmering in his irises. Living, and loving, came with risks. She'd been hurt. Her heart still remembered how it had shattered when she'd learned of Myra and seen them kissing in the palace corridor. She could be hurt again. But her heart also knew that it could heal and be pieced back together—and this time, she could do it with him.

"You're forgiven, El. Know it while we still draw breath." Her fingers brushed through his curls. "And know that I chose to return to the desert. I refused to leave another king behind to die in the Sancen. Not another man that . . ." She paused, the air alive, pulsing with the heat and the beat of their hearts. "I love you."

Elerek pulled her against him again, kissing her as if it were the last thing he would do in this life. One hand remained at her waist, the other cradled her head. A gust of hot air riled the tent, fluttering its canvas, as if the entirety of the desert gave exultation.

Lystra planted her cursed hands on his chest, clenching fistfuls of his shirt. *If these moments, few as they are, are all that*

I have with you . . . She would steal them. A bandit of the desert. Her hand moved to his collar, to the lacings, and tugged them free.

The tent shuddered, another gust of wind threatening to pull it from its stakes, accompanied by a shrill, unearthly shriek.

Chapter 26

Razhar

Razhar blinked, smearing the tears from his eyes. What was that? Before him, the shadowed corridors of the canyon shifted.

A mirage, much like the shimmering haze that appeared along the flatlands, but this held form, fluttering against the rock in the bell shape of a long thobe.

Oh no, not you. They weren't supposed to be real.

Behind the first mirage, a second, and then a third, floated down the canyon. They moved with grace, smooth, and entirely invisible save for the dull, silver edges. The form of a ghost.

A wraith.

As they stalked silently toward the encampment, the mirage at the front paused. Its domed head turned. In a haze of something like dust and smoke, a skull-like face appeared, as if from beneath a hood of invisibility. It leered, its eyes dark as midnight. Fixed upon him.

Razhar's knees weakened. What was worse—tungin, wraiths, drowning, or turning to sand? All of them seemed determined to plague them this day.

The storytellers' voices filled his mind, deep and as old as the desert itself. Their sober eyes swept over their spectators, usually children whose parents were occupied haggling prices with the market's vendors. Razhar remembered being among those children, his knees scraped from scaling the palace walls and his mind spinning with the marvels of a thousand tales.

The wraiths might have been the souls of the lost, those too tainted to walk among the stars, or ancient demons damned to the desolations of the Sancen. But Razhar knew one thing for certain. They were real.

A high-pitched scream echoed through the canyon with another gust of wind, stirring spirals of dust in their wake. Razhar reached for the cursed dagger, drawing it from its sheath. Behind him, Tiniah rose on all fours, arched her back, and growled. Razhar had a depressing feeling that her teeth weren't going to save him.

Another hiss shattered the air. Razhar spun around as the smoky, skull-like face bore down upon him. The shifting mirage pushed against him, knocking him to the ground with the strength of a muscled Jarkin.

Razhar slashed with the knife, but the wraith seemed unimpeded. He backed away, scrambling for his footing, just to be confronted with another haunt. Curved, bony grins mocked him. Soulless eyes froze him to his core. Everywhere he looked, another face, another death seemed bent to destroy him.

Death always follows me.

Rock and cliff, still visible through the wraith's ethereal body, spun and wheeled like the warped lens of a drunken mind. The specter before him raised its arms as if to strike. Air swirled over them. Razhar's clothes fluttered, his hair blew over his eyes. And sand—it blasted against the side of his face in a thousand tiny shards. One would think he'd be accustomed to it by now.

Fine as salt and as sharp as steel. Just as he wiped his hand across his eyes, another shock of sand hit him, digging into his skin with thin, fine slices.

The wind stirred and the wraiths seemed to form an agreement. With each wave of their shimmering hands, another drudge of sand was drawn up from the canyon floor and pelted against him. One after another after another.

"Augh! No!" Razhar tried to stand, only to fall again. Their onslaught beat his back, buried his legs, and shoveled up against his arms. Sand caught in his mouth, scraping his throat —awakening memories of terror. Of the curse. Of the death he couldn't seem to escape.

But he'd no intention of being conquered. Not today. He breathed in the dust-strewn air and threw his hands up. Sand streamed from his fingertips. Mountains of it. Enough to fill the canyon. More than he'd ever been able to conjure before.

The wraiths backed away. Razhar rose to his knees, and then his feet. Yes, no denying it now, his powers *were* growing. Spinning in a slow circle, he drove them back. The sand blasted against them, revealing their great height and the extent of their flowing figures. Even Razhar, with his broad shoulders and advantageous height, felt small in their presence.

He spun faster and shut his eyes. His feet caught on to a memory and fell to the steps of a common Instan dance, keeping to the rhythm of his heartbeat, the only music he needed. The sands flowed in tandem, a part of him now. A warmth stirred within that couldn't come from the Sancen sun, but nights in the market lit by multicolored torches and galas where Razhar attended uninvited and discovered no one turned away an eager dancer. Each new dawn, he courted life with arms wide open.

I will not grow weary of life.

Death danced in his shadow, a willing partner upon whom

he'd chosen to turn a blind eye. He counted those cursed to die as his closest companions, his tribe, his family. Forgoing sleep, he became a watchman upon the ramparts, slipping by candle-light into quiet chambers to do battle. To fight the only way he could—pushing back the curse.

And that was what he would do. Fight for life.

He might have danced till the stars appeared. Even then, he would have danced in defiance of the wrathgiver. Not even the stars could seal his fate. Not when he could preserve another day beneath the dancing constellations and the burning desert sun.

Why could he not also fight for his own life? Deep in his heart, he knew the sacrifice to be noble, beautiful even. He ought to have leapt at the chance to lay down his own life if it meant freeing his friends—especially Elerek. But a cold and terrible fear held him back.

Is my life not worth fighting for?

Across the canyon, the wraiths had amassed more of their ghostly companions.

Razhar raised his hands and planted his feet, but this time, only a weak and pathetic sputter of sand fell from his fingers. The wraiths advanced, their path unobstructed.

Terror ran his blood cold. He dashed back to camp, hastily grabbing their packs. "El! Lystra! We've got to run, now!"

The tent flap fluttered and Lystra dashed out, her tunic wrinkled and her hair wild. The queen took one look at the wraiths and shrieked. She ran to Tiniah, shouting commands to the reptile and heaving the saddle onto her back.

Razhar tied their packs into place with clumsy, frantic fingers. Lystra yanked a strap from his hand with cursed fingers, her eyes set aflame. "Help El. I'll get this."

Nodding, he turned back to the tent where Elerek sat

planted in its entrance. His arms were raised, palms flat, and his eyes blazed with intensity.

From his palms, a wall of water rose from the desert floor, creating an effective barrier between them and the wraiths.

Razhar stared, awestruck. This water bore little resemblance to the frothing rage he'd created in the canyon. Smooth and almost still, it shimmered like a mirror.

"Hurry!" Elerek barked.

Razhar collapsed the tent, rushing to roll the canvas and bundle their blankets. By the time he affixed the gear to Tiniah's back, the queen had the reptile ready to flee.

Not a moment too soon. He rushed back to where Elerek guarded the wall of water as a sentinel of the curse. The skin had fled his hands and receded up his arms like the Gungole's shores, replaced by water.

No, there was no stealing summer days and starlit nights. Razhar knew the truth, deep in his bones, that the end was drawing near—maybe for both of them. Even Elerek's curse mark, the slash of water across his body, had changed. Visible upon his chest, it crept nearly to his collarbone.

Razhar frowned at his open, unlaced shirt and tousled hair. *I leave you two alone for ten minutes . . .*

"I can't . . ." Elerek's shoulders dropped, his arms straining. The wall quivered, sending white-capped ripples across its surface.

The wraiths shimmered through the wall, outlined in silver. The leader moved closer. A ghostly hand moved through the water, parting it.

Razhar marveled at the way Elerek stared, eyes unblinking, into the skull-like face of the wraith—into death itself—and didn't even flinch.

But his arms, arms turned to water, *did* falter and the wall began to melt.

Summoning sands to his fingers, Razhar came alongside him and grabbed his arm, supporting it. Skin immediately clothed Elerek's arm, but the waters didn't cease.

If anything, they rose, intensified.

Razhar could feel it, his abilities channeled into Elerek's. Was that why his own sands had increased? Somehow, together, they became something more. Something powerful.

Elerek's eyes shifted toward him. He felt it too. The pull of the curse, that evil that had interwoven their lives, now forging them anew. Not one or the other, lowly Kushite or king, curse or consequence, but both, together.

Could they—together—save Instanolde?

Razhar managed a weak smile. No, they weren't so different, and Elerek had forgiven him.

The combined use of their abilities was draining. Fatigue assailed his senses, nearly causing him to waver.

"Come! Hurry!" Tiniah's shadow fell across them, Lystra in the saddle.

Razhar met Elerek's gaze. "Ready?"

The king nodded, his face drawn and haggard, and let his arms drop.

As the wall of water collapsed, crashing against the rock with a sound like thunder, the wraiths vanished beneath the waves. Before the water could reach them, Razhar hoisted Elerek into the saddle, Lystra then gave the word, and they bolted down the canyon.

They rode until they could ride no more.

The sun began its descent, burning at their backs as they continued east. Razhar wished to the heavens that the cardant would suddenly become *comfortable*. He gripped Elerek's shoulders, not to hold on, but to keep the king upright.

"I told you to rest," he muttered, unable to help it.

Elerek made no reply, his head hanging and shoulders hunched.

When they finally halted, amid rocky boulders and criss-crossing bridges of stone, Tiniah growled and thrashed.

"Easy, easy," Lystra crooned. "I think she's had her fill of us."

"Likewise." Razhar slipped from the saddle, landing in the sand.

All at once, Tiniah bolted, still with two riders in the saddle, and rounded a bend in the rocky labyrinth.

Huffing, Razhar pounded after them, his muscles screaming in defiance. Then he noticed the vultures circling in the pale afternoon sky.

The air filled with hisses, echoing off each boulder and crevice and Razhar found the source of the cardant's excitement. A dead vulture lay strewn across the rock. Its living counterparts had considered its sacrifice worthy and hustled for scraps. Tiniah snapped at the birds, lunging forward to claim the carcass for herself.

The sound of bones snapping and crunching grated on his ears. Decaying flesh covered the sand, Tiniah's claws, her teeth . . .

Lovely. Razhar moved closer. Lystra kept her grip on the reins, unperturbed by the sight of the cardant feasting.

Meanwhile, Elerek leaned over the reptile's side and vomited into the sand.

"Honestly, though," Razhar sighed. "She ought to leave some for us."

Elerek gagged, pinching his eyes shut.

"Steady, Your Highness." Razhar offered his arm and assisted him down from the saddle.

Lystra also dismounted, letting Tiniah have her fill. Once again, they took their packs and endured the tedious motions of making camp. Razhar kept watch on the canyons, waiting for some new horror to materialize. He took a blanket, tangled in a hasty bundle, and handed it down to Elerek.

Propped against a boulder, the king had already drifted to sleep.

Razhar didn't know what would happen when they reached the wrathgiver. It was easier not to think of it. To hope —like the patronizing ray of sunshine he so wanted to be again —that some miracle would occur. One where nobody had to die. At this juncture, that seemed a reality beyond imagination. But he knew one thing now: Elerek's death would not come from his hand.

Lystra stepped past him, snatching the blanket. Kneeling, she spread it over Elerek with gentle hands clothed again in the curse's mark. She loved him.

Here in these moments as they hastened toward the end, Razhar was glad of it. He almost felt ashamed of what he must do. "Your Highness."

Lystra glanced over her shoulder, a question in her eyes. Kneeling in the sand, the dying light glinting off her hair, she looked like an exquisite flower, defying all odds to bloom. The touch of the curse, of Elerek, streaked across her face, her lips.

Razhar reached into his shirt. He felt the emptiness where the writ once lay against the ink on his chest, but it was the dagger in its golden sheath that he grasped. "I think you ought to hold on to this."

Rising to face him, Lystra blinked once, dark lashes fluttering.

Razhar pressed it into her hand, closing her fingers about the hilt and pushing back the curse along her hands and arms. Whatever power or sway the dagger held over the curse, his vow, his determination to push back the curse was far stronger. "The crown belongs to you."

A tremor shuddered through Lystra's shoulders, the only evidence that fear dwelt in her body. "My duty is to my kingdom."

"*And* to the man who rules at your side—the man you love." Razhar heaved a dramatic sigh. "Surely worthy of an epic or two. A song, at least." He sobered. "Whatever happens . . . the future lies in your hands."

And not his, even if it cost him his life. The realization settled his soul, like the winds after a sandstorm. The dust would fall where it would, shaping valleys and building dunes. He felt no shame. He didn't need immensity, power, or prestige. No kingdom or crown fell on his shoulders. But that didn't make his own decisions any less important. Any less insignificant.

Razhar was made to hold back the curse. To keep his friends alive to do what they must. It was no punishment, no consequence, but an honor.

And perhaps, deep in his soul, he might yet learn to believe it.

Chapter 27

Elerek

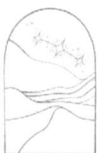

Darkness, from bleak horizon to bleak horizon. What mountains could be distinguished from the murk were sharp and cruel. Beneath them, where land might have spread, perhaps even the sands of the Sancen, lay submerged in water.

Raging, frothing water. Depths made to drown in.

But not for him.

He was the water, his consciousness extended to every drop.

Though the water covered the land, even rising to hurl itself against the mountains, chipping away at them stone by stone, the water wasn't satisfied. It wanted more. To consume. To destroy.

Elerek jerked awake. Pain knifed up his spine, sore from the boulder at his back. His skin was cool and damp, from the curse or cold sweats, he couldn't tell. Up above, darkness covered the sky, and for a moment he panicked, thinking the dream had bled into reality.

"El?"

No, the Sancen still surrounded him with its consuming bleakness. Their camp stood on a ridge, its pale stone just visible in the indigo murk. A blanket spread over him and a weight rested against his shoulder. Elerek found the comfort of starlight reflected in Lystra's upturned eyes.

"Are you all right?" She nestled against him, clutching another blanket around her shoulders. Her nearness still felt foreign, something forbidden yet desired. So close, and yet the layers of blankets separating them seemed too great.

His mind returned to the tent, before Razhar and the wraiths had so irritatingly interrupted them. The feel of her in his arms. The bare skin of her back soft beneath his touch. Her lips sparking a raging flame against his. Never had he imagined . . . *she's my wife.*

Theirs was not a relationship meant to be intimate, to even touch.

Now, he wished things were different. Fiercely.

The thought of even desiring such a thing stabbed his soul with guilt. His past sins still lingered upon the fringes of his mind. Memories he couldn't erase, they simply were. But she forgave him. All of it.

She loves me and she forgave me. And, by all the stars in the heavens, he loved her with his whole, broken soul.

Lystra blinked, still awaiting his reply.

Elerek looked away. "I'm weary, sore, and I keep dreaming."

"Dreaming of what?"

Tilting his head back, Elerek's gaze searched for stars. He spied the north maiden constellation, always the first to appear, twirling across the skies with her tambourine pointed forever to the north. For this reason, musicians stood positioned toward the north end of a celebration, following her lead.

His heart thudded against his rib cage at the thought that he would never hear music again.

The noise and thrum of the galas Cormek so often threw had never thrilled him. Too many people. Too many accidents waiting to happen. But now, stripped away, he found himself missing all that Instanolde held dear.

Breaking the curse would save Instanolde—because he would save Lystra.

A still, tiny voice within him whispered: it wouldn't be enough.

"I dream of starlight." His whisper seemed to float on the warm breeze flowing over the ridge. "The wrathgiver haunting me. The dark, furious waters of the curse. My fingers losing control. The curse shaping me into some terrible monster, much like the wraiths or the tungin."

"You're not a monster, El." Lystra tilted her head toward him, her dark hair hanging like a curtain of silk.

Her words echoed his own, spoken so long ago. Another night of stars and daggers. Then, Elerek had actually believed them.

"I've dreamed of Darcress," he murmured. "I've never been there. Never seen the kasbah fortress. But in my dreams, I see the place where my brother died—consumed by water. My water. My curse." His chest expanded, drinking arid air with lungs that would soon hold water.

"Are you going to do it?" Lystra's voice was hardly more than a breath, but her words belonged to the clever, logical queen that he'd come to love. "Drown them all—and take back Darcress?"

"Darcress must be liberated, and it must be done before the curse is broken." Elerek hung his head. "There's no other way." By him. One man—against an army.

Lystra continued to watch him, her gaze as sharp as the rough-cut cliffs.

"I . . ." Elerek couldn't speak. His heart pounded in his chest with the sound of war drums. If he pushed harder, went farther —he'd lose himself. He wouldn't die. What would become of the curse? Without the dagger spilling his blood beneath the stars . . .

Instanolde would be saved, but not his family. Not his queen.

Frustration burned hot in his chest. He cast away the blanket and hauled himself up onto the boulder, letting the wind touch his face.

Lystra stood, still clutching her own blanket about her shoulders.

"Where's Razhar?"

"Sleeping." She nodded toward the tent. "I didn't want to wake you, and you both needed a moment's peace."

Peace, something he might never feel again. What would happen to Razhar if he turned to water instead of dying? Would he turn to sand?

Elerek released a long exhale. His blood sizzled, hot, furious, and so terribly afraid. He needed to see the stars. His eyes followed the stretch of lonely landscape. The ridge dropped to a flat plateau, its rock turning cobalt in the fading light. Above, the sky reached the horizon. The mazes of rock, ridge, and canyon couldn't be bound by a map, but the sky he could read.

"Will the cardant suffer just a bit farther?" Elerek pointed to the edge of the plateau. "Just along there?"

Casting aside the blanket, Lystra strode to where the cardant rested, still saddled and harnessed. Soft wisps of her hair, like strokes of ink, blew back from her face. Last light glimmered in her eyes as she faced the west, as if searching for any shimmer of fair Instanolde.

And yet the whole of the golden city seemed merely a tarnish in comparison to her.

Lifting the reptile's head, Lystra scratched a tender spot beneath her maw. "Only if you remember that her name is Tiniah."

Its orb-like eyes slipped closed and, Elerek supposed, one could almost envision a subtle, sharply toothed smile on its jaw.

The sheen of gold caught Elerek's eye, tearing his gaze to Lystra's hip. The dagger.

He didn't know how she'd again come into its possession, but it always seemed to return to her. The weapon of another queen without a crown or throne, used to enact a terrible revenge. He feared nothing from Lystra, remembering well when she had surrendered the weapon to him on their wedding night. But would she surrender it again? When it came to the moment? Would she watch as he drove it into his heart?

Again, the feeling of rage and rising waters threatened to suppress his lungs. Even the Sancen's enormity hadn't the room for his crowded, disheveled, furious thoughts firing like rogue arrows from untrained soldiers. He needed air. He needed the sky. He needed to live.

Lystra brought the cardant—Tiniah—near enough for him to climb back into the saddle. Rather than take the reins, she instead pushed them into his hands and mounted behind him.

"She's weary and calmed, you can handle her." Lystra's arms tightened about his waist. "I'd like to see you sharpen your skills as a cardant rider."

Elerek blinked, catching the reptile's giant eye watching him from beneath its thick lid. He stared back, assertive, remembering the fury of scales and teeth that thundered into the palace courtyard on the day he decided to buy the reptile for his new queen.

"I'm glad to know an expert." His fingers brushed Lystra's

leg, nestled against his own. The numbness of the curse fled, replaced by a heat he couldn't quench.

Starkindler, it isn't fair. She's mine . . . and she's to be taken from me.

How would freedom feel tingling in his fingers? If his skin no longer held the touch of death? If the curse were broken for all time? If no one else had to die because of him.

His chest seized. Years had passed since he'd thought like that. Fanning the flames of impossible hope and now, he was liable to burn.

They woke Razhar, who begrudgingly, with eyes heavy with sleep, agreed to watch the camp. With Lystra's stern, but careful, instruction, he guided the cardant along the plateau. The wind blew against their faces, lonesome and wild. Elerek kept watch on the skies, on the daunting line of mountains and crags. As the sky darkened, more stars appeared, streaking across the sky and vanishing behind the rocky spires. Not yet defined enough to be identified, he found himself watching with rapt attention. Waiting.

Searching for the wrathgiver.

"El." Lystra's hold on him tightened, an anchor to the reptile's back, to reality. "Do you think there are more wraiths out there?"

A shudder assailed his skin at the memory of the wraiths' hooded heads and soulless eyes. "Maybe," he murmured. "I didn't believe they were real." In the stories he'd read—most myth and not meant to be taken as fact—the specters haunted places of darkness and desolation, drawn to it. Had they come because of them? Drawn to the death that he carried?

But they didn't come for him. Rather, Razhar had held their attention.

The cost. The consequence. Razhar's touch held death at bay, prolonging life. This didn't make sense. He wondered again at the Jarkins' musings. Could Razhar be a counter curse?

If he were, why hadn't he told them? Elerek shook his head. He didn't want to distrust Razhar. Not anymore. If these days were his last, he wanted to live without guilt, shame, or regret. He wanted to live.

As they approached the edge of the plateau, the rock sloped down to a steep precipice. Below, a dark labyrinth of canyons and crevices appeared as a sea of midnight with highlights of silver, like whitecaps, shining on the jagged edges of rock.

Above, the sky filled with the purest, white light.

Elerek beckoned Tiniah to halt. He'd loved the stars all his life, but he'd never seen them like this. So close he could almost touch them. Diving and dancing, they spun in a mesmerizing display of glory. The heavens where the Starkindler dwelled.

He so rarely visited the temple, that jewel of a building shimmering in the heart of Instanolde where the air hazed with incense and the priests' deep voices echoed over the marble. The curse kept him bound to the shadows in a way that even being crippled never had. And when Cormek had been declared heir, King Lorkin also gave Elerek a declaration—that he would keep out of the way. Cormek would be seen, Elerek would not, and the king that Instanolde had grown to hate cast his firstborn son aside.

Elerek blinked back bitter tears at the memory. Had he ever witnessed a single act of fairness? Had the Starkindler watched, even then, as sorrow after sorrow visited his years? The holy texts given him by the priests who tended the palace spoke of formality, tradition, and ancient rites. Stories of noble heroes and tragic cautions, of perseverance and diligence, set to produce worthy endeavors in the hearts they touched.

Meanwhile, he had known grief. Grief as dark as a starless sky.

He hung his head, broken by the sight. The skies of another world, a place beyond the mortal and the broken and the toil. No starlight remained for him.

"El?" Lystra shifted behind him, freeing an arm to point toward the east, where the mountains weren't quite so tall. "Is that it?"

The wrathgiver.

Elerek knew it as he would know any other constellation. It hung close, its movements precise and fluid, brighter than all the others, its knifed hand extending toward him.

The cold numbness spread across his body. He reached for his collar. The horizon of the curse mark had also spread, consuming his chest and shoulders. He wondered if the constellation also felt the strain of the unholy act that wrought the curse. Maybe the stars also wished for freedom.

"We're close," Lystra whispered.

He heard the taint of sorrow in her voice. Were they close enough to break it?

Everything his heart had yearned for, even in those early days, when the guards, attendants, and nursemaids rotated so frequently, their countenances bitter and angry at the prospect of caring for the king's crippled son. Years passed before Elerek realized why they were bitter, why the faces changed so often. Why his mother was dead. Why his father never embraced him.

The curse had done this to him. Stolen, ravaged, *destroyed*. Corrupted his soul and corroded his body. Sent him down spirals, punishing him as no one deserved to be punished. An existence he couldn't escape, a hold he couldn't break.

And the answer—was his death.

He understood the desperation that laced Razhar's voice, to suffer for something that they'd no hand in binding. To desire its breaking more than air, more than life, and to swear to do anything to see it done.

Elerek reached for the golden sheath tucked into the sash at Lystra's hip. Before she could react, he withdrew the dagger, the blade practically glowing with starlight.

His queen clutched his arm. "El . . . wait."

Immediately, his hand turned to water. No longer flesh and blood but cursed and terrible. He gripped the hilt tighter, afraid it might slip—or, without prompting, drive itself into his chest.

"It has to be broken, Lystra." His body turned cold. "It *has* to."

One more death and nobody else had to die. How else would he set her free? Rid her beautiful amber skin of the mark of his death?

Lystra dismounted, moving to the cardant's neck. Her eyes turned up to his, wide and filled with starlight. "Breaking the curse won't save us, El. Not anymore."

"And what of *me*?" The words came out as a growl, the monstrous voice of the inhuman creature he thought himself. "Haven't I suffered enough? I can't bear it anymore, Lystra."

"You must." Her voice was stern, insistent. "We need you whole."

We. That single word, spoken by the lips of his queen, seemed to encompass the whole of Instanolde. The people of the great houses, the outlying tribes, the merchants, and the rest who strode its streets. There were none ordinary or common, not in his kingdom. But they were threatened. They too, felt the fear of perishing before the stars faded.

Could this be what the Starkindler wanted of him? To use the curse to blanket the desert and cast the invaders into the torrent? To coat his cursed hands in blood?

But to come all this way, to survive this long, and *not* break the curse was a vile failure. To not die, to be absorbed into the horror and dark depths of the curse, sent his mind reeling.

An oath slipped over his lips, and he wondered why so much must be asked of him. Clenching the reins, water streamed from his fist, dripping over the reptile's scales. Tiniah shuffled and muttered, for which Lystra shushed her.

Elerek hunched, his shoulders bristled. "I was never whole, Lystra. I've been broken for longer than my memory knows. Don't I deserve freedom from this hell?" Even now, as he'd glimpsed heaven?

No, he didn't want to die. He wanted a place beneath the dancing constellations where darkness couldn't consume, and he wanted Lystra with him.

The queen climbed back into the saddle, this time in front of him, so near he couldn't ignore the burn of her eyes, the sway of her hair floating in the breeze, the soft, lithe shape of her frame. The curve of her lips, delicate against her amber skin, that he longed to kiss again.

"I don't mean unbroken, El." Her words were a breath. "We all harbor guilt and shame, cracks in our foundations."

"If I were stronger . . ." Perhaps the curse's murderous pull wouldn't have sunk its talons so deep into his soul. The clouds that hazed his mind and consumed his thoughts might have been pushed aside, forging his intentions with nobility and honor. Maybe the mistakes he'd made might not have outnumbered the sand.

Lystra ran her fingers down his face, tracing his jaw. "You're the strongest person I know."

Air shuddered in his lungs. No, weakness hadn't brought him this far.

"You're forgiven, El. Know it while we still draw breath."

If she could extend forgiveness, broken as he was, he wondered if it were possible to forgive himself.

Lystra neared, the scent of myrrh still clinging to her clothes, and drew herself to his lips. Water and tears mingled with their kiss, surrounded by desert sands and dancing stars. All else faded. All else besides Lystra.

She was the dawn, and he was left blinded. She was warmth and he no longer could feel the touch of death, even as skin fled her fingers as they moved down his neck and chest, taking the waters of the curse.

Weakness couldn't love Lystra. Not this queen who had loved and lost and loved again. No, her ferocity, bold as the dawn, required a strength to rival the Sancen itself.

Shame fell away as a garment. Desire fanned an unquenchable flame and seared across his heart. Hooking his arm around her waist, his hand planted against her back, he pulled her close, kissing her with a fierce and desperate longing.

"Stay with me." The words shuddered past his lips, air burning in his lungs. "Till the end. You've been my queen—gem of the Gungole, fire of the Sancen, fierce as the dawn, and mighty as the constellations. But as the man that I am, will you be my wife?"

Chapter 28

Lystra

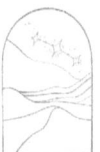

"*Will you be my wife?*"

The soft winds of the desert swept Lystra's breath away, consumed by the fire and intensity of Elerek's kisses. The thrill coursing through her soul reminded her of the moment she commanded her racers, when the air rushed, sand flew beneath pounding reptile claws, and all the world became a blur.

She already bore the crown, the title of his queen and his wife. Still, the simple beauty of it sent her heart soaring beyond the spires of rock and boulders.

Gazing up at him, the map of the skies spread across his eyes, she smiled. "Till starlight parts us, my love is yours."

An echo of the formality, the vows spoken before the priests and dressed in royal robes. The days since had been filled with chaos, but here, witnessed by the heavens above, the silence became somehow reverent, a testimony to all they had built of both beauty and pain and all they had broken to be tested by fire.

The words had hardly caught upon the desert wind before

his mouth closed in on hers again. A rich, deep kiss beneath the skies with all the spark of a dying star's last brilliance.

He's going to die, and I cannot save him.

Lystra's heart beat furiously, a longing in her body that went far beyond the desire stirred by his love. His touch was gentle, sweeping up her spine, avoiding the bandages he so carefully bound earlier, and into her hair. But his other hand still held the unsheathed dagger, the light of the wrathgiver reflected on its blade.

Elerek's work was saving Instanolde. Drowning the Jarkins and taking back Darcress. Whether by the heavens or the hells of the curse, he'd been forged for this task.

And her duty, bound by honor and the sacredness of their marriage covenant, was to stand by his side. To see him through whatever would come—even if it meant their deaths.

No. She couldn't think of it. Focus belonged to this moment. Right. Now.

She didn't want to feel sorrow—only to feel him. The gentle sweep of his fingers, the dance of his lips over her neck. The strong, solid feel of his arms, his shoulders, his chest—he felt like Cormek. But she and Cormek had only known joy. They'd never tasted sorrow, never been pierced by grief. Broken.

But somewhere in that brokenness, the loss, and the heartache, she and Elerek had come together like iron, glowing and hot, melted as one, aligning their lives as perfectly as the constellations above. Like they'd been meant to find their way through the haze and deceiving mirages to this moment, where the heavens shimmered above and Sancen dust lay beneath. They were the miracle. The extraordinary.

Beneath them, Tiniah shuffled. Startled from their kisses, Elerek's grip tightened, forcing the air from Lystra's lungs in a short gasp.

"Sorry." His eyes darted toward the reptile's head, as if in reproach.

"I won't let you fall." Lystra slipped an arm around his waist. "Certainly not from a cardant." This lighter conversation almost seemed a sacrilege with the lights of the heavenlies hovering so close, creation set afire with glory.

Starkindler, please, spare him.

A tiny prayer to an expanse of stars, the skies unhindered. And yet Lystra felt a beckoning. An emboldening. Perhaps they were not alone, even here, even now.

Lystra dropped her gaze, her finger tracing down his shoulder, his forearm, to flesh that had become the curse. "Let me carry it. Until it's time."

Elerek's fist, formed by water, grew tighter about the dagger's hilt. "The time may not come, Lystra."

Her heart constricted beneath the weight of the impossible journey they'd toiled. Lystra inhaled deep, speaking words that she knew she must believe.

"You've come so far, El. I don't know how this journey is destined to end. Whatever happens . . ." Despite her best attempts, tears filled her eyes and sobs choked her throat. She no longer could speak with the cultivated strength of the queen of Instanolde. Now she was merely a girl, holding on with the last of her strength and all her love. "Please, don't lose sight of the beauty you've given this world—and to me." His watery grip lessened. She took the dagger from him and slid it back into its sheath. For another day. Another time. "You are not your curse, so even if the curse must destroy our enemies, do not let it destroy you."

Even here, in the desolation of the Sancen, perhaps death could not always be the victor.

His eyes, bold and intense, stared hard into her own. She saw the strength in his soul. The resolve. Wrought from a prowling lion, a mighty cardant, a noble condor. A king of all the horizons beneath the star-cast skies. She loved him for it.

Elerek's hand traced her face, pushed through her hair, and pulled her head to rest against his chest, filling her ears with the pounding intent of his heart, the fight of his very being.

"I didn't know. . ." His voice murmured like the sound of many waters. "Like this . . . so quickly . . . I love you, Lystra."

A smile broke against her lips even as the tears fell down her face.

Their losses could outnumber even the glorious stars above. But they had *this*.

They could only linger so long before the night's chill drove into their bones.

Lystra took Tiniah's reins, directing them back toward camp. Elerek didn't speak, still seated behind her. He held a firm grasp on her waist, his thumb moving in a slow caress along the slight curve above her hip.

Stars. She longed for their cares to flee across the desert. A moment she could take him to herself. But a war lay ahead of them, a future of churning waters. A necessary work, what their kingdom required, and they would see it done.

Tiniah's harnesses and saddle were stripped, and the massive reptile settled near their solitary tent. Razhar had proved a terrible watchman, having retreated inside the tent as a slumbering lump with a pile of blankets smothering him. Lystra and Elerek shared a scant meal of crusty flatbread and the last of their dried meat. After the waterskins were filled, they cast one last glance to the dancing heavens, the wrathgiver eclipsed by the mountains again, before taking refuge for the night.

Razhar didn't move as they crawled inside and Lystra fastened the tent's flap—at least, until Elerek's elbow collided with his ribs.

"Ow!" Razhar stirred with a hiss. "Stars above, must all of me be sore?"

"That truly was an accident." Elerek yanked one of his superfluous blankets away. "But you were supposed to keep watch."

Razhar grumbled. "I did. It's your turn."

"It most certainly is not."

Lystra spread the soft skins out as best she could in the tight space. "Are you refusing an order from your king, Razhar?"

Thrusting aside the blankets, Razhar sat up, muttering beneath his breath. "You ask too much of your subjects." He huffed. "But I'll go. At least you can't kick me on my way out, *Your Highness*."

This time, the elbow to the ribs was intentional. "Comments like that will you get you exiled." Elerek drew the blanket over his legs and reclined, his face toward Lystra, and she glimpsed the smirk of comradeship on his pale face.

Perhaps they truly had forgiven each other, and the fact warmed her heart.

Razhar unfastened the tent flap again, spilling starlight inside. "You've been threatening to exile me for *years*, El. I still don't think you could stand by that decision—not that you *stand* by anything else . . ."

Elerek pushed himself up again with a monstrous glare. "Now you're just digging your own grave. Shut up and do as you're told."

"Actually, *I* will exile you." Lystra nestled beside Elerek, placing her hand on his chest. "I'd prefer this tent to myself—and my husband."

Razhar huffed. "Maybe you're right—I *don't* need sleep." He hurried outside and secured the tent again.

We need him. Jests and jeers aside, the fact sobered Lystra. Perhaps Elerek wouldn't lose himself to the curse. A way to keep him anchored, tethered, in control, Razhar could keep Elerek alive—alive long enough to die.

But these were far too heavy thoughts for the end of such a day. As Elerek lay down, he immediately flung his arms around her and pulled her against his chest. His hand found the hem of her tunic, sliding over the skin of her back. Warm and secure—and strangely peaceful—her fears and sorrows melted away, like cursed water seeping into the sands.

"I love you," she whispered with a smile.

Elerek responded with a kiss.

Chapter 29

Razhar

Razhar blinked sand away from his lashes, pale sunlight warming his skin. He rubbed his eyes, his fingertips revolting against the rub of sand and dried sweat. This vagabond life really didn't suit him.

True to his word, he'd kept watch—mostly. The night had been still, peaceful after the harrows of the day, and he was thankful for that, since he'd dozed off a few times.

He reached for his waterskin, pouring a few drops into his hands. An illusion of cleanliness, but it made him feel a bit more human.

Grimacing, he rubbed his fingers together, the motion reminiscent of that of merchants rubbing coins, listening to the song of profit. But instead of coins, grains of sand that didn't come from the desert shifted between his skin. No, the curse wouldn't allow them any humanity before this was over.

Shaking the sober thoughts from his mind, Razhar stood. The desert lay as immense and desolate as ever. Razhar cast off a slight shiver as the lonely canyons filled his vision. The sun hadn't yet made its traverse over the peaks, leaving the Sancen cast in a palette of pale violets and dull blues.

Razhar lifted a hand and concentrated, letting a curtain of sand rain from his fingertips to be caught in the winds. His mind conjured the image of the wall of water erected between them and the wraiths. An impressive feat from the cursed king of Instanolde. And when Elerek wavered, Razhar had become his strength.

The curse became magnified, strong, but not consuming, with their opposing forces working together.

Opposing forces. It wasn't quite true. No, the surrounding desert, with its canyons, dunes, and clean-cut rock stood testament to that. They were the forces that shaped the Sancen. Sand and water.

Razhar swallowed. This went beyond simply keeping the cursed alive. No, this was his part. Not just as the cost, the consequence, but as something more.

The sounds of stirring and gentle waking came from the tent. Razhar smiled to himself, imagining the couple wrapped in each other's arms. He grabbed their packs with their meager supplies. They had precious little left, and his heart sank. The finality of it all bordered on depressing. How many days did they have left? One? Two?

Lystra appeared, her hair tangled and her clothing rumpled. She looked nothing like the regal queen their kingdom knew, but the light in her eyes rivaled all the gold in Instanolde.

"Sleep well?" Razhar's gaze trailed on her lips, marked again with the pale sheen of the curse. When did the curse start doing that? That a touch provoked the curse marks?

Since this tedious, agonizing journey began. Since they'd begun to chase the stars.

"Mm, for once." Lystra tossed her hair over her shoulder,

turning her gaze to the horizon, as if in anticipation of the glorious dawn.

The closer we get to the stars . . . Razhar's stomach knotted. What would it be like at Darcress? Beneath the wrathgiver? His hand moved to his chest, to the fell stars etched in his skin.

The tent flap opened again. Using his arms, Elerek pulled himself into the tent's doorway and stretched his legs out in front of him. Razhar blinked. He ought to blame the desert, the Jarkins, and the toil of their journey, but Elerek looked as if he'd aged a hundred years. Darkness hung beneath his eyes. His skin appeared paler, despite the constant exposure to the sun, as if it intended to fade completely away—and turn to water.

"Razhar?" Elerek caught his stare, watching him with a hawk's intensity. "Are you all right?"

He moved a hand to his stomach. Perhaps he might stretch their rations a bit further. Stepping back toward the camp, he settled cross-legged on the rock, putting himself at eye level with Elerek, as he knew his friend would appreciate.

"The curse is stronger now, El. You know this?"

Sorrow shadowed the king's features. "Yes." At his collar, Razhar could just see the curse mark, reaching with finger-like tendrils up his chest, as if seeking to seize his heart.

"I think it's the stars. The closer we get to the wrathgiver, the more powerful you're becoming. Perhaps . . ." He huffed. "The curse doesn't want to be broken."

The severity in Elerek's eyes burned like a beacon from a watchtower. "I know. That is why breaking the curse must become our secondary mission. When we arrive at Darcress, I will eradicate the Jarkin army. Drown. Them. All."

Razhar blinked. There must have been sand in his ears.

Drown.

Them.

All.

In a matter of days, the king of Instanolde had gone from executing one Jarkin soldier in a prison cell, to facing off against the invaders, nearly swallowing the caravan in the canyons, and now he wanted to single-handedly take on an *army?*

"El . . . you'll permit the curse to go unbroken?"

Torment and strength fused in Elerek's gaze. An expression Razhar knew well, the same that the forsaken heir, the cursed prince, and the king who had risen from the ashes had worn all his life. The look of a man who still encountered his inner demons and had learned to fight them better.

Elerek lifted his head, his shoulders squared and broad as the horizon. "If I die and break the curse, what will become of Instanolde? Of my vows to my kingdom? Of all that I've sworn to protect?"

"But at what cost?" Razhar sputtered. Surely the curse wouldn't just *let* Elerek bend the power of the curse to his own will.

Alas, he knew the answer. The curse demanded a death, and a death it would receive.

He glanced at Lystra. Her curse-marked fingers, cast in a silver sheen of water, plaited her hair into a long, gleaming braid. The queen lowered her face, her skin stripped away by the brush of her lover's lips.

Stars above. Fury burned in his chest. This was wrong.

Razhar rose to his feet. Just as Lystra completed her braid, he offered her his hand, pushing back the curse marks and clothing her again in skin. No, he couldn't allow Elerek to do this. The king couldn't sacrifice Lystra, not even for the whole of the kingdom. Not after he'd fought so hard to save her.

And what about me?

"You can't talk me out of this, Razhar." Agony marred the fortitude upon Elerek's face.

Oh, yes he could. "You once called me a patronizing ray of

sunshine." Razhar puffed out his chest, heat rising at his throat. "At least, before you take matters into your own hand—and let the curse consume you—let me be patronizing."

"Excuse me?" Elerek raised an eyebrow.

Razhar marched forward, towering over the king. "Just like that? You'll leave us—leave *me*—out of the equation? All those who've suffered and carried the weight of this curse? Norbah, Driss, Cole—even, stars, Lystra? You'll sacrifice us all?"

Elerek's eyes flashed, embers burning with starfire. *"Razhar . . ."*

But once his tongue had let loose, Razhar found it difficult to stop. "El, you're supposed to be different—better than this, than all the other kings!" His voice echoed back at him across the desert expanse just as his baba's voice echoed in his mind.

"Kings send lowly men to pay in their own blood for what they weren't meant to pay."

"Razhar!" Elerek growled, his expression fierce. "As your king, I command you. Sit. Down."

Shame rolled over Razhar's shoulders, like the breaking of the curse's rolling waves. He took a step back, letting his shadow slip away from Elerek. The morning light illuminated the king's face again, pale against his cheekbones and bright in his eyes.

His baba spoke of one king. Not all. Not this king. Razhar seated himself, their eyes level once again.

"Are you done?" Elerek's tone cut sharper than the dagger meant for his flesh.

Grinding his teeth, Razhar glared down at his hands. Sand gathered along his fingertips. "I'm sorry, El. You can't."

Elerek opened his mouth to speak, but it was Lystra who gave reply. "Not alone. He needs you, Razhar. You can keep him tethered and prevent the curse from taking control—from taking him."

"I need you to find him." He'd done as his baba asked. He'd found the cursed king of Instanolde. A way to survive, to live. Now, Razhar prepared to go to war.

He hung his head, his hair hanging in clumps around his shoulders. What if he couldn't do it—fight? He'd never been a soldier nor held any desire to lift a weapon. He'd seen what violence had done to his own tribe—the bloodshed of the innocent and the bitterness of the survivors.

But it wasn't about the battle or the fight—it was about the curse, and his part in it.

"The starlight makes our powers stronger," he muttered. "We've come so far. We can't let the curse win."

Elerek's eyes skimmed the horizon, the muscles along his jaw taut. "And I don't desire its victory. I'm doing what I can with what I have—and I carry the curse."

But so do I.

Razhar's hands drew into tight fists. Perhaps Elerek wielded the authority of the crown, but Razhar held the curse and its secrets—and he'd been wielding them like weapons nearly his whole life.

One more secret. One more burning secret.

A secret to level the sands between them, just as Razhar had lowered himself to eye level with the king who could not stand without the aid of others.

"El . . . you're not the only one who's cursed. I carry it too."

The king narrowed his eyes. "You're the cost—"

"This?" Razhar reached out to clasp Elerek's hand. Sand and water flung from their arms until their contact was only that of skin. Real, human skin. "This isn't the cost part."

I will not be the cost any longer.

Lifting his gaze, he looked into the eyes of the king who had become his friend, his brother, the other half of the curse they both bore. "My powers aren't a punishment, El."

"Then . . ." Color fled Elerek's face, dark shadows swirling in the jade-hued depths of his irises. "It's true . . . you *are* a counter curse . . ."

Guilt ignited in his soul, searing Razhar with the hottest of irons.

"You lied to me. Again . . ."

A whistle blew against Razhar's ear. Heat seared the skin of his neck. He reached up and his fingers came away bloodied. A heavy *thunk* filled the air as the black-fletched arrow found its mark in Elerek's shoulder.

The king yelled, doubling over.

Razhar jumped to his feet, but found himself frozen, unable to act.

"El!" Lystra rushed to catch Elerek, holding him upright. The shaft protruded just above his arm. Blood and water both seeped from the wound and his body quaked with tremors.

Razhar spun around. His eyes darted about the landscape, catching on every shadow, every crevice. Searching. Barely breathing.

Behind him, Tiniah woke and gave a low, rumbling growl as she stalked in a circle. Her call resounded as other cardants gave response. The desert lizards emerged, bearing dark riders streaked with pale curse marks. More water than men.

"No!" Razhar drew his knife. But the weapon would be of no avail, not before the immense form of Gaudab Batu-Khasar standing atop a boulder, twin axes glinting in the emerging sunlight. Behind him, another Jarkin stood with a longbow, the string drawn taut.

Swearing, Razhar marched forward with a ferocity he didn't know he possessed, stepping between the invaders and his companions.

Gaudab raised an axe, in signal to his archer. His smile

leered, the grin of a skull beneath a layer of water and faint, fading skin. "Do you want an arrow, Kushite?"

Razhar snarled. "Only if you'll take one too."

Oi, you need to stay alive. El needs you. But maybe they'd never make it to the wrathgiver.

Water swirled about his feet. Razhar looked down. Only enough to darken the rock beneath him. Not a torrent. Not enough to drown their enemies.

He spared one glance over his shoulder. Elerek's face had gone terribly white, much too pale for Tribe Karim skin. Lystra supported him, her arms around his shoulders. He stretched out his hand, weak and trembling, the trickle turning to droplets from his fingers.

Razhar would not let Elerek die like this.

Growling, he lunged toward their enemies, raising his knife. Mid-swing, he realized a moment too late that he'd no idea what to do with it.

Gaudab swung his first axe. Razhar sidestepped, keeping his distance. This was a dance. He was nimble. But a dance required a partner, and Gaudab, despite his size, proved too great a warrior. A killer of kings.

Razhar gasped as the air left his lungs, forced out by the butt end of Gaudab's axe. He fell to his knees, blackness fringing his vision like tassels on a priest's robes.

A pair of bulky Jarkins with dripping, skeletal arms grabbed him—and touched his skin.

No . . .

Cries and curses filled the air. The Jarkins released him, raising skin-clad limbs to the morning light. Restored by the touch of a man tied to a curse, the cost, the consequence . . .

Razhar lurched toward the rock, bracing himself with shaky arms, cast with sand as he took the curse from the dying

Jarkins and expelled it to the wind. His lungs *burned.* He began to cough, sand sputtering from his lips.

It never happened like this.

He blinked up at the sun. That white light obliterated and scorched all, but he knew the stars were still there, even though he could not see them. The wrathgiver still watched.

"Well." Gaudab's rumbling voice sounded as if it lay underwater, gargling. "Not just another condor-scat mite of a Kushite?"

Razhar couldn't inhale enough air.

Laughing, Gaudab seized his arm, dragging him up like a limp puppet. Razhar distantly wondered if this was what Elerek felt like all the time, whole, but occupying a broken body. The curse retreated from Gaudab's hands and forearms, shrinking and shriveling.

"So, Tangu was right—about you."

Tears smarted in Razhar's eyes, swallowed by the sand. *Baba . . . Baba was right.*

Gaudab released him, sending him to his knees again. Coughs shook Razhar's body. Air fled away, replaced by coarse sand filling his lungs and scraping his throat. Panic lit a fire in his mind. He was getting worse, just like Elerek.

But Elerek's raging torrents seemed a thing of majesty and power compared to Razhar's crumpled figure coughing and fighting to breathe.

"Repulsive." Gaudab enhanced his disgust with a string of foul words in his own language. He turned on his heels, his cloak streaming behind him like the wing of a condor. "Men, we will see this curse broken. The filthy river rats' land will be ours."

Finally mastering control of his own lungs, Razhar drew a deep drought of air. Everything he'd done, everything he'd *ever* done, had been in the service of saving life—including his own. And he didn't want to die—not yet.

Cursed Jarkin hands grabbed him again. They pulled at his shoulders, securing his wrists, tying hands that could heal. Hands that had kept Myra, Norbah, Ishtal, Cole, Driss, and Lystra—brave, fierce Lystra who chose to take the curse—alive. Hands that had preserved the life of the king of golden Instanolde.

"But first, we must complete the rite spoken of amongst legend." Gaudab's voice echoed over the rock and lonely, desert wilderness. "The rites that demand that the opposites, the *counter curses*, must die."

Chapter 30

Elerek

Darkness veiled Elerek's vision. He grasped, straining for a handhold on reality. Rock beneath his broken legs. Water clinging to his fingertips. Lystra's arms encircling him.

But there was pain. Present and oppressive, more intense than anything he'd ever experienced. It shamed the dull numbness of the curse with a burning, furious agony. A pain that threatened to take everything away from him.

No, he couldn't go yet. He blinked, forcing the world back into clarity. But it was a world that he didn't want to see.

The bloodthirsty invaders were back. Somehow, amongst the Sancen's immensity, amid the tungin and the wraiths, they'd found them. Well, he'd told Lystra that the curse knew how to make him suffer. Perhaps the curse also knew its own.

Gaudab Batu-Khasar, the man who killed his brother and now chased Elerek along Cormek's doomed footsteps, stood as a monster more fearsome than any the desert had to offer. A warrior ravaged by the curse, yet with eyes burning in vengeance.

But his attention wasn't fixed on Elerek. Instead, he and his monsters encircled Razhar, mimicking the death swoops of vultures waiting to feast on their prey. They reached out, touched him, and discovered that Razhar's skin also held secrets.

The counter curse.

Elerek was meant for death, and yet they screamed for Razhar's blood. Could the curse require them both to die? Curse *and* counter curse?

Not Razhar. His friend, his anchor, his connection to humanity, the touch that enabled his own destructive powers to grow.

The brother who had lied to him. Lie after lie after lie.

Why, Razhar? Why would you do this?

Flames of pain rippled across Elerek's shoulder, his chest, his back, spreading like a wildfire. He fought back a moan, shuddering as spots of white light exploded over his vision.

Beside him, Lystra whimpered.

He blinked. Lystra he could see in perfect clarity. Each wild lock of ebony hair. The soft curve of her cheek. The terror swirling in the amber light in her eyes. His wife.

"Lystra . . . please." Torment strangled his voice. "Go . . ."

Her gaze grew glassy. A single tear cascaded down her cheek. Last night seemed worlds away—a world where she'd held him. Kissed him. Turned their bleak future into something precious. Vowed herself to him.

"El, there's nowhere to go."

Her whisper was swallowed by the crunch of boots. The invaders took the cardant, throwing ropes over her head and grabbing her horns. Elerek's ears filled with the reptile's fury, and he faintly wondered if she might trample them all.

Then, the Jarkins came for him. He screamed as they grabbed his arms, pain ripping through his shoulders. Lystra's hold slipped away and they threw him in a heap. Elerek ground his teeth until he thought they might break. The arrow's shaft rose toward the pale sky in his peripheral and farther above, the sneering, skull-like grin of Gaudab peered down at him.

Gaudab's boot crushed into his spine. Hard. Elerek's face scraped against the gravel. The heat of the Jarkin's breath blew over his neck. "You try another drowning, whelp, and she dies."

Screams cut through his consciousness. Forcing his head up, Elerek could only watch as two warriors seized Lystra. They drove her to her knees, yanking back her hair, and set a blade against her neck.

Starkindler, please, have mercy.

"I wouldn't move too much." Gaudab dug his boot deeper into Elerek's back. "Especially if you want to last to the constellation. Did you notice that we're almost there?"

Elerek couldn't speak, the air taken from his lungs.

"I need you to live a bit longer, and then you will die." Gaudab stepped back. "And your kingdom is ours."

Pushing himself up from the gravel, Elerek breathed in until it hurt. The Jarkins took the blade from Lystra's throat, leaving a trail of blood down her collarbone, and bound her. Her eyes met his, piercing his soul.

Gaudab stooped down, capturing Elerek in his shadow. Even the brilliant dawn couldn't illuminate the darkness in his expression. He snapped the length of arrow shaft. Elerek's vision swam. He wondered, if he closed his eyes, would it end?

No. He couldn't. Not yet.

"We rode hard to hunt you down. Lost several men. Drank their water." The Jarkin's lip curled back in a snarl. "So, I suggest you fill our waterskins. If not, I'll slit your queen's throat and you can watch her bleed out in the sands. Just like your brother."

"*I'll try, Cormek. I'll try to live.*"

Cormek didn't know it would be like this—that living would be so hard.

Impaled shoulder and all, Elerek attempted to fill each vessel brought to him. After the third waterskin, he passed out.

When awareness gradually returned, he didn't desire to wake.

The pain told him that he lived, that he hadn't died yet.

A string of oaths uttered in the Jarkins' harsh tongue fell upon him with an accompaniment of spittle. Elerek trembled in a bout of shivers while his skin became coated with feverish sweats. He lay back in their tent, the blankets and skins much as they had left them. Where Lystra had slept in his arms. The Jarkin kneeling over him held an open satchel. He withdrew a jar of dark salve and a small knife, which he used to cut the clothing away from Elerek's shoulder.

An arrow—there was no healing from such a wound. He should've already been dead. The pain had dulled to a steady numbness—a numbness that felt too much like the curse.

The Jarkin's knife fell to the sand and the man drew a hiss through his teeth.

Elerek craned his neck and saw only water.

The curse mark had spread. Up his shoulder, down his bicep. But beneath the watery skin, no muscles, bones, or veins remained. Only water, shaped to the dimensions of his well-muscled shoulder. And the arrowhead, dark and jagged, hovered in the midst of it.

His head flopped back. Could he not even die like other men? Like Cormek?

Razhar was right. The curse's power was changing, growing. He wondered how long till it consumed him. Till he became less.

Taking hold of the jagged shaft, the Jarkin withdrew the arrow with ease. Elerek didn't even feel it. Shaking his head, the Jarkin tossed the salve back into his pack and stationed himself across the tent.

Footsteps thundered outside the tent. Its canvas flew back, Gaudab's immense figure eclipsing the light. His heavy hands, marked by the curse, clenched Lystra's shoulders as if he meant to crush them. Then, he shoved her forward, sending her to her knees upon the threshold, her hands still bound.

Elerek's heart pounded in his ears. A trail of blood ran from her temple and a dark bruise welted on her collar. She trembled, but not from fear. No, rage burned in her eyes. If her hands had been free, Elerek didn't doubt that she'd strangle the Jarkin right then and there.

"I tire." Gaudab spoke slowly, deliberately. "Of this curse. The unfeeling in my bones."

This Jarkin knew nothing of suffering. Elerek's hands weren't tied. He pushed himself up. "Let's get on with it then."

"My men need water."

"I'd have filled the skins faster if you hadn't shot me."

Gaudab sneered as he took in Elerek's shoulder, flesh turned to water, and the broken arrow lying atop the blankets. Even the taint of his blood had been washed from the stone arrowhead. "You've recovered, which means I can do it again."

"If I'm to break the curse, I need to bleed blood. Not water."

"And we need *this*." Gaudab grabbed Lystra's hair. She screamed as he yanked back, forcing her eyes skyward. His hand reached for her hip, for the dagger stowed in its golden sheath. Once he seized it, he let Lystra topple.

Elerek lifted his fists, dripping water. "Touch her again and I'll—"

"You'll do as you're told." Gaudab sneered, signaling a guard with his arms full of empty skins. "I've no more patience."

Elerek drew a seething breath. "At last, something we agree on."

Soon. He would drown this man.

Trickle by trickle, he filled the skins to bursting. Gaudab greedily downed the first one and tossed it back onto the pile. Then, he left the tent, the dagger on his belt.

"They're too weak to travel," Lystra whispered. "We almost outlasted them."

Almost.

Elerek watched as the other soldier took the waterskins to distribute to the men, leaving them alone. He scooted closer, pulling the ropes from her hands.

The moment she was free, she flung her arms around his neck and buried her face in the shoulder that had become water.

He drew her against him, amazed at how naturally her form fit, at how quickly their souls had cleaved to one another's. He belonged to her.

"I'm sorry," he whispered.

Lystra shuddered in his arms.

Cupping her face in his hands, his fingers pushed stray hairs off her forehead. The sight of her eyes, filled with tears, broke his heart. This was where their story ended. As he always knew it would end, but not like this. Never beneath the star-cast skies did he anticipate this.

"Lystra, I love you." A whisper. A whirl of air amid a vast, barren wilderness. A drop of water amid a desert of sand. Elerek pushed his forehead against hers. "If I don't ever have the chance to speak it again, let me declare that you, my queen, are radiant and beautiful. Thank you. For ruling by my side, marrying me, and loving me."

The warmth of her lips and the taste of her stirred a thrill inside him that not even the curse could subdue. In a moment, all was forgotten. The desert. The Jarkins. The curse. There was only her and the melding of their hearts, the forging of something of hope.

"No matter what happens . . ." The air shuddered from Lystra's lungs. Her eyes fluttered to his. "I'll always love you."

Her arms still encircled him, her hands massaging the back of his neck. But the motion didn't disguise the tremor in her fingers.

He wanted to save her, but that was a day that had ended. One without a dawn, only darkness and a sky without stars. "Be brave," he whispered, leaning in to kiss her again.

Lystra hesitated. Her eyes began to burn. Perhaps the sky would not be starless after all, not with the embers of her starfire. "If they're going to kill you, make it count."

Elerek held her tighter, as if his arms were strong enough to uphold the heavens. "I promise. I'll take as many with me as I can."

Outside the tent, the noise increased. Boots, tack, the sounds of movement, of camp breaking.

Not yet. He wasn't ready. Elerek summoned water to his fingertips, washing away the blood on Lystra's face. "I . . . I wish . . ."

There wasn't enough air to give voice to all that he wished.

Gaudab's voice echoed across the desert, calling for the men to mount up.

Lystra kissed him. Deeply. Her fingers wound through his hair.

"I love you." He said it once more. One last time.

As a smile spread across Lystra's lips, her face became set like flint, like a warrior.

Then, they came for them.

Chapter 31

Elerek

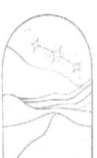

Elerek blinked against the sunlight as the Jarkins dragged him outside, the desert landscape shining pale and gold.

Gaudab waited atop Lystra's cardant, a terrible scowl across his features. Wrapped in the watery garb of the curse and his dark cloak streaming behind him, he looked more wraith than man.

Elerek clenched his hands, water rolling off his knuckles. His gaze searched the company. There were fewer, but still formidable, still too many. And they were worn. Too many hours beneath the sun without water.

He held their lives in his cursed hands, and their time was almost up.

Then, his eyes locked on Razhar.

Strong, bronzed shoulders were hunched. Arms crusted with sand and hands that had kept him alive were bound, the rope affixed to a metal stake driven into a crack of rock. The man who could turn to sand—the counter curse—anchored to the Sancen.

Through the sand coating his face and dusting his beard, a trail of dark skin was marked by a single tear.

Elerek's chest seized. He could only remember once seeing Razhar shed tears before. But no amount of tears could wash away his lies.

Gaudab wheeled the cardant in a circle. The reptile muttered and thrashed, but the soldiers managed to hoist Elerek into the saddle, binding his legs. As they pulled his arms back, securing his wrists, Elerek marveled that he felt no pain, no soreness. He glanced at his shoulder, at the mark spreading down his arms and across his chest, gleaming like crystal in the sunlight.

This was who he'd become. It would have to be enough. *Starkindler, please, let it be enough.*

A soldier led Lystra from the tent. The girl who had cried into his shoulder had disappeared. Transformed. Despite her bonds, she walked as if the crown of fire opals blazed on her brow. The bold queen of the desert, the survivor of Darcress, the ashes from Cormek's pyre turned to diamonds.

If she could carry herself with such courage, perhaps he too could become something more. If this was the day meant to be his last, he would live it without a single drop of regret.

"Mount up, men," Gaudab barked. "Darcress awaits us."

"Fitting." Elerek let his voice rise, filling the desert. "Where it all began."

Gaudab turned in the saddle with a sneer. "The key to the desert, the river, to your meager, river rat kingdom. One attack was all it took to cripple you."

Elerek met his gaze. "I counted *two* attacks, Khasar. And there's a profound difference between being crippled and being conquered."

A smile spread wide over Lystra's lips.

Gaudab's glare cut sharper than even the cursed dagger at

his belt. He looked to his men. "Make haste! The sooner we arrive, the sooner we slay a second Instan king."

The warriors swung into their saddles, full waterskins swaying with the motion.

No one claimed Razhar. No one loosed him from the stake piercing the rock.

Elerek's heart pounded. "The counter curse comes with me. Let the stars judge between us."

A shudder rippled through the Jarkins. A disturbance to the smooth surface of their watery skins. Razhar lifted his head.

Gaudab urged the cardant forward, approaching the place where Razhar appeared very small. The faded emerald of his beloved turban alone distinguished him from the muted colors of the desert, as if he'd turned to the Sancen itself. He didn't look at Elerek.

"Counter curses must die." Gaudab spat into the rock near Razhar's knee. "They empower the curse, letting it grow stronger." Then he barked a bitter laugh. "We'll leave his bones for the vultures. The Sancen will claim its flesh while we become free to claim our own again. His sands are a defilement, an omen of evil against this curse." He sneered. "This lowly scum allowed this curse to perpetuate."

Lowly. Razhar tensed, seeming to fold in on himself at the word's utterance.

Surely he doesn't believe . . . No, not Razhar.

"Why didn't you tell me?" Elerek whispered.

He wondered if Razhar had heard him. Lifting his head, a fire entered Razhar's eyes, the likes of which Elerek had never seen before. Embers enough to obliterate the entire desert. "You're wrong. Stars above, so wrong."

Another tear fell down his bronze cheek, provoking again the memory of tears upon Razhar's face. Stronger this time.

"If you can hear me, you'd better listen . . ."

How many times had Razhar lied to him? How many secrets had he borne behind a handsome smile? A melodious laugh? A well-aimed joke?

How many times had Razhar been there when Elerek couldn't even summon the strength to breathe? The war orphan who'd come to live in the palace, always in the right place at the right time. The right place to not turn to sand. The right time to save Elerek's life.

But he was also cursed—Razhar was saving *himself*.

"I'm listening . . ." Elerek drew a ragged breath. "Tell me the *truth*, Razhar. For once in your life." He felt as if he peered over the edge of a cliff, an endless plummet beneath. Such a fall would change everything.

"I'm *both*." Razhar sputtered, straining against his bonds. "Stars above, I'm both the cost of the curse *and* a counter curse. I'm turning to sand because I'm the cost of the awful thing my baba did but that's not all. I'm more. Something so rare all your books don't even describe it." He lifted his eyes, sunlight sparkling in his amber gaze. "And . . . am I still only a lowly Kushite? Even now? Stars, *I am extraordinary.*"

Elerek stared at him.

"I can hold back the curse because I counter it. That's what a counter curse does. It reverses the curse, stands in the gap, and pushes back the curtain of death. Surely that makes me an equal with the cursed king of Instanolde."

An equal.

Curse and counter curse.

The pieces fell together in Elerek's mind just as the words, the words that held the potential to change everything, left Razhar's lips.

"I also hold the curse's power in my hands." Razhar's voice faltered, choking on a sob. *"I can break the curse."*

Chapter 32

Razhar

Ow his baba had wept.

He wept for what was to come—and what had been done. He begged the Starkindler for forgiveness, for mercy.

Razhar hadn't understood. When his baba asked him to be brave, he didn't know that he would encounter death and become acquainted with grief. He'd carried secrets away from the canyonlands, a heavy burden. A truth built into the foundations of their shifting, star-cast world. That Instan kings knew only how to spill blood, and they would seek his death—to break the curse. A simple solution to fix what was broken.

Razhar shut his eyes, lost to all but the memory of his baba's voice.

"Yes, you can break the curse, but I don't want that for you. I want you to live. Live the life stolen from so many. I love you, my son, to the dancing stars above. Live a life that isn't cursed."

Razhar opened his eyes. He felt the stone, cast with sand, beneath his knees, the rope tight about his hands, and the heat of the burning sun above.

I tried, Baba. I tried to live.

Fahwal understood the world correctly. He knew that the moment Razhar spoke the truth, his life would mean nothing. A bit of sand blown across the desert. The legacy of a thousand Kushites before him, the children who bled into the Gungole, the soldiers murdered by Lorkin's warmongering. Of a Kushite archer who was driven to commit terrible acts.

He tried. Razhar would never discredit the fact. He'd built a life. A beautiful life. A lowly Kushite in the golden palace of Instanolde.

Lifting his eyes, irritated with sand, Razhar waited. The whole of the desert fell silent, afire with the Sancen sunlight and the blaze of Elerek's gaze. The heat wove tangled mirages, and Razhar didn't know if he watched the king of Instanolde or the brother who shouldered the other half of the curse. His baba hadn't lived to see this, what the two cursed children had grown to become.

Elerek's rage had run dry. His eyes became hollow, astonishment and grief spilling across his pale face.

The silence became a void Razhar was desperate to fill with words to make them understand. But, for once, Razhar couldn't speak. Here, at the end, he had only one thing left to offer—his most precious possession.

His life.

"That is my answer." He nearly choked on the words, sand clogging his throat. "That's why I've done what I've done. If you kill me . . ." How bitter the words tasted. "With the stars, with the dagger, I can break the curse."

The most imperfect solution. Save them all. Elerek. Lystra. The whole of Instanolde. Everyone but him.

Even the Jarkins stared, bewilderment twisting their harsh faces, leathered by the days spent beneath the sun. Razhar didn't mind them. They were strangers. But the eyes of his friends—of his brother—he could not bear.

"Don't leave me behind." Razhar kept his gaze fixed on Elerek. "El, please . . ."

A moment passed. Still, save for the wisp of wind through their dusty clothing and the twitch of the cardants' tails. The rope bit into Razhar's wrists as he leaned forward.

Elerek bowed his head.

"We've tarried long enough." Gaudab lifted his chin, shifting his hateful gaze from Razhar to the king tied behind him. "We ride for Darcress."

Despair strangled Razhar, choking the very life he wanted so badly out of him.

"No!" Lystra gasped. The queen strained at her bonds, tears streaming down her face. "Please, don't do this!"

Gaudab's eyes narrowed, as if he'd forgotten about her. A sneer caught his lip. "Jul, bind the little queen with the Kushite. Another offering to appease the desert."

Razhar couldn't breathe.

"No!" Elerek roared. Forged like iron and resilient like marble, the king of Instanolde turned fierce and terrible, exactly as he had the first time facing the Jarkin warlord upon the shores of his kingdom.

Gaudab paid him no mind. He laughed. "Let the Sancen have their flesh."

Razhar's skin numbed, as if he also bore the other half of the curse.

The warriors sprang into action. Weapons and tack rattled like chains. Hot blood stirred in the cardants' limbs as they kicked up dust, hazing the air around Razhar. He who shared kinship with the desert sands began to cough and sputter. He lost sight of Elerek amid the fray.

As for Lystra, the Jarkin dragged her, straining and screaming, and tied her down beside him, anchoring them to the rock to die beneath the endless Sancen sky.

"El!" Lystra pulled against the rope, tears streaming down her face.

As one, the contingent of cardants took off at a run. The men were dark shapes, indistinguishable from one another, their faces bent toward Darcress. And in a moment, they were swallowed by the canyons.

Razhar slumped forward.

Beside him, Lystra yelled. She struggled, thrashing against the ropes.

"It's no use." Razhar shook his head.

No water. No cardants. No Elerek. He hadn't even gotten to say goodbye. They would die, and the last thing Elerek would remember of him was his lies—lies that had defined their friendship, and his entire existence.

"Razhar." Lystra ground out the words. "Don't tell me what I can or cannot do."

She strained against her bonds, extending her foot toward a shard of a rock. A few nudges and kicks later, she managed to get it within reach.

"Help me," she commanded.

Razhar huffed, twisting to grab the rock with his tied hands, holding it steady as Lystra slid her ropes across its jagged edge. "It's no use."

But nothing would dissuade Lystra. Panting with exertion, she worked the rope until *snap*, the fibers split. Freeing herself, she quickly set to work on his bonds.

"We'll never catch them."

Light blazed in her eyes, a furious passion. Casting aside his ropes, she took his arm and pulled him to his feet, her movements desperate and frantic. Then, she broke into a run.

Somehow, despite the weight of his failures pulling at his

heart, Razhar managed to follow her. Each rapid footfall upon the worn stone felt like a slap against his sore soles. Wind tore at his turban, forcing him to unravel it and swing it round his neck.

Ahead of him, Lystra moved like a gazelle, nimble and delicate. She leapt across the rocks, running as if she were made for the land and the land for her. They didn't pursue the caravan, instead, they ran toward the edge of the rocky plateau.

A steep drop opened beneath them. A place where the rock had been beaten down by years of abundant winds, forceful waters, and blazing heat. The indomitable Sancen. A land cultivated to destroy.

They skidded to a stop at the edge. Sunlight belittled their faces. Razhar raised a hand, shielding his eyes as he peered across the lonely expanse. Desolation as far as the eye could see —as if they were the last of humanity.

No sign of the caravan.

He sank to his knees.

Lystra's chest heaved in gasps. She held back her hair to keep it from blowing. "You . . ." She looked at him, tears streaking down each of her cheeks.

Razhar drew his hands into fists. Grains of amber sand ground between his fingers.

"All this time . . .?"

The secret his baba commanded him to keep. It had taken such fortitude to even tell Myra, and he hadn't told her everything. Just enough to shape a partial truth, one facet of a gem that hadn't been cut to perfection. When he'd taken Lystra to the Kushite archives, revealing the writ of the curse, his risk had been birthed from desperation.

He'd trusted them, trusted that they loved Elerek as much as he did. And yet he could never trust Elerek with this, this ugly truth.

"Don't call me selfish . . ." Razhar pinched his eyes shut.

"Razhar . . ."

"Call me a liar. Call me a coward. Call me wretched." Hot tears stormed his eyelids with the frenzy of an advancing army. "But don't call me selfish. Can I not desire to live as much as anyone else?"

But what did it mean—to live? To fill with years? To watch as the heavens rotated in their dances for enough seasons to shrivel the skin and gray the hair? To linger for as long as one possibly could? Was that what mattered?

Razhar never desired to outlive the curse. Everyone he loved would then be dead. Instead, he'd chosen to push it back. To freeze time, like the grand murals on Instanolde's upper avenues. To keep his world in precious stasis, stealing days as the dawn stole the starlight.

But death had haunted those days anyways. He'd watched enough cursed burst into a thousand droplets and drown. He'd lived long enough to know that he couldn't save them, but also that he couldn't do nothing. Nothing beautiful could last forever. At least, not without fighting for it.

I'm tired of fighting.

"I tried . . ." Razhar's lungs heaved in a bitter sob. "And none of it mattered."

Lystra stepped toward him. "It mattered, Razhar."

He wiped his eyes, leaving a trail of dust across his face. "I'm not important. Maybe extraordinary, but not important. If I had been, I wouldn't have had to lie, to hide." He slumped, bracing his hands against the rock. "I asked you once, if the curse required something heinous to break it, would you be willing? Now you know. My death—or El's? And I know what anyone in their right mind would choose."

What's a lowly Kushite to the king of Instanolde?

"Razhar . . ."

"Years, Lystra! I kept him alive for years. I kept those he loved alive. Norbah, Myra, you . . ." He swallowed a sob. "All the while, he wanted to die. We—all of us—cared for someone who didn't wish to live." Lifting his gaze, he stared at her, the fierce queen. "Is that not love, Lystra? Shouldering the burdens that our friends cannot?"

Lystra didn't speak. Her chest shuddered.

"Still, my love wasn't enough. I wasn't enough. I'm the one that they'd kill the moment that they knew spilling my blood beneath the stars would set them free. After all, that's what you want, yes? For me to be loyal and steadfast and willing to give up?"

Lystra looked like a statue. Perfect marble, carved by the most skilled of artisans—almost divine. A maiden from the stars. Razhar marveled that she hadn't yet broken. After all they'd endured. After all she'd lost.

"I'll give you one thing, Razhar. One truth to your many, many lies." Even her voice ought to have belonged to a story crafter, perhaps a poet, or a reader of ancient texts at the temple. "*That* is love. Your deep, abiding love for the cursed changed the course of our world forever." She knelt beside him, her cursed hand reaching for his. "Curses aren't the only things that come with costs."

No, this felt heavier. His heart had been carved right out of his chest and what was left of him turned to sand—sand logged with water. Curse, cost, and counter curse, a burden he'd been carrying for so long.

Razhar clenched his eyes shut, holding back his tears as he'd held back the curse. The curse that would go unbroken. Without him, Elerek would have no anchor, nothing to keep him from slipping into the curse's power.

Lystra's hand, soft and gentle, touched his face, her voice a whisper. "Tell me, how many times have you told El that he's not his curse?"

Beyond count. Beyond the stars in the heavens.

"I'm sorry, Razhar, that I'm the only one left to tell you that *you* are *more* than *your* curse." Her breath caught. "You're the color that stood out even amid the garish silks and mineral-toned fires of the night market. You're the dancer who urged the people to dance beneath a sky full of stars, waking one queen from her own crushing grief. You're the loyal friend who inspired courage and befriended the cursed king of Instanolde. Don't tell me that *that* doesn't matter."

Razhar pulled away from her touch and stood. "Does it matter if we fail?"

Lystra closed her eyes.

"And we have failed. They're going to kill him, and we can't save him. We can't break the curse. We can't stop the invaders. Stars above, we can't even escape the Sancen."

The wind picked up, catching in his emerald scarf, and threatening to pull them off the edge. A world against which they could never win and had become fools to try.

Razhar wiped the tears from his eyes. "I wonder . . . what my baba would think of me. If he . . . if he knew what I'd done."

Well, he'd know soon enough.

Was he ready? To see his baba again? To look into Fahwal Emblino's eyes and tell him that yes, he'd lived well?

No. Not even close.

"I've lied to you too." He looked at Lystra again. Stars, he'd never blame Elerek for falling in love with her. "I'm sorry."

Rising on shaky limbs, she strode to the edge of the rocky precipice, facing the horizon. The azure of the sky and the gold of the desert reflected in her eyes. "I love him . . ." Her shoulders quivered. "Now he's . . . he's gone."

Razhar's heart ached.

Lystra covered her face with her curse-marked hands, muffling her sobs. "I love him . . ."

She began to break, here when all else had shattered. Razhar pulled her into his arms. He didn't speak. He certainly didn't think he ought to be holding the queen of Instanolde, but here he was. At the end.

Lystra turned her face to the wind, her voice a mere whisper. "No, Razhar, I'm not sure I want our failure to matter."

Her arms wrapped around him, and Razhar wasn't sure who supported who. Two souls shouldering the same sorrow. Scorched by the heat and light of grief, of struggle, of days lived cursed beneath the sun. No one could endure what they had and remain unscathed. The souls that they'd been before the summer—this last summer to live—had slipped away.

They could only reforge themselves, bits of old, bits of new, bits of broken.

Then, from somewhere above the desolation, a clear cry filled the air.

Both Razhar and Lystra turned their faces toward the skies and watched as pairs of bold, black wings eclipsed the sun.

Condors.

Chapter 33

Lystra

Five condors in all. Swooping in wide circles, gently descending.

Lystra waved her arms and screamed. They'd been found. They wouldn't die in the desert.

Her efforts were rewarded. The mighty birds veered in their direction. As they alighted, great ebony wings flapping in graceful unison, they stretched their long necks and blinked dark, beady eyes. Their Kushite riders wore cloaks of feathers that ruffled in the wind. Recurve bows were strapped to their shoulders and their skin gleamed bronze in the midmorning light.

Was this what Razhar might have become? If he'd stayed in Kushan? If his baba hadn't cast the curse?

If he hadn't become the counter curse?

Razhar stepped forward, lifting empty hands. "Peace, kinsmen."

One man dismounted, stepping forward. A yellow sash draped across his bronze chest, identifying him as the leader. "It emboldens our souls to find you alive." His kohl-lined eyes turned to Lystra. "Torra Lystra of House Arghan, I presume?"

They knew her? Dusty clothes. Dirty hair. Tear-stained cheeks. She hardly looked like the regal queen of Instanolde. *House Arghan?* Lystra raised her chin. "You were sent for us?"

The soldier nodded. "Queen's orders."

Lystra's heartbeat pounded in her ears.

"But she . . ." Razhar raised his eyebrows. "She's your queen . . ."

Not anymore.

Fury burned in Lystra's veins.

The Kushite looked to the man on his left. "Search them."

Lystra lifted her hands. For now, skin clothed her limbs, but she could feel it still. The numbness, an ever-chilling reminder that she would die—and soon, if Elerek couldn't break it. "Come no closer. I bear a curse. If you touch me, you will die." Vehemence and strength bolstered her voice. "Surely *she* told you that?"

"Stars above, what's going on?" Razhar's eyes darted between her and his kinsmen.

The Kushite warriors kept their distance, but roughly grabbed Razhar, searching for weapons. The leader turned back to her, darkness in his gaze.

"Where is the dagger?"

Lystra glared. "In the possession of your *king*. He was taken to Darcress, captive of Gaudab Batu-Khasar. Take us to him."

An order from a queen ought to have held weight as her cursed body held its deathly waters, but the captain only turned away, speaking to his men in his own language.

Two of the soldiers immediately mounted their condors, their wings flapping as they prepared to launch into the sky.

"Wait!" She stepped forward, her voice strained, like a child who feared being ignored. "Please, you must take us—"

"I'm to bring you back alive," the captain droned. "As I said, the *queen's* orders. But I need this information confirmed."

Queen's orders. Lystra's throat felt tight, as it always did in *her* presence. Then, the two condors soared into the air, becoming black silhouettes as they charted the skies towards Darcress.

"You've killed them." Lystra drew a sharp breath. "An army waits at Darcress. The same that slew one Instan king and waits for the blood of another."

The Kushite looked at her, his head tilted slightly to the side. A shadow engulfed his amber eyes, colored the same as Razhar's. "Instanolde has no king."

An Arghan Queen to rise again. And indeed, she had risen —and fallen—and another had taken her place. Now, Lystra saw her path set before her, one she had to trek.

Lystra glanced over her shoulder, drinking in one last, long look at the Sancen. The desert no longer struck her with fear, only sorrow. She'd always felt a kinship to its rocky spires, windswept dunes, and lonely canyons, but now, she knew a piece of her soul would always live here, in the wilds.

Perhaps the same part of her soul that belonged to Elerek.

Now she had to go back. Survive a second time. Instanolde burned in her heart, and she yearned for the glint of gold on its domes, the music of ouds, the thundering of cardants, the smell of mint and lamb. The kingdom she'd wanted so desperately to protect—and she'd left it unattended in the hands of ruthless invaders.

And Grandmother.

Tears misted her eyes and her heart cleaved against her ribs. *Starkindler keep you, El.*

Perhaps it was their fate to be kept apart, to always have distance between them. His destiny lay with Darcress, beneath the light of the wrathgiver. But the battle before her would wage back where it all began—the canyons of Kushan.

The riders doubled up, leaving a condor for them. Razhar mounted the bird with the graceful ease of one who had done this before.

As Lystra inched closer, the bird flapped its huge wings, stirring up dust in its wake. She shielded her gaze, appraising the bird's ominous eyes, leering head, and sharp beak. Surely it couldn't be so different from a cardant?

Its saddle, however, was distinct, flat, with grooves where their legs would lie, and no horn. Lystra quickly climbed up behind him. "When did you learn to fly?"

Razhar shifted in the saddle, taking up the long reins, attached to the bird's neck, not its head. "My baba had a condor." A sigh escaped him, deflating his shoulders. "We always made time for flying."

A distance hung in his voice, as if it lay across the mountains and fields of sand. Another wraith to haunt the canyons.

Razhar had been a child, just like Elerek. Two children with a curse they didn't deserve. Curses that shaped the men they had become. Lystra touched his arm. "I am sorry, about your baba."

The Kushites gave signal. Their birds wheeled round, preparing for the skies.

Razhar huffed. "It's in the past." He shifted, speaking low

over his shoulder. "I ought to be going forward. To Darcress. If El loses control, the curse won't be broken."

"How far is Darcress from Kushan?"

"As the condor flies, only a few hours."

Impossible time to fuel impossible hopes, but Lystra had little else. "Keep me alive to face Grandmother. We'll get you away before the sun sets. They won't dare kill El before then."

Razhar took his emerald scarf and quickly rewound it back into his lopsided turban, his eyes unsettled and uncertain. "As long as he doesn't do anything stupid. Now, are you ready?" He took a whistle from the saddlebag, carved in an oblong shape, perhaps from a small gourd.

Lystra took a deep breath. "I miss Tiniah."

"You'll want a bird of your own after this. No one needs to tell a bird to fly. We simply sit back and take in the view." Razhar managed the makings of a roguish smile. Then he raised the whistle to his lips and a soft, barely audible sound went forth. The condor responded, pivoting on its talons. Lystra's breath hitched, and she wrapped her arms tight around Razhar's waist, prompting an oppressed grunt. Then, the bird lurched forward.

Nothing could've prepared her for this. The rush upward into the brilliant skies, leaving the desert landscape of rock and jagged cliff to grow smaller and smaller, like markers on a map. Air sailed about them, so hot and fierce it stung her eyes. Slowly, gaining ground on the nausea in her stomach, the same intoxicating sense of freedom that a cardant ride provided filled her soul. A slow smile spread across her lips. A bit of stolen wonder from a world laced with evil.

Lystra craned her neck, watching the horizon. No stirring of dust. No sign of a caravan. No sight of the red towers of Darcress.

As the sun rose higher, the land changed. No longer desert, but just as barren. Rocky crags of dark stone, pointed and sharp, as far as the eye could see. No vegetation grew on these slopes. The heat turned harsh and vile. Their throats dried and their hair dampened.

They reached an outpost, a squat tower of gray stone standing between two sharp crags. A place only condors could reach. Their companions began to circle, gliding downward. Razhar blew the whistle again.

Lystra's stomach flipped as they glided in graceful circles that felt much too fast. The condor extended its long claws out in front of its body as they touched down. Thrown forward by the movement, Lystra gasped.

"Your Highness, you've got to let me breathe," Razhar muttered.

"Sorry." She let go, but her hands shook.

Thin and cold, the air took Lystra's breath away. The warriors hastened them inside. A chill that seemed to ebb from the stone itself perpetuated the bare structure, but it felt good to have a roof over their heads. Two more Kushites greeted them, providing water, dried, spiced meat, and a change of clothes. Lystra wept with relief as she shed the filthy garb of the desert behind a screen in the back of the tower. The simple, linen kaftan tunic was far too large for Lystra, but she fastened it with a sash and covered her hair with a scarf. Such a small thing to rejoice over, but she somehow felt braver. Bolder.

Razhar wore the clothing of his people, a long tunic tied with a sash over dark pants and a leather vest that made his shoulders seem broader. But nothing could undo the despair in his eyes. She thought of that night in the market, watching him dance with a smile upon his face and starlight in his gaze.

Grief had changed them, and it made her sorry. Lystra

wondered if they'd ever find those two dancers. Or, if they survived, perhaps they could learn to dance again. Old steps, new paths.

They departed within the hour. Away to their right, the Sancen faded into the horizon. The sun became their equal, blinding them with its radiance. Razhar kept his head bowed, squinting beneath his turban, while Lystra closed her eyes, pushing her forehead into his shoulder. She feared slumber, and plummeting to her death, so she clutched Razhar tighter.

Every so often, she looked over her shoulder, back the way they'd come. Whatever portion of the Sancen they'd traveled lay far behind them now. Elerek out of reach.

She marveled at the colors, the varied landscapes of a world far larger than she'd imagined. Wide plains, soft dunes, rugged cliffs. Rivers and canals. Mountains painted gentle greens, grays, and blues. A beautiful world.

Surely they could find a way. A way for Instans, Kushites, and even Jarkins to live in peace. She wondered what that peace would cost.

The first of the Kushite canals came into view. A deep gorge of azure. Whitecaps, like the smallest stroke of an artist's brush, lined its surface. No vessels sailed today, and while characteristic of the quietness of high summer, Lystra wondered if the Jarkin occupation had impacted their trade.

They descended, falling into the canyon's shadow. As they wheeled in wide circles, Lystra caught a closer glimpse of the cliffside dwellings. Elaborate edifices of wood, suspended above air, where human and condor lived alongside one another. Their inhabitants stood along the edges of the platforms, lined up like soldiers. Watching. Waiting.

A prickle worked its way up Lystra's spine.

Landing in the same village Razhar and Lystra had visited only a few days prior, Lystra shakily dismounted, her legs sore and stiff. Her eyes slid along the canyon walls, identifying the archive's dark doorway, and she wondered if everything would've been better if the secrets had been left in the dark.

As Razhar desired. She looked at him, the red canyons of his homeland reflected in his eyes. The counter curse. Not just the cost, the unfortunate consequence. Razhar truly was Elerek's opposite—down to the last detail. The most important detail.

"I asked you once, if the curse required something heinous to break it, would you be willing? Now you know. My death—or El's?"

Lystra hadn't given answer. How could she? Despite the love she shared with Elerek, she wouldn't use it as the justification to take a man's life. No one ought to decide such a thing.

If there were any chance of breaking it, that decision lay with Elerek—if the curse didn't claim him first.

Soldiers approached, speaking to the archers who'd accompanied them. They watched Lystra with wide eyes.

She wasted no time, marching into their midst. "I must speak with Chief Wuhaz at once."

The captain, an iron helmet capping his head and leather armor encasing his bronze arms, nodded. "Of course, Torra—"

"—Your Highness." Lystra raised her chin. "I took vows to my kingdom, to my subjects, broken only upon my death. And, as you can see, I am very much alive."

Razhar cracked a smile and the captain turned rather

purple. He bowed and then gestured forward. "This way—Your Highness. The emissaries from Instanolde wait in attendance."

Emissaries. Lystra's heartbeat quickened and she all but ran down the sandy path leading into the round, sunken arena cast in redstone. Her feet pounded down the steps, approaching the circle where the chief waited, flanked by his priests and his soldiers.

And there stood a gathering of familiar faces. Faces Lystra never thought she would see again.

Norbah, no longer dressed like an Instan general, wore a simple tunic and wrapped robe with a turban draped about his head. His scimitar remained belted on his hip, but he'd forsaken his glove, leaving his curse mark exposed, the bones of his knuckles pale in the afternoon light. Cole, the cursed soldier, accompanied him, the mark on his arm also visible.

Beside him stood her beloved cousins. Corsha looked small and fragile. Fear hovered in her emerald eyes and she stood with her arms wrapped around herself, her glorious hair bound beneath a scarf. Kimzi's long arms were folded, his bow and a quiver of arrows strapped to his shoulders.

And there, before the chief, stood Dalmah.

Grandmother. Lystra's hands clenched. *You cursed my husband.*

Unlike the others, she wore no traveling clothes. Instead, she appeared as if she'd just stepped through the gates of House Arghan's estate, clothed in silks, jewels, and a scarf of sheer black.

As one they turned, all eyes falling upon the queen of Instanolde.

"Lystra!" Corsha yelped, running toward her.

Lystra skidded to a stop. "Don't touch me!" She lifted her hands.

Her relief at seeing her cousin immediately turned to fear. The terrible fear of spreading the curse, of bearing responsibility for the pain of someone she loved, for an undeserved death.

Elerek had lived his entire life like this. Fear was no way to live.

For a moment, Corsha's brow crinkled, and then, her skin turned a horrid pallor. "Oh, Lystra, vianni . . ." She covered her mouth with her hand. Kimzi muttered an oath and shook his head.

Dalmah only stared. If disappointment could burn, Lystra's cursed flesh lay ready upon a pyre all her own.

"Torra. We meet again." Chief Wuhaz sat upon his circle of stone, flanked by guards who appeared more condor than man. Their helmets were fashioned with long visors that curved like their birds' cruel beaks and dark feathers lined their shoulders. "Much has occurred since our last meeting. I take it that Kushan will have no defense from Instanolde, seeing how it lies beneath Jarkin occupation?"

They needed their help. They could save them. And Lystra would have to convince them. She drew herself taller. "With sorrow, I proclaim it is as you have been informed."

The aged chief turned to Dalmah. An understanding seemed to pass between them. Lystra found herself small in their presence, shrinking as years and experience eclipsed her. Wuhaz had been chief of the Kushites through four monarchs, her grandmother included.

"I give thanks to the Starkindler." Wuhaz spoke slowly. "That Instanolde has found its rightful ruler again. Perhaps, when these threats have passed, we will see a new dawn."

Lystra stalked forward. "I never abdicated. These threats will not simply pass. They must be eradicated."

"Especially, it seems, this curse." The chief's eyes darted to

Norbah and Cole, their marks exposed, and their soldier adornments absent. They stood not as officers—but evidence.

Before she could speak truth into this madness, her grandmother cleared her throat. "As you see, Chief, even the disgraced queen bears this atrocity." Dalmah's voice sounded nothing like a queen's, but subtle, like the low threat of a whetstone upon a knife, and deadly like the numbness seeping into the skin of innocent souls. "If not stopped, this curse will destroy us all—even before the Jarkins."

When Lystra had first returned from the desert, she'd returned as a survivor. Broken and terrified and bearing the body of a dead king. But her people saw a queen, their adoration elevating her even above the prince-heir in reverence and popularity.

This time, Lystra stood in the center of stares. Those whom she counted her allies—Instanolde's intrepid general, her dear cousins, and Razhar—watched with wide eyes. The rest looked on as if she were some rotting, decaying thing meant to be abhorred and discarded.

Did Elerek ever feel like this? Oh, but she knew that he did.

"Grandmother." She spoke cool and collected. "What have you done to my kingdom?"

Dalmah stepped closer, eye to eye. Queen to queen. "It's not what I have done, granddaughter." She glanced over her shoulder, obsidian darkness in her gaze. "You have seen this curse, Chief, and its destruction."

Wuhaz dipped his chin. "You attribute it to—House Karim?"

Lystra felt as if she were underwater. Submerged. Drowning.

"The firstborn, spreading from the touch of the boy who should have never been crowned. Now the curse of bloody

Lorkin's son has infected the Jarkins who wreak havoc upon our fair kingdom."

How dare you . . . Behind her, Razhar swore.

"What has happened?" Lystra demanded, turning not to her grandmother, but to Norbah, for answers. A man she couldn't believe would tolerate these words spoken so cruelly of the king who had given what little he could to the preservation of their people.

Torment swirled in the general's eyes. "The cursed Jarkins spread it like mad. They wouldn't listen to reason and their soldiers keep control in the city." He swallowed, his face miserable. "So many have died, Your Highness. The curse has—changed, somehow. It strikes sporadically with a speed that we've never seen before."

Razhar drew a sharp gasp, and Lystra watched the sorrow deepen in his gaze. It had been him; he'd kept the curse moving slow when only thirty or so were kept within their own little community. They were his to care for just as they were Elerek's.

But if it had claimed the whole city, there'd be no stopping it. Instanolde would run with the water of drowned souls.

Souls that Lystra was powerless to save.

"In the wake of such a disaster, we look to you, Chief Wuhaz." Dalmah glided back to the side of the old chief, her silks slithering behind her like a snake. "Despite our differences, against a common enemy, we can prevail."

The Jarkins were their common enemy. It wasn't enough.

"Breaking the curse." Norbah spoke beneath his breath, his eyes still watching Lystra and Razhar.

The taint of disbelief. Lystra heard it as loud and as clearly as the silver trumpets that preluded the crack of Instanolde's grand, golden gates. After living so long with the imminent future hanging over their heads, the cursed had resigned themselves to their fate. Any hope of breaking the curse was too much to believe.

"Indeed." The chief's chest swelled, making him look a much larger man. "Despite our disagreements, our misfortunes, our opinion of the unholy act of curse binding was one shared even with Lorkin. The persistence of such a curse harbored by the pretender king of Instanolde was not something to be withheld from us." He turned a cold eye upon Lystra.

Dalmah interlaced her fingers, the rubies on her knuckles gleaming. "This wrong can be righted, O Chief, beneath the right leadership. The right alliance."

Enough. Lystra drew herself up, her posture one cultivated beneath her grandmother's tutelage. *Regal. Powerful. Something beyond the expectations of all who look upon you.* "I swore myself to the throne before the temple, my people, and the starcast skies above. With or without fealty, Kushan gives answer to Instanolde. To speak against its king—or queen—is treason."

Wuhaz scowled. "Under Kushite ordinance, any and all participants involved in the particulars of a curse face immediate execution."

"You've already done that."

Lystra's eyes widened as Razhar stepped forward. His clothing matched his kinsmen and his bronze skin gleamed in the afternoon sunlight. But his eyes held an intensity to them, the look of endurance that hadn't been born in the canyonlands. The Kushite from the golden palace of Instanolde.

"Is my face familiar to you?"

A murmur swept through the crowd. A ripple of familiarity, of whispers and speculation.

One step closer to the truth. Lystra looked at her grandmother and wondered what it would take to push back the curtain a bit further. To turn the guilt from the cursed to the binder? Surely Dalmah didn't know the truth about Razhar and his abilities?

But Dalmah's eyes gleamed. She entertained no fear, watching Razhar with the look of a lioness stalking her prey.

Lystra drew a sharp breath. No, she did know.

Chapter 34

Elerek

The sun shone hot and bright on the day meant to be Elerek's last. Taunting him. Reminding him that men were meant to die from the heat, the desert's unforgiving severity.

Not to drown.

It took everything in him to keep breathing, to keep the rage burning in his veins and not dripping from his fingertips.

Not yet. He had to wait. For the pale starlight to tighten its line, to bind him with the curse's cords, and turn his waters into a flow worthy of destroying an army. For vengeance to run with the ferocity of a swollen canal.

He didn't look at them, tolerating their sneers, their spit, and their curses. Head bowed, his jaw ached from the gag and his hands were bound tight. Beneath him, the cardant moved at a steady pace. The Jarkins were taking their time, saving their strength, and enjoying the luxury of endless water.

They. Will. Pay.

Let their bodies wash down the canyons for the vultures to find. Perhaps he'd even allow the cardants to feast on their flesh. He wondered if Lystra had ever needed to tell a cardant not to bite its owner.

Elerek shut his eyes against the sun's blinding glare.

Lystra . . .

Razhar . . .

Their faces seared into his mind as the caravan lumbered down the canyon, leaving them behind—to die.

They were gone. The thought made Elerek feel as if he'd never breathe again. As if he were already dead.

How foolish he'd been, to even grasp on to the hope of saving them—of saving anyone—with hands that could only destroy. Even breaking the curse and ending his wretched life would leave those whom he loved dead.

The queen he took for the sake of a new dawn would die in the Sancen. Lystra would never rule and reign in their golden city. Never again sit proud upon a cardant. Never smile, her hair swept back by the wind, with all the boldness of the dawn glowing in her eyes.

She would die because she loved him.

Had it really happened? Perhaps the sunlight played tricks on his mind, but he could imagine no better illusion than the touch of her lips, of the scent of her hair, and her body nestled against his as they held each other through the night.

I've lived too long.

How many times had he attributed the length of his sorrowful days to the curse's destructive nature? The curse wanted him to suffer, to watch those he'd cursed die in agony. But the guilt didn't lie with some notorious force of dark magic. Instead, it lay with his best friend, the embodiment of life itself. All this time, it was Razhar and his smiles, his patronizing optimism, and all his lies.

Elerek hadn't asked for Razhar to appear, almost out of nowhere, in his life—and certainly hadn't asked to be pushed into that fountain in the palace gardens. But Razhar had also helped him *out* of the fountain, dripping in smelly pond water.

After that, they were inseparable. No matter where Elerek chose to hide, Razhar found him. He mocked him, teased him incessantly, and laughed at everything. Without prompting, he would tell Elerek all about his adventures, which only grew more elaborate as they got older. Of course, Elerek grew jealous and hurled insults at every available opportunity. But Razhar stuck with him.

Most shied away. Fearful of his touch.

Razhar had stayed because he *had* touched him.

Elerek's eyes misted with tears. All those years, his father hunted curse binders. He tore them from the farthest reaches of Instanolde and the outlying tribes. Tortured them. Murdered them. Many were later proved innocent.

Only one had to die. The Kushite boy who lived in the palace. If he'd known, would he have done it? Sacrificed his best friend?

His father would have. Another casualty of the bitter violence his rule had waged. No one in his homeland would miss him. Elerek would have been free of the curse long ago. Cormek would've never been named heir, never rode out to his death. Perhaps Lystra might have attracted his attention anyways.

A mural-worthy life built upon the blood of an innocent man. Well, as innocent as Razhar could be, anyways.

Soldiers gave their lives to their king every day in the name of loyalty. Razhar was no soldier. He was nobody. But he was loyal, and he was Elerek's best friend.

The Jarkins called a halt. Gaudab dismounted as his men and their reptiles formed a large circle. They scrambled for their waterskins, emptying their contents so they could be filled again. So Elerek could be used.

Was Razhar any different? Using him to save his own skin?

He wondered if Razhar would find freedom if the curse could be broken. But they would never know. Razhar would die in the desert, with Lystra.

Gaudab untied one of his hands to refill the waterskins, keeping an iron grip on the other. "Won't be long now." His rancid breath blew hot over Elerek's shoulder. "Don't try anything."

Biting down on the gag, Elerek kept his focus on the steady stream of water pouring into the waiting vessels until the skins were full and the caravan set off again. Nothing remained to try. No grand plan or escape. Just the end, by the blade and the wrathful stars in the heavens.

At another time, he'd yearned for the end. Begged for it. How many days had he wasted cultivating his own suffering? Stewing in misery and burning with jealousy? Corrupting the gifts he'd been given by the brokenness he'd never even attempted to fix.

Until his brother died.

And I failed, Cormek. I'm sorry.

Even his task, this last task—avenging his brother and drowning the invaders—seemed beyond his ability. Without Razhar, he'd lose himself. Destroy the Jarkins, but he wouldn't break the curse.

Dying seemed simpler.

The cardants veered left, causing Elerek to teeter, the ropes cutting into his legs. As he peered over the edge, he realized the earth was packed and marked with smooth stones. A road.

Up ahead, the canyon widened, the cliffs sloping downward, as if they were ships slowly sinking and becoming submerged in the sands. The road followed a trail of deep red stones, as if they'd been painted with blood. The wind did its work, carving curious structures that towered toward the sky like spires. Gaps and holes opened like windows through the rock, revealing a deep blue sky beyond. The strange structures spurred Elerek to imagine that the shapes were ghosts of soldiers and cardants. The dead that would see no justice.

He craned his neck to look forward. But none of the spires were *the* towers, those built by man. Darcress. They were almost there.

Elerek then looked to the sky. The sun had left its apex, leaning toward the horizon in a slight tilt. Just after midday. The Jarkins couldn't slaughter him until nightfall, until the starlight came to claim him.

Only hours remained, hours left to live.

Memories of the dreams he'd dreamed in the desert filled his mind. The red towers of the Darcress Kasbah. The blinding white of starlight. The deep darkness of cursed waters cutting through the land. Such water wasn't life, no, it was fury. Fierce enough to re-form the land and wash away stone, sediment, and anything else unfortunate enough to stand in its way.

Can I be that fury? Can I be the wrathgiver?

Elerek swore that he would try.

Chapter 35

Razhar

When Razhar left the canyonlands of Kushan, he forsook allegiance to his people. Never again had his chest burned with the desire to live among the cliff dwellings or serve upon the back of a condor. Even in the golden city of Instanolde, he swore no loyalty to the people whom he'd known only as the enemy.

His devotion lay to his friends—to the cursed.

However, Elerek had been called to the throne. The new king had devoted himself to an allegiance, an idea, the hope of serving his people in a way that his forefathers hadn't. After all the bloodshed, injustice, and petty discord, Razhar knew that he must support Elerek in this endeavor—the only king to whom he would ever swear. After all, someone had to stand against mongering meddlers like Dalmah. Except Elerek wasn't here. He couldn't fight this battle against the woman who'd manipulated Razhar's baba to his own death, the false queen who created a charade to seize Lystra's crown, and the binder who sought to discredit him by way of the curse's condemnation.

But I am.

Here, in this moment, Razhar hadn't yet turned to sand. Standing here before the two rulers who had wronged those whom he loved, he still breathed. And he wouldn't hide anymore.

"My name is Razhar." He drew his hands into tight fists. "And I stand loyal to the king of Instanolde—and his queen."

Chief Wuhaz blinked his aged eyes—eyes that would've beheld the order for his baba's execution. "Emblino. The missing child of a condemned criminal. Have you lived in Instanolde all this time?"

"In the palace, actually. My baba didn't deserve to die."

"Razhar, wait." Fear infiltrated Lystra's voice.

"Impertinent words." Dalmah's eyes flashed wickedly. "The kingdoms I know—both Instanolde and the esteemed Kushan—would never tolerate such talk concerning such a curse. Tell me, how many cursed have you watched die? Would you have my granddaughter be next?"

Their eyes met. Razhar's veins pulsed with rage. It took an incredible amount of control to hold back, his boots firmly planted in the red earth of his homeland. But he couldn't very well go punching a countess. How he wished that he still had the writ of sale, that he hadn't lost it in the Sancen.

"Too many." He held her stare. "And every time I beheld a soul perish at the cruelty of this curse, I knew it was undeserved—that it didn't have to happen. I know this firsthand, like no one else does."

"Hmph." Dalmah eyed him with a curious fascination, as if he were a rare blend of spices on display at the market. "That you do."

Sharp, fine grains of sand poked through the flesh of Razhar's hands, crawling up his arms, and he was reminded again of what he was—and that Elerek was so far, far away.

No, there was no one like him. Even his sufferings, his trials, were unique. They had forged him into the man he'd become today, and right now, he had a choice. He could become that man, the one who could lay aside his lowly roots and cease counting himself as only a punishment and take up a mantle more glorious than that of any cape of glistening condor feathers.

The choice is mine.

Dalmah swept back toward the chief, speaking before anyone could counter. "Chief Wuhaz, your scouts did well to bring this one back. During my time imprisoned by the Jarkin invaders, this man came to visit the pretender king while he bore chains. I heard everything. How, because of his father's foul actions in binding the curse, he became a counter curse as punishment. He is essential to breaking this curse."

Razhar scoffed. No words seemed appropriate to combat the monstrosity of the countess's lies. Nothing he could say would bring his father justice. Nothing he could do would expose Dalmah's treachery.

"Unnecessary," Lystra declared. "This very moment, your *king* rides with the Jarkins, as their captive. He intends to destroy them with the curse's power and then sacrifice himself per the conditions of the curse." She turned to her grand-mother, her gaze as sharp as the blade that would pierce Elerek's heart. "Beneath the wrathgiver constellation with the curse binder's dagger."

An oath echoed over the sands. Razhar met Norbah's sorrowful gaze and Cole's wide eyes and gave a somber nod, confirming this grim fate as truth. Two more devoted friends that would die if Elerek couldn't break the curse.

Stars above, it should've been me.

Shame rolled over Razhar's soul like the breaking of a wave against a ship's prow. Elerek deserved to live and be happy, didn't he? Why couldn't Razhar give him that? Because he was afraid to die? Afraid to be the lowly Kushite who died to save the worthy Instan king?

The only one who could make him a lowly Kushite was himself. His choice.

"This is the king's decision, not ours." Lystra's voice didn't so much as waver. Not even now, speaking of the death of her own husband.

Razhar brushed the sand from his knuckles. What would Elerek say, if he were here?

Probably something insensitive.

Would Elerek ask him to die for him?

He released a long exhale. Perhaps the nobility of House Karim and the ferocity of House Arghan had finally rubbed off on him. If Elerek and Lystra could face what they had with their courage intact, with unyielding devotion and honor, perhaps he could aspire to a simple shimmer of their radiance.

I can break the curse.

His mission here was complete, he'd seen Lystra back to the arena of her expertise. Surely she would handle these old crumbling pillars and Norbah would lend her his strength, as he'd done to Elerek for all these years. He had to go back, and hear Elerek's answer. He had to keep Elerek from making a terrible mistake.

"The curse binder's dagger?" Wuhaz cast a shrewd eye on Razhar.

"An artifact lost to time." Dalmah tilted her head only slightly, the light catching in her blood-red earrings. "I remember days before bloody Lorkin's purge when research and literature were valued and not burned. Curses tied to weapons were most deplorable."

"It's not here." Lystra spoke through ground teeth. "The king knows what to do with it."

The countess responded with silence. A terrible, vengeful silence. Razhar took a step back, afraid to be scorched by the woman's burning eyes, as if she intended to incinerate her own granddaughter on a funeral pyre beneath the stars.

She took a decisive step toward Lystra, her chin prim and high. "I see no reason why we should expect this boy—the cursed mongrel—to do the right thing. I've come to expect that of no one."

Out of the corner of Razhar's eyes, he saw Lystra's hands tighten. The countess's implications were clear: She'd wanted Lystra to do it. To kill him.

How else had Lystra come to possess the dagger? How many people had Dalmah attempted to manipulate into destroying Elerek while her hands stayed clean?

He wished he could smile until his cheeks hurt, beaming with pride, knowing that Lystra had chosen not to kill Elerek—that her love would be enough to keep him alive.

He could live with that. He wondered if he could die with it too.

"Lystra, Your Highness." He edged closer. "I must go."

Her eyes pierced the whole of him. With all the grace and elegance of the perfect queen, she gave a solemn nod.

"What need have we, of this dagger?" Wuhaz demanded.

"A great need." Dalmah eyed Razhar. "If a false king won't break the curse, perhaps a Kushite who knows its evils will."

"Shackle him." This call didn't come from the countess who had spun lies around his life, but from the chieftain who knew nothing, who'd given the order for his baba's execution without asking enough questions.

For once in his life, Razhar didn't move fast enough.

Kushite soldiers surrounded him, their cloaks flapping, as if they were made of wings instead of merely feathers. Razhar squirmed and struggled, but they drove him to his knees. All the while, sand scraped down his arms. He no longer felt in control of it—the distance between him, Elerek, and the stars far too great.

"Stop!" Lystra demanded. "I forbid this."

"If Fahwal's boy is a counter curse, then he too must be killed." Wuhaz rose from his seat to stand beside Dalmah. His aged face appeared made of stone, hardly aware that he spoke of ending a life, particularly one who wore the skin of his own people.

"You don't understand." Lystra's hands curled into trembling fists. Her curse mark had spread across her hands again. "He heals the cursed. He's kept us—he's kept *me*—alive."

"And I'm sure, the cursed cur." Dalmah adjusted her scarf with a sniff. "Who should have died long ago."

Lystra's glare turned poisonous. "Stop insulting *my husband*."

Razhar strained against the soldiers' grip. Thrusting his hands forward, sand cascaded from his fingertips. Proof of his strangeness, his absurdity, the curse that kept doomed kings from drowning. "By starfire above and blasted Sancen sands below." He spoke through gritted teeth. "El is *not* his curse. Stars above, he's willing to destroy himself to save us."

Let me go. Let me save him.

Across the circle, a gasp echoed over the assembly. "Lystra . . .?"

Razhar had seen this girl the night he and Lystra had danced in the multicolored lights of the market torches. Tears burst from her eyes as she watched in horror. The panic spread, shaking through the foundations of stone beneath their feet as the entourage swept back from the queen who had twice survived the desert.

Skin *melted* from Lystra. The golden glow of amber slipped away, replaced by the sickly, wet sheen of the curse. Lystra's flowing hair hung limp, weighed down with moisture. Her eyes grew dull, pale. And beneath her skin, the leering grin of a skull appeared. The mortified silence broke with the sound of dripping water, cascading off Lystra's shoulders and clothing, forming a pool beneath her boots.

A sight Razhar had seen before—the sight of innocent souls as they burst into droplets and died. Each death seared a cruel scar across his heart, a reminder that someone else had drowned from the curse. That he had failed.

No. Not Lystra. Not when they were so close.

The queen fell to her knees. Her eyes rolled back in her open sockets. What humanity lingered in her bones seemed an island surrounded by the pool of water darkening the red stone of Kushan to the color of blood.

Elerek—was he dead? Maybe he hadn't made it. The curse unbroken.

Razhar glanced at Norbah and Cole. Their curse marks, exposed for all to gape at, remained unchanged. No, the curse knew vengeance. It came for Lystra, the girl Elerek loved.

As a string of foul words fled his mouth, Razhar jerked himself free from the astonished Kushite soldiers. He ran to Lystra, catching her just before she keeled over. Sand and water mingled together.

A sliver of soft skin ran down her arm. Not enough, but something.

"No, no, stars above." Razhar found his eyes filled with tears. "Lystra, please, hold on."

Dalmah gave an inhuman shriek, a sound more suited to the Sancen's wraiths. "See! See what this curse has done—what evil has done? Not my granddaughter. Please, not my granddaughter. The counter curse must die. We must take him to Darcress, find the dagger, and *kill him*."

Razhar took Lystra's pale fingers. His sands flowed out of

him and into her water, golden grains of desert clothing her once again in humanity's frail and beautiful garb. But the exchange happened *so slowly*. Razhar could feel the resistance, the curse raging against him with the same fury that caused Elerek to drown a man in a cell, to form a canyon into a canal.

He'd been here before. Fighting to push back death, the struggle that began anew with each sunrise. But he'd never won the battle, never saved anyone from drowning. If nothing changed, Lystra would die too.

Gently, he laid the queen down on the soaked rock. The midday sun cast a shimmer over her crystal skin, creating patterns of moisture and light. Razhar squinted at the sun, bright against the red canyons. Only hours remained. He had to reach Darcress before the stars appeared.

Razhar glared at Dalmah, despising her feigned tears. "*You* did this, Dalmah of House Arghan. Not El, not our king. If Lystra dies, her blood and water lie on your hands. Just like my baba's." He stepped closer. "I remember. I remember coughing and sputtering as sand grew inside my lungs while you told my baba that my life was the price he must pay. You wanted your revenge, you got it. But look at who has paid the consequences."

As the soldiers swarmed Razhar once more, clasping his hands in iron chains, he held Dalmah's gaze. Her tears seemed to freeze. Her face relaxed. And then, only for Razhar to see as they dragged him away, she smiled.

Chapter 36

Lystra

Voices swirled above, like the endless echo of moving water.

Lystra felt as if she were floating, even as a bed solidified beneath her. When she opened her eyes, water drained from her eyelids, flowing onto the pillow beneath her head. Everything felt heavy, even the heaving of her own lungs to take in air.

I'm next.

She knew. In her heart, in her soul, in every exposed bone beneath her watery flesh, that her end had come.

The walls around her were stone, rock hollowed out by the work of chisels. A shaft of afternoon light fell upon her arm, sending a shimmer over the wall. Diamonds created by the fusion of light and water.

Lystra wondered what it would feel like. To drown from the inside out. To die.

Movement stirred near the corner. Corsha sat on a stool, her back against the wall. Beautiful still, even without her colorful silks, she rubbed her forehead wearily.

"Oh, Lystra . . ." She leaned forward.

"Don't touch me." Lystra could hardly hear her own voice, distorted and gargled. Her mouth was full of water and, no matter how many times she swallowed, she couldn't get rid of it.

Corsha moved toward the door. "I know. I've been talking to the general. I don't understand, Lystra. All this time . . .?"

Lystra blinked, casting away more water. The last time she'd spoken to her cousin, she'd all but admitted to falling in love with the king. Now the only thing anyone knew about Elerek was that he was cursed.

Opening the door, Corsha stepped aside as Norbah entered.

The immense soldier seemed to fill the tiny chamber, even without his armor. "My queen." He dropped to one knee. "No matter what your grandmother calls herself, my loyalty is sworn to you and the king." As he rose, sorrow deepened the circles beneath his eyes.

Starkindler bless this man. "General." Lystra tried to smile. Her jaw hurt. "Thank you."

Shaking his head, Norbah sighed. "Your Highness . . . you look . . ."

"I'm close, aren't I?" Lystra pushed herself up, the simple motion draining her strength.

"You look like Azraa before she . . ."

Died. Lystra tried to close her eyes but found that her eyelids were made of water. She almost asked for a mirror, wondering if her own skull would grin back at her. But such a thing would be better not to see. It wouldn't be her. Only the curse.

Tears filled Corsha's eyes. "Vianni, did the king really . . . did he do this to you?"

Lystra gritted her teeth, real and solid within her watery

mouth. "El would never bring me to harm. This curse was my choice, just as I also chose him." She looked to her cousin with an expression that she hoped appeared soft. "Corsha, he . . . I love him. With all that I am."

Her cousin, the romantic that she was, stared at Lystra with wide eyes, the despair there fading into triumph. Even Norbah, the immense warrior, cracked a smile that broke the ice on his face.

"I wanted to save him . . ." Lystra didn't know if her cursed eyes were capable of tears, but the beat that still pounded in her chest was one of agony. "But El saved me, time after time after time. His powers kept us alive."

Squaring his shoulders, Norbah again took the stance of a general at attention. "Pardon my ignorance, Your Highness. I don't understand. The curse changed so suddenly. El changed. And Razhar, is he really a counter curse?"

Lystra summarized the situation as best she could, her words slurred as they moved like a river from her lips. Taking a towel from a nearby washbasin, she dried her face over and over.

Another layer of darkness shaded the general's face. "All this time?"

"He kept you alive because you're precious to El."

Norbah closed his eyes. "Now they'll die. Both of them if the countess gets her way."

Lystra's insides—what remained of them—twisted. "I don't know how to save him."

Admitting it, both out loud and in her soul, stabbed deeper than the dagger destined for Elerek's heart. A vow broken, but she belonged to her kingdom first. Instanolde had to be saved. If Elerek were the cost, so be it.

This voice sounded like Grandmother, not her.

"What have they done to Razhar?"

Norbah's hands clenched. "They locked him up. They intend to fly him to Darcress."

To sacrifice him. They would break the curse, and make sure that Elerek died. But no one knew that Elerek and Razhar were even more powerful together. Illuminated by the light of the wrathgiver, they would see their task through—and drown them all.

Lystra exhaled a long breath, a struggle with her water-logged lungs. Perhaps both men would be the cost. "General, what hope have we of taking back Instanolde from the Jarkins?"

Running a hand along his bearded cheek, Norbah frowned. "I've spoken with the Kushite commanders. There are numbers enough here if we attack from the air. I brought Kimzi to coordinate with the archers as he trained with the king's division. My men back in the city are ready to revolt. With the curse spreading and the Jarkins losing their hold, I'm sure it would be a short battle."

She held a smile, a mask to cover the terror and the sorrow. "Thank you, General. I can think of no one better to lead our soldiers. Make certain that the dawn rises upon Instanolde."

The general nodded. "I will do this in your honor, Your Highness."

She would take back her kingdom and be its queen again— if she didn't perish first.

The door burst open, and the room darkened. Shadows seeped from the inky blackness of Dalmah's silks, pooling about her feet and opening a deep void beneath them.

Her gaze swept between Corsha and Norbah. "Leave us."

Lystra clenched her hands, a steady *drip, drip, drip* falling from her fists.

Dalmah pushed the door shut behind them. "I should have known better." She shook her head, ruby earrings swaying. "Than to think you were ready, that your shoulders could bear these things. Perhaps if the Jarkins hadn't come, you might have been a pretty queen for peaceful times. Well." She huffed. "It cannot be helped now."

Lystra looked away. "I've little time left; I won't spend it listening to your insults."

Dalmah scoffed. "Now that we have the counter curse, we need only spill his blood to set you free." Her eyes narrowed to slits, like the heavy-lidded eyes of sand vipers. "A counter curse *and* the cost. Such a thing is rare, rarer than blue ivoress flowers. All the Kushite's strange powers and it's still not enough. Curses cannot be fixed with curses. Consequences are to be paid, not undone."

"You cannot kill Razhar for the sake of breaking the curse." Lystra glared. "When Elerek reaches the wrathgiver this very night, he will drown the Jarkin army, avenge Cormek, and use the dagger to break the curse himself." She inhaled, amassing enough air to give voice to the darkest of truths. "That is how you intended it, when *you* bound the curse."

"So noble." Dalmah floated across the room, eclipsing the afternoon light from the window. "But you see, after all that's happened, the boy cannot be permitted to live. The people would never accept one who has dealt so much devastation, all from a single touch."

Lystra leapt to her feet. Water cascaded down her clothing, puddling beneath her. "How dare you! El's saving the kingdom! Saving everyone!" Did Dalmah have no remorse? Did she think her actions evil at all? "You did this, Grandmother. You brought this horror upon the kingdom."

The entire room swayed, toppling like waves over a cliff. Lystra slid down onto the bed again, holding her head. Nausea rolled over her like a vessel on a stormy sea.

"You won't survive, Lystra. Even if your little king completes his mission."

Her blood. Her water. On Grandmother's hands. "Can't you undo it?" Lystra scowled. "You, who blackened your soul binding an unholy, horrible thing beneath the sacred stars and allowed a curse to strike a child who committed no wrongdoing?"

Pacing the room, Dalmah stepped into the shadows again. "I'm hardly the first binder among our line. You'll find the deed has haunted many a murky history. The curse wasn't directly cast against the boy, rather, his father. Lystra, vianni, I cannot imagine that you would know what it felt like when the throne was taken from me. To lose my king, my husband, the father of my son, to a thoughtless, bloody war, *and then* have the entire kingdom turned against me. To be shunned, cast out, and to lose all that was rightfully *mine*. Lorkin had no right." She shook her head. "Now, imagine watching the distress mar Lorkin's kingly brow as he discovered that his heir, his firstborn son, bore a curse. His agony as he must withhold himself and his queen from touching the child, sentencing servants to die in his care. Even when the child contracted skeetos, knowing that he couldn't allow the child to receive healing without revealing the terrible curse. To go mad hunting curse binders and having them killed. To watch as his queen fell prey to the curse and died quickly, unable to keep away from her son."

Lystra's heart sputtered. Elerek never mentioned his mother. It must've happened when he was young. Another agony that he'd carried his entire life.

Dalmah paused, breathing a deep breath that elevated her chest and somehow made her seem taller, more formidable. "No, you cannot imagine the feeling. Satisfaction—deep as the Gungole and as searing as the Sancen."

Lystra forced air into her waterlogged lungs. How could she not have seen the bitter hatred of her grandmother before? A woman who had indeed lost—a loss not much different from

Lystra's own—but had manufactured her loss into something wretched. What might have been if Dalmah had chosen not to enact the curse? To multiply her own suffering to so many others?

And now, all Instanolde lay beneath the curse's threat. How many would die because Dalmah wanted revenge?

Lystra's gaze dropped to her hands, more water than flesh. Even she'd been caught in its snare, cursed by her own grandmother. This couldn't continue. No one else would suffer because of her grandmother's hatred.

"To answer your question, vianni." Dalmah folded her hands and looked back at her. "Even if I could undo the curse—a task completed only by the curse's own stipulations, the rare existence of a counter curse, or the cost of a direct descendant—I would change nothing." She tilted her head to one side. "I would only see you safe, my granddaughter."

Lystra scoffed. "Even while I perish from the curse that you created."

But her mind had stalled, unable to focus on Dalmah. She dangled from a cliff, hanging by mere threads strung together by simple words. Words she wondered if her grandmother had meant to speak. Their weight enough to sink her into depths too dark to see.

The curse's own stipulations—Elerek's death would break it.

The existence of a counter curse—Razhar also could choose to die.

The cost of a direct . . .

Lystra's pulse pounded in her ears. It sounded like a river, a thundering canal. Rushing waters through the desert, where water wasn't meant to flow.

A direct descendant. Someone from the curse binder's line. Someone like her.

A strangled gasp escaped her throat, each breath more difficult than the last. She put a hand to her chest, coughing. When
she could speak, her entire body shuddered. Gripping the edge
of the bed, she pushed herself up. "Razhar . . . I must . . ."

A wave of nausea rolled over her. Water slipped from her
eyes, her ears, her mouth. The world flipped on its head, as if
caught adrift in a storm. Dalmah grabbed hold of her with bony
hands.

Lystra nearly cried out, but her grandmother spoke quickly.
"The curse is mine. It cannot harm me."

Dalmah guided her from the room and down a stone corridor. The passage curved as it descended, wide, uneven steps
cut into the canyon walls themselves. Each seemed a plummet
to Lystra, only able to stand while leaning heavily upon her
grandmother.

So, this was dying. Her eyes drifted upward. Toward the
light, streaming in long shafts from tiny round windows cut in
the rock. Beyond, pale afternoon sky shone above red, vibrant
cliffs and verdant alcoves. Beauty and wildness and all the
things that Lystra loved.

She didn't want to die here. Not in the darkness. Not
without the sun on her face and the wind in her hair.

Not without Elerek.

The whole of her soul seemed to cleave inward. Lystra's
shoulders hunched, shuddering with an emotion that felt akin
to pain. A raw, familiar pain. The void of separation. The
bitterness of loss. Grief's dagger wedged in her heart. Was it
only last night that she'd slept in his arms? That they'd kissed
beneath the stars?

That they'd bound their souls to one another with new
vows?

She couldn't die yet. She hadn't saved Instanolde yet, and
she hadn't saved him.

"Grandmother . . . *enough*." Lystra's voice rasped, her very breath snatched away.

Dalmah looked at her.

"What you have destroyed . . . I will repair." She returned the stare. "A. Direct. Descendant."

They halted on the stairwell. Two queens standing eye to eye. Frozen in their resolution.

Lystra didn't back down. She lifted her chin, listening to the *drip, drip, drip* of water falling down her body as the curse consumed her. How many years had it consumed Elerek, plaguing him with the guilt that he'd been killing his victims? No, this poison was older.

And it would end with her.

Lystra wrenched her hands away, stumbling back against the wall. The smooth stonework welcomed her transformation, like a stream flowing along smooth-cut cliffs.

"I know your grief, Grandmother. Your loss. The gaping emptiness. Look at how you have filled it."

Never again. Lystra had longed for freedom, for a life beyond Dalmah's influence. She'd set her sights high, choosing the same freedom that Dalmah had craved—the throne.

But the throne hadn't brought her freedom. Instead, it had given her purpose. The chance to fulfill her duty to her people, to save them as they deserved to be saved, to give them all that her grandmother had taken away.

To give Elerek the chance to be all that Cormek wanted him to be.

Dalmah's desert-amber skin turned pale. "Lystra, granddaughter . . ."

"Never again will you taint Instanolde, from the Gungole's depths to the Sancen's wastes. Twice I have returned from the desert and now I will go back—and save my people."

In that moment, Lystra no longer felt the burden of the

curse sinking her. As weightless as a condor in flight, as fast as a cardant, as strong as a warrior, and as lithe as a dancer.

Gem of the Gungole.

Fire of the Sancen.

Fierce as the dawn.

Mighty as the constellations.

Now, and always, the queen of Instanolde. And in her presence, Dalmah fell silent.

Chapter 37

Razhar

Razhar's knees hit the stone of the tiny cell where his own kinsmen had dragged him away and locked him up. Could this be the same cell? Where they'd kept his baba before he was executed?

Doubling over, his chains rattled as he yanked his hands through his oily hair. His lungs ached to breathe, the scratch of sand in his throat. After days spent exposed to the wilds, the stillness of the cavern prison weighed heavy on his shoulders, suffocating.

Time. They'd so little of it left. Each grain of sand, breaking free from among the pores of his skin and scraping down his arms, seemed to rend the tiniest shred of his soul.

He didn't have time to wait here.

Lystra didn't have time.

Elerek didn't have time.

"Stars above." He shook his head. The lies the countess had spun. The bitterness of his own people. Why did it endure? Why couldn't they just stop?

Outside the tunnel of cells, he could hear the commotion of

condors flapping and tack rattling. He hoped they were preparing for flight, to take him to Darcress. Back to the desert.

Back to Elerek.

Staring down at his hands, he watched as his skin began to shrivel, dry and cracked. Sand covered his forearms, seeping out from his sleeves. He considered the distance, the stretch of the Sancen where the Darcress Kasbah stood at the throat of the mountain pass. This was the farthest apart he and Elerek had ever been.

Footsteps hurried up the tunnel. The shape of a man filled the corridor. A man broad of chest and shoulders, with a scimitar at his hip.

Razhar pulled himself to his feet, gripping the bars with his sand-clad hands. "Norbah?"

The general didn't meet his eye, but produced a ring of keys and unlocked the cell.

As the bars swung back, Razhar remained rooted. "I suppose you're angry with me?"

Selecting another key from the ring, Norbah frowned at the shackles encasing Razhar's wrists. Then, he slowly met his eyes, hesitation's shadow lingering there. "You can touch me."

Razhar reached for his hand, watching with a sad smile as the curse mark shrank away like water ought in the desert.

Norbah had never shown bitterness at being cursed, despite having forsaken his home and family to protect them. Throughout the years, he'd always stood loyal to Elerek. A father when Elerek's own had overlooked him.

"You kept me . . ." Norbah's brows knitted together, staring at the hand he so often wore gloved, his mark hidden. "I've lived so long . . ."

"If you must know, I did a bit of sneaking about. Do congratulate me on my stealth."

The general scowled.

"Right. Myra helped me. And there's this tea, it's quite incredible—"

"You could have told us." Norbah's eyes sharpened like the blades of his scimitars.

Razhar stiffened. "Would you have slit my throat?" He lifted his wrists, shackles rattling. "To break the curse?"

"Of course." The chains fell to the ground.

Razhar's heart followed, sinking down among the stone and the iron.

Then Norbah, the stern, severe general of Instanolde, threw his arms around him in a comrade's embrace. "Surely all the jokes cannot belong to you?"

Grunting, the air forced from his lungs, Razhar clapped the man on the back. "Ah, it wasn't funny."

Norbah shook his head and released him. "Come, we've work to do." Ducking out of the cell, he swiveled his head from the right to the left. "And I may have left some damage in these tunnels. They seemed quite insistent that you remain under lock and key."

"Oi, now they want me? After spending my entire life with your lot."

Empty cells passed by in a blur. Razhar tried not to think of other prisoners, of those who had once waited upon execution, remembered only as ghosts in starlit corridors.

"Norbah, back in Instanolde." He almost feared to ask. "Is everyone—?"

The general's steps slowed, taking the tunnels with caution. "By the Starkindler's mercy, they're all right. Bushra, Driss, Ishtal, and Cole's here with me. The tribe's stuck together; we're a family."

Razhar smiled, his heart swelling. One tribe he was proud to be counted among their numbers, and thankful to have known them at all—and given them days to live.

Voices echoed down the second tunnel, the clamor resembling the growls of furious cardants. Norbah's hand went to his scimitar. "I heard them mention Darcress. Why there?"

"That's where the wrathgiver will be, the stars by which El has to die." Razhar winced at the harsh reality of his words. Terrible truths for terrible times.

Norbah glanced over his shoulder, his features stricken. "He'll do it, won't he?"

"We will do it." *One of us.* Razhar's vision skimmed the coating of sand upon his forearms. *Or both of us.*

Perhaps the myths and legends had gotten one thing right. From the storytellers of Instanolde's markets, the underground libraries of Kushan, and the campfire tales of the Jarkins, the counter curse couldn't escape death. Razhar imagined himself on the back of a condor, a creature he could not control. It flew toward the sun and a collision course was inevitable, a fate that couldn't be cheated or avoided.

Norbah swore. "So, I broke you out of prison to be saved *from* being taken to Darcress so that you can go *to* Darcress?"

"I'm sure I'll be much more comfortable this way."

The general peered round the next corner. With an effortless agility, he pounced forward, surprising a guard. Before the man could sound an alarm, Norbah slammed his head against the stone, rendering him unconscious. "Be ready to run."

Razhar eyed the Kushite, stepping carefully over his fallen form. "Where are we going?"

"To the queen."

Up ahead, golden sunlight streamed through the passage. Razhar inhaled a deep breath. "You do mean Lystra, yes?"

Shadows indicated movement up ahead. Norbah's stance tensed. "Is there another?"

"Absolutely not." Razhar hunched his shoulders, steeling himself for the moment the soldiers realized that he bore no chains and would escape Kushan a free man for the second time in his life.

"Tell me." Norbah adjusted his grip on his scimitar. "Does El love her as much as she loves him?"

A grin cracked over Razhar's face. "Stars, they're insufferable."

Norbah chuckled. "I'm glad of it." He stopped, his boots planted. "Steady . . . run."

And run they did. Chiseled stone gave way to gravel and soft tufts of grass. Razhar's lungs heaved, expanding wide for the wild air of his homeland. He drew his eyes to the sky, a deep azure above the heights of the red canyon walls. Gratitude for the sun filled his soul.

As long as the sunlight drowned out the stars, they lived.

Shouts rang from the clusters of shelters and perches, but they didn't stop. Norbah led the way down a winding path, keeping close to the canyon wall. They ducked into another passage carved into the stone walls. Razhar panted as their steps turned to stairs.

"I will go back—and save my people."

The echo of the queen's voice filled the stairwell, growing in its depth and its severity.

Razhar caught his breath. Save? He didn't doubt that Lystra would do anything and everything within her power, but how?

Rounding another curve of the stone-cut stairs, there, dripping and pale, stood Lystra, the one and only queen of Instanolde.

She wore the face of others—Azraa, Fin, Hassam, Yasmine, and so many others. The same face that taunted Razhar's nightmares—the ones he couldn't save from their watery deaths.

Only her eyes set her apart. The curse had taken her body, but her soul remained her own, burning with a determination fierce enough to strike the constellations down from the sky.

A soft gasp cascaded from her lips. "Razhar . . ."

Razhar bounded up the steps, gently taking her face in his hands. Skin blossomed from his fingertips, spreading across her cheeks, her brow, and down her neck. Lystra drew a deep breath, steadied.

Reaching for her hands, the sight of her restoration filled him with the hope of a new dawn. He grinned. "Instanolde needs you, my queen."

She gave him a faint smile.

Dalmah stood behind her. Aloof and cold, her eyes were vials of poison. Razhar turned toward her, opening his hands and letting the sand drop from his palms and pile at her feet.

"The least you could do, after all your lies, after the heinous things you've done to my baba, to my king, and to me, is thank me," Razhar spat. "For preserving the life of your granddaughter. For *saving* life, rather than letting it bleed or drown."

The countess's eyes narrowed, the slit-like pupils of a deadly viper.

"I've seen precious little justice in the world. I hope you receive a mite of it. Stars know you deserve it." He looked back at Lystra. "I must go to Darcress."

"I'm going with you." Her hands clenched and she took the stance of a soldier, ready to ride into battle.

Razhar shook his head. It was no use to claim the dangers and perils. Not now, in this last stage of their game.

Apparently Lystra didn't trust his silence. "You won't stop me."

"I'm not permitted to tell the queen what she can and cannot do."

She dipped her chin primly.

Turning to Norbah, Razhar forced his shoulders back and

his head high to match the general's giant-like stature. "If I don't come back, take care of our own."

Our own. Cursed and few that they were, but brave as the stars in the heavens.

Once again Norbah, the fierce general of Instanolde, wrapped him in a tight embrace. "You have my word. Take care of El. Tell him what he's been to us."

Razhar smiled and returned the embrace, thankful for the feel of another human being.

As he stepped back, Norbah clasped his shoulder. "I won't tell you, your head's big enough as it is."

"Another thing." Lystra's voice rang as clear as a silver trumpet, no longer distorted by the curse. "Norbah, general of Instanolde, please make it known to Chief Wuhaz and the nobles of Kushan and Instanolde that the woman you see before you is a curse binder. Guilty of binding the curse afflicting Elerek, the rightful king of Instanolde."

Norbah's face paled.

"As your queen, I order you to arrest her—she's in no danger from the curse—and keep her in chains. I'm sure Kushan will deal with her as in accordance with their laws."

Razhar watched Dalmah's face as Lystra spoke. Her features were cast in stone, like a statue carved of the purest marble. She didn't speak or protest.

If Kushan did deal with her according to their laws, then justice would be served, but Razhar knew that was too much to hope for. If he believed little in justice, he believed less in vengeance. None of it would undo the pain, the evil. Even now, as Lystra pronounced guilt upon her own flesh and blood, he wondered if he ought to feel satisfied. He didn't.

Perhaps it didn't matter whether Dalmah paid for her crimes or lived out her days in luxury. The powers that were would make their choices and play their games. Razhar felt only the burning desire to go to Darcress. Make his stand. Live with air in his lungs and blood in his veins.

Moments that no one could steal from him.

Beside him, Lystra took one last, long look at her grandmother. Her eyes turned to steel. Then she swept past Razhar, hurrying down the steps. He followed her.

Chapter 38

Elerek

The red towers of the Darcress Kasbah cast two long shadows, stretching down from the cliffs across layers upon layers of ribboned sandstone.

Elerek craned his neck to gape at the towers. Their height rivaled the tallest spire of his golden palace, straight as any archer's arrow, and as red as the blood spilled upon these sands. The fortress's stout wall ran along the canyon's edge, as if carved from the rock itself. Ragged, black flags flew from its heights.

Cormek died here.

Closing his eyes, Elerek bit down on the gag and drew in air that smelled of sweat and heat. Here, the stronghold stood like a sentinel over the gateway to the mountains where their enemies dwelt. This marked the end of his kingdom, the edge of the Sancen's desolation.

Cormek meant to inspire courage, to give charge to the soldiers who kept watch during the height of summer. He'd brought Lystra and her cardants as a promise of building loyal ranks who would see their kingdom in security and peace.

Elerek had come as a captive, a sacrifice, as blood to fulfill a curse's desire. Neither his nor his brother's death would accomplish what they intended.

"Riders!"

Gaudab wheeled Lystra's cardant around. Rope cut into Elerek's legs as he swayed with the reptile's momentum. Squinting, he watched the black shapes soar like drips of ink from a quill making their mark across the sky. Condors.

For a brief moment, hope stirred the embers in his dying heart. Thoughts of rescue, not for himself, but for Razhar and Lystra filled his mind. Had Kushan found them? Could it be that they hadn't died in the sand?

Elerek drew a wheezed breath, impeded by the gag. This canyon colored by blood and guarded by a fortress of war was not a place for hope.

"Loose arrows," Gaudab growled.

The Jarkins took bows from their backs and strung black-fletched arrows.

Silence hung in the air. A moment where all the world seemed to still. Even Elerek's heart forgot how to beat.

Bowstrings sang. The arrows vanished, lost in the speed and the distance. The condors' shrieks filled the air. The great birds lost their grace, wheeling and spiraling. Riders screamed before their voices were swallowed by the wind as their mounts hurtled to the jagged rocks below.

Elerek had watched plenty of men die. The moment came quickly, swathed in rage or the fury of battle and, most of all, the terror of drowning. But watching the Jarkins' cold countenances as they killed spiked his blood with wrath. They stole and exploited and killed without mercy. Even the land beneath them had been taken with the blood of his brother, the brother who belonged to the sun, a world without such horrors.

Cormek belonged to life. Elerek had never belonged to anything except death.

"We all have one life, Elerek. A mighty gift from the Maker of the stars. You say that you're not marked for life, but can't you see that right now, you've got the chance to live?"

The scene of the warrior caravan moving steadily onward to the red towers blurred with tears. Elerek drew a deep breath, a fresh resolve filling his chest. He still wasn't marked for life, but he had indeed lived. He lived while an extraordinary Kushite pushed back death, stealing cherished moments amid the rubble and the chaos. Lystra had stood beside him in those moments, digging them like gems from the sand. She had taught him to live.

If all that remained for him in this land of sand and sunlight was to die, then he would do it well.

Let me be starlight, Starkindler. Let me not be water.

"Filthy cowards." Gaudab huffed. "If you spy more, shoot them all down."

They neared the towers, the road entering a wide swath of land that sloped downward. As the cardant pitched forward, Elerek tried without success to settle himself in the saddle without feeling as if he were a pack strung to the cardant's back.

He turned his eyes to the canyon walls. Great, red monoliths that looked as if they'd been chiseled with tools wielded by the constellations themselves. Walls that could hold water.

"Are you going to do it? Take back Darcress? Drown them all?" Lystra's voice, rattling him with a courage he didn't know if he were capable of mustering.

Lystra and Razhar had made it easy to be brave. He wished that they were here. Without them, the task seemed a terrifying thing—as terrifying as the curse that could see it done.

If the curse took him . . . no, he couldn't think of it, only of saving Instanolde.

Toward the west, where his golden kingdom lay miles and miles away, the sun was well into its descent. The sky had faded from its deep blue, slowly sinking to pale yellow and the deepest oranges.

Elerek sat up a little straighter, straining against the ropes, and stared into the brilliance, letting it consume him. The last touch of the Sancen's rays upon his skin. The last light of wonder that illuminated the world, his world.

Another cardant sidled up beside them. The reptiles snapped at each other, Lystra's the clear agitator. Gaudab swore and jerked on the reins. "Fast demon but miserable mount."

The other warrior grimaced, giving his own mount some space. "Will we spend the remainder of summer here?"

"No choice. Tonight, we feast upon the stores of the fortress. No more cursed water." Gaudab cast a dark eye over his shoulder. "Instanolde will still be there at summer's end. Perhaps our men will have annihilated them by now."

"Or the other way 'round. We got more than we bargained for."

Spitting foul words, Gaudab shook his head. "We planned for everything, except a curse."

Hearing their snarls, their complaints, a fire ignited inside Elerek. His curse had become the sole obstacle in their plans. Not fortresses, kings, or armies. Not even the deadly Sancen. *His* curse.

He had to get his hands free—and the gag off his face. He needed to fight.

"The men camped here. I expect they'll be surprised to see us."

"Keep away until we've taken care of the curse."

Elerek twisted his wrists, shoulders straining, trying to wrestle his way out. Had they camped? Or were they occupying the fortress? Would he need to flood the towers too? Purge Instan land of the Jarkins' infection. These towers were his stage and the desert his audience.

As they drew nearer, pieces of humanity scattered the wildness of the desert. A helmet. A spear. Two great mounds rose from the sand and Elerek shuddered as he recognized them as the sun-bleached bones of cardants. Scavengers and the heat had done their duty, leaving no flesh. Gaping jaws lay open, studded with sharp teeth, and great empty sockets peered up toward the skies. Around arched spines and studded horns, the remnants of leather saddles could be seen, not yet claimed by the wilderness.

His brother had died here.

Instan soldiers, riding astride mighty cardants, unaware that they were about to be cut down. That the world was about to change. That death waited only a breath away.

Lystra had ridden among them, glorious and as free as the western winds. He was thankful that she didn't have to see this place again.

Finally. Elerek winced, working his hand through the loop of coarse rope. He loosened the gag, letting it fall around his neck, and licked his chapped, scabbed lips. Now, for the other hand . . .

"Keep still." Gaudab twisted in the saddle.

Elerek tucked both hands behind his back again.

Gaudab swore and turned forward, taking no notice of the slipped gag.

Two shadowed figures stood in the wide space between the two towers. Jarkins, mounted with long spears in their hands. Beyond them, shadowed by the immense cliffs down the

Darcress pass, he wondered how many waited, as unsuspecting as Cormek and the others who had died here.

The dagger lay in its sheath, tucked into Gaudab's belt. The ornate, gold designs glinted faintly in the fading light. Elerek leaned into the cardant's side-winding gait. He needed a knife and it may as well be that one.

He hesitated only a moment. Lurching forward, he seized the dagger, pulled it free—and plunged it into Gaudab's shoulder.

A feral, raging scream echoed over Darcress.

Elerek clenched his jaw, pulling the dagger back, the blade dripping with blood the color of the setting skies. He sliced the ropes binding his legs just as Gaudab recovered. The Jarkin clutched his shoulder, turning in the saddle with a poised fist.

Their eyes met, dusk gleaming red in their irises.

For Cormek.

Startled by the struggle upon its back, the cardant tossed its head and stamped its limbs. The upset provided Elerek the opportunity he needed. Water launched from his hand.

Gaudab tumbled from the saddle in a swirl of blood, leather, and cursed water. The cardant shrieked, sprinting forward. Elerek wrangled the reins into his grasp. He lay low over the saddle, praying that he'd keep his seat. With a tug, the cardant slowed just long enough for him to right himself. He'd never ridden without his legs strapped or someone to hold on to. One thousand unpredicted possibilities shot across his mind like falling stars.

Come on, girl. We've work to do. What was her name . . .? "Tiniah!"

The cardant curled its long talons into the sand, growling deep in her throat. Her head turned slightly sideways, just enough for one yellow eye to meet his. Elerek swallowed.

Behind them, Gaudab roared. The caravan moved as one, cardants racing toward them.

Elerek snapped the reins. Tiniah lurched, eager enough to outrun the approaching company. Air rushed about them, whipping his hair and clothing. For one beautiful moment, Elerek felt as if he were the freest man in the world. Free to sacrifice himself for his people, for his kingdom, for life beneath the star-cast sky. For Razhar. For Lystra.

Ahead, the two Jarkin scouts watched in bewilderment.

Elerek tucked the dagger into the band of his pants and raised a hand. Water shot from his fingertips. More than a stream, each drop seemed to multiply, becoming a vast and wild wave. More than Elerek and his curse had ever been before.

He saw the water reflected in their confused, terrified eyes, and then they were no more, men and cardant swept into Darcress.

Elerek gasped. Power tingled across his skin, more potent than anything he'd ever felt before. Water and death and vengeance.

He dreamed of Darcress. Red towers stretching to the sky. Blood stained the sand between them and the bones of cardants and men bleached white beneath the relentless summer sun.

Tiniah slowed upon the rise directly between the two towers. Before them, the land sloped into the pass. Tents made of hide dotted the shadows in ordered rows. Elerek pulled back on the reins. The water ceased from his fingertips, but the furious wave continued, marching down the pass like a stampede of cardants. It crashed and careened through the sand and rock and into the camp. Jarkins dwelling in triumph one moment and soaked the next in a churning mass of canvas, hide, armor, and the flailing arms and legs of men.

Not enough. He needed more—and they needed to die.

Instanolde would never be free until the filth had been washed away.

Elerek lifted his hand again, but furious voices filled his ears. Tiniah turned, snapping her jaws. Gaudab had remounted. As one, they surged toward him, ready to cut him down.

Drawing a hiss through his teeth, Elerek pulled a tent pole from the cardant's pack. Hardly an ideal weapon, but it felt solid in his hands.

Besides, his curse, his water, would end this war.

"Fall back, he's mine." Gaudab sat hunched atop his new mount, blood draining from his shoulder. He drew his scimitar, death gleaming in his eyes. Then, he charged.

Elerek prompted a tendril of water, like a long snake slithering across the sand toward his brother's killer. Gaudab didn't hesitate, riding in a rage of fury through the cursed water. As he drew close, his blade swung, singing in the air. Tiniah sidestepped, hissing. Elerek met the blow with his pole, splinters spraying. He pitched backwards, grasping the saddle.

Gaudab leaned over the side of his cardant and raised his scimitar again. "Your stars have arrived." He spoke as a sneer, a taunt.

Sparks of light appeared at the edges of Elerek's vision. Up above, the constellation that sealed his fate began its dance, the wrathgiver's movements faint, not yet in their full brilliance.

Skies full of endless stars. White light, pure and shimmering, more pristine than anything upon the ground.

A steadying breath inflated his lungs. Energy and light mingling with his blood and his curse. Here, he found the strength to do the impossible. The starlight called to the curse in his body.

Tonight, I am the wrathgiver.

Elerek lifted his hand, palm outward.

Gaudab's cardant lunged again. He raised his scimitar, moving with a warrior's swiftness—and sliced *through* Elerek's outstretched arm.

He cried out, but no pain followed. No felled limb. No spurt of red. His arm was no longer flesh, no longer human. Only water, untouched by the sword. Like the arrow.

Growling, Gaudab wrenched the pole out of Elerek's hands. The wood pummeled into his gut, knocking the air from his lungs. Indestructible against blade and arrow, and yet Elerek could do little more than fall from the cardant's saddle and topple into the sands. Gaudab dismounted, clawing like an animal. He yanked the dagger from Elerek's hip, the wrathgiver's light gleaming on its blade.

Drown him!

But before Elerek could act, the Jarkin sent a fist across his face. His head fell back. The stars seemed to multiply as his vision faded in and out.

Gaudab chuckled, standing over him with the dagger in his cursed hand. "Now, Instan rat, you'll die right here in the sands where I felled your brother. May your curse die with you."

Not . . . yet . . . Blackness fringed Elerek's vision.

And up above it all, the haze and the screams and the blood, he heard a condor's call.

Chapter 39

Lystra

Darcress. The kasbah. Bathed in a light as red as blood by the setting sun.

Lystra's skin tingled with gooseflesh. Not from the curse—skin clothed her limbs for now—but from the memories. The twang of arrows, the song of steel, the screams of dying men. The taste of a king's kiss. The terror that scalded her soul and the griefs she carried long after she left this place. What she had seen here had affected every area of her life and changed her world forever. And now, she'd come back to break a curse.

She flew atop the back of a condor, grasping Razhar, who had become her lifeline in more ways than one. They flew into shadow, chasing the moment between darkness and light, the exchange of sun and stars. The dying sun's rays burned at her back. If only she could hold it steady, command the very fires of the heavens to still, to wait. To let them live a bit longer.

Leaning over the condor's wing, she watched as the Jarkin caravan stirred up clouds of dust, cast gold in the fading light. They thundered toward the fortress, moving as one.

"There!" Razhar pointed. "Between the towers."

Lystra followed his finger. A circle of cardants gathered between the towers, Tiniah among them. From here, Elerek appeared small compared to the hulking Jarkins. Gaudab stalked toward him, scimitar in one hand and the cursed dagger in the other.

Why hadn't Elerek drowned him yet? Lystra tightened her grip on Razhar, water squeezing from between her fingers, as Gaudab smashed a bloody fist into Elerek's face. A cry loosed from her lips.

Razhar leaned forward, his hand outstretched. As the condor swept low, sand shot from his palm. Knocked off his feet, Gaudab collapsed, thrashing and struggling.

Thunk! The condor screeched, keeling sideways, an arrow lodged in its neck. For one terrible moment, they glided on air, free as the skies themselves. Then the bird stilled, diving headlong. Lystra screamed as darkness, starlight, and red earth spun over her vision. Sand eclipsed sky, the force of impact knocking Lystra and Razhar from the saddle and the breath from their lungs.

The red sands of Darcress covered Lystra. Sands that were once awash with the blood of her people. She dragged herself to her feet, limbs shaking.

She'd come back. The queen returned to the desert. Her desert. This time, she wouldn't run. She lifted her eyes. Up above, the wrathgiver moved through its stances, an assassin with a ready knife.

A king would not die today.

Razhar groaned, pushing aside the dead condor's wing. Coughing and sputtering, he blended in, his skin swiftly giving way to sand. "Stars above," he muttered, slapping the dirt from his clothes. "You all right, Your Highness?"

Lystra nodded. They'd landed on the far end of the canyon,

away from the armies. No turning back now. After tonight, no cursed water would flow on the paved stonework of Instanolde or the Sancen sands beyond. One summer to live all came down to a single night.

"Well, we're here and we're outnumbered."

Lystra raised an eyebrow. "Did you expect otherwise?"

Shrugging, Razhar gave a droll chuckle. "Well, El counts as a hundred."

Drip. Drip. Drip.

Lystra's gaze dropped to her hand. Here, in the starlight, her flesh withdrew, shimmering pale. Water dripped from her fingertips, darkening the sands below.

"Starlight," Razhar muttered, turning his eyes to the heavens. "We are *more* here."

A gust of wind stirred. Lystra grabbed hold of her scarf, its tail and tassels streaming behind her. Sand blew from Razhar as if he were made of dust and would simply crumble away across the Sancen.

Lystra's heart lodged in her throat. Time was running out for them both.

Razhar looked down at his hands. "I . . . I have to help him."

Lystra drew a steady breath. Only they could help Elerek, the only two who could save him.

"You . . . what will you do?"

She turned away, lest he see the secrets in her eyes, the hope of her soul laid bare. "Save my kingdom." The fierceness of the desert queen filled her voice. The queen she'd become— the queen she would ever be.

Razhar blinked, a question in his eyes, but he made no reply.

Together, they ran across the sands. Towards an army. Toward a war. Their shadows stretched across the plain, long fingers against the setting sun.

Lystra didn't think of the Jarkins as she approached the caravan. Their weapons, their cursed bodies, and their weary, disgruntled cardants were no obstacle. Not for her. These sands had seen violence before and, this time, she'd see the invaders' blood darken them.

Hope burst like the dawn in her chest. After tonight, her golden city, beyond miles of mountains, canyons, and dunes, would survive. Her people would see a sunrise beyond summer's end.

The warriors stood facing the center of the circle, the place between the two towers, where two kings faced one another.

Gaudab had risen to his feet again, his clothes dusty from the deluge of Razhar's counter-cursed sands. In one hand, he clutched the dagger, with the other he beckoned his men to wait. His movements were jilted, favoring one shoulder, where a dark stain leaked onto his cloak.

Across from him, crumpled in the sands, Elerek didn't wait. Water coursed from his hands, a monstrous, roaring wave. It rose high above their heads, covering the star-cast skies. With one flick of his wrist, Elerek sent it careening between the two towers, down the Darcress Pass where the enemy armies waited. His eyes were fixed on Gaudab, his sneer taunting him, his power on full display.

His hands, his arms, his chest—had all turned to *water*, the curse mark shimmering beneath the remains of his tattered shirt. The curse had transformed him into something cast from the purest starlight and the vilest curse. Something powerful, more than flesh and blood.

Gaudab's eyes turned. A sinister smile curled his lips. "Well."

The warriors backed away, clearing a path. Lystra stalked forward, remembering another battle, another circle, where she broke through the ranks to approach the king who carried a curse in his hands.

"She came to watch you die." Gaudab gave a cruel laugh.

The flow ceased from Elerek's hands. His fury faded as his eyes found hers.

I came back.

Again.

I'll always come back.

All that they had shared—and all that they hadn't—filled Lystra's mind. Dreams too beautiful to live. She wished there was more. She wanted more. A ruinous story had brought them together and they'd been given only one chapter. Precious pages that she hoped would burn like starfire amid the darkness.

Elerek had spoken of a future where he faded like passing starlight and she reigned with the glorious light of a new day. The king was wrought for death, a destiny written by a curse.

Well, he was wrong. So very wrong.

You, El, are the king of Instanolde and I will save you for your kingdom.

Lystra lifted her fists, poised for attack. Feet planted, seeking stability amid the shifting sands, her face turned toward the enemy who threatened not one, but two kings—the two men she had loved.

A stream of water shot from her fingertips. Her limbs grew numb, but the torrent spewed. The water seemed to absorb the light of the stars, turning silver. It shot toward Gaudab, knocking him back but not over.

"Stars above." Razhar stared at her, his jaw hanging open.

As for Elerek, the love and admiration in his eyes could outshine the wrathgiver itself.

With a shout, the clamor of steel rang across the desert. Scimitars sang as the caravan of cursed men swarmed to the aid of their leader. They had come with the promise of salvation, a future without drowning, and were ready for war.

Three—against an army.

Chapter 40

Razhar

Razhar had spent nearly his entire life as a counter curse—and he could cough sand. The queen of Instanolde however . . . he shook his head. Starlight didn't only strengthen the curse in Elerek. Perhaps he should've brought the whole cursed family.

He pushed sand in every direction. Swirls of a sandstorm of his own making hazed the air and caught in his enemies' eyes. Cardants reared, fearsome shadows in the dust, confounding their riders and thrashing wildly. More than once, Razhar danced and ducked out of the way of scraping claws. The sands kept him hidden, a phantom as elusive as the shifting wraiths. The ruinous swaths of his turban draped about his neck, his hair a tousled mess of caked dust, but he didn't care.

Here, with the wrathgiver shining above, his sands would prove their worth.

As he neared Elerek, he let the sands cease. The king's waters were a fearsome thing, but the mud created when their abilities mixed was not.

Elerek was not his curse. Razhar had held to this with all

the stalwart hope of a treasured faith. And it had never been more difficult to believe.

Water flowed in waves, rolling and frothing. It carved ruts into the land, drove silt from the rock, and turned the stone the color of blood. Jarkins were pushed to their knees. Orbs of water swirled about their heads and their bodies fell lifeless.

When the curse took its victims, it left no carnage. Only water to be stolen by the heat. Now, by the curse and the stars and the force of Elerek's vengeance, twisted bodies with water-logged lungs lay haphazardly across the sands. The violence sickened Razhar, but he swallowed his displeasure as one would a bitter medicine. He knew what they fought for. *We have to win.*

Elerek snarled like an animal. While his eyes burned in the starlight, the curse had laid claim to his body. The mark spread up his neck, reaching along his jaw. It had taken his arms, marking no distinction where his limbs ended and the cursed water began.

Then, Elerek stilled, the waves receding, watching Razhar with the stern countenance of a marble statute.

Typical. Razhar held his breath. Waiting.

"You're . . . alive."

"Ah, very good. I see the curse hasn't damaged your vision." Razhar smirked and lifted a hand to launch a plume of sand into the eyes of an approaching Jarkin.

An intense scowl darkened Elerek's features. "And . . . you came back?"

"Yes, El. Your lovely queen isn't the only one who'll come running back to you." Razhar knelt in the pool of cursed water puddling around Elerek and his crippled legs. He grasped Elerek's hand, but only the thinnest veils of skin covered his limb.

His heart sank. It wouldn't be enough. The curse had taken

him too far. Was this it? Did this mean that Elerek *couldn't* break the curse?

"I had to come back." Razhar met Elerek's emerald stare. "You have to answer a question."

Elerek set his jaw with the proud look of a king.

I need to know. Inhaling a breath ragged with sand scratching his lungs, Razhar mustered his courage and braced his soul. "Would you have done it? If you'd known that my death would've set you free years ago? From the first moment that we met when we were children?"

What a life he might have lived. The prince-heir. Instanolde's king. Lystra's husband. But even as he thought it, Razhar realized the profound truth. Elerek had been all those things. Destiny as sure as the stars themselves, forged in the fires of turmoil and heartache. Grief had become a catalyst, a spark brighter than the noonday sun.

Razhar saw the war in Elerek's gaze. An ever-present battle, the one he had to fight. To live. But this time, the sorrow shimmering there wasn't bitter or resentful. Not insensitive, but *compassionate.*

"I never had to consider it." Elerek spoke slowly, deliberately. "You didn't give me the chance."

Razhar swallowed.

"You made me want to kill you half the time with your patronizing optimism." Elerek gripped his shoulders with both hands. "But I wouldn't trade our friendship. All those years, you stood by me, stalwart and loyal. You protected those whom I've loved. You kept me alive." His eyes steeled, severe and sure as the heavens themselves. "Not. For. The. World. Razhar. Not for all the glittering sands beneath the dancing constellations."

Not for the world . . . The world Razhar could give him. He could give Elerek everything.

Could this be why he became a counter curse? The lowly

Kushite standing at the side of the king cursed to drown? They'd both borne curse and consequence. Both suffered from the vengeance festering in the souls of others. Perhaps this was why they both could undo the death in their bodies.

Because they were the same. Equals, and they could *choose*.

Elerek wouldn't die by the Jarkins' hand. No, he'd destroy them all and take his own life.

Razhar wouldn't let his life be taken from him. No, he'd give it willingly.

"You're my brother." Elerek pulled him into an embrace, flinging his arms around him. "My true brother."

Crushed by arms strong enough to destroy an army, Razhar clenched his eyes shut. He didn't want to cry. Not now. Instead, he returned the embrace and forced a smirk. "Congratulations, El, that's the most un-insensitive thing I've ever heard you say."

"I told you, I'm not insensitive."

My brother. Relief lifted every burden, every fear from his heart. As they pulled back from the comrade's embrace, Razhar grasped Elerek's shoulder. "I never had a brother. I only had you."

Elerek's intensity broke with a smile, his eyes glassy. Then, it shattered, the king's gaze shifting to the furious scene surrounding them. He released Razhar and water rushed from his hands, rolling up over their heads in an elegant arch and sweeping a row of Jarkin soldiers off their feet. The wave didn't stop, smothering and burying the warriors, pushing them down into the sand. But before they could drown, another pair of warriors rushed toward them. Elerek twisted, fixing his attention on the next threat.

Razhar jumped up. Arms raised, a spray of sand shot across the expanse. The warriors lifted cursed hands to cover their faces, screaming and swearing. Razhar knew their pain, the feeling of razor-sharp grains digging into their skin.

When the Jarkins attacked Cormek's regiment, they fought as men, with weapons and the tactics of ambush and ruthless slaughter.

Now, the sands of the earth, waters of the skies, and the light of sun and stars had joined the warfare. Even Tiniah, hissing and thrashing her horned head, circled near them, ready to pick a fight with the other reptiles. Razhar grabbed her reins, commanding her to halt. Using the cardant's body as a soldier would a wall or rock, Razhar slid his arm beneath Elerek's shoulders and hoisted him upright. Elerek gripped the saddle, his eyes murderous as he scanned the Jarkin warriors. Both sides seemed to stall, inhaling a deep breath, waiting.

Razhar lifted his eyes. Up above, the wrathgiver constellation, the same stars etched on his chest, shone brighter than he'd ever seen. They spun and wheeled, dancing the same trails they'd danced for thousands of years. Onward and upward, never changing.

I wonder if there's ever been anything like us.

There didn't need to be. They were extraordinary. Living while dying. Breathing in this moment beneath the stars. Alive.

"El, how do we begin?"

Elerek's gaze narrowed. Many of the warriors had turned away, waiting for word from their commander. But Gaudab gave no orders, his mouth full of cursed water as Lystra pelted him with wave after wave streaming from her cursed hands.

No one attacked her. No one dared.

"She . . ." Elerek couldn't speak.

She was fire and fury and light and glory. Without weapons, without armor, and yet unstoppable. Lystra the queen of the desert standing against Gaudab Batu-Khasar of the Jarkins.

"What are we here for?" Razhar grunted, adjusting his grip on Elerek so as to not let him fall. "She can clean up this mess on her own."

"But why—?" Elerek's eyes remained transfixed on his wife. "Is it the stars?"

Always the stars. Razhar huffed. "Unless it's because she's related to the curse binder?"

"Speculation."

"Ah, perhaps." Still. Razhar wondered. She *had* said that she'd save her people.

"Awaiting orders, Your Highness." His eyes located the dagger, abandoned where Gaudab had dropped it. How close it lingered to where Lystra stood planted like a centerpiece fountain, every eye drawn to her brilliance. He had every confidence that she'd retrieve it when her work was complete. Razhar's voice dropped to a whisper. "Please, El, let me break it."

A dark scowl contorted the king's brow. "I'll never ask that of you, Razhar."

"I've followed you this long on this horrendous adventure." Razhar sent another vortex of sand spinning through the air and into the eyes of their enemies. "I'm *legendary*, El. A counter curse. Besides." He looked at his friend, his king. "I'm not asking for permission. You could *live*."

Elerek shook his head, but a bit of light struck his eyes. Something of sorrow. Something of hope. A yearning as fierce as the battle they faced. "Saving our kingdom is more pressing than breaking the curse." Elerek spoke sternly, astutely. "That's something only you and I can do."

"Ah, a challenge then?" Razhar allowed himself a laugh, a ringing sound to rival the songs of scimitars. "Let us be curse and counter curse and one of us wins the prize of shedding our blood when this is over?"

Elerek nodded grimly.

Curse and counter curse.

The lowly Kushite and the cursed king of Instanolde.

My brother.

Razhar also felt the starlight, stirring the curse in his lungs. His bronze arms, muscles taut as he lent Elerek support, became riddled with fissures, cracks. Sands shifting. The opposite of the empowering that made Elerek capable of drowning an army.

It felt like dying.

But here, now, Razhar almost didn't care. He didn't fear. Standing here, at the end of the world, the farthest reaches of the kingdom he called home, at Elerek's side where he no longer needed to seek the shadows to brush the sands away, he could think of no better adventure.

Chapter 41

Elerek

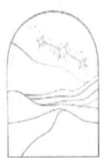

Elerek held on to the cardant's saddle with a desperate grip. Beneath him, legs that wouldn't hold ached. Razhar stood as his support, his arms lending him their strength.

So many had died for him. Too many. Their faces haunted him, their voices whispered in his ears, and their touch heaped ashes of shame and guilt upon his head. He would not allow Razhar to die for him too.

The Kushite boy who'd come from nowhere and became everything. The sands that shaped his world with a carefree smile, a terrible joke, and a patronizing word of encouragement. The starlight when the darkness threatened to swallow him whole. No one could replace Razhar, the brother who had kept him alive time after time after time.

Razhar would not break the curse—the curse was *his* responsibility.

Tiniah released a long hiss. Lunging forward, she bit the shoulder of another cardant, this one bearing a Jarkin. The saddle's leather strap ripped through Elerek's hands and he fell.

Razhar tried to catch him with a lung-flattening "oof." The cardant wheeled, its long tail flying far too close to their heads. The warrior fell as the two reptiles ripped into each other's scales.

Before the Jarkin could rise, Elerek summoned water. He couldn't be a warrior, not like his father or his brother. Empowered by the eternal stars, he didn't even feel much like a man anymore, only this inhuman force wrought of a vengeful desire mixed with the hope of saving his people. A prism of both darkness and light, a hero cast down from the stars to destroy and cleanse.

When the warrior lay dead, his lungs full of curse, Elerek bowed his head, panting for air. It didn't matter if it were a Jarkin invader who would bring unspeakable horrors upon his people. A man died, and Elerek, the king cursed not to feel the touch of humanity or draw comfort from skin, *felt it.*

Razhar let him sink back down to the stones, standing over him like a sentinel. Elerek blinked. Cracks, like the baked desert earth, scaled across his bronze skin, snaking beneath his eyes and across his cheeks.

Would he die anyways? Crumble away to dust? Would anything that Elerek could do stop it? Could he save him?

Then he looked down at his own hands. Fingers formed of liquid in the shape of the man he once was. The curse had consumed him, his shoulders, chest, and neck all turned to water. He wondered if anything remained of his face.

"Razhar," he breathed. "If . . . if you help me . . ."

His friend looked doubtful, cocking one eyebrow. "Together, the curse is stronger."

"I need the curse stronger." Elerek spoke through gritted teeth. "But not strong enough to take me. You won't let me lose control?"

Razhar knelt beside him. His hand clenched, sand

squeezing between his fingers. "Something only you and I can do." He repeated Elerek's words. "Neither of us might survive."

No, and that's the cost they would both pay for their kingdom.

The air filled with a dull roar and beneath them, the earth began to quake. Elerek and Razhar craned their necks, staring over the ridge of Tiniah's spine. Movement stirred near the base of the towers. The glint of starlight shone on polished leather and dull armor as the parasites of Darcress spilled onto the sand. Elerek narrowed his eyes. An army within the fortress, an army beyond, scrambling in the pass, and the cursed caravan.

Waiting for him to drown them all.

A great split in the earth, running the length of rock between Darcress's twin towers. And from this great split, a canal emerged. Waters bursting from the depths of the earth, crashing and foaming, raging against the desert rock. The water flowed between the two towers, spilling through the pass like an army. An army no man could command.

This was why he was here. This was why he was cursed. To save his kingdom.

Elerek closed his eyes. Faintly, he heard a rushing, rhythmic pattern of water that had flowed in the same channel for eons. Water that knew its stone, the places where it hit, spraying delicate diamond drops. It sounded like a heartbeat, a reminder that he was still here. Still alive, even after all this time.

"Razhar," he whispered, opening his eyes. "I accept your challenge."

The amber gaze of his friend shone dark, filled with all the sorrow of years taken. Life cut short. Unlived. Much like Cormek. Razhar gripped Elerek's arms. At their point of contact, Elerek immediately felt life flood through his arms and up into his shoulders. A power, pulsing with a furious energy.

But his skin didn't return to his body, nor the sight of blood flowing through his limbs. No blood to spill, to break the curse.

Perhaps some curses weren't meant to be broken.

"Starkindler," Elerek whispered, lifting his eyes. "Let us be enough."

The stars seemed to intensify, bold and bright. He wondered if he were just a bit taller, if his legs weren't broken, if perhaps he could reach the lowest star. To grasp a hold of the heavens and leave the earth behind.

Razhar rose to his feet, stretching his sand-strewn arms behind him. The light of the stars that he had never learned filled his gaze. Then, the lowly Kushite who had sworn allegiance to no one except the cursed, lifted his head and smiled an intoxicating smile.

"Well, then, for Instanolde."

Chapter 42

Lystra

"**I** told you, Gaudab Batu-Khasar." Lystra's posture tensed. Her heart beat wildly against her ribs like a feral animal, desperate to be free. This man had made an enemy of her when he'd threatened all that she loved. And now, her time had come, facing the foe who had caused whole armies to tremble.

She thought of Elerek, the crippled prince from the shadows, standing on the strength of others to defend Instanolde, lashing with cursed water. His advantage had become her own.

Fury billowed within her soul. A rage she wasn't sure belonged to the curse or herself. All the grief of the past three months welled within her body and shot from her fingertips. The decades of poisonous vengeance that had consumed her grandmother, the bloodlust of Lorkin as he nearly tore a kingdom to pieces, the weight of seemingly endless evil.

How did I get here?

Better men had stood against Gaudab Batu-Khasar. Better generals, armies, and kings had stood against the Jarkins.

Only she remained.

The surrounding warriors no longer resembled men, not even bloodthirsty invaders. More water and bone than muscle and blood, they were weak from the curse and worn from their days in the Sancen. They crumpled beneath the brunt of Lystra's torrent. Though water leaked from her eyes, she felt no pity. No remorse. Her tears were that of relief.

They'd never threaten her kingdom again. She had returned to the desert, the place she'd fled—and executed judgment.

The fear and the noise and the adrenaline filled her senses. Gaudab sank to his knees. The dagger had fallen from his hands, lying in the sands. Lystra stepped closer, the stream from her hands intensifying.

The cursed caravan circled. Their cardants thrashed at the sounds and sights of the water. Several warriors dismounted, rushing to the aid of their leader with drawn weapons. Lystra turned one hand on them, pummeling them with wave after wave.

Gaudab collapsed. The water flooded about his head like burial wrappings, omens of the funeral he would never have. Lystra didn't think, didn't consider the fact that she was about to snuff out a life forever. She only knew that she *had to drown him.* The Jarkin who put an axe in Cormek's chest stilled, his body limp.

Lystra shuddered, falling to her knees. It was done.

Lifting teary eyes to the starry skies above, she let out a quaking breath. She'd avenged Cormek. The blood had been repaid, but it changed nothing. No wars or vengeance would ever bring Cormek back.

But Instanolde would be satisfied. Their king had not died in vain. And Gaudab Batu-Khasar would never slaughter again.

Hanging her head, damp hair clung to her scalp, her cheeks. Her breaths grew shallow, the curse rearing its ugly head. She leaned forward, reaching for the dagger with a skeletal hand.

Her skin-turned-water prickled at the touch, the meeting of flesh and steel. This dagger had seen blood before. The fell stars etched into its blade had drunk of men's lives—cursed men's lives.

Her heart, still flesh within her chest, beat loudly in her ears. Drumming. Thumping. Reminding her that life was precious. Life was *powerful*.

Obliterating it changed the course of the future forever. If some hadn't died, some might not have lived.

Lystra gripped the hilt, resolve burning in her breast. Cormek had died to ensure that she lived. Now her turn had come. She would perish to give Elerek life. The man who was cursed to die would live.

How she hoped he would live. A life full. Bursting with joy. Bleeding with beauty. Everything that had been stolen from him returned with the brilliance of a constellation's ethereal dance.

Lystra sniffled, turning her attention to the heavens. The wrathgiver hovered above, watching. She wondered if she'd meet Cormek again among the stars.

She wanted to tell him what she'd done. She hoped he'd be proud.

Hot breath blew over her neck, followed by a low growl and the scratch of cardant talons.

Lystra turned, staring into Tiniah's keen, yellow gaze. The cardant bore wounds, rips in her scales that leaked tiny rivers of blood. Her saddle lay empty but still intact. Lystra saw a warrior in her eyes. "Hello, my fierce girl."

The cardant wagged her head, hissing, wanting to flee but lingering.

Then, Lystra rose to her feet, taking in the scene around her.

Water.

This was nothing like the Gungole. Nothing like the smooth Varkei lake. Nothing like the soft springtime rains.

A wave. As high as an estate. Capped in white. Writhing, foaming, and furious. It crashed against the towers, the sound a deafening roar, and barreled down the Darcress Pass. Only the towers and the distant mountains remained visible above the churning mass.

Nothing could survive that. Nothing could survive Elerek.

Chapter 43

Razhar

The light of the wrathgiver burned on Razhar's skin, hotter than the Sancen, more searing than the noonday sun. It pulsed in his veins, this strange inversion of the curse as equally fearful.

Well, the stars weren't daft. They knew that they were tied to his blood too.

He braced his knees against the rock, his hands gripping Elerek's shoulders. The king's hands stretched toward the horizon, toward the advancing army, toward the pass that had to be conquered and protected. Water poured from his fingers.

Razhar wondered what they looked like to the Jarkin invaders. Two ragged travelers—nay, adventurers—cast from the Sancen, one flaked with sand and the other turning to water. Two men against an army.

Of course, if they got through them, they'd stir the anger of the mighty queen of the Sancen.

He glanced over his shoulder. Lystra's onslaught had ceased. Most of the cursed Jarkins lay dead, including Gaudab. The infamous warrior had become nothing but skin and bones and drowned lungs. Now, clutching the dagger in her trembling hands, Lystra took Tiniah's reins, speaking softly to the reptile. The curse hadn't yet taken her.

Razhar huffed. He wondered why he had so many items to keep track of—and how much time the stars would permit him before he turned to sand.

Elerek's water spread into a wide surge, as wide as Darcress Pass itself, stretching from tower to tower. It sped toward the soldiers, smacking against the knees of the frontlines. They slowed, but it hardly hindered them.

Scrunching up his face, Razhar scoffed. "Oi, El. What happened to your plans?"

Growling, the king gritted his teeth. "Nothing. The curse is stronger here."

Elerek was stronger here.

Razhar swallowed. He looked down at his hands, perfect sculptures of sand. As for Elerek, the curse striped his face like mourning paint, clear water beneath. His hair lay dark and soaked, diamond droplets catching in his curls.

Cold fear shot through him. Were Razhar's powers waning? Were they doing anything to help the king?

"El, are you in control?"

Elerek's shoulders dropped slightly. "For now . . ."

Steeling himself, Razhar tightened his grip on the cursed king. "Don't hold back. I'm here." He grinned. "Save Instanolde—maybe us too, if you can fit it into your schedule."

Muttering beneath his breath, Elerek leaned forward. His arms were taut, his palms flat, fingers splayed wide. A gust of wind moved over the waters, rippled their clothing, and in a mighty surge, the water *rose*. Cresting to meet the sky, the wave shone silver. Wide as the canyon itself, capped with foam, it swelled and grew. Just before it broke, for one splinter of a second, starlight shone through the wave, illuminating the dark shapes of men's bodies. Then, with a sound like a thunderclap, the wave crashed, storming into Darcress with a fury that no army could ever command.

Instanolde could ask for no better defense.

Razhar bowed his head, hissing through his teeth. As for him, he was still here.

He remembered the pain, the curse's strange design as it infected his body. Sand prickled in his lungs and the sharp grains pushed through his skin. The cost—the consequence of someone else's sin. He remembered his terror the night that Elerek drowned the Jarkin assassin in the palace prisons. When the curse saw fit to remind him, yet again, that there were consequences to bloodshed.

It all surged from his contact with Elerek—he could feel the curse, the power, the rage. A monster contained, like the high walled pens for unruly cardants, by Razhar's own strength—and he could feel himself weakening.

If the stars made Elerek more, they made him less.

As the wave crashed, it foamed and swirled, a great mass of churning water. It clawed at the earth, dredging the stone itself. Great splits cracked in the rock, and the place where Razhar and Elerek perched became a ledge, a plummet beneath them stretching into shadowed depths. The desert had become a canal, a place no army would dare encroach on again.

"Steady, El. Steady." Razhar willed strength to his voice.

Up above, the stars became eclipsed by black shapes circling. The call of a condor rang out even above the roar of the water.

"Oi, you lot had to come." Had Dalmah's orders gone out? Had Norbah failed to arrest the countess? Had they come to make certain that he and Elerek died?

Not only die, but break the curse.

One of the birds swooped low. The rider lay bent over the

condor's neck, a long spear in his hand. Razhar saw the glint of steel in the starlight—just before the shaft sliced into his side.

No. Why?

His lungs, raw with sand, could no longer hold air. Pain filled his vision with darkness and spinning stars. The force of the spear's impact knocked him back, sending him sprawling. Shuddering, he gripped the rock beneath him, his contact with Elerek severed, the spear's shaft protruding from his side, just beneath his rib cage.

The condors wheeled, gracefully descending. Coming to finish what they'd begun when they executed his baba. His baba who wanted him to live well. Didn't Fahwal know that this wasn't the sort of world in which they could live well?

A world that destroyed. A world of curses and counter curses. A world bent on crushing every last ounce of courage.

He looked up, blinking as sand coated his eyes. Water from the wave surrounded Elerek, wrapping around his legs and torso. He kept his hands outstretched, upholding the torrent. But he looked over his shoulder. Elerek no longer possessed flesh, blood, or skin. He was water. Only his eyes remained his own—and they were wide with terror.

"No! Stop! I beg you!"

This shriek came from Lystra. With Tiniah behind her, the queen stalked closer. Her hair and clothing dripped with water, a stream still flowing from her fingers. Swathed in silver, shimmering in the starlight, she looked as if she belonged to the heavens themselves.

"Stand down!" she screamed at the Kushite archers. "As your queen, I command it!"

The condors alighted on the stone. Their riders' faces gleamed dark.

Razhar bowed his head, grunting. He needed to cough, but

the spear lodged in his body held him back. Beneath him, sand slid from his arms, carried on the air stirred by rushing water.

"Razhar!" Elerek's voice. Drowned out by the roar, by the curse.

Lifting his eyes, Razhar's soul gave way to grief as the water swept up over the precipice—dragging Elerek over the edge and into the depths.

Chapter 44

Lystra

Lystra stood still, her gaze transfixed on the narrow ledge, its edges slanted like the prow of a ship.

El . . . Gone. Swept away by the throes of the curse. Taken by the depths. To drown.

Her fingers, slick with moisture, tightened about the hilt of the dagger. Her soul, still ragged from drowning Gaudab, unraveled like a once lovely tapestry that had been trodden upon, dragged through the dust, and now lay in shredded threads.

If Elerek perished, the curse wouldn't be broken. No dawn for Instanolde. How many innocents had drowned in the streets? The survivors would turn to hatred, sown by Dalmah's poisonous seeds. No one would ever know of the cursed king who had dared to live. They would only know scorn.

"We . . . still . . ." The sound of a dry cough mingled with the roar of cursed water.

Razhar. Lystra hurried to his side, kneeling before him. What skin he still wore lay pale beneath a layer of sand. Glittering, amber sand. Lystra tried to wipe it from his cheek but there was *so much* of it. It smeared her hands, ridding her own skin of the curse's mark.

And the spear. The Kushite spear impaled his side. No blood leaked from the wound, his clothing dark with water and yet more sand.

"Still . . . alive." Razhar's body shuddered, his breaths short and ragged. "If we . . . still alive . . ."

Lystra hastily nodded. "Then El's still alive too."

There was still hope.

Razhar's face scrunched, pain written across his brow with an ink deeper than the tattoo on his chest. "Take it out." His voice grew stronger. "The spear. Please, Lystra . . ."

Her eyes fell to the wound. The sight of the shaft, wood polished to precision, embedded in his flesh brought bile up in her throat. Rising to her feet, she spun toward the archers. It took everything in her to not throw the precious dagger in their faces.

"If you want to remain as my subjects, fly over the water. Scout the pass. If you see any remaining Jarkins, kill them. Not one must be permitted to survive this day. If you see the king"— she glared—"let him live."

One by one, the Kushites and their condors took to the star-strewn skies. Her heart seethed. "I'll never forgive them." Tucking the dagger into her sash, she knelt before Razhar again, her trembling hands reaching for the shaft.

"You have to." Razhar lifted his eyes, his gaze clear in the pale light. "Lystra, it can't be like this. Not between Instanolde and Kushan. You . . ." Coughs wracked his chest. "Your Highness, give them a kingdom where they can live."

Lystra's eyes filled with tears. "A kingdom where they shan't grow weary of life."

The ghost of a smile curled Razhar's lips. Lystra dared not breathe. Deep in her soul, a truth rang with the clarity of ram's horns as the gilded, golden gates of Instanolde swung wide. A sound meant to welcome a member of some high house, royalty even. She wondered if the stars possessed such heralds. Surely a soul being welcomed to dance among the skies was worthy.

You'll dance again, Razhar. Dance and dance and dance.

Perhaps she would dance with him.

Lystra cupped his face in her hand and leaned close, planting a kiss on his sand-strewn cheek. "I'm not the one to create such a kingdom, Razhar. You know there's only one who can do that."

A pair of tears cascaded down Razhar's face, leaving fissures in his skin. "Take out the spear, my queen. Let me save him."

One deep breath wasn't enough to steady the soul. Lystra gave herself two, her lungs half belonging to the curse already. Then, taking the spear with both hands, she pulled.

Razhar cried out, collapsing forward.

It gave way, sliding easily. Too easily. Lystra watched in horror as sand spilled from Razhar's side, leaving a jagged hole where his bronze skin ought to have been beneath his brightly colored clothes.

Heaving for air, he pushed himself up. His boots had vanished, pillars of dust, earth, and the finest of amber grains. His eyes found hers, full of sorrows to fill a thousand desolate Sancen canyons.

Razhar seized her hands. "I don't know if . . ."

Lystra could feel him. Life ebbing from his touch. Away from him and into her. Skin covered her limbs again.

I need myself. I need my blood. The price that her grandmother would never dare pay. Lystra stared down at her hands. "It'll be enough."

It must be enough.

Razhar laid gentle hands on either side of her face. "Forgive me, Your Highness. I only wanted to live." His whisper sounded like the moan of a slight breeze. A lonely sound crying across the wilderness.

"You've lived well, Razhar. No life is ever wasted that is spent in the love and duty of others." She pressed her forehead to his. "This moment, you are alive. You are free."

"I'm not . . . I can't break it . . ." A sob broke from Razhar's throat. An earthly sound, like the cascading of stones. He tilted his head back. His finely chiseled face and lips made for smiling were bathed in the last light of an endless day. Starlight shone in his eyes.

The dancer. The counter curse. The warrior who smiled.

"The curse was never your burden to bear." Lystra withdrew the dagger again. The wrathgiver above gleamed on the wrathgiver below. Two blades wrought of starlight. "Now, we find the king."

Chapter 45

Elerek

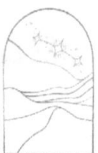

The stars themselves had drowned.

Blackness blanketed the world, a world of rage, of darkness, of water.

Elerek no longer belonged to himself. The curse consumed him, its roar to rival a lion's, a cardant's, and all the monsters of myth and legend. Water filled his lungs. The whole of the abyss swallowed his vision. The current's pounding replaced the beat of his heart. His awareness permeated as far as the flood could reach. He knew every body, broken and battered by the torrent. Their faces, jaws agape and eyes frozen in terror, haunted him. The water, the curse, as if sensing his repulsion, pushed them tumbling down the pass and toward their homeland. Perhaps their bones would wash up on Jarkin lands and they would know that they were not welcome in Instanolde. The desert was theirs. Now and forever.

If there remained a desert.

Water. Only water.

Maybe he wouldn't exist at all. Maybe no starlight awaited him. Maybe he would only be water, and flow forevermore.

Skin and bones no longer bound him. His crippled legs were no more. He wanted to breathe. He wanted to feel. He wanted to blink and see the starlight one last time.

He wanted to die. Finally. Here at the end, couldn't the curse give him this one mercy?

"El? Stay with me."

He knew that voice. The memory sliced through his consciousness. He'd been brought back from oblivion once before. That time, he'd bled blood instead of water, having taken a knife, dragged it down the length of his arm, and waited for death. He'd been found by those who'd cared, those who wanted him to live.

One was a king who belonged in the glorious sun. This king didn't deserve such sorrows, particularly not a brother given to darkness like him. Still, he'd come running when the call echoed down the palace corridors and fled to find a physician.

The other was Razhar.

"I'll stay with him. I don't intend to lose him."

Elerek remembered the pain buzzing in his head, dulling his senses. Everything felt slow, wet, and sticky with blood. He remembered wondering if drowning would have been better.

Now he knew.

These waters, the water that he had become, were also death. A death without ending, much like his curse that would now never be broken. These depths were the void that sealed him in nothingness. Here he would drown without dying.

The memory broke across his thoughts like the dawn, shining with a clarity his dying mind had forgotten.

Someone touched him. Took his arm, cold and drained of blood, and bound it tight to keep what life he had left from spilling out. Arms slid beneath his shoulders, cradling him. The frantic beat of another heart filled his ears. If he'd been stable, aware, he might have protested this closeness. He couldn't kill anyone else. Wasn't that why he'd tried to kill himself in the first place?

"If you can hear me, you insensitive idiot, you'd better listen. You're not dying. You're not doing this to yourself. I came all this way to find you and I'm not losing you."

A hand grasped his, holding on tight. That touch kept him alive.

The water's roar intensified. Furious and vengeful, full of the lives it had taken.

And it receded.

Hard earth rose to meet him. Sand gathered about his fingers, pressed against his face. Air filled his lungs—what a relief to know that he still had lungs. And a hand grasped his, a hand made of sand.

Elerek pushed himself up. Both water and man, the curse had left him somewhere in the impossible in-between. Still connected to the deluge, water pooled about him, draping from his shoulders like a burnous. The remains of his tattered shirt, pants, and one boot clung to his strange semblance of a body. The shape of a man formed of water.

Behind him, the wall of water stretched as high as the Darcress towers. Up beyond, the stars still blinked. The wrath-giver watched. Caught between the heavens and hell.

Razhar blended into the damp earth. A statue sculpted of sand, each breath of wind stirred by the water blew bits of him away. He knelt in the water, having pulled Elerek from the depths yet again.

Behind him, Lystra stood beside her cardant, the reptile equipped to scale the cliff his torrent had cut. Nearly every trace of Lystra's lovely, Instan skin—skin he had touched, caressed, and kissed—gave way to the curse. Instead of her smile, her skull leered at him, framed by ebony waves of hair. In one skeletal hand, she clenched the dagger. The other clutched

Razhar's arm, and this connection dressed her fingers in skin that belonged to her.

Here, where death had hung its banner, the two that he wanted most to live had come for him—because they loved him.

"Forgive me." Elerek's voice held an echo, the sound of many waters. "I failed our challenge."

Razhar hung his head. "Me too."

Sand and water. No longer flesh and blood.

They couldn't break the curse.

Elerek reached for him, his hands-turned-water lying on Razhar's shoulders. Sand cascaded down his thick arms like a landslide. "I'm sorry, so sorry, Razhar." His chest heaved, desperate for air to form words. "If it isn't broken . . . we can't . . ."

Razhar bowed his head. "We saved the kingdom, El. Let that be enough."

The quest fulfilled. Elerek's vengeance satisfied. Why didn't it feel like enough?

Because they were dying.

Razhar drew a rasped breath. "Counter curses can't be broken, they're meant to come alongside the curse. This is what I was meant to do. I've been holding back my whole life. Lies. Truths. I chose this—for *our* kingdom."

Our kingdom. "No." Elerek spoke in a low murmur. "*You* saved the kingdom, Razhar. You saved Instanolde—and me." Over and over and over again.

Razhar, his brother, lifted his gaze. His eyes were unchanged, pulsing with life, burning with starfire. His hand clasped Elerek's shoulder, resting upon the water as if it were still flesh. Here, at the end, no healing came from his touch. They were only curse and counter curse. "El, be good to my people. Tell Kushan that you're not like the rest."

I'm water. Elerek stared at him, begging the image to be

some cruel manipulation of his worst imagination. A nightmare, wrought of curses and starlight. He wished himself anywhere, anywhere but here watching Razhar fade away to sand. Watching Razhar die.

The wall of water behind him foamed, whipped into a frenzy by his grief. Its wind blew sand, glittering like starlight, from Razhar's coffee-colored hair and bronze skin.

"I can't . . ." Sobs strangled Elerek's throat. "I can't do this without you. Razhar, if it weren't for you, I would've lost hope. Never once did you give up on me. Know this, you are my brother."

An insufferable smirk curled onto Razhar's lips, the same that illuminated the shadows and breathed life into the turmoil. The smile of a warrior who never gave up. He exhaled a soft chuckle. "There, not so insensitive after all, eh, El?"

A shrill sound split the air. It rang off the cliffs and sang to the stars themselves. The wall stirred, frothing with rage and vengeance. The wrathgiver seemed to intensify.

It was the sound of the star-cast dagger, being drawn from its sheath in the hands of the cursed queen of Instanolde.

And one of those hands, even stretching up her arm, still bore skin.

Chapter 46

Lystra

L ystra felt heavy with the weight of drowning from the inside out.

The dagger's hilt numbed her fingers, pulsing with what sounded like a heartbeat, except she didn't have a heart anymore. She was cursed. She was water.

Her eyes lifted, following the towering wall of water created by Elerek. A barrier between this, the farthest reach of Instanolde's dominion, and the wild lands beyond. Would Instanolde be protected? Could such a thing be accomplished by something as vile as the curse?

But here, in the end, they had little else. No other resource had saved their kingdom.

If only there remained a way for them to save themselves.

Lystra blinked. Water fell from her lashes, cursed tears for a cursed hour. The image of Elerek blurred before her, blending into the raging wall of water. His body had been taken by the curse, water shaped into the man who was her husband. Water swirled where his curls had been, but his eyes were the same, severe and shining like starfire. For the first time in his life, he'd become his curse. His body was lost, but his soul still held on.

She had to save him. Before all the stars in the glorious heavens, this was her task. The reason she'd survived, time after time. He'd given her the dawn, the tomorrow that Instanolde needed to see and now, she'd give it back to him.

But here, before the monstrosity of the curse's power, she felt small—and terrified.

The hand that held the dagger began to quiver. She looked at her other hand, the one still clothed in skin along with her arm up to her elbow.

Starkindler, please . . .

Would it be enough? Enough to sever the hold of something so dark and vile, something that had twisted generations and doomed too many to drown?

"Wait, Lystra . . ." Razhar stumbled to his knees—what was left of his knees. As Elerek had turned into a man shaped of water, Razhar had become sand shaped of man. His eyes, gleaming amber, went wide. Did he understand now? What she must do? Did he know that she might save him too?

"It'll be all right, Razhar." She met his gaze. "Everything will be all right."

"No, no, you can't—" Razhar lifted his hands, glittering sand falling from his fingers.

"I'm the only one who can." Lystra's breath shuddered. A frantic tremble scurried across her body, a deep and awful dread. This was it.

My days end here.

"What . . ." Elerek stared at her, fury burning in his eyes. "What are you talking about . . .?" His voice was drowned out by the water. Powerful and vengeful, the cascade lurched toward her. Elerek raised his arms, shoulders stretched wide, chest heaving, holding back the torrent—from *her*.

Shaking, Lystra took a step back. Water surged around her calves, anchoring her in the mud. Cold as death, its currents were strong, seeking to pull her down, to absorb her into the frothing fray.

The waters couldn't rob her humanity, her skin, the blood that still pulsed in her arm. Lystra looked down at her upturned palm with a whimper. She wondered if it were right to feel fear when she was about to commit the act that would set every-thing right?

Unless, it wouldn't be all right . . .

No, she couldn't waver. In everything she'd faced, she hadn't been wholly brave. There had been fear, more fear than she'd ever wanted to feel. And now, if her courage were to be mixed with fear, here at the end, so be it.

She met Elerek's gaze, memorizing every line of his water-etched face. Its beauty, its bravery, and all its brokenness. How she wished for one last moment, to feel once more his strong arms around her. She longed to kiss him, to touch him, to love him. But such a risk was too great, greater than the risk of touching the cursed king had ever been. Their moments were now past, but not gone or forgotten. No, they blazed with all the glorious fires of the stars.

"Elerek, rule Instanolde. It's your birthright. They're your people. Love them. Serve them. You . . . you are their king." Lystra drew as deep a breath as she could. "And, El . . . I love you."

She raised the dagger.

"Wait!" Razhar's voice rasped with sand.

She lifted her arm, her arm clothed in human skin. Then she turned her eyes to the heavens, where the wrathgiver watched, and beyond, all the stars stood in rapt attention.

"Starkindler," she whispered. "Let it be enough."

"Lystra . . ." Elerek's voice was a breath.

The world seemed to freeze. A moment cursed. The waters stirred with fury.

"You will live, El. *You. Will. Live!*" Lystra sank the dagger into her arm, at the crick of her elbow, and dragged it down to her palm.

Blood spilled from her skin. Dark, slick, red. Human.

Down to every last drop, she would bleed out the blood that the curse wanted—what it *required*.

It *had* to be enough.

Her ears filled with the sound of rushing water. Somewhere in the deluge, she thought she heard Elerek, a mournful yell torn from his throat. Darkness fell over her vision, spinning depths dragging her deep. She pitched forward into the red sands of Darcress. Here she had returned, and here she'd come to die.

It happened more quickly than she'd anticipated. Life draining out. Sound began to fade, slowly seeping into silence. The darkness blanketing her vision deepened, and everything became empty.

She yearned to feel it, the shattering of the curse. She wanted what she had died for.

But she felt nothing. No release. No burst of starlight. Only nothing.

Chapter 47

Elerek

*L*ystra...

"What have you done?"

Elerek fought, agonized, against the water—the curse. The roiling mass of water behind him threatened to collapse and bury them in the depths forever. It hissed and frothed, raging for blood, for a victim to drown. The weight strained against his back, his shoulders, as he held it back—back from her.

"No! Please . . . you can't have her!"

Stout tendrils of water wrapped about his arms, his neck, and enveloped his torso. He shuddered, cold numbness seeping into the sliver of being, of soul, he had left.

And before him, Lystra—his light, his queen, his wife—bled out. Starlight shone sickly on the dark puddle forming beneath her. The smell, poignant and metallic, brought back memories that Elerek would have rather forgotten.

How her eyes had burned, the breath fluttering at her breast. The fierce determination of the queen that he'd come to love with the whole of him. The girl who returned to the desert twice for him—the girl who showed him beauty amid the sorrow.

She lay in the sands, dark with water and blood. She didn't drown. She bled.

And she'd grown still.

Wrath, raw and primal, rose in his chest. Elerek clawed at the water, fighting like an animal. He needed to reach her, but the waters only tossed in white waves, almost in mockery. Nothing would stop the curse, and Lystra was dead.

Despair, as poisonous as a young viper, as strong as the most intoxicating wine, as deep as death itself, drowned him.

I am my curse.

"She . . . she said she could break it." Razhar remained. He blinked, staring at Lystra's fallen form.

Nothing could break this. No one.

Up above, the starlight intensified, the dance of the wrathgiver closer than it'd ever been. Razhar turned his gaze upward, the light of the constellation that lay etched on his chest filling his gaze. He heaved for breaths, the gaping hole in his side still pouring sand onto the desert.

Elerek blinked, water covering his vision. No, not him too.

"Razhar . . . please . . ." Elerek stretched out his hand, reaching for him.

But Razhar didn't turn. In the wrathgiver's light, he began to crawl, painfully inching his way across the earth. He grunted and strained, approaching the queen's body. Blood seeped into the sand at his knees. Then he lifted his eyes, looked at Elerek, and smiled the biggest grin in the world.

A cough shook his chest, sending another veil of sand cascading from his shoulders. As the starlight glinted off the amber grains, turning them silver, it almost appeared as if Razhar, the war orphan from the canyons of Kushan, wore royal robes.

"Live well, Elerek, my brother. Live the life stolen from so many. Live a life that isn't cursed."

Here, in this moment, this terrible moment, Elerek felt *only* cursed.

Razhar reached Lystra, kneeling beside her. A tear rolled down his face, carving a canyon across his cheek. His throat worked and he lifted hands that shook, hands that had paid the costs of evil decisions and committed a few of those of his own.

With a long exhale, he touched Lystra. Over her still and lifeless form, trails of skin traveled up her arms, her chest and throat, and across her lovely, pale face. Razhar restored her, holding back the curse as he'd done countless times before. Preserving those whom Elerek loved.

And Razhar himself had been among those whom Elerek had loved most.

His work complete, Razhar's figure sagged. He glanced over his shoulder, meeting Elerek's gaze. Like a dune caught in the desert winds, he began to crumble.

"No . . . no, please . . ." Elerek whimpered. Heaving, he launched himself forward, fending off the watery tendrils and crumpling in a heap in the sands darkened with blood and water.

One last smile carved across Razhar's face, and then, with one final breath of desert air, he vanished. A swirl of dust, dancing on the wind, and scattered across the wilds of the Sancen.

Elerek felt as if the whole of his soul had been cleaved from what remained of his body. Whatever monster he'd become, the vengeful torrent of water and death, he *despised* it. Whatever world remained beneath the glorious sun and glittering stars, he wanted no part of it. Even now, the stars that had once granted him hope now only mocked him, tied to the curse that had taken those whom he loved and doomed him to drown.

The unbroken curse left Elerek to linger here between life and death. His only tether, the brother of his soul, was gone. No one remained to hold back the curse. And before him lay his love, his wife, his *Lystra*.

In the light of the stars, he crawled to her. Beneath him rested the sands that belonged to Razhar, now smeared with Lystra's blood. Both trailed along his clothes. Her eyes, once burning fierce with the light of the eternal sun, lay closed. Even now, shrouded in death, she was beautiful.

Elerek slid his arms beneath her, cradling her against him. The blood dripping from her arm mingled with his body-turned water, swirling like ink.

"I'm sorry, Lystra . . . don't leave me . . . I'm so sorry." Inside his soul, something broke. The roar of a crashing wave escaped his lips. He pressed her head to his chest and wept.

No. He couldn't—*wouldn't*—live. Not without Lystra. Not without Razhar. Not losing them both. A reversal of all his desires. His best intentions thwarted. Perhaps Instanolde would endure, but they would see none of it. Those who were cursed weren't meant for the dawn, and all those who had loved him were dead.

"You were meant to live! Not die—live!"

Why had she done this? Lystra had faced every danger at his side—choosing to take his curse. A choice born from her love for him. She'd determined to seek his salvation, to uncover secrets, to bring the curse binder's dagger into his bedchamber the night of their wedding only to show mercy—and change the course of their kingdom forever.

The same dagger lay in the sands, glistening with her blood, the constellation just visible along the blade.

"*She said she could break it.*" Razhar's words. Razhar who had given the last of his strength, of his life, to restore her. Not even Elerek's touch as he held his wife obliterated her skin. Her body had become whole—but still held no life.

"Why isn't it broken?" Elerek lifted his eyes and screamed up at the heavens, at the wrathgiver.

A sudden gust of desert air descended into the canyon, the gorge that his water had cut. Behind him, the wall of water quivered. It reached toward him, blending into the water of his cursed body. It tugged on his soul, whispering poisonous thoughts. Willing him to drown as the curse intended—as he always knew he would.

This time, he hadn't the strength to fight it.

But then, there was starlight.

The wrathgiver came down from the heavens, its light brilliant against the darkness. It shimmered even here, in the depths of the cursed earth. Elerek bowed his head, unable to look at the stars.

He traced his finger along Lystra's face and smoothed back her thick, dark locks. Here, at the end, he wanted to remember her sitting tall astride the cardants she loved so much. The wind in her hair and fire in her eyes. The queen who had chosen to love him.

The water pulled away from him, receding into the cauldron of cursed water and dead Jarkins. With a great *crack*, fissures broke through the rock, the water crashing into the depths of the earth.

It's time.

Elerek braced himself. He lifted his gaze, wanting to see the heavens one last time, but the wrathgiver's light blinded him. Curling forward, shielding Lystra, he clutched her tighter.

A roar filled his ears, a sound to shatter stones. The earth trembled, the cliffs shuddering. Then, the wall of water *burst*. It crashed against the walls of the canyon, surrounding them but not touching them. A swirling vortex of water. And there, in its center, the eye of the storm, Elerek waited, Lystra in his arms.

With the force of a thunderclap, the cursed water swept away, down the pass, and down into the deep, deep depths of the earth. Darcress, built of redstone and blanketed in the blood of kings, queens, and loyal soldiers, stood intact. The Jarkin army and camp washed away. The only water remaining flowed from Elerek's body.

But he didn't flow with it.

He remained on land.

Solid.

Elerek lifted his eyes, blinking in the starlight. Air drew into his lungs. Real lungs. Skin that could touch and be touched spread across his body. A heartbeat pulsed in his ears. The numbness that had inhabited his bones for as long as he could remember seeped away.

Tears filled his eyes. Real tears. Made of salt and hope.

A wholeness filled his heart, chasing away the curse's deadness with the fury of a thousand cardants. Years of waiting for death all dissolved in a moment. Life began anew.

Life after death.

The curse . . . is broken.

Elerek looked to the skies, to the stars and their maker. Dancing lights full of pale, pristine beauty. The wrathgiver returned to its place, freely spinning through its stances. Its hold on him broken.

And his was not the only heartbeat. In his arms, Lystra stirred. Her chest rose as breath entered her lungs. Warmth flooded her glorious, sun-kissed skin. Her eyelids fluttered, and the starlight burned in her eyes. The faintest of smiles glowed on her lips.

Elerek caught his breath. "You . . ."

It was her. The cost—the death—paid with her blood. Lystra broke the curse.

But she lived. How? All at once, Elerek's chest shuddered as he realized the truth. Razhar. She'd become his curse and he'd pushed it back, giving her days. Giving her life—*his* life.

My brother . . . thank you. Pain and grief and joy collided inside him with an intensity that made his heart ache. Lystra—and he—were alive. Flesh and blood and human. Broken and scarred and healed. They were everything they had always been and bursting with all that they could be. Whole.

Pushing his fingers through her hair, his hand fit against the curve of her head as he drew her near and kissed her with all the promise of this newness, this *life.*

When they broke apart, Lystra heaved a sob, her body quivering. Her chest rose in rapid pants, gasping for air as if she feared she might run out.

Drip. Drip. Drip. The ominous sound no longer belonged to cursed water, but to blood. The wound in Lystra's arm remained, rent from her elbow down to her palm, cut clean through her flesh. Deep enough to break the curse and still deep enough to be dangerous.

The sight sickened Elerek, drawing a growl from his lips. "We've got to get you out of here." He pulled the remains of his tattered shirt over his head, his bare chest healed of the curse mark, and bound her arm as best he could—just as Razhar had bound his wounded arm so long ago.

He turned his gaze from the blood seeping through the makeshift bandage, to the sands where Razhar had faded. A life poured out in sacrifice so that they and their kingdom could live. He reached out, his fingertips stirring the sands. *Be at peace, my brother.*

"How did you break it?" His voice sounded foreign to his own ears. It vibrated in his throat, real and authentic.

Lystra's eyes dropped to the dagger in the sand. "My grandmother mentioned that descendants of the curse binder had power, power to count the cost. To die and break the curse, same as you." Her fingers reached for it, its blade stained with her blood. She touched the hilt weakly. "I wanted to do it—to save you."

Elerek snatched the dagger, not keen on seeing it in her hands again. Beneath the sheen of blood, the wrathgiver constellation had faded from its blade. The curse broken.

A low, guttural growl echoed across the canyon. Elerek looked up and smiled. "Tiniah."

Lystra gave a faint exhale. "You . . . you remembered."

She'd lost too much blood. Even in the pure light of the stars, her skin grew pale. Her eyes drifted softly closed.

"No, you're not leaving me now." Elerek clenched his teeth. "Oi, Tiniah, get over here."

The cardant growled again, disgruntled with his tone, but obeyed. Approaching them, she lowered her belly, her girth flattening against the sand.

"Good girl," Lystra whispered.

Elerek stowed the dagger in Tiniah's pack. He kept his hand on Lystra's back as she climbed into the saddle. Leaning forward like a wilted aloe, she grasped at the reins. Elerek grunted, hoisting himself up behind her.

"Tell me what to do."

"Don't let go."

His arms encircled her, hands sliding into place along her waist. Holding her steady as her stalwart soul had steadied him. "Never."

We . . . we have a future. The thought was almost too incredible to believe.

Lystra whispered a command and the reptile spurred

forward. Tiniah scaled the cliffside, leaping from ledge to ledge, her claws catching in the cracks.

Leaving the treacherous earth behind, they emerged back onto the solid ground between the two towers. Elerek blinked. While more of the star-strewn sky lay visible, fringed by black mountains and cliffs, the landscape seemed darker covered in dampened earth and the limp bodies of fallen warriors. Men who had drowned in the desert.

The threat eradicated. Instanolde delivered. But the work lay far from over.

Elerek gazed skyward, watching the condors of the Kushite archers wheel in wide circles. Tiniah lifted her head, her attention keen as the great birds descended before them. The archers, five in all, wore the bronze skin of Kushan and feathered capes cascaded from their shoulders.

"Upon whose orders are you here?" Elerek's voice carried over the stone, reverberating off the towers. Now wasn't the time to be arguing with the king who had drowned an entire army.

"Dalmah of House Arghan," the leader replied. "Acting queen of Instanolde."

Rage kindled in his chest.

In his arms, Lystra stiffened. "She . . . arrested, unfit to serve." Her voice wavered, weak, not at all like the true queen of Instanolde.

Elerek glared at the assembly. "Your orders are moot and further action cannot be taken until this investigation is complete. You saw what was done here. The Jarkin threat is destroyed. The curse fallen to myself is broken. Whatever complaints Kushan may make against me, I will challenge in the presence of your chief. For now, *you* submit to *me*."

One by one, the archers, the men who had aimed a spear

through Razhar's ribs, bowed their heads and said no more. He wanted to hate them. To scream judgment and threaten a cruel, harsh future once the throne was restored to him.

"El, be good to my people. Tell Kushan that you're not like the rest."

Air inflated Elerek's uncursed lungs. Perhaps Razhar believed in him too much, seeing virtue where there was only vengeance. But if Razhar himself could give so great a sacrifice, perhaps Elerek could try to live up to his lofty expectations.

"We get to choose what sort of men we are to be." Cormek's voice. A young king who was given a kingdom torn by strife, a king who didn't know how few his days would be—and had lived well, choosing peace.

I'm not like them. But Elerek knew there was only one path forward. For Instanolde, for Kushan, and for him.

"You are forgiven." He forced the words out, words to echo to the stars themselves. "For the attempted murder of Razhar Emblino, my brother. I will hold no charge against you. Kushan never was, and never shall be, my enemy."

The archers stared at him. They seemed to shrivel, at last seeing him as Instanolde's reigning king.

"Grant us passage," Elerek ordered, squaring his shoulders. "The queen's wounds must be treated immediately."

"War wages at Instanolde; your general leads an attack against the remaining invaders," the archer responded. "Kushan is a shorter distance."

Elerek could almost smile. Well done, Norbah.

Lystra gave a shallow exhale, her body slumped against him. "Grandmother . . . in Kushan."

Elerek's jaw clenched. After all they'd endured, after all they'd survived, they still had to face the woman who had bound his curse and sentenced so many to die. But first, he would make things right with Kushan.

406

For the years of violence between them.
For the innocents who had suffered and died.
For Razhar.

Chapter 48

Razhar

As the light of the wrathgiver descended, shining bright over Lystra's sacrifice, her blood poured out, the curse's hold *shattered*. Razhar felt it, the snip of the stitch that allowed the entire garment to unravel. As the seams of the world faded, he didn't notice the vengeful water, the shifting sands beneath, or the wrath of the constellations above.

He didn't have all the answers, and none of them seemed to matter any longer. Everything would be all right. Lystra would take care of Elerek now and the kingdom would be safe in their capable hands.

Never again would the sand cling to his skin.

Never again would his lungs scratch and burn.

Never again would the effects of the curse weigh from his shoulders.

He'd died as he had lived—holding back death. His life given to the lengthening of days, chasing the sunlight, stretching the moment. The present. Now, the present stretched into a forever illuminated by starlight.

Would those who had perished be waiting for him? Those who had been taken by the curse? Azraa, Fin, and countless others in whom he'd rejoice to see well and no longer bound? Myra, who had kept his secrets, and died for the sake of the man she loved? Would he see Cormek standing whole and hale? Have the chance to tell him all that his brother had become?

Would he feel the arms of his baba again? Welcoming him into a warm embrace?

As the shadows of the world fell away, replaced by a heavenly light without blemish, Razhar couldn't wait to find out.

Chapter 49

Elerek

Never. Again.

As the condor swept to its landing with swift precision, Elerek's drumming heart threatened to flee his chest. He stared dazedly at the earth beneath the bird's perch. Even in the torchlight, the rich soil shone with a deep red that could only belong to the canyonlands. Never in his life had he been so thankful for dirt.

For most of the journey, he'd kept his eyes shut fast, praying desperate prayers that he wouldn't vomit. The deepness of night helped, shadowing the height and the devastation of impending plummet. They'd given him a spare thobe to ward off the altitude's chill and, upon Elerek's insistence, tied his legs to the saddle. Razhar would've laughed at him, being frightened of flying over the desert.

But Razhar wasn't here.

Leaning forward, he gripped the edge of the saddle. He couldn't think of Razhar. Not now. Now, he had to be king.

Torchlight played on the sentries' faces as they rushed to

catch the birds' reins. The Kushite archers dismounted, except the one cradling Lystra.

"Bring a stretcher!"

A lump rose in Elerek's throat. As the men laid her limp form on the stretcher, even the torches' glow couldn't mask the ghostly pallor of her skin. The wraps of Elerek's shirt about her arm were soaked with blood.

Before they'd taken flight, he'd ordered that one archer remain behind to watch Tiniah, guarding the cardant as one would royalty. Reinforcements would return to Darcress soon enough. The fortress couldn't be left abandoned and a plan had begun to form in his mind. Still, he felt sorry whispering to Lystra that they would retrieve the mighty cardant at summer's end.

The queen had only nodded distantly, spurring his dread.

"Take her to the healers." The head archer stood tall. "And alert the chief—the king is here."

Expressions of wonder and bewilderment passed among them. Elerek drew a deep breath, realizing that a king had not entered the canyonlands without ill intentions in generations.

And here he'd come, missing a boot, wearing borrowed clothing, and worn thin by the Sancen. "Tell him that I will see him at dawn." He let his voice carry, echoing off the steep cliffs. "I'll go with the queen."

Even as he spoke, his mind began to slow, overwhelmed by the fight, the grief, and the monumental events of the last hours. Fatigue sank upon his shoulders, a burden he hadn't the strength to carry anymore.

"And . . ." His voice wavered. "I need help. I can't walk."

The Kushite sentries swiftly obeyed, assisting him down from the condor's back and onto the wagon where Lystra's stretcher lay. Elerek closed his eyes, bracing himself against the wagon's uneven rumbling across the gravel path. He craved silence, the stillness to process, to grieve, but he also knew the things he had to process, to grieve, weren't easy.

No, he couldn't think of them. He twisted in his seat, watching the shadows flirt across Lystra's lovely face. Reaching down, his fingers brushed a lock of hair from her brow.

The wagon lumbered to a stop before an imposing section of cliff. Torches burned in the holes cut as windows. Arched pergolas adorned the cliff's exterior, the architecture blending into the wildness of the cliff dwellings. The sentry leapt down from the wagon, giving orders, and healers in pale robes assembled.

"What's happened?" A man in a yellow turban worn in the same manner that Razhar would wear, approached the wagon.

"The queen, she's lost a lot of blood."

Elerek's jaw clenched. This scene mirrored a memory, one where *he'd* been the one whose skin needed to be stitched closed. A healer had joined the ranks of the cursed that day.

No more. The curse had ended. No one else would die.

"Get her inside." The healer waved to his associates. "Prepare a room."

The healers lifted the stretcher bearing Lystra. Elerek did his best to follow, but the healers barred him from the operating room, built like a cave into the cliffside. With nowhere else to go, Elerek beckoned the sentries to help him onto a bench hewn from the wall. Hunching forward, he held his head in his hands, exhausted.

"Your Highness." The head archer approached him, bowing. "If it pleases you, we can prepare accommodation nearby. One of my men will send word the moment the queen has recovered."

Elerek blinked, the fatigue heavy behind his eyes. He probably looked nothing like the king of Instanolde, but a battle worn warrior. And still, the chief would come at first light, and the matter of Dalmah . . . yes, maybe he ought to rest. He nodded wearily and thanked the archer.

"I need reports concerning the fate of my kingdom, as soon as you have them," he added.

True to their word, the Kushites gave him a room on the lower levels of the cliff dwellings, the healers' alcoves just across the canyon. A soldier stood at the door and an attendant gave him aid. After bathing away the sand of the desert and shaving the stubble along his jaw, he felt some semblance of humanity return to himself.

I am human. Not cursed. Human.

Elerek hardly recognized the face that stared back at him in the mirror by the dim light of meager candles. The darkness beneath his eyes deepened, pairing with the bruises, scars, and scrapes splattering his skin. But this skin belonged to him. These weary bones, fatigued muscles, and crippled legs were his own. A home for his battered soul.

He waited for the reports, but none came. Not from the chief, Instanolde, or the healers entrusted with Lystra's care.

He needed sleep. The chastisement lay distant, a far-off echo amid the chaos warring through his head. After the nights spent on the rocky ground, a bed beneath his back felt like luxury. The air left his lungs in a long sigh, the tension ebbing from his shoulders. His fingers traced the creases of the sheets, the solitude closing in as deep as the darkness of the canyons.

I . . . I don't want to be alone. If only Lystra lay nestled against him, her soft skin beneath his touch. Did she yearn for him as much as he yearned for her?

He shut his eyes, but the moment he did, his mind spun, images flashing over and over in a dizzying cycle. The great wall of water formed by his hand. Warriors floating limp, screams dying on their lips. The pull of cursed water dragging him into the depths.

Razhar fading away to sand. Blood pouring from Lystra's arm. Over and over and over.

Elerek rolled onto his side, pulling the alpaca wool blanket over his bruised shoulders.

Don't think of it. All that he'd lost. All that he'd gained. *Don't think about Razhar.*

The curse was broken. They were safe. Lystra would be well. They had a future.

He could live.

Pinching his eyes shut, his lungs deflated with an exhale. *I don't know how to live.*

When the first rays of dawn cut in broad shafts over the edge of the red canyons, Elerek welcomed its warmth on his face, on skin that no longer held the curse's numbness. As he watched from a couch near a window, the canyons burst into glorious shades of umber, red, and white, he felt again as he had that first morning as the king of Instanolde.

Terrified—but burdened with purpose.

But this time, he, like his kingdom, no longer had one summer to live.

Mere moments after the sunrise, soldiers brought reports. Instanolde had successfully been liberated from the Jarkins. A swift campaign, jointly executed by the city militia, the palace guards—including Elerek's regiment of archers—and an ample supply of Kushite warriors.

The whole kingdom working together. Just the thought gave Elerek hope that a future was possible.

"And the queen?" he demanded.

The Kushite captain blinked. "I'll go to the healers immediately."

"See that you do." Elerek narrowed his eyes. "Tell the healers to expect me."

Once the captain departed, two soldiers remained. Elerek turned in surprise. One of the men, crowned with a head of gray hair, was seated in a wooden chair—a chair with wheels—his pants sewn where his leg ought to have been.

He rolled his chair forward and bowed his head. "Your Highness, my name is Jarrah. If Your Highness will hear me, I've come with a request."

"You may speak."

Jarrah bowed again. "In Kushan, so little has been known of His Highness's person. We were not aware of your disability. My request is that for the duration of your stay, my chair would be of use to you."

The warmth of the man's generosity dawned in Elerek's heart. "I am honored, Jarrah. But I know what my chair is to me, and I wouldn't dare part you from yours."

"Please, Your Highness, allow me this honor." Jarrah took a cane from his side, using it and the aid of the remaining soldier to help him rise from the wheelchair. "My condor will get me about too, and, Starkindler knows, I prefer wings to wheels."

Elerek offered a gentle smile. "Our tastes there differ, I'm afraid. I thank you for your service to your king."

Joy burst upon the older man's face, which only intensified as they brought the chair to Elerek's couch. The chair moved a bit more stiffly, lacking the refinement and polish of his own, but climbing into it still felt like coming home.

A third soldier appeared at the door. "Your Highness, Chief Wuhaz has arrived."

Elerek squared his shoulders, once again making a chair with wheels his throne. He would face the chief feeling himself at least.

The small parlor grew crowded as a host of soldiers and officials darkened the doorway. Elerek kept a stern countenance as the chief's ancient form, clad in yellow robes and bearing a staff, approached him. His last council with Kushan, when they'd denounced the bloody history of House Karim and denied him fealty, took place in the throne room of his golden palace. Now, he met the chief in his own lands, surrounded by the red canyon walls.

"Your Highness." Wuhaz bowed, his entourage mirroring his actions.

Elerek gripped the chair's armrests. "Chief, it is an honor to meet you face-to-face. You have my deepest gratitude for the aid you have given me, my queen, and my people."

Lystra's absence formed a canyon, cutting through his soul. Her words, her skill in diplomacy, were always sure to flow like silk, and he appreciated her giftings.

As the chief straightened, a shadow darkened his face. Elerek's heart pounded. Did he see Lorkin's ghost lurking in his eyes? No, he would not carry that weight. He was here, and he was someone else. Instanolde was their work.

"Much has been said and done, Your Highness." Wuhaz's tone grew stern. "But the testimony of your return, the curse's breaking, and the restoration done unto those who bore it is a remarkable feat. Am I to believe that the counter curse completed his duty?"

"El, be good to my people."

Razhar hadn't given his life for the curse's breaking. No, he'd died for this—the salvation of two kingdoms that ought not to be enemies. To end a rift of bloodshed and violence. To give him and Lystra the days to see it done.

Elerek set his jaw and maintained his posture of strict regality, masking the ache of pain and loss. "Is there not a Kushite proverb that states that life is not measured by its number of days, but the bounds of its generosity?"

Razhar, my brother, I miss you more than I can articulate.

Wuhaz regarded him with a skeptical lift of his eyebrow. "Your Highness is indeed well-read to know our proverbs."

Elerek's fingers drummed on the arm of the chair, an anxious fidget. He needed more than compliments. "I'll be direct, Chief. You gave aid to my general, preserving my city, *our* kingdom. The Jarkins' threat has been eradicated by joint efforts, thus it seems wise to place provision for our preservation in hands firmly clasped."

"Hands that bore a curse, a thing that shouldn't have been kept secret from us. A breach of trust."

Elerek pushed his shoulders back. "That breach of trust began with the countess of House Arghan." His heart beat wildly, knowing his every word had to be strategic. "I believe that, upon the subjects of curses, you and I share sentiments. I know their depths of suffering. Kushan, upon principle, judges those involved with these dark manipulations harshly. The countess judges the same, only using these methods to execute her verdicts. Surely Kushan sees that an alliance with her, of any form, cannot hold weight."

A heaviness settled upon the chief's shoulders. "Kushan will form no such alliance, Your Highness. The countess's manipulations have run their course, a river that has worn a trench far too deep. Upon the departure of your queen and the Emblino boy, she confessed."

She—what? Elerek stared at the chief, knowing he'd betrayed his noble countenance.

Wuhaz nodded. "She feared for her granddaughter's life. The queen accused the countess and ordered her arrest, but her own words, sealed with tears, convinced us of her guilt. A severe tragedy."

"A tragedy that has claimed victims from among both our peoples." Elerek sat a little taller. "Between us lie the remains, the ashes. The choice falls to us to let strife's poison fill our veins or to forgive what lies behind and look to a new sunrise. This morning, this day, we stand in a victory earned not by ourselves, but by the loyalty and endurance of our people, working side by side."

The chief gave a *hmph.* "You ask for Kushan's fealty?"

"Yes." Elerek didn't let his voice waver, empowered not by the curse or threat of death, but the hope of service to his kingdom, to his people.

Movement stirred the entourage, their yellow robes fluttering. Light shifted between their eyes, watching their chief—watching *him,* the rejected king of Instanolde who had survived a curse and the desert, and had come back to build a new world.

Finally, after an expectant pause, Wuhaz dropped to one knee. "Elerek of House Karim, son of Lorkin, king of Instanolde, to you Kushan pledges its loyalty, its blood, and its courage. For peace, for hope, until the stars rain from the heavens."

Elerek released a slow exhale. Peace, like still waters, settled over his soul. He wished that Razhar was here, to see what his sacrifice had achieved. "Until the stars rain from the heavens," he repeated, his voice soft.

Chapter 50

Lystra

It's broken. The curse. Ended forever.

Paid with her own blood.

The world after lay hazy, a landscape of shadows and wheeling stars fringed by the wings of condors soaring between the sands and the heavens. Had the great birds come to take her to the Starkindler? She had died—hadn't she?

What were these memories? The surge of breath into her lungs. The warmth dancing on her skin. The eager longing of the kiss from the king of Instanolde.

And she remembered sand, blowing away on the wind. Flying free.

Then came the darkness. The muffled sounds. Jarring movement. All distant, as if she lay underwater, buried by the curse's torrent.

She awoke to a searing pain. Still in darkness, but halos of soft light surrounded the flame of oil lamps. She lay on a bed surrounded by walls of stone. A cave, or perhaps they'd dug her a tomb. Men and women with bronze skin worked frantically. They held her arm over a bowl of bloody water. The shreds of her bindings, hardened with blood, were being torn from her wound.

El's shirt. Where was he? Why wasn't he here? Lystra blinked, her eyes jumping from face to face. All strangers.

"It's deep," one of the men muttered. "How did this happen?"

"Knife work. Disinfect and stitch quickly."

Lystra tried to lift her head. Sweat dampened her brow. "El? Where is . . . where . . . ?"

"Shh." A woman touched her shoulder. "It's all right, Your Highness. You're here, in Kushan." She lifted a cup, steam wafting from it. "You need to drink this, it will make you sleep while we stitch your arm."

Hot liquid burned her lips, trickling down her throat. It tasted of strong tea, bitter and pungent. The room began to spin, the halos of light dancing like the constellations themselves. Lystra moaned.

"When you wake," the woman whispered, "you'll feel much better."

Lystra's eyes drifted closed on that promise—that she would wake up.

And she did, blinking in the light of glorious morning. Her surroundings were familiar, a simple bed with wool blankets woven in bright patterns surrounded by walls of chiseled stones and irregular windows revealing glimpses of a brilliant blue sky.

The last time she'd woken in Kushan, she'd lain dying from the curse. Now, she lived—and the curse was broken.

Her arm lay stretched out from her body. White bandages wrapped from her elbow down to her fingers. There wasn't a single drop of blood in sight, not on the bandages or the sleeve-less nightgown, colored the same glorious shade as the sky, that replaced her desert clothes. Lystra felt no pain, only fatigue.

The silence broke with a rustling sound. The turning of a page.

She wasn't alone.

Beside the window, an alcove had been cut from the wall and lined with cushions. There, Elerek reclined with his legs stretched out in front of him, an open book in his hands.

Lystra held her breath, transfixed by the sight. *He's beautiful.*

A king. Regal and noble, each line cut like the sharp peaks of the desert mountains—from the severe slant of his jaw, the rise of his cheekbones, and the intensity of his stare. Not a hint of the desert's dirt and grime clung to him or his clothes. The dark green thobe, lightly adorned with orange embroidery, couldn't compare to the robes of a royal, but the proud set of his shoulders wore it well. Beneath, a simple white qamis lay open at his chest, a chest made of skin and tight muscle and not water.

Lystra could no longer see Cormek's ghost haunting Elerek's features. She'd gone past his dark curls, the hue of his eyes, the build of his body, and into his heart—the soul that wanted to give up but had chosen to fight, to burn like starfire. The soul she had bound herself to with a love that no curse could destroy.

Not unbroken, but together they were whole.

Across the room, the door creaked open. Elerek's eyes

shifted. The sunlight turned Corsha's auburn hair to gold, a smile wide across her lips.

"Lystra, you're awake!"

In a flash, her cousin stood at her bedside, stroking her hair and kissing her forehead, tears dripping from her cheeks. "Oh, vianni, I've missed you so much. I was so afraid . . . afraid that we'd lose you."

"I'm all right," Lystra whispered, finding her own eyes filled with tears. She squeezed Corsha's fingers with her unbound hand. "How long has it been?"

Corsha briefly glanced toward Elerek. "You returned last night, very late. The king brought you back."

"You don't need to call me that." Elerek closed the book and set it aside. Beside him, an empty chair stood. A chair with wheels.

As he climbed into it and wheeled closer, Lystra noted his ease, his confidence, the way such a chair had given him freedom.

"You're family, after all." A soft smile graced his lips.

Lystra's heart fluttered. It took such effort to tear her gaze back to her cousin. "Please do, it's a title he's earned a thousand times over."

Corsha smiled, her cheeks turning pink. "I ought to give you a moment." She reluctantly released Lystra's hand and backed toward the door.

"More than a moment," Elerek spoke after her. "Please inform the healers that Her Highness has awoken and is certainly not spending another night alone here."

Corsha fled the room.

Lystra's cheeks flushed. She contemplated pulling the blankets up over her head to hide the smile that she tried, unsuccessfully, to pull back. She'd a feeling that Elerek would need

422

no encouragement to join her—and she rather hoped that he would.

"It's lonely here." Elerek's fingers brushed through her hair, along her cheek. "Stars, I missed you." His gaze wandered farther, from her eyes, to her lips, her neck and—Lystra's face burned as she reached for the blanket.

"Has there been word? From Instanolde?"

He gave a sober nod. "The Jarkins are routed. Norbah took back the city with Kushan's aid." His voice dropped to a whisper. "Everything will be all right now."

She caught it. The grief tainting his voice, like the essence of mint mixed with strong tea. An edge of shadow emerging in his piercing eyes. She wished she could erase it, let the light chase away every darkness, but she'd lived with enough shadows to know that it wasn't so simple. They lived on, marching forward.

Not unbroken.

"Why am I alive?" she scarcely dared to whisper.

Elerek bowed his head. His jaw hardened. The words he spoke ached. "You died, Lystra." His fingers lightly touched her bandaged arm. "And Razhar pushed the death back, at the cost of his own life."

Oh. Lystra closed her eyes.

"He died for us. For Instanolde. For a new dawn." Elerek's throat worked. When he lifted his eyes again, they were full of tears. "Lystra . . ." The way he said her name ignited a flame in her heart. "What you've done . . . you broke it."

Lystra reached for his face with her wrapped hand, catching his tears with its gauze. Each drop was precious. Water not shed from a curse. Tears of grief, yes, but tears also of hope.

"I've only lived my broken and shattered life knowing that I would die. Now, because of Razhar, because of you . . ." Elerek drew a deep breath, his chest heaving. "I'll live. How do I live?"

Oh, El. An echo returned to Lystra's mind. A memory that seemed to come from another life. A wedding feast for a king and queen who couldn't touch, whose love belonged to their kingdom. A man of secrets who could hold back the curse with the touch of his sand-clad hands, speaking of Elerek. *"Living—like never before."*

Her fingertips, exposed from the bandages, entwined in his curls. "Razhar believed that the crown gave you purpose, a reason to live." She smiled. "That doesn't have to end now. Not just because you are a king of a kingdom, of a people, of my heart—but because you are alive. You don't need a purpose to live, just to know that each day, each moment, each sunrise, is a gift."

At the mention of Razhar, Elerek closed his eyes.

Gently, she caressed his face, his beautiful, noble face. "You're not alone, El. I'll share that gift with you. I'll mourn with you. I'll laugh with you. This life—this *moment*—is ours."

His eyes turned to hers. Tears washed his irises clear, polishing them like the most perfect emeralds. Full of brokenness and hope—of starlight.

Elerek cupped her face in his strong and scarred hands. He pushed his fingers through her hair, cradling her head and gently lifting her toward him.

Heat surged through her the moment their lips touched, the burst of first light as the sun rose from the horizon. A new dawn in the world that belonged to them. Gone forever was the chill, the note of death that haunted his skin, the curse banished to the depths.

When they separated, Lystra caught her breath. Her vision filled with the whole of his eyes, intense and pure. Perhaps it was always meant to be this way. He was hers. She was his. Together they had shattered, together they would heal.

"I'll show you how to live." This promise hovered between them, in the heat, the lingering air between their lips. Flinging her unbandaged arm around his neck, she closed the distance again. Kissing him deeply, fiercely, with the whole of her heart.

Elerek sighed into her kiss. His arms encircled her, his hands moving down her back. Strong. Warm. *Him.* Pushing the thobe from his shoulders, Lystra burned with the distance, as if the whole of the Sancen separated them as it had yesterday. Yearning to never be parted from him again.

"Do you . . .?" His breath blew hot against her neck. "Is this what you want?"

Lystra stared up at him. Her king. Her husband. "I want *you.*"

Elerek drew back, smiling a smile that wasn't broken. He yanked her blanket aside. A shudder of cool air crept along Lystra's legs, chased quickly away as he drew her onto his lap, his hand against her thigh. His kisses turned fierce, a fire set to flare and burn to the heavens themselves. His lips moved to her ear, her jaw, against her neck, her collar. Lystra closed her eyes, her hands, slowly with the bandage, slipping beneath his shirt with its open neck, to muscled shoulders that she knew were bruised. Shoulders that had carried the weight of the world.

"I love you," Elerek murmured, his breath hot against her throat.

Smiling, she leaned back, still held steady in his arms, the wheeled chair beneath. "I think we ought to lock the door."

He laughed, lifting her onto the edge of the bed that wouldn't be empty for long. "Perhaps you're right, my queen."

The harrows of their journey faded behind them and a new one lay before. Each kiss, each touch, became something precious, cherished. A promise of the lifetime before them where they now belonged to one another, wholly and completely.

Chapter 51

Elerek

As the daylight waned, the reds of the canyons deepened. White rock turned to dusty blue and the river of sky up above faded into a glorious display of orange just as the first constellations came out to dance. The skies in Kushan were as bright and colorful as Razhar's clothing.

The wrathgiver lay obscured, claimed by the cliffs and the distant horizon. Elerek was glad of it.

Wuhaz invited them to dine with him and the other nobles of the tribe, his table prepared upon a balcony cut from the cliffs themselves. Elerek kept himself and his borrowed chair away from the rail, having had his fill of heights, but Lystra swiftly approached the edge, accompanied by her cousin and a cloud of nobles. As she leaned over the open expanse, the wind caught in her hair, blowing over her shoulder like a condor's graceful wing. A kaftan dress of a delicate lavender adorned her figure, procured by Corsha, detailed in black and silver embroidery.

Lystra glanced his way. Her smile burst with joy, with love —and the secrets they had shared together.

Elerek's heart beat faster.

"I'm glad Her Highness is well," Wuhaz commented, slowly lowering himself to a silk cushion at Elerek's right.

"As am I." Elerek turned his attention to the chief. "Our kingdom is in debt to your healers."

His eyes wrinkled as the chief gave a soft smile. Then, he poured a goblet of wine, extending it. A flash of panic shot through Elerek, his hand immediately going to the chair's wheel. *I'm not cursed.*

There was no danger, no threat. He accepted the goblet— and the newfound truth that he had no need to fear. It would take some getting used to.

"I crave your pardon, Your Highness, but I am curious." The chief poured himself a goblet. "Your queen's wounds. If the Emblino boy didn't break the curse—how was it broken?"

He has a name. Elerek's hand tightened about the goblet. He inhaled deep, an attempt to dispel the rising flood of emotion consuming his soul. "Razhar granted salvation to many —including Her Highness." Meeting the chief's eyes, he let the grief show on his face. "For now, let it be enough that it is broken."

Wuhaz nodded and said no more.

Before long, the scent of roasting meat filled the air and servants laid the table high with lamb, flatbread with garlic and spices, couscous, palm dates, and heaping bowls of moonfruit. Elerek blinked, suddenly aware of how few and far between his meals had been. When Lystra seated herself beside him and a blessing whispered to the Maker of all stars, a swell of gratitude and contentment filled his heart.

Razhar was there, with the Starkindler.

Not about the table, stuffing his face with palm dates. Not

caught up in riotous laughter over a joke or cracking one of his own. Not grinning like an impish child or cheering as another jar of wine made its rounds.

Not with me.

Elerek tried to smile, to laugh, to enjoy the festivities, but grief became a cursed dagger of another sort, one that had pierced his heart and pierced deep. He didn't want to think about Razhar—and the fact that he'd lost another brother.

Lystra reached for his hand, her fingers soft and enveloped in white gauze. Her eyes met his, shining brighter than the oil lamps on the table. The glow of a flame he never wanted to fade.

"We don't have to linger," she whispered.

Elerek nodded.

Rising, Lystra announced their departure, bidding the nobles words of satisfaction and gratitude.

"Your Highness." Chief Wuhaz bowed. "Whenever you are ready, a vessel will set course for Instanolde. But what of the countess of House Arghan?"

Lystra's face fell, melting the image of her regality. Elerek watched her, wishing they could leave now, sail as fast as the winds would take them for the home he'd never thought he'd see again. Their kingdom, alight in a glory that would outlast summer's end.

"I'll send word," Lystra replied. "I intend to take care of the matter."

"You're sure?" Elerek turned to his wife, brushing a stray hair over her shoulder, letting the lamplight gleam on the soft curve of her collarbone.

Lystra bowed her head, cradling a cup of steaming tea between her palms. Fatigue drew deep lines across her face. "The sooner Grandmother's handled, the sooner we can go home."

As darkness fell over Kushan, the shadows deepened by the steep cliffs, they'd retired to Elerek's rooms, taking tea in the small parlor illuminated by the soft glow of candles. He'd left the borrowed chair, nestled against Lystra on the couch.

"What will you do?" Across the table, Corsha sat primly, so still that not even the tassels on her cushion dared to move. Elerek suspected that the girl realized that her presence stood as a solitary barrier between him taking Lystra into his arms again and kissing her until she was breathless.

"Kushite ordinances would have her executed as a curse binder." Lystra's voice ran bitter, like strong coffee. "She deserves it."

The curse binder who cursed him. Elerek sipped his own tea. He knew he ought to be angry, furious even. The woman who'd destroyed so many lives, including his own, deserved judgment. If Kushan did execute her, they'd receive no protest from him.

But he didn't feel angry. Only weary. Only sorrowful.

If not for Dalmah, Razhar would still be alive . . . No, he wanted nothing to do with the matter. Lystra's hands were more than capable.

"She was also a queen . . ." Lystra said softly. "A queen who suffered."

Compassion radiated from Corsha's eyes. "You're not like her, vianni."

"You are not your curse." Razhar's voice echoed in his ears. Elerek bowed his head.

Corsha leaned her elbows on the table. "I witnessed her confession. I believe she truly feared for your life."

Elerek sniffed. It was far too late for sympathy.

"I killed, Corsha." Lystra's voice held a pain to it. "I drowned Khasar. Perhaps it might be justice, the rules of war, vengeance for Cormek's blood—but Grandmother has just as much blood on her hands as the Jarkins. Who am I to say whether she should live or die?"

Elerek shifted his gaze toward her. "My hands are bloody too, Lystra."

She looked at him, sorrow lingering in the soft glow of amber.

"Your grandmother raised you to be a queen, but you were never a queen like her." He leaned forward, planting a kiss on her forehead. "You never lost your kindness. Your compassion. At Darcress, you did what you believed to be necessary—which also saved my life. Discernment, knowing when to execute justice and when to show mercy, shouldn't be overlooked or ignored." Elerek gave her a small smile. "I believe you'll make the right decision."

Her chest rose and she held her head high, as if the crown of fire opals sat radiant upon it. The glint in her eye turned solid, like polished gold. *Starkindler . . . she's beautiful.*

And she was his.

Outside, a commotion stirred. The flap of condor wings. The rattle of tack and metal. The stomp of boots.

"General, wait, you can't—" the Kushite soldier stationed outside protested.

"Try and stop me."

Elerek's heart rose in his throat. *That's . . .* He grabbed the arms of the borrowed wheelchair. Pivoting around the table, he made it halfway across the room when the doorway darkened. The immense man wore no armor, yet appeared formidable anyways in a leather hauberk and twin scimitars strapped to his hips.

But the moment Norbah caught sight of him, his face lost its ferocity. The general had always been a man of emotion, showing compassion to a prince overlooked by his father.

Dropping to his knees, his eyes full of tears, Norbah bowed his head. "My king."

This man had won the kingdom back. While Elerek drowned the invaders, he protected their people. Swallowing, he forced strength to his voice. "Let me see your hand."

Norbah rose, presenting his hand without its glove. Cleared of the curse. Elerek clasped it like a brother-in-arms. Skin to liberated skin.

"It's broken," Elerek whispered.

"And you're alive, El. You're *alive*." Norbah threw his arms around him, nearly lifting him from the chair.

Never once had Elerek been embraced by his father. His mother had perished from the curse in a time nearly beyond his memory. His brother had been kept at arm's length. But these, these precious individuals. The men and women who knew their end would come because of his touch and chose to love him had become his family. One not built of blood, but of cursed water.

The curse took so much, but now, in the end, I see it also gave me much.

Then, his defenses shattered, Elerek wept. And his friends allowed him, standing beside him until his tears ran dry.

Norbah knelt before his chair, gripping his shoulder. "It's all right, El. They're all right. Ishtal, Driss, Cole, Bushra. I've gone home, to my family. Held my son. I kissed my wife for the first time in years." His glowing smile created creases about his eyes. "I hope you've done the same?"

The touch of Lystra's soft hands caressed Elerek's shoulders. What a wonder that someone could be both fierce and gentle at the same time.

"Of course, General." He could hear the smile in his queen's voice. "Thank you for what you've done for your kingdom."

Norbah inhaled deep as he rose to his feet, his hands falling comfortably to the hilts of his scimitars. "We couldn't have done it without Kushan, my queen. With the frontal assault from the air, we had little loss of life. My men in the city were prepared, waiting. When the sun rose, we realized that the curse had been broken. The Jarkins had done their damage spreading it, but when the people were restored, it gave them the courage to take back the city."

"Spreading . . .?" Elerek felt a chill as the blood drained from his face.

Norbah's gaze darkened. "It took the kingdom, El. Without precautions, without understanding, without Razhar to hold it back."

The room seemed to blur. Elerek leaned forward, holding his head in his hands. "Do they . . ." His voice sounded strangled. "Do they know that it came from me?"

Norbah sighed, clasping his shoulder again. "Does it matter? They'd just as soon blame the Jarkins. Tell me, El, hasn't Razhar told you countless times that you were never the curse?"

Razhar . . . A great chasm cracked across his heart. A gaping emptiness. It left him numb in a way that the curse never had, a brokenness that couldn't be healed.

Elerek shut his eyes. *Don't think about Razhar. Don't think* — He felt as if he were back at Darcress, upholding the swirling mass of cursed water by a small, single thread of control. A torrent ready to crash and consume.

Norbah blinked, and twin tears streaked down his cheeks. "Did . . ." His voice held the same weight. "Did Razhar break the curse?"

"No," Lystra replied softly. "He saved the kingdom, giving of himself for the hope of a new world. Without him, neither myself nor El would have survived. He gave us a gift, a world that will see another sunrise."

But what sort of sunrise would it be without him? Without his glowing eyes, alight with adventure? His smiling lips from which poured laughter and far too many terrible jokes? Even his colorful clothes and lopsided turbans. Everything that Razhar did burst with a love of living. And he chose to live among the cursed, to keep them alive like lamps lit against the night.

Losing Razhar felt like losing half of Elerek's soul. And he'd felt this way before.

Cormek. Myra. Countless others. Yes, he'd gained much, many beautiful things. A future. His kingdom. His bride. But that would never mean that he didn't feel the loss running like the Gungole through the Sancen.

They needed their grief like they needed the river, to survive, to remember that they were frail and beautiful and alive.

Elerek drew a shuddered breath. He would think about Razhar. He would think about him every day for as long as he lived.

This time, he wouldn't merely try to live.

He would live.

Chapter 52

Lystra

Lystra awoke with the dawn.

Light streamed from the rough-cut window in long shafts, falling over the bed with its soft alpaca wool blankets where she lay tucked beneath Elerek's arm.

Several days had passed. Days their weary bodies and worn souls sorely needed. Their duties still required their tending, but between the chief's attention to his tribe and Norbah's swift return to Instanolde, they were given stillness. Lystra looked down at her hands, clothed in skin and not curse. Though she'd borne the curse for such a short time compared to others, she still caught herself checking. Likewise, as she slowly sat up, she traced her finger along her husband's chest, where no trace of the watery mark remained.

The curse was broken, and today they would return home.

Home. The beauty of the Kushite canyons was captivating, but Lystra missed the desert. The wide horizon. The great sky above. The sweep of a dune as a cardant shifted its weight, using the slope to build its momentum.

Lystra heaved a short sigh, thinking of Tiniah left at

Darcress. She'd already conversed with the archers who'd flown back. They'd spoken fondly of the reptile and assured her that the next rotation of soldiers would treat her as royalty—and probably spoil her rotten.

Per Elerek's negotiations, Kushan would assume the task of fortifying and expanding the Kasbah fortress. With the aid of condors, Darcress would become accessible and defensible all year round. Word had spread that the pass had filled with wild-flowers, life awakened by the waters of death. Eventually, a cardant stable would be built there, as Cormek had once promised.

Beside her, Elerek stirred. The sunlight burned in his eyes as a smile appeared on his lips. "My queen."

She'd never tire of his smile, of the shadows pulled back and hope burning in his soul. As she leaned down to kiss him, he pulled her into his arms and the warmth of their freedom enveloped them.

They had time. Time to live, to love, to thrive.

All that had been torn down they would rebuild. From her cardant stable, to relations between the tribes both great and small. Even the shattered pieces of their grief-torn hearts would mend—and they would do it together.

"You're beautiful." Elerek brushed her hair back from her face.

"Hmm. I'm glad you think so."

"I do." He touched his lips to her forehead. "And I mean to remind you each and every day, till the stars rain from the heavens."

Such words warranted another kiss.

"We ought to hurry." Lystra huffed, reluctantly backing out of his arms and swinging her legs over the side of the bed. As the cool stone touched her bare feet, the reality of the work set before her solidified in her soul.

Today. I face Grandmother.

On the table beside her bed, a rolled scroll sat tied with an orange silk ribbon, sealing her decision. The sight of it rolled her stomach.

Elerek moved behind her, laying his hand on her shoulder. "I trust your judgment."

Even he didn't know the contents of that scroll, insisting that this duty belonged to her. Lystra was glad that this burden wouldn't add to the weights already stacked upon his shoulders.

"Thank you," she whispered, thankful to not be alone.

Rising, she crossed to the washbasin to tend to her arm. Unwrapping the swaths of gauze, the sight of the deep gash made her dizzy, the line of stitches linking her flesh like the seam of a worn garment. The healers had given her enough herbs to spice a feast, and they claimed it was healing well, but restoration would take time.

Watching her, Elerek's jaw tightened. A familiar march of ghosts passed through his eyes. "It will scar, you know."

Lystra cast aside the old bandages and reached for the roll of clean ones. "I know." She watched him as he donned a gold-embroidered jabador, an ensemble worthy of a king making his triumphant return to his kingdom, and a smile lilted her lips. "It means I've lived."

He bowed his head, his fingers stilled on the fastenings at his chest. Lystra could almost see the weight settling onto his broad shoulders. His chest rose and fell, and she could feel it, the single heartbeat, all the time it took for grief to return. "It'll match mine."

Her gaze strayed to his forearm where intricate embroidery and dark silk covered the mark that cut like a deep canyon along the pale parchment of his skin.

She glided closer, laying her hand, the last of the stitches sealing her palm, on his. "It's not a mark of ending, El."

"I know." Elerek exhaled, turning his face toward the open window. As morning dawned, the light shifted, touching the rise of his cheekbone, catching in his glossy curls. "One of a thousand rescue attempts. Cormek. Razhar. You. None of you gave up on me."

Razhar. Lystra heard it. The softness with which Elerek spoke his name. They would find a way to honor him. She laid her hand on his chest, leaning into him. "They would both be so proud of you—as I am."

When the king and queen arrived on the shore of the azure canal, the mighty canyons emptied as the Kushite people assembled to see them off. Many wore adornments of yellow over their simple, homespun clothes. A scarf, a turban, a tasseled sash, a display of their heritage, their pride, and their loyalty.

Lystra also wore yellow, a flowing kaftan of layered, nearly sheer silk. Gold stitching adorned the collar, the shoulders, spreading down to her hem. The sleeves draped over her bandages, hiding her scars as Elerek hid his. Today they would appear as monarchs. The glorious rulers who had survived the harrowing dawn of their reign.

Norbah returned to escort them, arrayed in full armor and a flowing cape of Instan orange, flanking Elerek's right while Corsha, likewise dressed in orange, stood at Lystra's left as they met the contingent of Kushite officials. Wuhaz wore his own cape of condor feathers, fluttering in the breeze stirred by the canal waters.

They sank to their knees in deep, ceremonial bows. Lystra caught her breath as the entirety of the Kushite people did the same. Even Norbah and Corsha joined, the orange silk of Instanolde rippling in the morning light. This reverence and loyalty was owed them, but Lystra vowed that they would rule to be worthy of it. They would be good to Razhar's people.

And there, behind the chief and his entourage, stood Dalmah.

Her lips were dull, lacking the vibrant stains of deep red. No scarf or veil covered her hair, leaving her black, streaked with silver, locks to be tossed by the wind. Stripped of her silks and jewelry, dressed in a simple kaftan of black, she looked ordinary. Certainly not the fearsome figure that had raised Lystra with a harsh hand and even harsher words. Not a curse binder, taking vengeance upon kings, princes, soldiers, and lowly Kushites with blood and fury.

Just a woman vanquished.

Lystra bowed her head, her jewelry glittering in the light. She wouldn't let Dalmah see her soul, the tumult of righteous anger, the deep sorrow, and swelling remorse. She'd painted her own face enough to hide it, presenting the icon, the queen of Instanolde raised from the ashes of one king's pyre. She held the scroll, the words inked by her own hand. Words that would change the world.

It seemed fitting. Another such scroll had been read here in the Kushite canyons, brought to the light by the courage of a man who loved his brother. That scroll had heralded death.

The one in Lystra's hand would not.

Stepping forward, Lystra didn't look at Dalmah. Her skirts fluttered about her ankles, her every step poised with grace and dignity.

"Chief Wuhaz." She bowed her head.

The chief bowed again. "My queen. We of the canyons, of the redstone and the skies, wish you and the king safe journeys back to your fair city. May the heavens shine over your reign forevermore."

"May the heavens shine!" The refrain rose from the crowd.

Lystra handed the scroll to the chief. "In this you will find all you need concerning the prisoner, the former countess of House Arghan, convicted of the binding of curses and multiple attempts against the king's life." She lifted her chin. "I can give no pity, no clemency, no pardon to these heinous acts. As a victim of the curse itself, who felt its effects in her body and beheld its dark agony in her soul, I cannot be made to understand any motive to cause such suffering. Nonetheless, I won't perpetuate this suffering. I spare Dalmah her life, but I will take the necessary steps to protect my kingdom from her person."

Lystra wanted to look at her grandmother, to see her surprise, astonishment, or perhaps her disgust at her actions. But Lystra gave no weight to what her grandmother thought of her. Not now.

You made me a queen, but my choices are my own.

Instead, she looked at the chief, a man who had seen horrors beyond measure—Kushite children's blood draining into the canals and desperate soldiers fighting endless wars. "This woman shall never set foot in Instanolde again. She shall never see my face for as long as she lives. And if she ever threatens my kingdom—my family—again, let her death be swift." Lystra bowed her head. "So be it."

Wuhaz also bowed. "So be it."

Lystra turned, her eyes seeking Elerek, his strength. He gave a subtle nod, but his eyes were cold as steel. Her grandmother had done terrible things to them both, but none of it mattered anymore. She was nothing to them.

The scroll would tell the chief the rest. How Dalmah would be kept to the confines of a humble home in one of the remote, outlying villages maintained by Kushan for the care of the elderly. Soldiers would guard her day and night and she would live in useless obscurity.

As Lystra and Elerek boarded the vessel, its crimson sails ready to catch the air and deliver them home, the people of Kushan took up the refrain.

"Gem of the Gungole."

"Fire of the Sancen."

"Fierce as the dawn."

"Mighty as the constellations."

Lystra smiled as she stared out over the brilliant red canyons and its people, their cheers echoing off the heights.

Chapter 53

Lystra

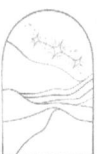

When the oars of the river vessel were retracted and the great crimson sail furled, Lystra stood at the prow, clutching Corsha's hand. Golden domes and spires pierced the deep blue sky and the familiar stonework of Instanolde filled her vision. The pale mosaics, the rich tones of silk canopies, the fluttering flags in royal orange— the colors of her people welcomed her home.

Elerek waited in the vessel's cabin, absolutely and predictably seasick.

People lined the docks, clustered the balconies, and leaned out the windows. Eagerly waiting.

Evidence of the Jarkins' occupation lay everywhere. Scorch marks in the stone. Several docks obliterated. Makeshift shelters for displaced families and refugees occupied corners and lined the walls. And the fear: Lystra could see it in her people's eyes, even from here. They would heal. Together.

"I'm glad we're back," Corsha whispered.

"Me too." Lystra breathed deep. The smell of the water, the harbor, and the city filled her nostrils. But there, somewhere beyond, the wildness of the Sancen permeated her senses. Her people belonged to the desert.

The vessel docked, its deck outfitted with soldiers. They chose to forgo a carriage, instead requesting a pair of cardants to ride through the city to the palace. Back on land, Elerek recovered and managed his cardant well. Along each and every avenue, the people cheered their arrival. Lystra couldn't help but smile as the chatter filled her ears.

This time, a king returned from the desert, and the streets lined with his subjects, welcoming him home. The sight only made Lystra hold her head higher. They had survived, becoming symbols of hope, of a new sunrise.

They weren't the only survivors. She didn't know how many the curse had claimed. Perhaps no one really did. But her people still drew breath, the curse broken, and she would cherish this victory.

At the palace, another sort of homecoming took place. Kimzi and Jethro waited to welcome Lystra and Corsha, throwing their arms about her. But Lystra soon broke free from their embrace, watching with elation as the assembly of Elerek's family spilled out of the palace.

They rushed his cardant, bringing with them his beloved wheelchair, and helped him down. They smiled, they laughed, and they wept. Embraces were given, hands and shoulders clasped, the affection of touch no longer harboring the cold chill of death.

Elerek smiled and laughed, tears streaming down his face as he embraced each and every one of them. Lystra was certain he'd never experienced such an onslaught of affection—*closeness*—before.

But the palace still hung with ghosts. Lystra could see it plainly in the little tribe's eyes. The memories of those lost.

She felt it too. The noise and the laughter hearkened back

to the era of another king. A tall, dark-haired king who loved to dance and smile. But the losses rang louder. Even as Elerek and his little family talked and smiled, they'd lost one of their own. Surely Razhar wasn't really gone. Perhaps Lystra need only tilt her ear to catch his jokes. To turn around, and he'd be there with a charming smile and flash of colorful flamboyance.

But he wouldn't.

At the highest point of Instanolde, closest to the stars, a fire burned.

Not a body; all that remained was dust scattered across the Sancen and the waters of Darcress. Only a fire.

The constellations had changed. The wrathgiver no longer danced in the darkness above, now well below the horizon.

As the priests had set the kindling to light, a proclamation had been read. A scribe penned it, a herald read it, but the words were Lystra's.

When children asked for the story of the wrathgiver, and fathers told of the stars to their sons, no longer would he be known as a dark assassin wielding a knife. Now, they would hear the tale of an orphaned Kushite who stowed away from the canyons to live in the glittering city of Instanolde, of the Karim prince who became his brother, and the curse that bound them together. Of his sacrifice, the giving of his life to save Instanolde, to the hope of a new dawn. In remembrance not of a wrathgiver, but of a warrior who smiled.

No smiles encircled the fire tonight. Sober faces and glistening eyes faced the flames.

None drew closer to the fire than Elerek and Lystra, the firelight dancing in the opals on their crowns.

Dressed again in royal orange, Lystra blinked a multitude of tears. Had it only been months since she'd stood here before? Watching Cormek's body turn to ash? That she'd heard the sound of wooden wheels and realized that she was not alone?

She'd stand here again. Maybe tomorrow, maybe years from now. Their time was short, but it need not be empty.

Today, they would live.

She looked at Elerek, his face stern and noble. For Razhar, he had already wept till his eyes were dry. Now, he looked brave. Bold. Strong. He wore a dark tunic with sleeves cut at the elbows. There, upon his taut forearm, fresh ink gleamed black, a string of stars adorning the scarred skin. A constellation. The same that had danced on Razhar's chest.

Lystra stepped closer to his faithful chair. Elerek glanced up at her, his hand reaching for hers, their fingers locked. His eyes were full of pain, of hope.

And of love.

"We were different people, the last time we stood here," he whispered. "We didn't know how hard it would be."

She caught her breath. "We didn't know how far we'd come."

Her husband closed his eyes, bracing himself against the grief. His fingers clenched, holding her hand tighter.

Lystra drew herself up, her chin high as she faced the pyre. "Razhar told me something the day we went into the desert. I told him that I was weary—weary of death."

Elerek opened his eyes, a single tear drifting down his cheek.

"He told me that we ought to make certain that we don't become weary of life." Even as she said it, Lystra felt healing bathe her soul.

Elerek exhaled and matched her posture. "And so, we won't."

The End

Acknowledgments

I didn't know that I was writing a duology. I thought I had a very long book in need of edits. But when a friend suggested that I just split it in two, give the first a cliffhanger, and use Razhar to expand the second book, I was thrilled. There was more to the story—to these characters. More depth, more adventure, and more of the healing that Elerek, Lystra, and Razhar so desperately needed. I'm beyond thankful that I got to tell this story. There's something about this one, the themes, the moments of rawness and forgiveness between the characters, and the climax—that there were beginnings as well as endings, and life after curses.

Even at the time of writing *Queen of Shifting Sand's* acknowledgments, this story wasn't over. The book that I had poured my grief and longing into released into the world while we lived out of our suitcases in the NICU with our brand-new baby who came to us via adoption. I cried many tears of amazement, seeing how all had come full circle, by God's grace and how He authored our journey to our baby as well as this story of curses, grief, and two broken people finding their way into each other's hearts.

First off, thank you to the amazing team at Whimsical Publishing, especially the incomparable Micheline who has believed in this story sooooooooo much. I still am in awe that this partnership occurred and that you love my characters just as much as I do. Especially thank you for loving this second installment, and I'll never forget those tears of relief when you finished reading it and *got it*. All of it, and agree with me that this one is even better than the first.

Thank you also to Christina, Lucy, Hannah, Deborah, and the rest of the team who have contributed above and beyond in taking care of the whimsical stories, keeping us on track, and designing epic things, you guys are fantastic! Also thank you to all the reps who have made such pretty promos and showed off our pretty covers.

Speaking of covers, thank you from the bottom of my heart to Salome Totladze for the epically beautiful cover art (Elerek got his own cover!) and bringing beautifully cursed El to life. Also, thank you to Kateryna Vitkovska for the outstanding "beneath the jacket" art for the exclusive edition, bringing on the drama of the climax beneath the stars. It's always an honor and privilege to work with so many wonderful artists, including Jenelle Hovde for the lovely, romantic portrait of Elerek and Lystra and Hannah Rodgers for the stunning portrait of Razhar and Elerek's cursed powers. And, of course, a billion thank yous to Micheline for her painting of Lystra and Elerek together and her work on the header portraits and making this book just the most absolutely beautiful package.

To my friends and family, thank you. Browns, Logans, Gosnells. To my writer friends, Liz, Mary, Michelle, Andi, Brittany, for standing alongside me through this adventure. A special thank you to Brigitte for taking care of us while we were in the hospital with baby, and opening your home to us, giving us a bed to sleep on, feeding us, and warming our souls through that time. Those who laughed and cried with me. Thank you to all the other Whimsical authors for being such lovely authors and wonderful publishing sisters. To everyone who has shown up to my signings, read, reviewed, and endorsed, you guys are fantastic!

To Michael, my husband and soulmate, to whom this book is dedicated. There's a passage in here that I wrote purely from the place of holding your hand as we drove to a scary doctor appointment. It was an unromantic, rather terrible moment, but it is one that I remember loving you more deeply than I ever had before. That was the feeling I wanted captured for Elerek and Lystra as they dared to love despite the hurt, the hopelessness, and the hard things that lay before them. We've been through so many hard things, and I doubt they'll end, but I want you with me, by my side. Thank you for reading this book a billion times and taking care of our baby so that I could finish it and meet my deadlines. On that note, thank you, dear Aiden, for letting mommy edit while you napped. Many of these chapters were edited while you were curled up in my baby carrier against my chest.

Thank You, Jesus Christ, for entrusting me with this story. For showing Your love in what writing it has taught me and doing beyond what I could ask or imagine.

And you, dear readers, thank you for letting me tell you a story.

About the Author

Kaitlyn Carter Brown, an avid adventurer both on and off page, crafts fierce fantasy filled with high stakes, sweeping worlds, and courageous characters stories while taking inspiration from her treks across the US' National Parks. Off the page, you'll find her decorating cakes, drinking plenty of coffee, and surviving the Arizona heat much like her army of houseplants.

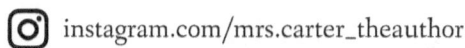 instagram.com/mrs.carter_theauthor

www.ingramcontent.com/pod-product-compliance
Lightning Source LLC
Chambersburg PA
CBHW030756260626
47169CB00001B/70